nancy (handwritten)

Flight from
a lurid
family secret...

She pushed the door open a bit wider. All
the breath left her body and her mind
reeled even as she saw that Millicent's arms
were around Jason's and that one of his
hands caressed her back. A lover's kiss.
They were so lost in it that they did not
hear Julie's muffled gasp or her swift flight
down the hall.

"Incest"—the word repeated itself over and
over in her brain—"incest."

MARY KAY SIMMONS

A *Fire* *in the* BLOOD

A KANGAROO BOOK
PUBLISHED BY POCKET BOOKS NEW YORK

A FIRE IN THE BLOOD

POCKET BOOK edition published June, 1977

This original POCKET BOOK edition is printed from brand-new plates made from newly set, clear, easy-to-read type.
POCKET BOOK editions are published by
POCKET BOOKS,
a Simon & Schuster Division of
GULF & WESTERN CORPORATION
1230 Avenue of the Americas,
New York, N.Y. 10020.
Trademarks registered in the United States
and other countries.

Printed in the U.S.A.

Acknowledgments

The author is deeply indebted to Gary E. Hicks of Great Western Champagne's Pleasant Valley Wine Company at Hammondsport, New York, for his information on New York's wine industry, and for his compilation of historical data on the Finger Lakes District; to Nellie Torres of Great Western's New York office; and, last but not least, to Sheila McHugh Simmons for her invaluable aid in general research.

To Martha Winston,
who remains the *sine qua non*

PART ONE

1

A summerlike stillness covered the prairie and a full May moon turned orange above its vaporous heat. The moon poured molten paths of light over the convent gardens; it stole into the dormitory, where the sleeping students of St. Veronica's Young Ladies' Seminary stirred fitfully and threw aside their coverlets without waking.

In one room Julie Fontaine stood deep in the shadows between her bed and wardrobe, buttoning her navy cotton uniform over corset and petticoats with shaking fingers.

Across from her lay the sleeping form of her roommate, Eileen Butler, and as Julie bent down to tie her laces, Eileen moved and sighed. For a moment Julie froze, and then, assuring herself that Eileen still slept, she crept forward to the window and stepped over the sill and onto the porch roof. She stood there briefly, her back to the convent wall. Save for the normal night noises, all was quiet. Cautiously, she edged her way to the trellis now thick with leaves and the closed buds of newly flowering morning glories. The trellis creaked under her weight and she reached the bottom with hammering heart, half expecting one of the nuns to appear. But the convent's inhabitants slept on undisturbed.

Skirting the paths of moonlight, she made her way to the gardener's shed. It was dark beneath the overhanging trees and the lush hedge growth bordering the back wall, and she could not see the ladder she had placed there just before confession that evening. She felt for it slowly, fearful of knocking it over. Encountering it at last, she seized it gratefully. Within a few minutes she had skimmed lightly up over the wall, drawn it after her and was down in a flash.

Free! She could have shouted aloud with joy. Night after night this spring she had remained awake in her narrow bed, tossing, turning, unable to sleep while May grew seductively hot. She would imagine herself out from behind the walls and . . . She frowned. Confession that evening had forced a reluctant admission to Father Calhoun that she had been thinking of a boy. Father Calhoun's chastisement still rang in her ears and the long penance he had invoked rankled her.

She flushed and bit her lip, her violet eyes darkening. Lord, she was nearly eighteen. Her own mother had been married at nineteen. What did Father Calhoun know or understand? "Carnal thoughts," he had called them. Thank God she had not told him the exact nature of those thoughts! Or that they involved Bill Robertson, who worked at the village general store.

Bill. She gave a little start and began to walk toward the road. Eleven, he had said. Would he wait? It must be past that now. She began to hurry, not pausing in her flight until she saw the first stand of trees. She slipped between them, hurrying through and across the fields that led to the grove of willows. The dew-wet grass pulled at her heavy skirts and the windless heat of the night beaded her forehead with perspiration and curled the tendrils of hair at her temples.

In the back of her mind, she knew she was risking more than breaking a convent rule, but she pushed the thought away. Bill waited just ahead. Bill had contrived under the watchful eyes of Sister Thérèse and Sister Celeste to steal moments alone with her on the weekly shopping expeditions to Elton's Grove. She could still feel the touch of his right hand on hers as they pretended to sort through ribbons, the tingling sensation of his other hand slipping up her wide sleeve to run his fingers along her inner arm. And today! Her heart began to beat faster. They had come close to discovery today.

He had seized her around the waist while they stood behind the stacked bolts of thick cloth. His lips had barely grazed hers when Sister Thérèse's heavy tread shaking the floorboards alerted them.

"Tonight," he had whispered, "by that grove of willows, at eleven." He released her as Sister Thérèse rounded the corner of the counter and he began to whistle as he got down bolts of cloth for Julie to examine.

Julie shivered in anticipation. Ahead lay the drooping branches of the willows, although Bill was not in sight. She hurried forward eagerly, stepping into the grove, and then he was before her, his face a pale blur in the shadows.

"Julie," he whispered. He took her hand and led her forward through the trees to the edge of the still pond. He had turned to look at her but she suddenly became shy now that they were alone, and she could not meet his eyes.

He drew her down with him to the base of one of the trees, and for a long moment, they sat side by side without speaking until at last he said, "The water is beautiful in the moonlight."

He pressed her hand gently, but she made no response. Where was the exciting feeling? Somehow in the mad rush to meet him it had disappeared. What was she doing here in the grove risking discovery, risking expulsion, risking a far worse penance than the one she had received earlier? She started to withdraw her hand, but he tightened his pressure. There was a brief, silent struggle and his hand left hers and encircled her waist.

"Don't." But as she turned toward him in protest, his other arm was around her and his fingers brushed against her neck. It was back again, that giddy feeling that made her grow hot and cold at once. She swayed toward him, her body going soft beneath his arm, and he bent his head to reach her lips.

That first kiss was strangely disappointing—tentative and unpressured. He drew away and looked down at her. She let her head fall back against his arm, half closing her eyes as they met his.

"Your hair," he said wonderingly, "I never really saw it before." He reached out and loosened the ribbon that bound it and it flowed around her, black and silky and thick. She felt his hands moving through it, drawing it back from her face, and this time when his lips met hers a wild surge of feeling shot through her so that she pressed closer against him. She could hear him breathing heavily, feel each kiss probing deeper and deeper. She ran her fingers over the back of his neck, twisting them in his springy wheat-fair curls. His hands moved over her, touching her breasts, and it made her moan. When he stopped she reached out her own hand to draw them back, but he shook it off, fumbling now with the buttons of her neckband, moving his head down to kiss the hollow of her throat as he opened the heavy cloth to expose the binding corselet. She heard the faint ripping sound of one of the straps breaking. Her own hands went up then, pushing his away, but he was too strong for her. She could feel him seeking the way to unbind her, and at last her flesh was free of the restraints. His hands fell on her bare breasts, cupping them, and she ceased to struggle against him, giving herself over to the feeling that surpassed all her wildest imaginings. They lay now on their side, kissing frantically. He pressed her closer and closer, and through the folds of her skirts she could feel his body, hard and demanding, as he moved her against him in a rhythmic motion. Blood pounded in her ears and she murmured wordless sounds against his mouth. But when she felt him tugging at her skirts some vestige of reason returned and this time she succeeded in stopping him. They lay apart, breathless and trembling. Julie pulled her clothing together, buttoning up her bodice with clumsy fingers and rising on unsteady legs.

"I have to go back," she said.

He rose, too, leaning briefly against the tree. "I'll go with you," he offered.

"No. It'll be bad enough if I'm caught alone. With you . . ." Suddenly the realization of what she had done swept over her. "I . . . I don't know what they would do to me," she finished. "No," she said as he moved toward her. "No. I'm going now."

"Meet me tomorrow?"

"No!" She had turned and was running back through the trees. He came after her, catching her as she emerged on the road. He pulled her into his arms, holding her firmly.

"I won't let you go until you say yes," he threatened.

She capitulated, telling herself that it was only so he would let her alone. She promised herself that all the way home, promised it going back over the convent wall, and climbing once more through the window of her room where Eileen lay sleeping and her own bed was as she had left it, the pillows arranged as if a figure lay beneath the coverlets. She undressed quietly, breathing a prayer of thankfulness and promising herself once again that she would not meet Bill the next evening. Her body felt warm and good and yet curiously achy, and it was a long time before she was able to fall asleep.

The morning bell woke her from a delicious dream that clung pleasurably to her consciousness, even as she evaded Eileen's promptings to hurry. She dawdled over her toilette, letting Eileen go on ahead so she could have a minute to herself. As she pinned the torn strap of her corset cover, memory caused her to flush with pleasure and, a moment later, to pale with the knowledge of her present fall from grace. She had been to confession yesterday. She would be expected to receive communion this morning. But she could not. She had sinned—really sinned. And even as she told herself fiercely that she didn't care, she knew that she was not carefree enough to go to the communion rail in this state. Yet, barring illness, mass and communion were mandatory.

The chapel bell pealed in the first call just as Sister Celeste tapped and said, "Julie, you are late, come along."

With sinking heart Julie followed the nun down the broad stairs to the reception foyer where the school had gathered to march through the covered passageway that led to the chapel.

Mass was endless. The sermon droned on. Yet all too soon Father Calhoun was holding aloft the host in the sacrifice. The acolyte's bell tinkled and the rustle of fists striking breasts sounded. "Mea culpa," Julie murmured with the rest. "Mea culpa." She wondered vaguely if God would strike her dead when she approached the rail.

She rose with the other girls in her pew for the procession to the altar, and as she stepped out into the aisle behind Eileen she felt light-headed and faint.

Faint! The word sprang into her brain like a beacon of hope and a moment later she gave way to her trembling knees and felt them buckle. There was a startled hiss from the nuns and then she was down, lids fluttering over her eyes.

As fake faints went, it was a good one. Her pallor, her thready pulse, and her paralysis of fear were convincing. She did not make the mistake of remaining unconscious too long. As hands sought to lift her, she moaned, her lids fluttered, opened and closed and opened again, and she allowed herself to be raised and led tottering out of the chapel.

The faint turned out to be a double blessing. It permitted her to spend the day in bed, sleeping, resting, reading, and marshaling her thoughts.

She could not faint regularly each Sunday, yet she could not confess to Father Calhoun. At best, she would have to make an imperfect confession. Remembering how he had behaved over her imagined kisses, she had no doubt that he would order public penance if the events of the night before were unfolded to him. She thought briefly of running away, but she had no money. She lay there, alternately deciding to brave it out and confess and never see Bill again, then thinking that perhaps she might meet him and seek his aid in running away.

She was able to malinger through supper, with a worried Eileen bringing her a tray. If only she could confide in Eileen it would help greatly. But Julie knew that was impossible. Her roommate was known among the other senior girls as "Saint Eileen." But there was no mistaking Eileen's genuinely good nature. Julie remembered the night she had been torn with pain from a badly infected jaw, and Eileen had sat up all night, rosary beads in her hand, alternately praying and murmuring soothing sounds whenever Julie started up from fitful dozing.

Eileen, with her gentle eyes and smoothly braided brown hair, thought that a kiss resulted in downfall, ruin, and an utter disgrace brought about by illegitimate pregnancy. There had been many a time when Julie had been on the verge of giving Eileen a few pertinent facts. A kiss! It was laughable, although a kiss could do many things. It had sent her to this dreary landlocked convent at fifteen.

She sighed and Eileen said quickly, "Are you feeling worse?"

"No," Julie replied shortly. "I'm bored—bored with this convent, bored with these stupid uniforms, bored with women, women, women, day after day. One day I'll get even with Holt Prescott."

"Your cousin? What does he have to do with it?"

"Nothing. I'm just out of sorts. And I'm not hungry." She eyed the chicken stew and rice pudding with loathing. "Take it, will you, Eileen?"

Eileen lifted the tray, saying, "But you should eat. You need it to feel better."

"I'll be fine," Julie said. "Once I leave here, I'll be fine. One more month and I'll see the last of St. Veronica's and of fat old Sister Thérèse and Sister Celeste with all her prayers and . . ." Eileen began to look scandalized and Julie said hastily, "Oh, I don't really mean that, Eileen. I *am* out of sorts. I don't feel well." And slipping down into bed, she drew the sheet up around her, closing her eyes.

She heard Eileen shut the door gently. No, there was certainly no talking to Eileen, and as for any of the other senior girls, the gossip would be sure to reach Sister Thérèse, who had the eyes of a ferret and the ears of a lynx, and looked like an ox—a red-faced ox.

She had been at St. Veronica's for three years—three years of rules and regulations, and not a man around save the gardener and Father Calhoun. It was a world filled with girls and nuns. There were summers at Camp Joy, run by another group of nuns from the same French order. Camp Joy, where she played lawn croquet and embroidered and weaved altar cloths; where French conversation dominated dinner and the evenings were given over to musicales and crowned with prayers; where even the picnics at the lakeside were chaste forays where one gathered wild flowers and herbs for the nuns, who made sachets and various herbal remedies. And if that weren't enough, even her winter holidays had been spent at her elderly third Cousin Bertha Fontaine's house in Vincennes, Indiana.

It might as well be Victorian days instead of 1915. A war raged in Europe and threatened to draw America in. There were rumors of a revolution in Russia. Some king or duke had been assassinated. Women were getting arrested for making demonstrations to get the vote. Quite respectable women, too.

Elsewhere, they had put aside their heavy corsets and raised their hemlines to reveal a glimpse of ankles. Even here in Elton's Corners, Iowa, one could see proof that the old ways were vanishing—but not at St. Veronica's, nor at Camp Joy, and certainly not at Cousin Bertha's, where tight corsets and prayers and good works were advocated.

It couldn't go on forever. This would be her last

summer at Camp Joy. Another summer—it was suddenly more than she could bear to contemplate.

All those dreary days to come and the nights when she would lie with her body burning and her mind raging as she tried to subdue her thoughts. Home—that was where she longed to be.

May, at home, when the waters ran bubbling clear in the lakes and rivers that rushed to the sea; summer, when the grapes hung heavy and sweet on the vines and the intoxicating scent of roses filled the air; autumn's crisp nights under big yellow moons; and winter howling outside the big old Prescott house, alight with log fires —fires that in happier days had warmed her.

She sat up abruptly in bed. There must be some way out. She thought briefly of the reception she could expect at home. Uncle Jason might be easy to win over, but not Aunt Millicent, who had caused her exile to St. Veronica's in the first place. And all because Holt had caught her behind the grape arbor in the act of being pecked on the cheek by bashful seventeen-year-old Andrew Clay. To hear Holt tell it, Julie's conduct had bordered on harlotry. And Holt was his father's pride and his Aunt Millicent's idol.

No, it wasn't Millicent's fault—poor spinster, keeping house for her brother and his wife and then for Jason and Holt alone after Sara Prescott had run off. It was Holt's fault. Four years older than she was, he had treated her with indifference while her father was alive, and she still lived in the Fontaine house, behind which stretched her father's vineyards. After her father had died and she had come to live with the Prescotts, Holt's indifference had turned to a resentment he barely bothered to conceal.

Julie had long since lost any memory of her mother beyond the recollections that stirred sometimes when she got a whiff of an elusive perfume or heard an old lullaby. But her father was still vividly before her: tall, black-haired, with a white flashing smile beneath his big black mustache. Even now, five years later, the memory made her heart ache a little.

That day they had brought her the news of his death, a cold November day with the sun glittering on the icy crust of the first snow, she had been numb with shock and disbelief. When the merciful opiate of the shock wore off, she had had nightmares of her father riding along an old Indian trail at Watkins Glen and of the horse bolting, and then of herself on her own mare, Blythe, trying to catch him—and a soundless terror as the glen fell away beneath them both. Only, somehow, she always woke before she reached the bottom, woke and knew her father was dead.

Thinking of it now, her eyes stung with unshed tears. If he were alive, she would not be here. He would never send her to a place like this. Her father, in spite of the fact that he made the outward show of convention, had possessed a secret irreverence for rules and regulations that would have shocked the staunchly Presbyterian Prescotts had they known. For that matter, the marriage of their younger sister to a Roman Catholic had been shock enough for Millicent and Jason.

Jason Prescott was an elder of the church, as his father had been before him, and he was stiffly proud of his eminent position in the business community and of the Prescott name. The only comfort he drew from what he otherwise considered a *mésalliance* was the old local belief that the Fontaines were descendants of the Dauphin of France, who, legend had it, was spirited away from the Bastille and taken to America.

It had never pleased Jason to hear her father disclaim this bit of questionable history by laughing and saying, "It is more probable that the first Fontaine was simply a royalist sympathizer who was lucky enough to flee the Reign of Terror."

Jason could never move John Fontaine from his position, and even the supporting bit of evidence—an heirloom lavaliere bearing a miniature oil of an eighteenth-century lady who resembled Marie Antoinette—brought Jason fresh discomfort. "Not a royalist, then," John Fontaine would tease, "but perhaps a thief of low birth who stowed away on a merchant ship."

Julie smiled, thinking how much her father would dislike the convent and how well he would understand her feelings. The idea relieved her sense of guilt and unease, but it did nothing to solve her problem.

She spent the rest of the evening deciding between one course and another: now firmly resolved to run away; now to confess and be shriven.

When Eileen came up to bed, Julie feigned sleep, lying motionless between the sheets while her mind raced feverishly. Father Calhoun had left after the early mass and would not return until next Saturday evening, in time to hear confessions. Of course, if some spiritual disaster should overtake the convent, he would be summoned from St. Michaels in Des Moines, some twenty-five miles away from Elton's Corners. Barring such an unforeseen event, she would have six days to make up her mind.

Soothed by this notion, she tried to relax, and yet, even as Eileen's deep breathing proclaimed her asleep, Julie was rising from her bed and automatically plumping the pillows beneath the sheet.

Somewhere between one thought and another she had decided she might as well be hanged for a sheep as a lamb. Outside, the sultry night beckoned her away from the confines of her quasi-imprisonment. Perhaps, after all, she might decide to run away. She could find a priest who didn't know her, confess to him, and somehow it would be all right. She pulled her uniform on over her nightdress and, leaving her boots, drew on her black cotton stockings, knotted them, and rolled them to her knees.

One part of her stood appalled, but overriding that was the thought of the night before and the night to come. Her purpose was strong, her spirit rebellious, and her passions primitive. Before them, years of teaching melted away like sugar over heat. By the time she reached the grove and found Bill waiting with newfound impatience born of the previous night's frustrations, all other thoughts left her head.

He drew her deep into the grove to a small space where he had laid a carriage blanket over the damp ground. She went willingly into his arms this time and heard his exclamation as he felt the softness of her corsetless body melting against him.

Moments later the uniform lay discarded beside them and only the thin batiste of the nightdress covered her trembling body. They kissed and kissed again, growing dizzy with passion, and suddenly he moved away from her. She made a half-unconscious sound of protest and raised herself on one elbow just as he came back, shirt and trousers gone, and then he was beside her once more. The rough texture of his underclothing excited her and she surrendered to his caresses, scarcely aware of her surroundings in the intense heat that suffused her body.

He slipped his free hand under her nightdress, kneading her flesh, squeezing her breasts, his fingers pulling gently at the nipples. She pressed closer and his hand caressed her thighs, moving them apart to touch the softness of the inner flesh and then moving up between her legs. A tremendous thrill of excitement shot through her and her legs fell apart almost involuntarily. Deep sounds emerged from his throat and he took his hand away to draw hers along his body, beneath the unbuttoned underclothing, placing it around his organ with a moan. The feel of him aroused her to fever pitch. In a moment he had pulled her gown up over her stomach and was on top of her. She stiffened at once, closing her thighs against him. He thrust his hand down, trying to pry them apart.

"No!" she gasped. "No!" They fought silently for minutes and then he rolled away from her, drawing her hand back to him, showing her how to pull in an up-and-down motion before his hands sought her body again. She pushed against his hand, hoping he would never stop, growing more and more excited, and finally there was an ecstatic seizure of her entire body and she jerked spasmodically with a long, soft cry. It seemed to agitate him more and his hand closed over hers, guiding her, instructing her until he uttered a groan and a warm wetness spread over her stomach.

She was covered with sweat, her mind hazy in the aftermath of excitement. They slept then until the cool predawn winds sprang up and the moon and the stars disappeared.

By the time Julie had climbed back over the covent walls, the sky was light.

Halfway up the trellis she thought she heard someone whispering, but when she paused to listen, all was quiet. Then she stepped softly over the sill into her room and was in the act of removing her uniform when the door opened and Sister Thérèse stood there, kerosene lamp in her hand, her red face redder than ever in its flickering light.

2

In the days that followed Sister Thérèse's triumphant discovery of Julie's absence that night, the recurrent theme of "confess your sins and be pardoned" ran beneath the orderly convent chorus like the repeated statement of a mournful oboe.

It unnerved her, but it did not sway her. Father Calhoun, summoned to the convent by Julie's adamant refusal to explain, found that cajolery, patience, and, finally, warnings as to the state of her immortal soul, were to no avail.

"She is beyond redemption," Sister Thérèse announced, which statement sent Sister Celeste hurrying to the chapel to pray for Julie's soul.

Eileen was sent by the nuns to plead with Julie. "You must tell the truth," she said. "At least you must confess and do penance."

"I have nothing to confess," Julie lied, and the more often she said it, the more certain she became that it was true. Slowly, she came to believe that what the priest and nuns would consider sinful was no sin at all. Surely sooner or later everyone felt as she felt and did what she had done. "Or else," she told herself, "who would ever have a baby?" God certainly had made it attractive, and if He hadn't waited to do so until the banns were read and the vows were taken, what did anyone expect of her? The idea that her thoughts were heretical did not occur to her. Uppermost in her mind was the reception she could expect at home and the longing to see Bill again.

In the end, Father Calhoun sent a letter home and she was ordered to remain in her room to await the requested telegraphed reply. Save for Eileen, she spent the final week at St. Veronica's in what amounted to solitary confinement.

"I wonder," she said to Eileen one night upon receiving her bread-and-milk supper, "why they let you stay here. Aren't they afraid I'll contaminate you?"

Eileen blushed. "They think I . . ." She stopped. "It's silly," she burst out. "If you have nothing to confess, why don't they believe you?"

"They think I'm lying," Julie answered with a short laugh, then added recklessly, "and I am, for that matter."

But to Eileen's pleadings she turned a deaf ear.

"It's better that you don't know anything," she advised her. "That way you won't be caught between loyalties."

"Were you with . . . someone?" Eileen asked.

"And if I were?"

Eileen looked doubtful. "I don't know. I mean, if you were just talking to . . . to . . ."

"I wouldn't risk my neck just to chat with a man," Julie said.

"You didn't . . . you couldn't . . ." Eileen, out of her depth entirely, looked stricken.

"Couldn't what?" And at Eileen's bashful answer, Julie laughed and said, "Well, before I go, I think I ought to at least tell you. There's more to having a baby than just kissing someone, and," she added hastily as Eileen's cheeks flamed, "I am not pregnant, if that's what's worrying you."

Poor Eileen fled before the frankness and Julie thought she would probably follow Sister Celeste's example and head into the chapel. With all these people praying for her soul, she supposed she'd be safe enough until she got home. It occurred to her that Father Calhoun might well be right and beneath her hard stubbornness there beat the pulsing fear of retribution.

If she could be like Eileen, compliant, obedient, sure of the teachings she received, and not tempted to stray, she wasn't sure she would like it. Serenity born of a clear conscience struck her as dullness born of timidity. What did Eileen have to look forward to? Back home to Chicago this summer and a life devoted to charity and good works and the Church and presently marriage to some suitably dull man.

The Butlers were rich, richer than any of the other girls' families, and Eileen was very eligible, a desirable, dowered debutante with an ambitious mother. Julie thought of the one night she had stayed with the Butlers in their big stone gingerbread pile of a house along Lake Michigan. Mr. Butler was a hearty, ruddy-complexioned, self-made man who doted on Eileen. Mrs. Butler, thin and ascetic of face, of an old family that had fallen on hard times, was clearly anxious to marry her daughter off to a boy from her own background. And Eileen would meekly follow her parents' designs.

"It isn't for me," Julie said now. "I won't marry at all if I can't marry someone . . . someone who makes me feel alive and . . ." Her mind drifted to Bill and she felt a bodily ache of longing to be back in the grove, with the moon shining silver on the pond and the trees sighing over them and . . . A vivid, wordless picture sprang into her mind and the ache became unbearable. Hastily, she began to sort through her belongings, marking what was to be packed and what was to be discarded. The uniform would remain. Never again would she be encased in navy serge for winter and navy cotton for summer and endless petticoats and high-laced boots and those curious bonnets that covered all the hair and hooded out on either side like horses' blinders.

She went to the wardrobe and drew out the one dress that was wearable. She had bought it one summer on her way back from Camp Joy. It was a silky violet cocoon of a dress with the skirt hobbled but discreetly slit. Hidden in the back of the wardrobe was a pair of low-cut shoes. She wouldn't dare wear those out of the convent. But she could change to them once she reached New York and, perhaps, if she was lucky, she might be able to buy some lovely black silk stockings with clocks at the sides.

She drew her hat from the top shelf and removed the tissue paper. It was really too childish a hat to wear with the violet silk, but she had no other, save the school bonnets. She put the black big-brimmed pancake on her head and surveyed the effect in the small mirror. It looked silly with the streamers trailing behind her head. A school girl's hat. Well, she would fix that. Cut off the streamers and it would do, with perhaps some of the lavender hair ribbons she had bought in town wound around it. Inspired, she went to her desk, on which reposed a small compote filled with waxed green grapes. A few of those tied together and sewn into the ribbon would give some appearance of style.

When she got home she would buy clothes. Her money was tied into a trust fund until she was twenty-one, but on her eighteenth birthday she would receive an as yet undisclosed sum, no matter what Uncle Jason did or Aunt Millicent or Mark Douglas—Mark! She had hardly remembered about Mark.

Co-trustee of her estate with Uncle Jason, Mark had been her father's assistant and then a junior partner in the Fontaine winery. Since her father's death, he had run the winery and overseen the vineyard.

He and Uncle Jason never had gotten along. She knew that Jason resented a then twenty-three-year-old man being made trustee with him, but her father had trusted Mark enough to arrange it that way. She herself hadn't seen Mark for years, but he had dutifully sent an accounting twice a year, and always with a pleasant, if formal, note.

He was vague in her mind now, a mere impression of a tall, broad-shouldered man with dark red hair. And, for some reason, she remembered him as angry. She sighed, thinking that perhaps he would not be any more understanding than her Prescott relatives.

A knock on the door broke her reverie and she hastily put her low shoes back into the wardrobe before answering. It was Sister Celeste, there to tell her that the telegram from home had arrived and she was to be ready to leave in the morning.

The drive to Des Moines with Father Calhoun and Sister Thérèse passed in silence. As the priest's old touring car rattled through the village, Julie had caught a glimpse of Bill Robertson standing in the doorway of the general store talking to two town girls, and a stab of jealousy mixed with resentment pierced her. He looked up to watch the motorcar pass and she half hoped he would look at her, and then, hoping he would not, she sank back into the far corner. She had come this far without anyone being able to prove their suspicions and, whatever they might think at home, in the absence of proof they would be helpless.

At the Des Moines station, Mrs. Miller, the bustling and plump head of the altar society at St. Michael's, waited to escort Julie and Sister Thérèse to New York, where, according to the telegram from Jason, Holt was to meet her.

Why they had chosen Holt, she couldn't imagine. But why he had agreed to do it was even more perplexing. She felt certain that whatever the reason was, it meant no good for her.

She smiled a polite greeting as Father Calhoun introduced Mrs. Miller, a large, austerely dressed matron who did not return the smile. Her response was as grave and chilling as Sister Thérèse's offended silence; both foretold the atmosphere in which they would travel.

Julie moved aside deferentially to let them precede her onto the train, but Mrs. Miller stood back, indicating that she was to follow Sister Thérèse, and so, with only a perfunctory farewell from Father Calhoun, and sandwiched between the two women, Julie began the silent journey to New York.

She remembered very little of the trip. Union Station in Chicago no longer seemed familiar. She had always enjoyed eating at the Harvey Restaurant on her way to and from Cousin Bertha's at Christmas. This time the meat was sawdust in her mouth. The factories in Gary, Indiana, the fields of Ohio, and the rolling hills of Pennsylvania passed day and sleepless night like a stream of meaningless pictures, and the lonely whistle of the engine at the crossings echoed and reechoed in her mind.

Sister Thérèse and Mrs. Miller chatted amiably and spoke to her only when it was necessary to the business at hand. Once Julie looked up and caught Mrs. Miller staring at her with cold eyes in which an avid curiosity flickered.

I wonder what they would do if I suddenly said, "Oh, let me tell you all about it," she thought, and she imagined hurling the details of her nights with Bill into their astonished faces.

It made her smile, and Mrs. Miller said sharply, "You have very little to smile at, my girl. I understand that your family is very angry."

Julie's smile faded, but she continued to return Mrs. Miller's stare, boldly and with a leaping defiance in her eyes. It was Mrs. Miller who looked away, two spots of mottled red color high on her plump cheeks.

If the trip to New York had been difficult, the meeting with Holt made it seem pleasant in comparison.

As they came into the vast domed waiting room of Pennsylvania Station, Holt walked forward to greet them, trailed by two nuns who had come to meet Mrs. Miller and Sister Thérèse and take them to the sanctuary of some local convent where they would rest before their return.

Holt was no favorite of hers, but the sight of a face from home for the first time in three years brought an involuntary smile to Julie's face and she stepped forward eagerly. He looked wonderful, she thought. He had the thick, fair hair of the Prescotts and their brilliant blue eyes, and, as always, he was impeccably turned out. Today he wore a dark summer suit, white silk shirt, and a slender, neatly knotted maroon tie. He carried his gray Homburg in his left hand, his right extended, but as Julie put her own out to take it, he walked past her to grasp Mrs. Miller's hand and thank her warmly for "her kindness in a most difficult task."

Julie's face flamed and the smaller of the two New York nuns, the one who rather reminded her of Eileen by the sweet gentleness of her face, took the hand Holt had ignored and said, "I am Sister Josephine, my dear. You mustn't worry. It will come out all right in the end if you follow what you know in your heart is best."

They were the first kind words she had heard in days, and Julie, feeling a thickness in her throat, batted her lashes rapidly to keep back the tears.

"Thank you, Sister," she managed to say in a low voice. For the first time since she had seen Sister Thérèse's angry face in the doorway of her convent room, guilt and remorse swept over her. Now she would gladly have confessed—sure of pardon and compassion.

She started to mumble a penitent answer when Holt was beside her, his voice cold. "Well, Julie, I see you have managed to disgrace us again."

Anger and humiliation swept away all other emotions, and, forgetting they were in a public place, she flared: "Since when did you become so proper, Holt Prescott? You're the same miserable little sneak you always were. Go to the devil!" And without bothering to say good-bye to the others, she stalked off across the lobby toward the exit sign, heedless of the fact that her luggage still remained at the gate. Early morning travelers stared at the sight of a well-dressed girl scurrying as fast as her hobble skirts would permit, head high, hat shaking as she bounced along while, behind her, pale green waxed grapes rolled along the floor like scattered marbles.

Holt caught up with her at the stairway leading to the street. He grasped her by the arm with such harsh cruelty that she cried out.

"Where do you think you're going? Must I call the authorities to keep track of you? Perhaps I should do that. Then you'd be remanded to a home for wayward girls and we'd be rid of you once and for all."

He had let go of her arm and he was smiling, but his eyes were glittering with anger and his voice was venomous. Julie had always feared Holt a little. There was a cruelty in him that lurked just below the surface, and when she was younger and was reading Bible stories, the devil somehow always had Holt's face in her mind.

A chill passed over her and she shuddered. She saw his satisfied smirk and for once held her tongue. Until she was back in Prescottville, she was at Holt's mercy, and she had too often seen him in a passion of rage not to fear that rage now directed at her.

"Don't be silly, Holt," she said with a calm she was far from feeling. "I'm not running away. In fact, I'm dying to get home. When does the train for Hammondsport leave?"

"That's better," he replied, "much better. And as for dying to get home, you aren't going to be happy with the reception committee, save of course, for Mark Douglas. He seemed to think it was all a joke. But, then, whoring around as he does, he admires a harlot."

Julie felt a hot retort spring to her lips and bit it back. "I'd better see to my luggage," she said instead, and she followed Holt meekly back to the gate.

Not only would it not be a happy homecoming, but it was to be worse then she had feared—except for Mark Douglas. Well, one friend was more than she had counted on. She lifted her chin in a spirit of renewed confidence, and from that moment until she mounted the steps of the Prescott house she gave Holt no further cause for anger.

Her pulse began to race from the moment they reached the outskirts of Elmira, and reaching Bath half an hour later, scenes familiar since childhood began to restore her sense of well-being.

Amos, who had driven for the Prescotts as long as she could remember, greeted them at the station in Hammondsport in Uncle Jason's new Packard motorcar for the drive north to Prescottville.

"Miss Julie," he said, his face splitting into a wide grin, "we've sure missed you around here. Margaret's in the motorcar with me. Said she had to get a look at you." He ran his gnarled hand over his silvery hair before replacing his cap and opening the rear door.

"It's good to see you, Amos." Julie smiled back, grateful that there was at least one warm greeting. She looked down at him, smiling again, remembering how her father used to say that Amos might look like a small, truculent fighting cock, but he had the soul of a lamb.

"Let me say hello to Margaret first," she said, and Amos opened the front door.

Margaret, who topped Amos by three inches, pinked with pleasure at Julie's greeting. "You look like a proper young lady," she said, and her soft palm patted Julie's cheek warmly. "Hard to believe you ever were that baby who used to come into the kitchen begging for bread and jam."

"Well I'm not a baby anymore," Julie laughed. "But I'll be begging for your homemade bread and jam, Margaret. You can count on that."

Behind her, Holt said stiffly, "Julie, will you get into the motorcar, please. You can have your conversation at home."

When they were in the car and on their way, he said, under his breath, "Butter wouldn't melt in your mouth, would it, Julie? You're just full of sweetness and light on the outside, aren't you?" She did not answer, smoothing her skirt and tugging off her gloves.

As they bounced along the old carriage roads, Julie, holding her hat on her head with one hand, peered eagerly through the windows at the surrounding countryside, smiling at the riders of each horse and carriage they passed.

Landmark after landmark rose before her: Crater's Mill on the outskirts of the small lake where she and her father used to swim; Douglas Dairies, where Mark's cousin Art had been the first to modernize, and was even now engaged in building a dairyman's cooperative; the little

farm the earliest Prescott had built that still belonged to
Jason Prescott and was now leased for tenant farming;
then the vineyards, stretching as far as she could see; and
in the distance her old home, rising white and lonely
among the oaks that surrounded it.

Her heart caught in her throat and her eyes filled with
tears. Home. How she would love it if she could just
move straight into that house. Impossible, of course.
Mark Douglas lived there now, or at least in one part of
it, and the rest was shut off, the furniture covered with
dustcloths that were removed twice a year by Amos'
wife, Margaret, for the spring and fall cleaning.

Someday, she promised herself, someday when I am
married I'll move back into it. But sell it, never. She felt
a surge of gratitude to Mark for refusing to consent to
the sale that Uncle Jason wanted; for offering to maintain it as his rental for living in one section so that he
could preserve it for her. At twenty-one she would be
able to control the disposition of her property. At twenty-
one she would be free to come and go as she pleased,
and no one could stop her then.

Sighing with satisfaction, she leaned back in her seat,
letting her hat fall askew and then drawing out the large
pin that secured it so precariously, laughing, running her
hands along her hair, wishing she could take out the hair-
pins and let it flow down her back.

"You're very gay for a girl who is about to face the
lions," Holt said sourly, breaking his sullen silence.

"Once they're faced, it will be over," she answered.
"And that will be soon. We're nearly there," she said
and pointed out as the motorcar turned into Seneca Avenue and the Prescott house came into view.

It was the largest house on the street and the oldest,
as befitted the scion of the town's founder and the owner
of the town's bank. Built in Southern colonial fashion, it
faced Deer Hill Park and Wide Waters Pond, where
swans and ducklings nested each summer.

"The lilacs!" Julie exclaimed. "I had almost forgotten
they'd be in full bloom now!" Masses of purple and white
blossoms filled the park's lawns, sending their heady,
sweet odor over the pond so that it seemed to distill their
essence and perfume the air.

She drew deep, satisfying breaths as she emerged from

the car, whirling about on the lawn and flinging her arms
wide open. "Home!" she exulted. "Home at last!"

"Behave yourself, Julie," Holt commanded.

But feeling safe now, she made a face at him. "I
needn't worry about you anymore, Holt Prescott. Go pick
on someone else." And without waiting for a reply, she
ran up the steps of the wide-columned porch just as the
door opened and Millicent Prescott, her thin face a mixture of greeting and disapproval, stepped out.

"Julie," she began, but got no further.

Julie, in her own delight at being home, flung her arms
around her diminutive aunt, nearly smothering her in her
exuberant embrace and crying, "Don't be too angry, Aunt
Millie. I haven't committed a crime, and I promise I'll
be as good as gold from now on."

For a moment, Millicent Prescott wavered, determined
to be severe, but she was assailed by a twinge of guilt
when she remembered the reasons why she had sent Julie
away—reasons, she acknowledged to herself, that had little to do with that silly flirtation. The twinge left her.
She returned the hug briefly, saying, "For heaven's sake,
Julie, do start now, then. You're too old to be acting like
a child and, anyway, I can't promise you Uncle Jason
will be very lenient."

The first battle was over. Julie sensed that and sensed,
too, that if Millicent was not going to rant and rave,
Jason wouldn't do more than bluster for appearance's
sake.

"Let me look at you," Millicent said, drawing back
and running an appraising eye over her niece. "Grown
up, really grown up," she said at length, and in her
voice there was both regret and satisfaction.

She looked past Julie and called, "Holt, dear, how
was the trip?"

"Filthy," Holt replied. "And quite unnecessary. Julie
could have come on alone. She has her own way of
getting what she wants." The sneer was unmistakable,
but Julie, knowing she had won on this front, at least,
took pleasure in a sweet reply.

"Poor Holt," she said, laughing. "To be forced to
pick up a silly girl cousin and worry about her. Do you
know that when I started to walk away in the station,
he actually thought I was going to come to some harm.

He ran after me like a mother hen. Dear Holt," she said, turning a smiling face at him, "I am sorry if I worried you." She took immense satisfaction from the smoldering fury in his eyes.

3

Dinner that evening was less of an ordeal than Julie had expected. She had been up in her old room when Jason Prescott arrived home from the bank, and it seemed prudent to remain there, delaying as long as possible the lecture she felt certain Uncle Jason would be obliged to give.

Her clothes of three years ago, freshly washed and pressed, hung neatly in the wardrobe, and she had tried on one garment after another, discarding each one as too small or too hopelessly childish. One, a light blue cotton with the old kimono bodice and wide short sleeves, had the best possibilities. And her linen slips still fit, although they were a bit short.

She washed thoroughly, standing in an old wrapper at the flowered porcelain basin and pitcher in her room. She wanted a full tub, but that would necessitate going down the hall to the bath, and she was determined not to chance an accidental meeting with her uncle.

Standing in her long Poiret brassiere and bloomers, in the act of pulling on her slip, Julie caught a glimpse of herself in the pier glass and moved toward her reflection.

Looking at one's body was strictly forbidden at St. Veronica's, and she had not seen a full view of herself since Christmas. She had changed. Her body was slimmer at the waist, rounder at the hips, and her breasts had acquired an enticing fullness. She looked taller. Lifting the slip, she surveyed her legs, encased in the despised black cotton stockings. Long and well shaped and tapering to slim ankles, they showed a band of alabaster-white where garters met the stocking tops.

Satisfied, she finished dressing, going once more to the mirror when she had finished. Blue was a good color for her, although the lavender deepened her violet eyes and seemed to make her hair and brows and thick, sooty lashes even darker in the camellia-white of her face.

She brushed her hair again, hearing it crackle through the bristles of her tortoiseshell brush, and then caught it, smoothing the springing tresses with light hands, catching and twisting it into a low knot at the nape of her neck. There! She gave a last critical appraisal, tucked a linen handkerchief in her belt, and went downstairs.

The others were already in the dining room when she entered. Holt was drawing the chair on Uncle Jason's right for Millicent, and he did not look up as she entered, going instead to the foot of the table, opposite Jason, his normal place, except for formal dinners, when Millicent acted as hostess.

Julie slipped quickly into her own seat across from her aunt and said quickly, "Hello, Uncle Jason. I'm sorry I'm late."

There was a brief silence before Jason said, "I should think your lateness is the least of your failings, Julie."

She looked up at him, seeing at once how much he had aged.

"I'm sorry I caused any difficulty," she answered. "But it was a lot of fuss about nothing. It was hot, the room was stuffy, and I only wanted to be out for a while to . . . to see what it was like at night, how it felt to be alone." She stumbled only briefly over the lie, which by now had become almost rote to her.

"It was against the rules," Jason said heavily.

"I know that, but there wasn't any real harm in it." She had a quick impression of Bill, a swift memory of the last night, and she blushed, furious at the telltale sign. Thankfully, both her aunt and uncle took it as embarrassed penitence, but darting a quick look at Holt, Julie saw that he was not so naïve. He met her look with a faint smile of contempt and she lowered her eyes.

"We'll say no more about it at dinner," Aunt Millicent declared. "Please, Jason," she added, and before he could answer, the pantry door opened and Jenny, the waitress, came in bearing the tureen of soup, the ritual beginning to every Prescott dinner, winter and summer.

There was little conversation during the meal. Jason Prescott, a heavy man with jowls that bulged above his high starched collar, was too fond of his food to be distracted by talk. At fifty-eight, his fair hair was threaded with gray and getting white at the temples. Millicent, six years younger, had held up better, Julie decided. Small, thin of body and face, she wore her hair piled high, and if there was gray in it, the careful arrangement concealed it. Apart from the difference in their physical stances, they could have been twins, so alike were they in coloring and features. From the pictures Julie had seen of her own mother, all the Prescotts bore a strong family resemblance. Holt was often taken for Millicent's son when they were among strangers. Her own mother had been very like them, except for the tender, short upper lip that Julie had inherited.

"Not a true Prescott," Millicent used to say of Julie. "All Fontaine, except for the eyes, and, my dear child, I don't know where you got those lavender-blue eyes." When she was little it rather made her feel like a changeling. Now she was glad enough to be called all Fontaine.

Idly she wondered what Sara, Holt's mother, had looked like. From the moment Sara had run off with what Aunt Millicent termed "a passing whiskey drummer," Jason had burned every picture and had forbidden the mention of her name. What bits and pieces about Holt's mother Julie had been able to gather had come from Margaret, the cook. Holt seldom mentioned his mother at all, which Julie found curious. He was four when she left, old enough to remember something. Once Millicent had said to Julie. "You are like Sara, very gay and flirtatious, and you know what happened to her." But when pressed, Millicent would not say more. What had happened to Sara? According to Margaret, she had simply packed up one night and left a note, the contents of which Jason would reveal to no one aside from Millicent. She had not been seen or heard from again.

Once, just before Julie's father died, a letter had arrived from New York. She had seen a great sadness transform his face as he read it. He had gone to his desk immediately and written two replies. Curled up in a chair, reading, Julie had heard him sigh from time to time and had wondered what the letter could be about.

When he had finished writing, he drew his checkbook from the middle drawer, made out a check, and slipped it into the smaller of the two envelopes he had addressed. Just then, he was called away to the telephone, and Julie, curious, had chanced a peek at the envelopes. The smaller one said simply, "Sara." The other was addressed to a Mrs. Paraglie or Pargalie in New York. She knew Sara was the aunt who had run away, but the other name she had never heard before.

After her father returned to the library, she saw him seal the smaller envelope and slip it into the larger one. And then he had done something surprising. He had torn the letter that had come for him into pieces and thrown it into the fireplace, stirring it with the poker while he watched it burn.

"Julie," Aunt Millicent said loudly, and Julie looked up, startled. "You must be in a daydream. Uncle Jason is speaking to you."

"Sorry. I always seem to be saying 'sorry.'" She turned to Jason.

He grunted and said, "Mark Douglas is coming by this evening. We are going over the terms· of your father's will again. Also, you're coming into a larger sum than I think wise for an eighteen-year-old girl. However, it was your father's idea that you might like to have a good sum at this point for some special reason. I think that you should reinvest most of it. After all, you have an allowance increase then, too, which means that there will be less reinvestment in your trust fund. It's true that you have a substantial trust, but the market is fluctuating, and if Wilson is re-elected, your trust might be reduced considerably three years from now. We have this war in Europe and that imbecile Wilson in the White House thumping on about peace—peace! How can we have peace when the Germans are killing innocent Americans? Look how many died on the *Lusitania*." He stopped and gnawed his lip, a habit he had when he digressed, as he often did, from the main point. "Fools," he went on, "fools, all of them! Who told them to sail on a British merchant ship in the middle of the war? Still, the Germans had no right to sink her. Wilson'll sell out this country. Never trusted that addlebrained college professor, anyway. Said so at the time. He's ruining business. Where was I?" He appealed to Millicent.

"Trying to convince Julie to reinvest her lump sum."

"Eh? Oh, yes. Now you want to think over what I said, Julie. After all, you'll be controlling all your money soon enough. And you'll also want to think about the winery, now that you can vote your stock. Prohibition is coming down on us like the wolf on the fold. Better be thinking about how to convert Fontaine's or sell out.

"Personally, I think eighteen is too young for that kind of responsibility. Not that Mark Douglas paid any attention to the future while he still controlled your votes. Never did understand John—bringing Mark in from California when there were plenty of good young men right here in Prescottville. For that matter, I never understood Mark's father—leaving Prescottville, selling his share in the Douglas land and dairies to his brother, and then going off to San Francisco and marrying into God knows what and staying there. Wild blood! All the Douglases are, although, at that, Mark may not be as crazy as his cousin, Art Douglas, up there at the dairy, trying to start a cooperative with his father hardly cold in his grave. Cooperative! Buying up mortgages on dairy farms and then he doesn't turn the farmers out, he helps them. Socialist thinking. Why, he's as crazy as that Eugene Debs. They all ought to be locked up. Ruining this country. . . ." His fair skin was very red and the broken veins in his cheeks had turned a deep fuchsia.

"Jason, dear, please," Millicent said in alarm. "You mustn't get so excited, especially after dinner. You know the doctor said it was bad for your blood pressure." She laid a hand on her brother's arm and smiled into the angry face that he turned toward her. It was a gentle, affectionate smile, and something in her eyes seemed to calm him.

"Yes, well, if the socialists don't get us, those doctors will," he grumbled, but the steam was gone.

"Father," Holt spoke up for the first time, "I wanted to see you about the Schultz mortgage before tomorrow. There's a problem—nothing I can't handle, but I think you ought to be in on it."

"No more of that business tonight," Aunt Millicent said firmly. "You can talk to your father in the morning. What with Julie's return and Mark coming over. . . ."

She turned back to Jason: "Now, you don't want to be sick again, Jason, Early to bed and no more worries to-night."

It settled the question of Holt and of any lectures to Julie. Millicent had a quiet and gentle manner, deferential in every way to Jason and Holt, but when she spoke up, as she rarely did, she generally had her way.

Jason and Millicent retired to the living room, as was their wont, to listen to the crystal set and to play Caruso records. Holt was still sulking and passing Julie in the lower hall on his way out for the evening. He brushed against her rudely, saying, "Well, you got away without so much as a lecture. Very clever. Actually, what you need is a good beating."

"Leave me alone, Holt. I'm not a child anymore," Julie flared.

He didn't answer, slamming the door as he went out. She stared at the closed door and suddenly remembered a day long ago when she was perhaps six and Holt was ten. As a mean joke he had tried to pull down her bloomers as she climbed the low branches of an apple tree in her father's garden. She had screamed and her father, who was having a visit with Uncle Jason, had hurried from the house. Holt had jumped away from her at once, but she remembered sobbing in her father's arms and telling him what Holt had done. "He was trying to make me fall," she said. Her father had seized Holt as he attempted to run and hustled him into the house to confront Uncle Jason.

Julie, following them in, still crying, saw Holt strike his father's hand away from his arm. Jason had whipped Holt then, right in front of everyone, whipped him until Julie's father had said, "Good Lord, Jason, you'll hurt him if you go on like that." And Jason, red-faced and breathing hard, had released his hold.

"I hate you!" Holt had screamed at them all. "Hate you! Hate you!" And he had run out of the house.

Julie shivered. Holt today was as hateful as ever. Saving Millicent, she didn't think he had any feelings for anyone, not even his own father.

It wasn't going to be easy living in the house with Holt again. The best she could do would be to stay out of his way. She sighed restlessly. The house was suddenly too confining. Outdoors the twilight had lengthened with the spring days and she went outside to wander aimlessly about the lawn and finally to cross Seneca Avenue and lose herself among the lilacs in the park.

Now that she was back, the days at the convent seemed far away, as if they and Camp Joy and Cousin Bertha were all part of a bad dream from which she had thankfully awakened. Even Bill's face blurred in her mind, although the memory of his touch was still warm on her flesh.

Tomorrow she would look up old friends. Tomorrow she would become part of the social life of Prescottville again: boating on Wide Waters; playing tennis; walking in Deer Hill Park up to the top of the hill; shopping at Brenner's Department Store on Main Street; and, if she could persuade Millicent and Jason, driving into Elmira to buy some clothes—only a few, because she would save the lump sum for shopping in New York City at McCreerys or Franklin Simon or Best's or that new French Shop near Fifty-seventh Street that Alice Bradford had written her about.

Tomorrow she could begin to live. The soft-scented air, the flowering cherry and dogwood massed at the foot of the hill, the sky turning pink and turquoise on the western horizon, and the first faint stars gleaming in the darker eastern sky filled her with nameless delight. She felt light and floating; her skin was cool, but there was a glowing warmth inside her body. Impulsively, she buried her face in the purple lilacs beside her until the angry buzzing of a late bee made her draw back, laughing a little at her own foolishness.

She came out of the park and saw a large roan horse tied to the old hitching post in front of the house. The sky had deepened to navy blue and behind the drawn draperies of the house lights gleamed. The soft breezes of twilight had changed to cool night winds, and, chilly in her light frock, she ran across the road and across the broad lawn, taking the shallow steps in one bound to arrive at the door, flushed and breathless.

Giving little thought to how she must look, and carried forward by her own impetus, she burst into the living room, skidding to a halt as Jason and Millicent turned astonished faces toward her.

There was a third person in the room—a tall, broad-shouldered man with an air of vitality about him that made her catch her breath. Hazel eyes regarded her with some amusement, and in the light, his dark red hair shone polished cedar. She had barely time to notice that he wore his hair unparted and longer than was fashionable when he was advancing toward her, saying, "Well, well, Julie, back from the nuns and all grown up, I see." His eyes swept over her from head to foot, and there was no denying the frank admiration in them.

Flustered, she pushed the pins back into her hair, knowing she must look disheveled, wishing now that she had saved that lovely violet silk for her first night at home. She couldn't quite meet his eyes, and she held out her hand, saying primly, "Hello, Mark. I hardly recognized you." Her slim fingers were lost in his warm hand, and at his touch some instinct made her draw back as if his very presence would somehow envelop her whole body in the same way that he now imprisoned her hand.

From his place near the newly lit fire, Jason said, "Well, I suppose we had better get down to business. We'll go into the library." He rose heavily, patting Millicent's shoulder as he passed her chair.

Mark was still holding Julie's hand, saying something about how nice it was to have her at home in spite of the escapade that had brought her there.

At the word "escapade," her lids flew up and she looked full into his eyes, eyes that held so much laughter and challenge that they seemed to shoot sparks. She felt a rush of conflicting emotions. She wanted to smile back and frown at the same moment and something else. She started to withdraw her hand. He held it firmly in his for a moment, almost as if he were proclaiming his mastery, and then she was free.

"Now," he said, stepping aside with a faint bow to let her precede him, "on to the intricacies of an eighteen-year-old girl let loose with all that money and the right to vote on Fontaine's policy."

"Really, Mark," Millicent said, annoyed.

"I am only teasing, Miss Prescott," he answered. "After all, she's still under guardianship for three years. Hardly free to come and go as she pleases."

In the library, Julie settled herself demurely in one of

the leather chairs a little apart from the two men. She kept her hands clasped loosely in her lap and her eyes down.

Jason cleared his throat several times before he spoke. "I said at dinner," he began, "that you were receiving a larger sum than I think is wise. It's nearly ten percent of the entire amount in trust. That's ten thousand dollars."

Julie's lids flew upward and her mouth opened in surprise. Ten thousand! It was far more than she had imagined. With that much money, why, she could do just about anything. She could . . .

"Now, of course, it's yours," Jason went on. "But I am still your guardian, and Mark agrees with me that you'll want to do something sensible with it."

Julie murmured a brief "Of course," thinking that what Jason and Mark might consider sensible would be far different from her plans for that money. Ten thousand! She settled back in her chair and listened carefully.

Jason did most of the talking, and Mark appeared to be in almost total agreement. They differed, however, as to what she should do with the money. Mark wanted her to invest part of it back in the winery, while Jason wanted her to put it into his keeping at the bank for what he termed "more prudent investment."

Over this, they had a heated discussion. Jason kept pressing the point that with the prohibitionists hot on bringing the remaining fifteen states into the dry camp by the means of constitutional amendment and the bad crop of the previous year, the winery was in danger of going out of business. "Unless you'd convert it. Do what Charles Welch is doing over in Chautauqua County. Make grape juice. Or else sell the winery to Steuben. Or pull up the vines and plant crops."

"How many times must I tell you, Jason? I can't rip up acres of Isabellas and Catawbas. I won't. That stock has been there for decades. How long do you think it takes? You don't cultivate a vineyard overnight. It isn't a damned potato patch. As for that fantastic prohibitionist, Charles Welch, he'd pour sulfur and molasses into bottles and hawk them if he thought it would keep the country dry. The fifteen states won't follow. California never will! And the federal government won't pass the law."

"They will," Jason said.

"Well, if they do, they'll have a tough time making it stick. There are stills in all the hills of all the dry states this very minute."

"You're talking about illegal operations."

"I'm talking common sense. Pass all the laws you like. People are still going to drink wine and spirits. Hell, they've been drinking wine since Caesar's time, and before that. You don't imagine that the good ladies of the Christian Temperance Union are going to prevail over human nature, do you?"

"You've got to admit it's chancy, Mark. Even if it does as you say, the winery is a long way from being as solid as the bank."

"All right, I'll concede to that. But Julie has a vested interest in that winery. She's inherited a major share of stock. If it sinks, so does her money, save, of course, for what is 'prudently' invested in stocks and bonds through your bank. If it comes to that, Jason, if the winery does sink, there will be a loss around Prescottville itself, and your bank will feel it. Don't forget the men we hire and the business they help support with their purchases. It's like a pebble in a pond; the ripples go out beyond the point where the pebble strikes."

Julie, watching the two men, marveled at their difference: Jason, getting older, paunchy, and thick, with a stubborn conservatism that never wavered; Mark, mercurial of temperament, slim in spite of his width and hardness of bone and muscle, his features just missing handsomeness by the rugged structure of his bones and the crescent scar above his left eyebrow, a mark that gave his face a faintly sardonic look even when that eyebrow wasn't raised in mockery.

So far she had said nothing, and at last they finished their private argument and turned to her.

"Well, Julie, what will it be?" Mark asked.

"Neither," she said quietly. "I want the money for my own use, as Papa intended."

Mark laughed, but Jason was unbelieving. At once, less enthusiastically supported by Mark, he began to dissuade her. She said no for some minutes, trying to pick the time when she could win what she most wanted by conceding the least.

At last, when Jason had paused for a moment to wipe his perspiring forehead, she said, "Well, I might invest half of it if I could use the rest and if I could go down to New York with Aunt Millicent to get some decent clothes."

Jason was past speech for a minute. His face grew so dark that Julie became frightened that he would have a fit of apoplexy.

"Five thousand dollars is a lot of money for clothes," Mark interposed. "Don't you agree, Jason?"

"Not to be thought of," Jason growled. "Ridiculous."

"Then I'll keep the money, and when I'm free to come and go as I please, I'll spend it and everything else on a trip to Paris to get clothes."

"In the middle of the war?" Mark inquired.

"The war won't last forever, especially not if we get into it." And at this Jason threw up his hands in wordless amazement.

"Five thousand is still too much," Mark persisted.

"Very well. I'll keep four, then," Julie agreed. "And I'll never vote to sell the winery, Uncle Jason."

"Where does she get these ideas?" Jason said to no one in particular. "We've sent her to a convent school and she comes home filled with notions that wouldn't occur to any other girl her age."

"Oh, yes it would," Julie answered, "even if they hadn't been stuck in the middle of a prairie in ugly old uniforms. Only most of them don't have ten thousand dollars of their own."

She settled back in her chair, an obdurate expression on her face. She knew she was going to win at some point or other, and it was just a matter of getting the best bargain she could.

In the end, she agreed to divide all but twenty-five hundred dollars between the bank and the winery. In return she wanted a shopping trip to New York, as well as a preliminary shopping expedition in Elmira. "I have nothing at all to wear," she said firmly. She refused to promise not to spend the whole twenty-five hundred dollars on shopping. "We'll stay at the Waldorf," she announced. "I'll pay for it, of course," she added grandly. "And I want to be there for at least three days, and I want to go to the theater at least once and to nice restaurants like Delmonico's. And then I'll come home."

Jason gave up. Hard as he might be in business, for all he seemed to rule the house, he was never any good at dealing either with Julie or with his own son, Holt, unless he had Millicent to back him up. And Millicent was fortunately lost in the golden tenor notes of "Ridi Pagliacci," which even the tinny mechanical reproduction could not fully mar.

Mark did not return to the living room with them. He said good night at the front door. Jason left Julie to see him out, and as they stood together at the doorway, Mark said softly, "I admire your spirit, Julie. Who would have thought you'd turn out this way?"

"What way?" she asked.

"Well, for one thing, you appear to have a brain—a very shrewd brain—beneath all the fluff about clothes. I'm sure you planned your strategy well in advance."

She smiled. "Not too well in advance—only since I found out just how much I had."

"Thank God your father had the wit not to leave you in control of the winery, at least not in full control. That, dear Julie, is my department, except for the other stockholders, all of whom but one are men."

"You may be glad of my help one day," Julie answered. "You might need me to put back income, if what Uncle Jason thinks is true."

"If what Jason thinks comes true, you won't have very much income, dear girl." He laughed and took his departure, leaving her to frown with inexplicable annoyance at his retreating back.

At the convent the days and nights had seemed endless despite the rigid schedule that left few free moments. At home, the two weeks leading up to her birthday flew by, although they were filled with pleasures and lacked any real duties. Occasionally, Aunt Millicent would mention that Julie should be thinking of some suitable way to occupy her time, mentioning, among other things, the library guild and the new local Red Cross chapter. Millicent, busy seeing to the running of the household, managed time for both, as well as the Missionary Society of the First Presbyterian Church.

Religion still hovered like a dark cloud over the rest of Julie's occupations. Sunday meant church, and if she didn't go to Mass at St. Stephen's, she would have been carted along to services with the Prescotts. Of the two choices, it was easier to make Mass.

While she had been gone, Father Cassidy had died and Father Gannett had taken his place. He might wonder why she did not receive communion, but it would be some time before he would approach her on the subject, if, indeed, he ever did. One more plus: all of Holt's dire predictions when he met her in New York had so far failed to come true.

She kept as far away from Holt as she could. It was not a difficult task. He was not any fonder of conversation at mealtimes than his father, and he was seldom around in the evenings. Once, however, as she stepped into the hallway from the bath, he caught her by the arm and said, "Riding high these days, aren't you, Julie? Just remember about the pride that comes before the fall."

She wrenched her arm away. "If pride precedes a fall, you should have split your head at least a dozen times by now, Holt. I can take care of myself, so leave me alone."

"Who is it to be this time? Andrew Clay again? Possibly some new bit of callow youth? Or maybe an older man. Maybe Mark Douglas? He's been around a lot more lately since you've been home."

"Don't be stupid, Holt. Mark comes on business only."

"Really? Then why not see Father at the bank? Or have you out to his office in the winery?"

She walked on without answering. Mark. She didn't like Mark at all, not really. He made her feel timid and unsure of herself, and he always seemed to be laughing at her, as if she were a performing poodle.

The following morning, Alice Bradford, who had been Julie's closest friend all through childhood, telephoned to invite her to tea that afternoon.

"I couldn't believe my ears when I heard you were back," Alice bubbled over the wire. "I was going to come straight over this morning, but Mother's having all these ladies in to tea, and I must be here. You've no idea how fussy Mother's become since Father was elected mayor."

"No matter how fussy she's become, she can't be as fussy as the nuns," Julie replied feelingly.

"Oh, I've so much to tell you, and there's so much I want to hear about. Wasn't it awful to be exiled that way? I kept thinking surely you'd be home at Christmas or for the summer holidays."

"It was awful," Julie said. "But it's all over now. It'll be lovely to have a good gossip again."

"Yes, and your Aunt Millicent declined—something about a doctor's appointment that couldn't be changed. So you won't have her within earshot. Oops!" she broke off. "It's Kenneth. He wants to use the telephone. I'll see you at four."

Sitting in the Bradfords' pleasant living room, sipping sweet tea and nibbling at a watercress sandwich, Julie was conscious that she was under the covert scrutiny of several of the ladies present. It made her uncomfortable. She found it difficult to believe that either Jason or Millicent would have made the reasons for her return known. And Holt. Well, anything was possible with Holt, but he, like the rest of the Prescotts, never liked family affairs talked about publicly.

"I swear," Julie said in a low voice to Alice, "that I must be the subject of some gossip. Mrs. van Houten has been peering at me as if I were something rare and strange. Don't tell me there's gossip about me!"

"Not that I know of," Alice said. "I think Mrs. van Houten is like the rest. You have changed, Julie. You're . . ." she said and waved her hands, ". . . oh, beautiful and . . ."

Julie blushed. "Don't be silly. It's the same face I've always had. No one stared at me before I went away."

"You're grown up."

"Well, so are you," Julie said. It was true. She had remembered Alice as skinny and small with merry brown eyes and an innocently round face. Over the three years, Alice had grown in inches and in width. While she wasn't fat, she was definitely plump in a pleasing way. The dimples on either side of her full mouth were deeper and there was a definite mischievous look about her.

"Tell me," Julie said in what she devoutly hoped was a casual manner, "speaking of people changing, Mark Douglas isn't quite as I remember him. And my family keeps hinting that he's turned into a rake of some kind."

"Mark?" Alice echoed. "Mark? Oh, I don't know, I

hear he's been seen out at Viola's Roadhouse, but, then, I'll bet my sainted brother Kenneth has, too. Actually, Mark is very popular, at least with the ladies. He took Elizabeth van Houten to the Christmas ball last year, and you know Mr. van Houten. Elizabeth would have been in chains before her father let her go out with a rake."

"Elizabeth? But wasn't she always rather prim and bookish?" Julie asked.

"Still is. Mark doesn't see her anymore—not since he picked up with Miranda Latham. Well, of course, now it's in the open. I heard that they've been seeing each other ever since her husband died. That was the year after you went to St. Veronica's.

"Ray Latham owned stock in Fontaine's, and when he died Mark had to see her on business a lot," Alice said and giggled. "Of course, he never brought her about to parties or anything until her year of mourning was up. But once it was, they were seen everywhere together. Miranda is looking for a new husband, I guess."

"But Miranda is old," Julie said. "Why, she must be thirty . . . five."

"Thirty-three. My youngest aunt was in boarding school with her," Alice returned impishly. "No secrets in Prescottville, Julie. Surely you remember that? Of course, Mark doesn't seem to mind gossip, or Miranda, either. He ties up that horse of his in front of her house even in broad daylight."

"Why does he ride all the time?" Julie asked. "He has a motorcar. I know that, and our old carriage is still out at the house if he prefers horse-drawn cars to motors."

"Must be his California upbringing," Alice said. "He's usually in cowboy clothes, too. Oh, not at a party, of course. He looks positively handsome in evening clothes, and, of course, he doesn't bring Miranda on the back of his saddle. He drives in his Buick touring car then."

"Is Mark going to marry Miranda?"

Alice shrugged. "His cousin Art Douglas says Mark is doomed to be a bachelor. But I don't know. Miranda's the sort of woman who likes to have her own way. She and Mark are a pair. Miranda's a terrible flirt, and Mark Douglas, well, he's different—a rebel, people say. I mean, he wouldn't ranch, and then when his family got him an appointment to West Point, he resigned after two years."

"I'm not too fond of Mark," Julie confessed. "He's my trustee—or one of them—and I know my father thought he was just perfect, but I don't know. Mark's, well, hard, if you know what I mean."

"He's nobody's slave. I'll say that. Know how he got that scar on his forehead?" Julie shook her head. "He got it in a fight in a winery in California where he went to work right after he left West Point. It seems the other man broke a wine bottle and slashed Mark with it. Mark broke the man's arm."

"How?" Julie asked with a shudder of excitement.

"I don't know. Kenneth said Mark probably broke it over his knee."

"It's funny. Mark was my father's friend and I've known him for years, yet I never heard any of these stories. How do you know so much about him?"

"Julie, while you were out in Iowa, I was right here in Prescottville. Once you get to a certain age, people don't shoo you out of the room when they want to gossip. But don't worry," she teased, "I'll bring you up to date."

"What are you girls whispering about?" Mrs. Bradford said chidingly. "You'd think you were twelve instead of eighteen. Mrs. van Houten has just invited you to a dinner party for her niece who is coming up from Philadelphia next week."

In the flurry of apology and acceptance, the talk of Mark was forgotten and Julie did not bring it up again. But it stayed in the back of her mind, and the following day she asked if Amos might drive her over to the winery on the premise that she would like to see it again after such a long absence.

She arrayed herself in one of the best costumes she had managed to buy in Elmira, a summery white voile skirt and blouse inset with bands of eyelet embroidery and girdled by a bright pink sash that matched the flowers on her straw hat. Her feet and ankles, encased in white silk stockings and cunningly cut low white shoes, peeped beneath the hem, and she observed them in the mirror with great satisfaction.

Cool and elegant, she thought, and a match for Mark Douglas. He might treat her like a child at home, but dressed as she was and in his office, he would have to be more deferential. After all, he wasn't that much older than she was.

He might be the catch of the town and set every girl's heart beating faster, for all she cared. He had no such effect on her, and somehow this afternoon she meant to make him treat her with some respect. Better yet, it would be nice to make him like her, and then she could have the pleasure of laughing at him.

With all the romanticism of eighteen years and a confidence born of her recent experiments with love, she sailed forth, imagining a sullen, importunate Mark Douglas at some mistily conceived gathering where she treated him with cool indifference and was the envy of every woman in town.

4

Mark was in the vineyards with Joe Damien, Fontaine's winemaker, when one of the workmen at the winery came to tell him that George Schultz was waiting to see him and that Miss Julie Fontaine had arrived.

"I'll be along in a few minutes," he told the man, and then turned back to examine the vine flowers.

"It's the early spring we've had and the heat," he said to Joe. "If it keeps up like this through the summer, we'll have a vintage crop this year."

"To make up for last," Joe said, wiping his seamed face with a bandanna handkerchief. "By the way, I hear that Schultz has got some problems down at the bank. That's probably why he wants to see you. Shame to lose his crop this year of all years. Might have to bail him out."

Mark made a gesture of impatience. "We're working too close to the edge now. Avery Bertram is at me constantly to cut operating costs."

Joe shrugged. "Two years of bad weather, Mark. Summer before, mildew wiped out too much stock, and last summer was so short, you could wish for the old days before the government put a limit on adding sugar."

"That was back in the nineties," Mark said.

"Before you were old enough to know a grape from a huckleberry." Joe grinned. "But I can still hear my father hollering about it. Ever tell you about the time . . ."

"Can't hear it now, Joe. I'd better get back to the winery and see Schultz. I wonder what Julie Fontaine is doing here."

"Looking over her property, I expect," Joe answered mildly. "I'll stay up here for a while. I want to see the stock higher up the hill." He waved and started to move up to the next level, his short, muscular body straining against the cloth of his jacket. Mark watched him for a minute. Joe was looking a bit under the weather these days, and his son, Peter, while showing every promise of turning into the master vintner his father and grandfather were before him, was still too young.

Pity that Joe's older son had shown no interest in winemaking and had turned instead to dairy farming. He was eight years older than Peter, and the children in between were girls. At thirty, Armand would be ready to take over in case anything happened to his father, in the same way Joe had when his own father, the first Armand, had died.

Fontaine's had been lucky to get the Damiens. The Phylloxera epidemic that had nearly wiped out most of the French vineyards in 1865 had given Julie's great-grandfather the opportunity to hire a great winemaker.

"It's in the blood," John Fontaine used to say of Joe Damien. Well, if it hadn't been transferred to the second Armand, it had certainly found a ready home in young Peter. Under Joe's tutelage, he would one day become his father's equal. Until then, he could only hope that Joe was able to keep working.

Mark took a handkerchief from his pocket and wiped the perspiration from his neck and face. Standing among the vines, in Levi's, open-neck shirt, and the Western boots he discarded only when protocol demanded formal attire, Mark looked more like a cowhand in a Biograph film than he did the manager of an eastern wine company.

Halfway up the hill, Joe turned back and Mark waved a hand at him. Joe was all right. Joe was the best there was. He could have left Fontaine years ago for more money, but he had refused the offers of some of the bigger companies. "I have enough," he had told John Fontaine. "I like it here. Here is my home." Five years old when he had arrived in Prescottville, Joe remembered nothing of his home in France. And the house where he grew up, not far from the winery, was still his home.

Again, Mark thrust aside the gnawing worry that Joe might be ill. There was Schultz waiting and there was also Julie. He had an idea that she hadn't come to view her inheritance. If he read her right, she was ripe for a love affair. He hadn't believed for a minute that her convent escapade was as innocent as she pretended. There was something about her, some way she walked, the way she held herself, the habit she had of looking at a man with slanting eyes that proclaimed a sensuality to him.

As he strode back to his office, he wondered idly who the boy had been out in Iowa and found himself resenting the idea that there should have been someone, after all.

What the hell. What was going on here, anyway? First Joe and now this crazy business about Julie. Heat must have gotten to him. It was the hottest June he could remember outside of the California valleys.

He stopped outside the winery door, wiping his face again, moving his shoulders more comfortably beneath the damp shirt. Annoyed with himself, his face grew grim and he stepped into the welcome cool of the old stone building looking angry. George Schultz was seated in his office talking to Avery Bertram, but Julie was nowhere in sight.

"Miss Fontaine has gone along with Peter to see the cellars," Avery told Mark and, shaking hands with George Schultz, he went back to his own office to mull over figures and count costs and click his false teeth against each other in mounting alarm.

"George," Mark said, extending a hand to the smaller man, "what can I do for you?"

George Schultz coughed nervously, alternately opening and closing his hands against the thighs of his good Sunday suit. All dressed up, Mark thought rapidly. Slicked and clean shaven, and he's plastered his hair with Macassar oil. He hadn't seen George dressed that way since his youngest daughter's wedding last spring. His Sunday-go-to-meeting clothes. And if I went to church on Sunday, I'd see him just this way—only not quite so slick and not quite so nervous.

"Something wrong, George?" Mark inquired lazily, leaning back in his chair and pulling out his pipe, taking his time, reaming it, filling it, drawing easily against the flame of the match while he waited for the other man to speak.

"Er, ah, yes and no." George coughed again.

"Just came from the vineyards," Mark said. "If this weather holds, we'll have the best crop in years. Must be that way through the whole valley, wouldn't you say? Benson's got a fine crop, he tells me. And I hear that Selkirk's is even better. Nice after the past two years."

"Crop's good," George said hastily. "Like you say, if the weather holds, and the almanac says it will, no reason not to expect the best."

"Then what is it, George?" Mark sat up suddenly, laying the pipe aside and leaning forward.

"It's . . . well, it's that Prescott is calling my mortgage, and, well, thing is, I got a good offer from a winery down in Hammondsport. Top offer." He mentioned a figure that exceeded Fontaine's by a good fifteen percent.

"How did you get the offer, George?" Mark asked, his face expressionless.

"Fact is, Mrs. Prescott told me that this winery fellow was looking to buy crops, even willing to take a chance and put a bit down against the harvest."

"I see. And have you taken the offer?"

George shook his head, tugging at the high starched collar over which his flesh bulged slightly. "Wouldn't unless I saw you first. Figured I owed you that. Not to bargain," he added hastily. "Thing is, I can't get an extension from Mr. Prescott. Might have, but young Holt Prescott handled it first, and his father wouldn't change Holt's decision. He did tell me where I could get top dollar. Mark, I can't lose the vineyard and the house. You can see that."

He looked earnestly at Mark, saw Mark's face darken with anger, and his own paled. Mark Douglas had a reputation in a fight, a reputation few men in the valley cared to challenge, least of all, George Schultz.

The bastard, Mark was thinking. Deliberately, if I know Holt. Too late now to point out to Jason that this kind of move would hurt Julie and other stockholders along with the winery itself. If he paid George what he'd been offered, he'd have to pay the same thing to every other grower whom they bought from. Cut down the kind of eventual profit that would offset those two bad years. Not to pay and let word get out, and he'd lose the crops. Have to pay. He could hear Avery Bertram's whine of outrage now.

For the moment they were all right. The winery was doing well on the previous vintages. In three years' time they would begin to feel the pinch. In three years Julie would be in control of her stock. "You may need me to invest my money when I'm of age." He could still hear her say it and he began to smile.

George Schultz sank back into his chair with relief. It was over then and, emboldened, he spoke up: "I wouldn't have decided to do this if I hadn't needed to," he said.

"Of course not, George." Mark smiled directly at him. "Supposing we meet the offer from Hammondsport?"

"Meet it?" George's jaw dropped. "But, well, of course. I've got no call to sell someplace else except for more money."

"How soon do you need the advance?"

"In about a week."

"You wait here, George," Mark said, rising. "I think we can settle this today."

He left his office and went across the wide entrance room to Avery. Bind Schultz to an agreement before he got a chance to let the cat out of the bag. Call on the others. Now. Get the crops sewed up. God knew how many other mortgages Holt Prescott might have reason to call in.

Avery was too stunned to object. Dazed, he prepared a series of checks payable to all the growers who sold to Fontaine, and when it was over he fell back into his chair, his face pinched, his skinny body looking frailer than ever.

"If anything happens in the making of the wine," he managed to say, "Fontaine's will be wiped out."

"Nothing will happen," Mark said. "I trust Joe Damien, whoever else I don't trust."

He went back to his own office to give George the check. Forgetting about Julie, he left the winery moments later to make his deal with the other growers.

It was after five when he got back, satisfied with the day's work, and taking grim satisfaction from having outwitted Holt Prescott.

He was surprised to find Julie still there, Peter Damien beside her, his dark face bemused and flushed.

"I was just leaving," she informed Mark coolly as he came through the door. "I'm sorry you were too busy to see me, but Peter was very kind." She flashed a wide smile to young Peter Damien, who mumbled something indistinguishable.

"You'll be walking back?" Mark queried.

"Why, no, Amos is outside."

"Amos has left," Mark interrupted her, smiling at her discomfiture. "I imagine he went to pick up Jason and Holt at the bank. Of course, he'll probably be back. On the other hand, I'd hate to leave you alone here."

"Alone?"

"Peter is going home for dinner, I expect. Mr. Bertram has already gone, and I am about to follow."

"But I can't walk back," she said, looking down at her shoes and tugging at the hobbled skirt. "It would take forever dressed like this."

"Very charming," he approved, "but hardly practical for a long, dusty walk. Well, I suppose I'll have to take you myself. Come along, then."

She followed him meekly enough, but when she realized that he meant to put her in front of him on the roan, she balked.

"I can't ride a horse like this," she protested. "It will ruin my dress."

"I'm doing the riding," he said. "You're only coming along as a passenger. Can't put you on behind. You can't straddle anything in that skirt. Here." He swung into the saddle and, leaning down, he scooped her round the waist and hauled her up in front of him.

"Good thing I ride a Western saddle," he said, grinning. "We'd be mighty uncomfortable on one of those high English things."

She said nothing, sitting stiffly upright, her back barely touching his encircling arm. He clicked the horse to a walk and started off, moving easily in the saddle while Julie jolted up and down in front of him until he urged the horse into a light canter. It forced her to

lean back against him and he tightened his arm to hold
her firmly.

He was conscious of the softness of her body and of
an elusive fragrance emanating from her hair and skin,
fresh and yet sweet. As they rode, she relaxed further
against him, loosening one arm and slipping it around
his waist. It brought the fullness of her breasts up
against his shirt, and he muttered under his breath,
reining the horse to a walk again. She did not move,
except to settle against him more securely.

Deliberate, he thought. This is something she meant
to do. He knew she was aware of the effect she was
having, and from the quickened rise and fall of her
chest, he could see that she was not entirely immune
herself.

He leaned his head back and looked down at her
sideways. Her wide hat brim left the upper portion of
her face in a shadow, but the full mouth and soft chin
were bathed in the late sunlight.

She looked up suddenly and, meeting his gaze, smiled
and said softly, "You are coming to my birthday party
tomorrow night, aren't you?"

Something in the eyes, a wanton kind of flirtatiousness,
and the pleasure his discomfort was giving her fired his
temper. He pulled the horse up short, moving forward
to keep Julie from falling, and as she turned to look back
at him in startled protest, he bent his head and covered
the full, pouting lips with his own, tightening his arms
until she was crushed against his chest.

He had meant only to teach her a lesson, to relieve
some of the pressure that was building up in him, but
at the first touch of her lips he was seized with a desire
for her that left him shaken. She squirmed in his arms
and he held her more firmly until she stopped and then
he let her go, looking down at her, feeling the excitement spring up between them. The blood was pounding
in his ears. Her eyes were enormous, darkly violet,
almost black, and her face was pale in contrast; only her
lips lent color in their moist red softness. He groaned
and bent his head again and, this time, it seemed that
she met him halfway. Passion clouded his mind and he
thought, shaken, I'll be dragging her off into the bushes
next, and he wrenched away so violently that the horse
started and strained forward. Mark tightened the reins

just in time, sawing gently to keep the roan from rearing. Julie clung now with both arms around his waist while Mark eased his mount into a walk. They were silent at first, and then he said abruptly, "Sit up, Julie. You're too tempting as it is. I seem to have forgotten myself." He heard her indrawn breath of insult and went on: "I hope you don't make a habit of this sort of thing. First your farmer in Iowa, today Peter at the winery, and now me."

"Peter!" she said. "Peter! Do you imagine that I'd carry on with a hired hand?"

"Hired hand! Why, you little snob. Peter is Joe Damien's son. And Joe Damien was Armand Damien's son. And, without the Damiens, the Fontaines would have been making grape jelly or selling their crops to another winery. Hired help! You better pray that Joe Damien and Peter stay with us. Fontaine's is a small winery in comparison to some of the others. Peter one day will be able to go anywhere he likes. If it hadn't been for Joe's loyalty to your father, he'd have been hired away long ago. Why do you suppose they own stock at Fontaine's?"

"I didn't know," she said in some confusion. Then she added heatedly, "Well, it's all your fault, Mark Douglas. Accusing me of . . . of . . ."

"I apologize about Peter," he said, "but not the rest."

He half hoped she would deny that, too, but she said only, "How could you know there was someone in Iowa?"

"I only suspected it until a few minutes ago," he told her. "But that wasn't your first kiss—not by a long shot."

To that she said nothing, sitting stiffly before him. A moment later, the Prescott Packard came into view and Mark reined and dismounted. He held up his arms to help Julie, but she had turned in the saddle and managed to slip down herself. She wrenched her ankle in the process, but outside of a muttered exclamation, she gave no indication that it hurt.

Amos was standing beside the rear door and he opened it at Julie's approach. Mark heard her say, "Thank you, Amos, I'm sorry you had to make the extra trip." She said it in a voice so full of sweet concern that he couldn't help smiling.

"Good-bye, Julie," he called, but she made no attempt to answer, and he stood beside his horse until the motor-car had turned around in the lane and started back to town.

Mounting up again, it struck him that he had never wanted a woman as badly as he wanted this eighteen-year-old girl—John Fontaine's daughter, Jason Prescott's niece. He had loved the one man like his own father and had disliked the other cordially. Julie. He suddenly remembered John Fontaine saying to him, "Ah, Mark, if only I end up with a son-in-law I like as well as you."

Son-in-law, not lover. Marriage? Never, he assured himself. Women, yes; wives, no. The memory of his own childhood and youth remained vividly before him: his father, sinking slowly under the constant shrewish nagging of his mother; his older sisters, Grace and Carrie, first bedeviling him and then bedeviling their husbands.

He had loved his father; loved his gentleness with animals, with plants, with his own children; loved his ability to teach and to explain; loved, above all, his clarity of thought and his detached, cool logic. With the ranch hands his father had been kind but firm, and it had puzzled Mark that the man who could command respect from the men under him could not command the same respect from either his wife or his two older daughters.

His mother, always the martinet, had ruled them all with an iron hand and acid tongue. His sisters emulated both characteristics, assisted by the coldness of nature that had marked their mother with everyone—everyone save her youngest child, Valerie. With Valerie, so frail in health since her childhood illness, she had been as kind and as affectionate as was possible for a woman of her temperament to be.

With Mark, she had been hardest of all. He could not remember a time when there had been any affection between them. When he thought of his mother, it was always as a woman advancing from middle age to her present elderly state without having enjoyed any youth. Yet he had seen pictures of her in her youth, pictures that showed a blooming, voluptuous girl with masses of fair hair and a coquettish tilt to her eyes, a coquettishness that he had seen in Julie Fontaine this afternoon.

He wanted Julie Fontaine, all right, but not at the price of his freedom, and yet that was the only way he could have her. She wasn't just any woman. She certainly wasn't Miranda Latham, who brought a certain wit and easiness to their relationship, who abhorred the idea of remarriage, and whose expertise in any bed they happened to share kept the excitement constant.

The differences between Julie and Miranda were vast. He might want the first, but he would get along just fine with the second.

He prodded his horse with his heel and sent him off at a gallop across the fields that led away from the winery and came out at the orchard behind Miranda's house.

Miranda was in her bedroom when she heard Mark reining his horse at the door and thought with a mixture of amusement and annoyance that his particular insistence on riding certainly alerted everyone for miles around of his presence.

More than once she had suggested that his car or even a carriage would be a more seemly approach for his "business visits," but he had simply shrugged off the suggestion. "I sit too much as it is," he said. "I like riding. I use the motorcar only when I have to. And it isn't necessary when I want to cut over from my place to yours."

She had to admit he was right about that. Mounted, he could come straight across the roads and fields to the orchard.

When Ray had first brought her to his family home as a bride, she had hated its isolation. For years she had agitated him to sell it and buy a house along Seneca or over on Tuscarora Road, but Ray, indulgent with her on almost any issue, balked. After he died, she had almost sold the house, and then Mark had come along, and now she blessed the fact that, save for distant neighbors and the odd carriage or motorcar passing by on the way to Douglas Dairies, a mile down the road, no one really knew of her comings and goings.

She had been dressing for dinner when Mark arrived, and she continued to move placidly, excitement mounting beneath her calm exterior. It lent a flush to her pale blonde coloring and made her eyes sparkle. In one way it was a pity that Lenore and Fenton were in tonight. She and Mark always had to be discreet in case one of the Fentons should knock with a message or an inquiry as to household arrangements. In another way, it lent a fillip to their lovemaking. There was something in the idea that she and Mark might be discovered that increased her passion. There was something in the very need to be secretive that made him more desirable.

He was an ideal lover: passionate, with a flavor of cruelty held in check; demanding where Ray had been placating; boldly inventive where Ray had been timidly gentle.

Lenore's soft knock sounded at the door and Miranda drew a deep breath, smoothing her skirt, twisting to look in the mirror, and calling, "Come in."

"Mr. Douglas is downstairs," Lenore said, her face correctly expressionless, although her eyes were knowledgeable.

"Not more papers to sign?" Miranda exclaimed in a bored voice.

"I don't know. Mrs. Latham. He's not carrying papers," Lenore replied.

"Some other fuss at the winery, then," Miranda said petulantly. "I wish Ray had sold that stock to Jason Prescott. It's more trouble than it's worth."

"Yes, ma'am," Lenore said. It was a game she had played with Mrs. Latham more than once. They both knew it was a game, but not for the world would she or Fenton say anything. It was a good job. It paid more than they could have gotten elsewhere, and they both knew that the raise offered shortly after Mark Douglas started to come calling was a silent bribe.

On days such as these, she and Fenton kept to their own quarters—both on nights when Mr. Douglas would bring her in from some party or affair and leave promptly, and when Mrs. Latham took the motorcar herself, saying she was going out for an evening drive. Fenton swore they'd probably find her at the old Fontaine place in Mark Douglas' bed.

"Well, say I'll be down presently. And ask Fenton to bring the car around. It's after six and I am due at the Fremonts' house at seven."

"Yes, Mrs. Latham. Will you be driving yourself?"

"No, not tonight, but Fenton can bring the car back. The Fremonts will see me home."

"You look," she said to Mark as she entered the parlor, closing the door behind her, "as if the furies were in pursuit. Don't tell me there is more trouble?"

"A run-in with Prescotts again," he answered as he sat beside her on the sofa. "I'll tell you about it later."

"I'm dining out this evening," she told him. "In fact, I have to leave in half an hour." She reached out and drew a tentative finger along the line of his open collar. "You should have come earlier."

"Don't be coy, Miranda," he answered roughly and caught at her hand. There was a tension in him she hadn't seen before, but she wisely made no mention of it; instead, she leaned toward him.

Moments later, she said, "You'll ruin me for going out to dinner," and then, "Mark, be careful, the servants." And he laughed.

"You like that, don't you? The idea that we'll be caught at this one day." She drew back in reproof, thinking, damn him, he reads me too well, but he said again, "Don't be coy, and don't deny it."

They were expert with each other now, having learned over the year to accommodate to whatever situation they found themselves in. The chemistry was still strong enough to arouse them, and their experience at innovation enabled them to reach the final throb of mutual pleasure without effort.

Afterward, reassembling her clothing, Miranda thought, We are good together and he never bores me. And one of these days I'll maneuver him into that marriage he doesn't want. Older than he was by three years more than the two she confessed to, she had been clever enough so far to lead him into believing marriage was the last thing on her mind. They were settled into the relationship now. In a little while she could begin to avoid seeing him, taking trips away, accepting other men's attentions. Mark wasn't average, but there wasn't a man alive who couldn't be maneuvered into a proposal under these circumstances. She would have to be careful, though. The slightest hint that that was what she had in mind, and it would be all over.

"What are you plotting now, Miranda?" Mark broke in on her thoughts.

"I'm plotting how to avoid changing again before I leave," she lied.

"You're fine. A bit of powder, fix up the hair, and no one will ever know how you whiled away the minutes before your departure." He grinned at her. "See you tomorrow evening."

"Oh, yes, Julie Fontaine's birthday-*cum*-debut. What's

she like after three years at the convent? I always thought that was probably the best idea the Prescotts ever had. That girl matured a bit early. Must be all that French blood."

"Julie's fine," he answered shortly, and something in his voice alerted her. She looked at him keenly and, although his face was unreadable, there was a tensing of muscles along his jawline.

Without knowing why, she sensed that he was attracted to Julie. She had a swift memory of Julie's slender, high-bosomed body, of her flawless complexion, and what she herself recognized as a tempting way with men. Casually, she said, "You really ought to begin teaching Julie something of the way the winery works. She'll soon be in control and it wouldn't do to leave her to the Prescotts. Shall I bring her out one day and you can show her around?"

"She's been out," he answered. "Peter Damien took her on a tour today."

So that was it. That accounted for the shortness of tone and for the impetuous, unexpected visit to her. Miranda felt a searing throb of angry jealousy and busied herself with smoothing her skirts for a few seconds before she spoke.

"Oh, I will have to repair some of the damage. Darling, excuse me, will you? I've got to go upstairs." She pressed a light kiss on his cheek, saying, "Tomorrow night, then. About nine?"

She smiled at him, was still smiling as she saw him out the door, and then, as it closed behind him, her face tightened with the anger she had suppressed.

He had come from a flirtation with Julie Fontaine to her, as if she were one of Viola's girls. Her rage mounted and for several minutes she couldn't get herself back into control. When at last the anger ebbed, she felt weak. She went up to her room, prolonging her toilette, conscious that she would be late, but determined to wear a mask of gaiety. Tonight, in bed, she would plan her next move. Julie Fontaine. Stupid. Ridiculous. A girl. No match at all for me, she thought, and, comforted, she smiled.

5

On the evening of her party, Julie stood in the reception line next to Millicent and welcomed guests with a fixed smile. The house was ablaze with lights, and in the foyer against the stairwell a three-piece ensemble played old-fashioned waltzes interspersed with current tunes.

Aunt Millicent's and Uncle Jason's birthday gifts had been real surprises. Not even Holt's token of a sewing basket could dim her pleasure in the beautiful new gown and the accessories Millicent had ordered from New York.

Gone were the hobbled skirts that still graced the upland emporiums. The brilliant deep blue dress had a wide skirt that rose a few inches about her ankles. Gone, too, were the long drawers and in their place was something new called knickers—short bloomers coming just above the knee. They and her new slips were embroidered crepe de Chine. And she had evening slippers, blue to match the gown. She had piled her hair up, securing it with her mother's old *brillante* hair ornaments, and fastened around her neck the filigree gold necklace set with tiny diamonds that belonged to her great-grandmother Fontaine.

She knew she looked beautiful, but in the confusion of emotions that now raged in her breast she took small pleasure from the fact. She had been unable to think of anything except the ride with Mark the day before. She was torn between the dazzlingly sweet memory of his kiss and the humiliation of his angry accusations. One moment she wished to be in his arms, the next to insult him as cruelly as he had her.

Now, as she smiled and smiled and pressed hands until her fingers ached, she was feverishly anxious to catch a glimpse of him. But shortly after ten when the receiving line broke up, Mark had not arrived.

Julie moved among the guests, sipping the Château de

Brugarde champagne, which Uncle Jason had insisted on ordering from a French import house in New York, and nibbling at the hors d'oeuvres without appetite. Some of the younger crowd had begun dancing on the polished floor of the wide foyer. Andrew Clay came to claim her for a dance.

He looked different somehow. She had remembered him as rather tall and thin. But he was not much above her five-feet-six frame, and he had broadened out. His hands were perspiring through his gloves as he pumped her about the floor inexpertly to the strains of "Syncopated Walk."

Aside from a shy compliment on her looks and an even shier reminder of the incident behind the grape arbor, he was too busy trying to follow the music and keeping from treading on her toes to say anything else. She was relieved when one of the van Houten boys cut in.

At eleven, listening to Mr. van Houten and her Uncle Jason discourse on the coming senatorial election, she gave up hope that Mark would arrive. She was hardly following the conversation and it gave her a headache. Murmuring an excuse, she started for the hall, determined to slip away up the back stairs to her room. And suddenly Mark was there, looming up in the archway, head and shoulders above Andrew Clay, standing near him, and topping Holt's height by at least two inches. His dinner jacket was impeccable and his suntanned face glowed above the stark white of his shirtfront. He met her glance and she felt a strange little thrill start somewhere along her ribs and spread up and down in radiating circles.

His eyes darkened and their brown depths burned so fiercely that they gave off a reddish glow. She stared back, too shaken to smile. He looked away and the spell was broken. Her knees felt weak and her hands trembled.

It was almost as if she were in love with him—with Mark! She had liked kissing him. But then she had liked Bill Robertson, too. Really liked him. She tried to remember how that had been, but she couldn't summon any image. Mark. She didn't really like him nearly as well. He made her angry. He had hurt her feelings. Still, she moved forward to greet him and at that moment realized that Miranda Latham was with him.

"Julie, dear, how are you?" Miranda cooed. "My goodness, you're all grown up. Mark, doesn't she look sweet?"

"Very nice," he approved, smiling.

"Thank you," Julie replied sourly. She knew she was giving herself away and was frustrated because she couldn't seem to help it.

"It seems only yesterday you were a little schoolgirl," Miranda went on.

"It *was* only yesterday," Mark added, then turned to speak to his cousin, Art Douglas.

Julie, feeling rage about to break, veered toward the front door, opened it, and left the house. As the door closed behind her, she could hear a burst of laughter and, caught in her own turmoil of emotions, she fancied that it had been directed at her. This only heightened her anger, and she stood for several minutes on the porch, trying to decide on some course of action. At length, she went around to the side of the house and out into the back garden, where several people had gathered to escape the noise and the warmth of the house.

"Ah, here is our birthday girl!" Mayor Bradford hailed her. "You remember my son Kenneth, don't you?"

Julie smiled at Kenneth, thinking, He's nice looking and his father is important, and if I go back into the house with him, it will look as if that's what I'd had in mind all along.

"Of course, although you've changed," she said. "You're taller than I remember, and, well, I don't know. . ." She feigned some slight embarrassment and slanted a quick look up at him and then turned away.

"I might say the same for you," he answered with awakening interest. "The last time I saw you, you had braids and were playing dolls with Alice."

"Oh, Kenneth, you're surely teasing. I was fifteen when I left for St. Veronica's."

"Well, perhaps I didn't pay much attention to Alice's friends in those days—a sophomore at the University of Rochester and all that."

"Excuse me," his father murmured. "I'm sure you two won't miss me, and I see your mother is about ready to go inside, Kenneth. I can tell because she keeps looking this way and raising her eyebrows, so I must rescue her. It's nice to have you home, Julie," he added and gave her shoulder a friendly pat.

After he left there was a small silence, which Julie broke by saying, "I suppose I must get back."

"I'll come with you," Kenneth offered. "Perhaps we can have a dance."

"I'd like that," she answered, feeling her confidence flow back.

She danced until supper was announced. She smiled, flirted, and gave the impression that she was enjoying her own party as much as any guest.

At supper, Kenneth Bradford filled her plate and Andrew brought her a glass of punch when she said she had a headache from "too much champagne." She ate sitting between them on the stairs. From time to time she had caught glimpses of Mark either dancing, or talking, moving from girl to girl and group to group with an air of easy affability.

The party was nearly over before he approached her, Miranda at his side.

"I haven't seen you all evening, Julie. I looked for you, but you'd disappeared." (Liar, she thought savagely.) "You look lovely. Congratulations, my dear," he said, then grazed her cheek in an avuncular kiss. "Oh, and before I forget, a little remembrance." He reached inside his jacket and extracted a small flat box. "Happy birthday," he said.

"Well, aren't you going to open it?" Miranda spoke up. "I'd adore seeing a gift from my guardian . . . if I had a guardian."

"Mark isn't my guardian," Julie answered, hearing the jealousy in Miranda's voice and taking pleasure from it. "He's just a friend of the family."

"And one of your trustees," Mark added. "Trustees always give birthday gifts to the wards of the trusts. I remember how I used to send you books and games, but I thought at eighteen you'd probably outgrown that."

Miranda laughed and said, with a light tap on his arm, "Oh, do be serious, Mark. You talk as if Julie were a child." She said this in a voice that plainly meant, Don't hurt the poor child's dignity.

"For pity's sake, open the present, Julie." This from Alice. "I'm dying to see it, too."

Julie couldn't refuse without looking childish, so she undid the wrapping and opened the lid. There was a gasp of astonishment from the onlookers. In the center of the

satin lining lay a·brooch in the shape of a star, its golden
points outlined in seed pearls and a heart-shaped garnet
in the center.

"Why, it's . . . it's lovely!" Julie said. "I . . . th . . .
thank you, Mark!" She reached up on tiptoes and be-
stowed a light kiss on his cheek.

"Put it on," Alice urged.

"Not now," Julie demurred. "I . . . there are some
people leaving whom I must speak to. Thank you again,
Mark." She did not look at him, but she gave a blind
smile in his general direction before hurrying off.

She did not see him again that evening, and it was just
as well. Her mind was racing with the knowledge that he
had given her something that had belonged to his family,
and, more, that he knew she was aware of it. Why?
How could he ignore her, insult her, laugh at her, and
then turn around and give a gift he should be saving for a
wife or a . . . well . . . a close family member. Unless
he . . . but that was impossible. She remembered the
only other time she had seen the brooch. It was the year
after Mark's father died and she had been not more than
eleven. The brooch had belonged to Mr. Douglas' mother,
and there was Mark's grandfather's watch, a slim gold
watch with chains and fobs that Mark seldom wore, and
his grandmother's ring, a small but perfect sapphire with
a star in the center.

Mark had shown them to her father, who had suggested
that they be put in the safe. They had talked after that,
a sad and bitter conversation that she hadn't quite understood—something to do with Mark's breaking up with his
family in California and why he had never wanted to go
home again and how he felt closer to his Prescottville
Douglas cousins than he did to his sisters.

Undressing that night, she remembered her father saying that Mark was the brightest Douglas in either branch
of the family. Her uncle had said that Mark was arrogant
and bad-tempered, and her father answered in Mark's defense: "He's hardheaded, Jason—brilliant, hardheaded,
and his own man. He'll never bend to anyone. Time
might give him more diplomacy, but it won't change his
will to win."

Lying awake in bed, the events of yesterday and of this
evening began to merge and to make sense. He was in
love with her and he thought she was just a silly flirt. So

he pretended he didn't care at all. Well, she would change that. Tomorrow, armed with the knowledge of what his gift had meant, she would not be afraid to face him and to wring an admission from him. She fell asleep smiling.

Contriving to see Mark again proved more difficult than Julie had imagined it would be. Amos was unavailable the next day, and when she suggested that she might go for a walk, Aunt Millicent reminded her that it was their at-home day and that Mrs. van Houten and Elizabeth were calling, and Julie's presence was specifically required.

The mention of the van Houtens reminded Julie that, in her mad efforts to flirt with just about every man in the room the night before, she had promised James van Houten to go to a touring repertory company's production of *As You Like It* down in Elmira that evening.

By the following day, she had lost some of her conviction that it would be easy to see Mark and wring anything from him. She could hear him laughing at her, denying any motive more than that of a kindly trustee bestowing a gift on a young ward. She spent the day in idle pursuits and wound up after dinner feeling headachy and dreary.

Coming downstairs later that night, she heard voices in the library, raised in anger.

" . . . deliberate attempt to sabotage the winery." It was Mark.

And then her Uncle Jason: "Damn it, Mark, Fontaine can't afford to compete with the big companies. If you were smart, you'd vote to sell out now, before the country goes dry. Conserve Julie's estate. I know for a fact that Steuben Wines would make you a sound offer. There are other stockholders who feel the same way."

"I'm not selling. I control the majority of votes, at least for the present. And if you want to conserve Julie's estate, kindly tell your son not to go around behind my back calling growers' mortgages and then setting them up with Steuben or someone else to sell their harvest to at top prices. If Fontaine goes under, do you think Steuben will continue to pay like that? No! Trouble with you and Holt is that you're shortsighted. You can't remove me without cause. If I have any more of this, I'll move the Fontaine account down to the First City Bank in Elmira. I can do that, you know. And if I do, I'll convince my cousin to take his account with me. And you know the influence Art has with the other dairymen. Think it over. You try one more thing to jeopardize Fontaine's and I'll make every effort I can to bring a run on the bank."

"You do that and you'll finish Julie along with whomever else can't take the pressure. I can." Jason was bellowing now. "I'm not completely dependent on Prescott Bank, and Prescott Bank isn't dependent on Fontaine's or on Douglas Dairies. If it comes to a fight, there are plenty of businessmen in town who'll stand with us."

"Will they?" Mark's voice was so low that Julie had to strain to hear. "Once a thing like this gets going, Jason, you might find out that you have fewer friends than you think. In any case, if Fontaine is in danger, I don't give a damn who gets hurt. Try it, that's all. Whatever happens, Jason, you'll know you've been in a fight."

The lowness of his tone and the venom with which he colored his voice made it far more menacing than Jason's roars. There was a silence and finally Jason said, in a less belligerent way, "You always were stubborn, Mark. I'm not trying to ruin Fontaine's. As for Holt calling that mortgage, it was good business. All I tried to do after that was save George Schultz. After all, he's been a bank customer for thirty years."

"I'll accept you in the role of good samaritan, Jason, if you'll give me your word to ride herd on that son of yours when it comes to anything connected with the winery."

"Holt is with me in wanting to sell out now. He sees the handwriting on the wall, even if you don't."

"Spare me another lecture on the drys pulling off prohibition laws. I won't deny they've got a hell of a chance, but I told you before, and I'll tell you again—even if they do, they can't make it stick for long."

"It might be long enough to finish the winery."

"I'll take my chances," Mark said. Julie heard the sounds of chairs being pushed and slipped away from the door and out onto the front porch. Behind her, the voices were coming closer and she skimmed lightly down the steps and out to the corner of the property, standing at the edge of the road as if about to cross. Several minutes went by, and when no one appeared she headed over to the park, where she lingered, one eye on the front door, until at last it opened and Mark stepped out.

She waited until he reached his horse and then, stepping to the edge of the road, she called softly to him. He looked up, startled, and with a finger over her lips she beckoned to him. He hesitated a moment and then walked over to where she stood.

"What's all the mystery?" he asked as he reached her.

"No mystery. I heard you and Uncle Jason arguing and I wanted to know about it without Uncle Jason shouting at me, too. It's something to do with the winery and money, isn't it?"

"Yes, but it's nothing you'd understand." He smiled at her.

"Explain it to me. After all, I'm the one you both keep saying has the largest share. Don't you think I should understand some of what's going on? I will be twenty-one someday," she added.

He eyed her speculatively and then said, "You may be right. Let's see what you can grasp of it."

"Can we walk while we talk?" she asked. Without waiting for a reply, she started forward along the path that wound through the lilacs, nearly finished now, their scent fading to a delicate reminder of their former glory. Ahead of them lay the shores of Wide Waters and the path that followed the curve of the pond to the tall rushes where the swans nested.

Mark talked uninterruptedly for several minutes while she, silent, tried to absorb the importance of his remarks. At the banks of the pond, he stopped talking and, catching her by the arm, drew her to a halt.

"Not a question? Did you understand any of this?"

"Yes, I think so. Holt tried to lose crops for the winery by calling the Schultz mortgage, and that made you have to pay more, and if the crop isn't as good as expected, it will be bad, anyway, and even if it is, the winery is going to be short of capital because of it."

"Those are the essentials, anyway," he said approvingly. "We're working very close to the edge now. That's why I wanted you to reinvest your lump sum in Fontaine's. Just how much money you'll eventually have depends on how well the winery does."

"All right. I'll invest it all . . . except the twenty-five hundred."

"You've promised Jason half," he reminded her. "And

in any case, while it wouldn't hurt to have it, it won't make or break Fontaine's."

"I'll do it anyway. It's my money."

He said nothing for several minutes and presently they began to walk again, heading around the far side of Wide Waters.

"Why this sudden capitulation?" he asked at length.

"Oh, I don't know. I suppose because the winery is really my family's. I remember my father telling me that the very first Fontaine, the one who built the house, started to cultivate the wild grapes he found and made wine for himself at home, and then it just grew and he began to sell some, and the vineyards got better and . . . oh, it's a story I always liked. Anyway, I wouldn't want Fontaine's to become part of Steuben Wine, the way so many of the smaller wineries have. I'll never vote to sell."

He stopped abruptly, turning her around in the path to peer down into her face. "You're a curious girl, Julie Fontaine. The minute I think you're just another foolish female, I find out you have more intelligence than . . ."

He broke off as she leaned toward him, saying, "I'm not like you said the other day, Mark, when . . . when you were taking me home and . . ." She couldn't go on. He was staring at her with such intensity that it flustered her.

"Mark," she said in a whisper, and somehow, she never knew how, she was in his arms as if it had happened without either of them moving, as if they had melted toward it. He was kissing her now, slowly and softly and then with gradations of passion that fired every nerve in her body. The world spun around her and she pressed close to him, feeling the long length of his body as it became hard and unyielding.

Time stood still. There was nothing except his mouth parting her lips, his hands moving along her back. She felt her heart beating like the frantic wings of a snared sparrow and his heart hammering against her own. How long it went on she never knew. She knew only that it seemed she could not get close enough to him. His lips wandered downward and he bent her backward, arching her body high against him. Suddenly it was over. With an incoherent exclamation, he put her away from him and she swayed dizzily, unable to get her bearings.

At last some of the dizziness passed and she was able to look at him. He was leaning against the bark of a tree, lighting his pipe with trembling fingers.

She moved toward him and he said in a low voice, "No, Julie, don't. It can't be this way. I'm not what you think. There . . . there isn't anything in this for you." The statement seemed to steady him and he straightened up as if he were once more his own master. He smiled at her. "I won't deny I want you," he said. "You . . . well, never mind. But I don't want to marry you, and, Julie, you're as ready for marriage as any woman I've ever seen. One day I'll be leaving Fontaine's. I've already begun to acquire property—vineyards. When it's time, I hope you marry someone who can take over the winery. I'll be heading west for a time and then to France, and when I do come back it will be to experiment, to try to grow the kind of grapes that will make a red wine comparable to the great Bordeaux and Burgundies of France. I hear there's a monk in Strasbourg who has had some success with grafting other varieties on native rootstock. No one is paying much attention to it now, but I think someday it could be used to introduce the vinifera grape to the eastern stock."

He was talking feverishly, as if what he said wasn't nearly as important as saying something. She couldn't make sense out of most of it. Standing out in her mind were the only phrases that meant anything to her: "I don't want to marry you" . . . "One day I will be leaving Fontaine's" . . . "Marry someone who can take over the winery."

"Perhaps I should try for Peter Damien, after all," she said in a lifeless voice. "He's young and he knows about wine, and I guess that takes care of all the requirements. I don't think I'll have any trouble getting him to propose, do you?"

"Don't be foolish," he said roughly.

"I'm not being foolish. In fact, I think I'll go out to the winery tomorrow, late. Perhaps Peter won't be in a rush to go home to dinner, after all."

"Please yourself," he said. "I'll see you back to the house."

"Don't bother. I know my way." She walked past him, head high, her eyes bright with unshed tears. Never would he see how he had hurt her. Never.

She heard him moving down the path behind her, but she neither turned nor spoke again, and coming to the edge of the park, she cut across the road and the lawn in front of the house, reaching the front door before Mark had untethered his horse. As she stepped into the foyer, she heard the roan's hoofbeats going up the street and each one was like a fresh blow to her heart.

Julie did not make good her threat to go out to the winery the next day. Instead, seized with a desire for strenuous physical activity, she went out to the old stables that lay behind the gardens just off the narrow mews leading to Tuscarora Road. They had been unoccupied since Holt was given his Oldsmobile and since her pony, Blythe, had been sold before she went to St. Veronica's.

Separated from the shining new garage by a high hedge, the stables were overgrown with climbing vines, and as she entered the musty interior she heard the scampering of mice.

It took her nearly three days to clean out the accumulation of three years of dust and grime and misuse. In an excess of enthusiasm, she even made an attempt to clean the carriage. However, it was too rusty to be of much use, so she abandoned the idea. When she had finished, she went out to Bekins' Stables on the edge of town and bought a young mare named Fancy that had been sired by the same stud that had sired Blythe. "Strong, but gentle," George Bekins said. "Took to training like a champion. She's just ready, Julie. Had someone coming up from Elmira to look her over for his daughter, but you're first, so she's all yours."

Buying the mare lifted her spirits and her days were occupied in feeding and grooming and taking long rides. One morning, a week after she bought Fancy, Julie packed herself a lunch and took off for Watkins Glen, the scene of her father's accident. It was something she wanted very much to do, although she had not thought she could ever enter those trails again. But as she urged Fancy forward, the years fell away, and she was a little girl once more, out for a ride with her father, who was mounted on his black gelding.

Driven by a newly born recklessness, she urged Fancy over the trail where her father had ridden on that fatal day until she reached the spot where his horse had

plunged and reared and fallen into the rocky glen below. There she reined up, staring down, trying to visu-
alize how it must have been, how it had seemed in her
old nightmares, but the glen gave no hint of the disaster,
and she could not envision that day long ago.

At last she went on, this time at a fast canter, her own
head bent low, the tree branches clearing Fancy's head by
inches until at last a sharp bend in the trail made her
slow down. She was breathless, excited, as if somehow
she had reached a conclusion as yet unknown to her.

Going to bed each night, exhausted from her physical
exercise, she would fall asleep almost at once. In the odd
moments before sleeping or on waking or at some task,
Mark Douglas would rise vividly in her mind and a bewildered kind of ache would possess her brain and her
body. On such occasions she would say fiercely to herself, Don't think about it, and she forced her mind onto
something else.

On the morning after her ride through the glen, she
went to the stable as usual, fed Fancy, exercised her
briefly, and spent the morning trying to answer letters
she had long neglected. One from Eileen Butler in Chicago, telling of her coming-out party and inviting Julie to
attend, had been there for over a week.

She had found writing impossible; it required too much
introspection, and when she came to it, she could not
think of anything to report. To Millicent's surprise, she
had put off the trip to New York, saying she would rather
make it in the fall when the new clothes were in.

There had been one scene with Jason when she informed him that, after all, the winery needed the money
and she was investing all but her original stipulation in it.
Jason had blustered, but his blustering died away when
she brought up Holt's calling in of the Schultz mortgage.

"It is my property," she had said. "For good or bad, I
am going to invest in it." He did not try to change her
mind after that. Holt, hearing of it, caught her one night
as she was coming in from a walk, holding her on the
porch as she tried to enter the house.

"You can fool Father with that talk of Fontaine's being your property, but not me. It's all for Mark Douglas,
isn't it? He's not your family. You should be standing
with us, not Mark. But, then, if I were running Fontaine's, as I should have been, you'd be putting your

money in Douglas Dairies or whatever other enterprise Mark Douglas was involved in. And you'd vote to sell Fontaine's, too, if that's what he wanted."

"You were seventeen when Daddy died," Julie said calmly. "Let go of my arm, Holt, or I'll scream till the neighbors come out of their houses."

He flung the arm from him with a brusque laugh. "One day, Julie, one day you'll get what's overdue for you . . . and I'll be the one to give it to you."

She had not answered him, nor did she let him see that his threats still had the power to frighten her, bluff though she might. After that she took care never to be in the house alone with him. On the odd evening when he might be at home and her aunt and uncle were away, she would drop by to see Alice Bradford or accept one of the invitations she had received. She had not been very social of late, and Aunt Millicent was beginning to comment on it. "Moping around the house again this evening, Julie?" she was wont to say. "Why did you refuse Kenneth Bradford's invitation to the Summer Ball in Hammondsport?"

To all this Julie had only the answer that she was tired from riding, that she needed the practice on Fancy, that the convent and Camp Joy had kept her from riding for three years. Any mention of the convent generally had the effect of discomforting Millicent and causing her to either change the subject or to acquiesce.

Julie looked down now at her half-finished letter to Eileen, added a few hasty sentences, signed her name, and addressed the envelope. Her writing desk was full of other correspondence, and just as she had begun drawing some from one of the crammed pigeonholes, the luncheon gong rang. She had dreamed the morning away, hardly conscious of the time passing.

The afternoon stretched before her like a void. Fancy had been overworked yesterday. She wouldn't take her out until evening. Meanwhile, how would she make the day pass? She thought of the winery and discarded the idea. She thought of shopping, of calling on Alice and having some gossip, of finishing her letter-writing. In the end, she did none of these things, but she took the letter for Eileen and walked all the way into town to the post office, a small gray building that clung next to the big courthouse as if seeking protection. She mailed her letter, bought some new stamps, and then went along to the library on the other side of the town square.

There were no new novels, but she selected a couple of old favorites: *Scaramouche* and *The Mill on the Floss.* Then, browsing along the rows, she came across a dusty volume entitled *Sutter Mill Days: A History of the California Gold Rush*, and she took that, as well.

The excursion brought her home late and she barely had time to change for dinner. That night there was a particularly stultifying feeling at the table. The weather had continued unseasonably hot and there had been no rain for weeks. The sultry air outside wrapped the stuffy house in its humid blanket. Millicent looked very pale and hardly touched her food, while Jason ate heartily from a full plate of beef and potatoes and vegetables, his face red and perspiring.

Halfway through the meal, Julie saw Millicent wince and put her hand to her breast. She started to say something, but Millicent caught her eye and gave an imperceptible shake of her head.

Julie watched her covertly and saw that her aunt was looking paler as the meal progressed, and toward the end of the dinner she gave a little gasp and clutched at her shoulder.

Jason looked up, startled, and made an anxious inquiry.

"It's all right," his sister assured him with a smile. "A bit of indigestion, that's all."

"If you aren't feeling well, Millicent, we can cancel with the Bradfords," he offered solicitously.

"No, Jason. It's indigestion, that's all, and it's this awful heat. I love auction bridge, and we haven't played very much lately. I think it will take my mind off the weather. It's sure to be cooler at nine."

Holt, who had been sulkier than usual that evening, brightened perceptibly and said, "Well, I plan to stay in this evening. It's too miserable to do much of anything else. I think we're due for a good thunderstorm, as it is."

"And I suppose you'll be in as usual, Julie?" Millicent addressed her with resignation and something else, some anxiety, as if Julie's behavior was a source of worry to her.

"No," Julie said quickly. "I haven't exercised Fancy. I

thought I'd ride over to Alice Bradford's. She just got a new McCall's fashion book, and I want to see it."

Not for anything would she remain in the house alone with Holt. She'd an idea that he was staying in deliberately because Jason and Millicent would be gone. He was quite capable of harassing her, driving her to a rage of temper, and then taking pleasure in some physical cruelty. It was nothing that could ever be brought back to him as evidence of anything unnatural, but she had suffered too many bruised arms and twisted wrists at his hands to want to risk anymore.

Shortly before Millicent and Jason left, Julie went out to the stable and saddled up Fancy. The divided riding skirt felt heavy against her legs and the shirt clung damply to her body. The riding boots made her feet hot and uncomfortable. She walked Fancy out through the rear gates to the narrow lane that cut across the back of the property and led to Tuscarora Road. For a while she walked, leading Fancy as she stepped daintily behind her. At the end of the road where it forked, she mounted the mare.

For a moment she stayed at the fork and then, without thinking where she was going, she turned Fancy right, on the road leading to the winery and away from town. In the distance she saw flashes of sheet lightning and heard the low rumble of thunder. Still she went on. The farther north they went, the cooler the air grew, with the outriding winds of the distant storm dissipating some of the unbearable heat.

She tapped Fancy lightly on the flank, and the mare, as if sensing that the lifting of the heavy heat lay ahead, quickened smartly and broke into a light canter.

The electricity in the night, the oncoming winds, and the lightning and thunder sounding louder as they went along, stirred Julie and brought an eager flush to her body. Her long hair, tied back in a ribbon, whipped from side to side as if seeking to loosen itself from its confinement. By the time the winery loomed ahead, the ribbon had fallen far behind and her hair was tossing wildly in the wind.

To her right she saw the outlines of her old home and the gleam of lamplight. She reined so sharply that Fancy reared back in whinnying alarm.

"Easy, girl." She stroked Fancy's neck. "Sorry." Fancy

subsided and Julie nudged her to the left, along the back path. Raindrops splashed her shirt. She lifted her face to them, shivering deliciously.

Something fierce and elemental rose in her. The winds, the wildness, the feel of her hair blowing free, the first bit of rain upon her body, the animal's sides between her knees, and the ever-approaching storm exhilarated her and she raced Fancy the last distance to the house, dismounting and throwing the reins loosely around the back porch railing all in one fluid motion.

She did not knock at the door but turned the knob, bursting into the kitchen, glowing from her exercise. Seeing Mark, who had stopped in midstride toward the door, she flung herself forward without a word, catapulting into his arms and burrowing against him.

"Julie" was all he said before he swept her into his arms and carried her from the room. She heard him kick a door with his boot and then they were in the dark, and he was turning her in his arms, kissing her, murmuring her name over and over.

His lips fell upon her throat and traveled down, and where he encountered a barrier of clothing, it seemed to melt from her body. His hands were warm and firm on her flesh and his mouth traveled over it, gently but with increasing urgency, until she moaned and then cried out, caught in a fit of passion that drove everything else from her mind.

Somehow she was free of all her clothing, and somehow she was on the bed, with him beside her, his flesh burning into hers.

He bent his head, kissing her breasts, licking softly at the nipples. He held her with one hard arm and his free hand moved along her thighs, rubbing the flesh softly and slowly and then more quickly. She reached her hand out to touch him, making inarticulate cries, and he moved up and over her. There was a moment, and only one, when she stiffened in resistance, but he urged her on until she arched her body to meet his.

He was hurting her now and yet she couldn't bear to have him stop. She clung to him, pressing closer and closer until, with a piercingly sweet pain, her body knew the ecstasy of utter surrender and the storm breaking overhead was somehow part of it all.

She had gone to sleep in Mark's arms, quivering in the aftermath of emotion, and some time later she awoke, hearing the rain falling and the storm moving off, feeling drowsy and desirous, knowing that he had awakened her with gentle caresses. She caught one of his hands and moved it up to her breast, feeling a sweet ache as he pressed it and bent his head. She held him against her, her hands running lightly down his back and coming back to cradle his head. They made love slowly now, savoring it, after the headiness of that first encounter, and yet in the end it was suddenly more urgent than it had been before. She felt weak and disembodied, as if she floated somewhere above herself while her body still trembled. He made soothing noises, stroking her, bringing her back to quietude.

He pulled the covers around her, tucking her in as if she were a child. Contentment spread over her and her heart ached with the love that went beyond any physical assuagement.

Of love they had said nothing, and now he whispered beside her, "You're mine."

"I know," she replied.

There was no further need for words. What they had was forged between them like an invisible bond, and despite the little experience she had had, Julie knew it was unbreakable. She had known it since that first night back home when the air crackled with the excitement of his presence.

She began to drift off again, wondering that she had come to him when she had never planned it, remembering the ride through the wild night and how Fancy reared. Her eyes flew open. "Fancy," she said aloud.

Beside her Mark stirred and said sleepily, "What is it, darling?"

"My mare. I rode her over. I left her outside."

He was rolling away from her and out of bed, suddenly wide awake. He pulled on his Levi's and buttoned them as he ran for the door.

He came back a few minutes later, his body damp.

"Gone," he said. "You must have left her untethered. She's back in the stable by this time."

Julie sat up in bed, clutching the covers around her. "What if she's hurt?" she asked.

He shook his head. "Not likely. Anyway, we'll find out

soon enough. I'll take you home. The rain has almost stopped."

"What time is it?" she asked.

"Nearly three in the morning. You'll have to tell them Fancy threw you and you walked here."

"Instead of walking home?"

"Here was closer. It's all right. Don't look so stricken. You really are incredibly young," he said, and a shadow passed over his face. He rose abruptly, saying, "Come on, get dressed. I'll go and saddle Rusty."

He was silent, almost morose, on the way back. She rode behind him this time, her arms about his waist, her face resting against his back. At the lane leading to the stables he reined up. "We'll walk through," he said. "If Fancy did come back to the stable, you can go on into the house and no one will be the wiser."

He took her hand as they walked, but still he said nothing. There was a preoccupied air about him, as if he were miles away from her in his thoughts. It frightened her and she whispered, "You aren't angry with me, are you, Mark?"

"No," he said enigmatically, "not with you."

He waited outside the gate while Julie checked the stable. Fancy was there, all right, still saddled, and shivering with cold. Julie threw a blanket over her and went swiftly back to tell Mark.

"I'll leave you, then," he said, and when she raised her face he brushed her lips lightly. "Good night," he whispered, then was gone as softly as a cat threading its way through tall grasses.

It was nearly dawn when Julie finally finished rubbing down Fancy. Poor Fancy had shivered and whinnied during Julie's ministrations. She forked hay over the stall and put oats and water inside, where the mare could reach them.

At last she crept into the house, going slowly up the side of the stairs, trying to avoid the middle sections that creaked. It was like being back at the convent, only no one emerged suddenly from the shadows of the upper hall, and she got to her room in safety. She smelled horsy and sweaty and longed for a bath. She washed up at her stand, getting rid of the worst of it, and finally sank into bed. Her muscles ached everywhere.

Her bed felt alien, as if she no longer belonged in it,

and she thought of Mark and his room off the kitchen of the old house, and that was more real to her, more familiar than this blue-and-white room with its carved bedstead and bureau and its massive old wardrobe.

He had been so quiet at the end, so withdrawn, and his face had worn the old angry look, but not toward her. For whom, then? She fell asleep before she could answer her own question and woke the next day in time to hear the luncheon gong.

She dressed hastily, repairing what ravages she could, and went down late with her prepared explanation that Fancy had thrown her, bolted, and she had had to walk home through the storm. It was received without comment, although from the swift exchange of looks she gathered the silence did not mean acceptance of her story.

It was only later, when she had gone to the stable and found Fancy lying on her side, burning hot, and summoned the Bekins' veterinarian, that Millicent's stern look softened. Not Holt's, of course, who said to her under cover of the flurry, "Bolted, my eye. I saw her come in a good five hours before you arrived. Where were you really, Julie?"

"You saw her? And you didn't go out and take care of her?" Julie exploded.

Holt shrugged. "Why should I? It's your horse. I'm not your groom."

"But it . . . it's only decent!" she cried. "I wouldn't let any animal go uncared for. Why," she paused, "why, if you wrecked your silly old car, I wouldn't just sit by and file my nails. Didn't it occur to you that if Fancy came home alone, I might be out there somewhere, hurt?"

He smiled thinly. "Well, yes and no, dear cousin. First of all, I thought you'd probably found something better to do than ride Fancy. And then, of course, the possibility that you might have been killed occurred to me. I regret to say that it caused me no pain. I believe it might have helped us. After all, as next of kin, we do inherit your Fontaine stock along with everything else. We could do as we pleased with it then. Mark Douglas would be out and I'd be in. Yes, your death wouldn't cause me grief."

She stared at him, sickened. She had always accepted

Holt's dislike as a dreary fact of life. She had no affection for him, either. But this was more than dislike. Why? She voiced the thought, adding, "What could I ever have done to you, Holt, to make you wish me real harm?"

"Nothing," he said insolently. "You just are, that's all. You *exist*. And I always saw what you were beneath the sweet face you put on. You're a whore. You see, I watch you, Julie, and I know. Just like I know where you were last night and what you were up to. Do you think I'm so stupid that I don't know what a woman looks like after she's been with a man."

But he hadn't seen her last night when she came in. He couldn't know. Or could he? Something in her face gave away her thoughts and Holt said, "You see, Julie, you don't fool me for a minute. I even know who you were with—Douglas." He spit out the word and she whitened and reddened in turn. "You had better run along," he said with contempt. "Here comes the good doctor—probably going to shoot your horse." And she broke away, running back toward the stable as if demons pursued her.

6

The *Prescottville Weekly Banner* had its offices on the north side of the town square. The building had originally been a saloon, but in 1875 the town passed a law forbidding saloons within the town limits, and the building had remained vacant until Sam Howard purchased it in the nineties and moved his press and other equipment into it.

Sam was nearing sixty now, a large, silver-haired man with a narrow saturnine face and keen eyes that appeared to view the world with a mixture of cynicism and humor. His editorials had sometimes been reprinted in the *New York Sun* and occasionally were picked up by other big-city dailies. In this way he had achieved a mild sort of fame outside the town and it lent him a sense of prestige within Prescottville itself that he otherwise might not have been accorded.

Sam's editorials were bipartisan politically, a fact that irritated the conservative and influential Republican elements in the town. He could not be persuaded to endorse either party in any election unless in his own view one of those candidates was hopelessly inadequate or was suspected of being less than honest. To have Sam come out for a candidate was tantamount to calling his opponent a fool or a thief, or possibly both. In the more than thirty years he had printed his paper, he had made only one endorsement in a local election—for Mayor Willis Bradford over one Horace Chantler in 1912. Two years after Mayor Bradford won, Horace Chantler was indicted for attempting to bribe a United States Senator, and the town thought Sam omniscient.

On the Tuesday night following the big thunderstorm Sam sat in his office mulling over a police report concerning one of the girls at Viola's Roadhouse who had been assaulted the night before—beaten and raped. The girl had claimed rape as well as a beating, but that had been discounted by the police. After all, everyone knew how Viola's girls earned their living. But the beating had been especially vicious, and the girl could not identify her assailant—couldn't or wouldn't. The police had tried to get some admission from her but had failed, and Sam had a hunch that she was afraid to tell.

Twice during the past eighteen months there had been cases of robbery and assault at Viola's. He had seen those girls, and the marks on their bodies had been ghastly.

It was all too much to be a coincidence. Sam's own view was that someone from Prescottville or one of the nearby towns who frequented Viola's and was known to Viola was responsible for the episodes.

He sighed. No use in stirring up the town with speculation. And no use running a story that hinted at rape with nothing more to back it up than the girl's word. His was a family newspaper. Better wait. He'd go out to Viola's himself and try to interview the girl. He rolled a sheet into his ancient L. C. Smith and slowly began to type: "A waitress at Viola's Roadhouse was set upon by

thieves last night and was severely beaten when she re-
sisted their attempts to rob her. She is resting comfortably. The assailants are unknown." He would set it on
the third page of the six-page paper. The headline that
week was: WILSON URGES PEACE, NOT WAR. Two feature
stories went as follows: "On Saturday, during a thunderstorm, Miss Julie Fontaine was thrown from her mare,
Fancy, on Hillcrest Road. The mare bolted and ran.
Miss Fontaine was unhurt but Fancy is still recovering
from exposure." And: "Mr. Mark Douglas, of Fontaine
Wine Company, predicts that this year will give Valley
grapegrowers a vintage crop." His editorial of the week
was a thoughtful analysis of just what the effect of America entering the war might be nationally as well as lo-
cally.

When he had finished, he took some folded newsprint
and stuck it in his pocket, turned out the lights, and
left the office. It was nearly five, a good time to head
out to Viola's. There would be many customers in the
bar at this hour, and that meant the girls would be more
available for questioning.

Viola's was set back from the road leading to Penn
Yan. There was a high, carefully clipped hedge in front
and the place looked at first glance like a family style
inn. It had once belonged to a Prescott cousin, and when
Viola Remsen bought it from the estate, no one had any
idea that she meant to found the town's brothel there—
at least, no one with the possible exception of Jason Prescott.

Behind the original house, Viola had built an addi-
tional wing. There were two entrances: one a normal
path to the house itself; the other a lane at the side that
cut through a thick copse of trees and opened onto a
clearing where those customers who wished to be discreet
tethered their animals or parked their motorcars.

The large frame house had a genteel and welcoming
air about it. The paint was never allowed to gray or peel,
and even the sign proclaiming VIOLA'S RESTAURANT was
kept fresh, its hinges always oiled.

The contrast between the exterior and the interior
was startling. The doors opened onto a large barroom,
with a cloakroom on the left and a curving stairway on
the right.

The bar was furnished in Victorian style, with brass cuspidors and velvet hangings fringed in gold and a large ornamental mirror over the bar that reflected the opposite wall's painting of a Rubenesque woman reclining on a sumptuous couch and draped with a red satin throw that left her legs and arms exposed and covered the torso, save for one voluptuous breast.

Beaded curtains at the far end separated the bar from the dining room. Here, tables were set with white napery and heavy cutlery. Along one wall there was a series of recesses. When not in use, red velvet draperies were looped back with gold tassels to reveal a couch with a table in front of it. When occupied, the draperies were discreetly dropped.

Viola charged handsomely for these alcoves. The men who used them brought their mistresses there. "When a man uses a girl that ain't one of mine," Viola would say, "it takes away from business and has to be made up for in some way."

Sam, entering the bar that evening, found Viola standing at one end of it, talking to Jack, the barman. In keeping with her decor, Viola and the girls would be costumed like dance-hall girls from the Old West. Tonight, however, Viola was still wearing her regular clothes and had yet to twist her bleached hair into its high pompadour. She looked different this way. Save for the color of her hair, she was like any other middle-aged woman from an ordinary background. Her dark blue dress was low-waisted and full-skirted. Her hair was knotted at the back of the neck and her face, innocent of makeup, looked white and tired.

"Well, if it ain't Horace Greeley himself," she said, greeting Sam. "Come out to get the news? No news, Sam. Francie's all right and she never saw the thief."

Sam grinned at her. "May as well have a drink, then," he said. "Bourbon, Jack, please."

Jack looked at Viola and Sam saw her give a slight nod. He poured an extra measure, then set it in front of Sam, saying, "First customer this evening. It's on the house, Mr. Howard."

Sam thanked him, picked up the drink, and walked down the bar to stand next to Viola. "Here's to you," he said, tossing off the drink. "And good luck, Viola. I hope there aren't any more robbers around for a while. How many did this make? Three? Four?" She stared at him coolly, but Sam saw that one of her hands was twisting at her skirt. "You know, Viola," he said mildly, "I never publish rumors and I never publish anything that would offend the good ladies of Prescottville. Now, why don't you let me talk to Francie? I'm not going to talk out of turn."

"Francie don't want to talk," Viola said shortly.

"Mind if I ask her myself?" Sam prodded. "I'm not a stranger around here, and I'm not a policeman. I'd like to get the story straight from the horse's mouth. Makes it more believable, don't you know? That way, when I write that a waitress here was set on by thieves, it'll have the ring of truth about it."

"Well, it is the truth," Viola said. "So just print it."

Sam sighed. "See, that's just why I came out here. I kept writing and rewriting that story, and it kept sounding more and more like an excuse."

"You're trying to frighten me," Viola said accusingly.

"I? Frighten you? Now, Viola, haven't I been a good bar customer? And don't I treat you and the girls well? And have I ever printed a thing that would cause you any trouble?"

"Well," Viola said reluctantly, "I don't think Francie . . ."

"You tell Francie I'm here, and I think she might see me," Sam said quietly. There was a silence. Jack was wiping glasses, his head slightly bent to catch the conversation. Viola had lowered her eyes, biting on her lip indecisively. Sam waited, leaning easily against the bar.

After a moment or two, Viola straightened up and met his eyes. "All right," she agreed. "But you've got to promise me not to keep at her and just to take her story and write it that way."

"Done," Sam said promptly.

"You wait here. I'll see if she's awake." She left the bar and went up the stairs, reappearing shortly afterward to beckon Sam from the landing.

Francie's room was at the end of the hall in the new addition just off the outside stairway door. Viola led Sam to it and motioned for him to enter.

"I've got to change," she said. "Be back when I'm done."

The room was shrouded and dim and the girl who

lay on the bed neither moved nor spoke when Sam entered. Her arms were crossed over her face. He went softly across to her, looking down at her, and saying quietly, "It's Sam Howard, Francie."

"I know." The voice was a strangled whisper.

"Hear you got hurt pretty bad. Want to tell me about it?"

"There's nothing to tell." Francie's voice was stronger. "Like I said to the sergeant, this fellow was waiting for me. Must have come up the back stairs. Anyway, he jumped me, tried to take my money, and then when I screamed, he beat me. I kept hollering, but no one could hear what with the music and all downstairs."

Sam coughed. "Where were the other girls—all downstairs?"

"Guess so," Francie muttered in reply.

"After midnight?" Sam's question was mild, but the girl stiffened at once and her hands came down from her face. Sam couldn't stop his audible gasp of pity and horror.

One of Francie's eyes was completely closed, and the other badly bruised. Her lips were swollen and split, and multiple welts and bruises covered the rest of her face.

"I know how I look," Francie said sullenly. "Doc says it'll heal itself in a couple of weeks. Said I'd look a whole lot better in a few days."

"All right, Francie." Sam's voice became crisp. "I don't believe you took a beating like that and never screamed loud enough for somebody to hear. Who was he?"

Francie shook her head and moaned.

"Francie, you can't let him get away with this. Who was he? Not a burglar. Burglars don't stay around beating girls until they scream. And for the matter of that, neither do rapists when there are crowds of people around to hear."

"I told you," Francie said resentfully. "I told you it was all the music and no one being in their rooms."

"Let's have the truth," he prodded. "Francie, have I ever told something on you or any of the girls?"

"No. But I can't tell his name because . . ." She stopped, realizing that she had given away half of the truth.

"All right." Sam seemed to capitulate. "I won't ask

you his name again, but I want to know why you're shielding him."

"You'll tell the police."

"I won't. You have my word on that."

Francie half raised herself from the bed and looked pleadingly at him. "I'd be killed, Mr. Howard. And if I wasn't, Viola would throw me out. I'd lose all the money she keeps for us. Like Greta last year. Talked and blabbed about which men came to her and Viola just threw her out. I can't. I been working here a year. Another four or five years, and I'll have me enough to quit, like Mabel did. Took pretty near two thousand dollars, and I stand to take more, what with my regular trade. Five years you got to promise Viola. Five years and you're pretty near finished, anyway. Customers get used to you and want a new face and body. Me, I been lucky. Had this fellow ever since I come here. He keeps me for himself and he pays a lot to do it."

She sank back on the bed, breathing hard, and Sam saw tears glistening on her puffy cheeks. God, she wasn't more than nineteen. He remembered when she first arrived—a pretty little thing, quiet, with a sweet smile and a beautiful figure that the nineteenth-century costume brought out to the fullest. Yet in a few months she had changed: her eyes had hardened and her manner was sharper and wiser. He sighed.

"Why, Francie?" he asked. "Why this kind of a life?"

"What else is there?" she asked. "Marry some little farmer like my ma did? Have a kid a year and get beaten if you say no to anything your man wants? Ma hated Pa. But she went to bed with him every night of her life and did just what he said, because otherwise she'd be out of her house or dead. Don't matter. She was so old by the time she was forty, and she was dead less'n two years after that. Pa wanted me to stay home and take care of the baby and the little kids, me bein' the oldest girl. Had to quit school. He'd come home hollering and drunk, and I knew he was going to this woman in town and paying her for what he wanted. First chance I got, I took some money from his trousers and left. Met Mabel down in Albany and she told me about Viola's. Same thing. But I make money and I get taken care of. Same thing," she repeated. "And when I don't do what he wants, I get beaten."

"So it's your regular customer who beats you?"

Francie started up again in alarm, whispering, "God Almighty, don't even let Viola know I told you. I didn't mean to. Please. Please. He's one of Viola's best. That's how come I got this room near the stairway. Any of the girls he picks for regular get this room. And more money. You tell the police, and if he don't get me, Viola . . . you got to promise." She was tugging at his sleeve and crying.

"Hush," Sam said. "I won't tell anyone anything. But you've got to promise me something. When you leave this place, I want you to name him to me. Will you promise that?"

Her hand fell away and she lay down again. "Yes," she said in a tired voice, "once I'm gone—if he lets me go. Figure he will. Figure he'll get tired of me soon enough, and then I won't be having him to worry about no more."

Sam laid a gentle hand on her shoulder. His throat was constricted with pity. Foolish and not very smart. She never did have a chance.

He met Viola in the hallway on his way out of Francie's room. "She's all right," Sam said. "You've got them well trained, Viola. Or maybe she is telling the truth. You want to watch out for the next robber, though. One day one of these girls will get killed, and there'll be more than a robber-rapist story to tell."

"I got a man on guard out in the back," Viola said. "Should've done that a long time ago. Feel real bad I didn't."

Sam said nothing. He was filled with a mighty anger not only at the man who had beaten Francie, but at Viola, as well. She stood before him, powdered and painted and wearing a low-cut dress that bared her shoulders and half her bosom. The cosmetics hid the aging lines in her face, but the body was still good. A woman in her prime. Making money on girls like Francie. Protecting a good customer for profit.

"I need a drink," he said. "That girl looks bad. Sure she'll be all right?"

"Doc says so. She's young and healthy. I've seen worse."

"Yes, I guess you have," Sam said. He walked past her and went down into the bar.

The place had filled up. Jack was busy pulling steins of lager, and another barman, unfamiliar to Sam, had joined him. The girls were out in their finery. One of them, a pretty blonde, was talking to Mark Douglas at the other end of the bar. When he got his drink, Sam went to join them.

"Just the man I was looking for," Mark said, greeting him. "Stopped by your office on my way out. Figured I might run into you here."

"Something on your mind?" Sam asked.

"Let's move over to one of the tables," Mark suggested. "Sorry, Dawn," he said to the girl. "I'll see you later."

"But I wanted to tell you about . . ."

"Later," Mark said, interrupting her. "I'll be back." He fished into his pocket and put a dollar on the bar. "When you get a minute, Jack, buy Dawn a beer." He winked at the girl and gave her a light pat on the rump in passing. She flashed him a wide smile as she collected the dollar and stuffed it in the bodice of her dress.

"Every little girl's friend," Sam said morosely.

"They're not bad girls," Mark answered good-humoredly. "I don't fancy tying up with one of them, but they're okay. Any woman who tries to please is good company. It's the nags you have to watch out for."

Sam lifted an eyebrow. "That's quite a speech," he said. "Didn't realize you'd come into contact with nags; bachelors seldom do."

"Even bachelors have mothers," Mark said, his face darkening.

"I just saw Francie," Sam said casually, changing the subject.

"The girl who took the beating?" Mark asked with interest. "Did she say anything?"

Sam shook his head, slightly surprised at himself. A minute ago he would have given Mark some of the details, relying on his silence. It's not that I suspect Mark, he thought. God, no. But that girl . . . that battered face . . . the fear in her eyes . . . no. Until he knew who the man was, he'd keep this much to himself "Same story about a robber-rapist."

Mark gave an unamused laugh. "It certainly figures to be that way," he said. "Must be somebody important for Viola and the girls to keep quiet about it."

"Yep." Sam tilted back in his chair and said, "Now, what was it you wanted to talk to me about?"

"I need a little advice, Sam," Mark said.

"Shoot."

"I'm in a spot of trouble with the Prescotts—father and son, that is." He grinned. "I'm going to give you a hypothetical situation, and you tell me what the *Banner* would do about it. It began with them driving up the price of the crops this year." Slowly he outlined the circumstances while Sam listened and nodded.

"And, so you see, although Jason has more or less agreed that he'll call a halt to this kind of thing, I don't trust him, and if he or Holt does move against us again, I will make good my threat."

"And you want to know if I'll back you? Move my own accounts? Write editorials? In what way, Mark?"

"I want to know how you feel about it, first of all, and then if you're on my side."

Sam shifted about in his chair, frowning. "Tell you what," he said slowly, "first I'd have to have proof of some kind of underhanded skullduggery. These family feuds—and even if you aren't related, this is something like one—I stay out of. It's a tangle. You're a trustee of Julie Fontaine's. You run a place she's inherited the bulk of. Jason is a trustee, as well, and her guardian." He shook his head. "I'd have to see more than you've told me. If it comes to a head, give me something solid. I'll back you then. But it will have to be solid. I'm not taking on Jason Prescott and Willis Bradford and Ned van Houten and the rest unless it's a hundred percent justified. I agree that if they ruin Fontaine's, it will ruin a lot of other things here too. That I'll fight for, but not a family argument."

"Don't worry about that. I don't waste my time with personalities. But if the Prescotts do try to take control of Fontaine's—and I think that's what they're after—I'll have proof . . . all you can use."

"Done." Sam's face lightened. "And where does Julie stand in all this?" he asked.

"Don't know," Mark said shortly, and something in his face make Sam shoot a keen look at him.

Like that, I see, he said to himself. Those vague rumors are true, then. John Fontaine would have liked that. Jason Prescott won't.

Aloud, Sam said, "I hear her horse threw her over on that winery road last Saturday. Foolish girl, riding that far with a storm brewing. Lucky she wasn't hurt."

"Yes."

Mark stood up and it seemed to Sam that the blood had come up in his tanned face. People are easier to read than they know, Sam thought, even the ones with the tightest control—*especially* the ones with the tightest control, he amended. The terse answers. The tightening of facial muscles. After all, it was only a situation that called for suitably concerned remarks.

"Well, Julie's young and she's stubborn, from what I understand. She'll outgrow the first, but it will take a strong man to gentle her."

"I hope she finds one, then," Mark replied. "Look, Sam, I have to get back. How about a game of poker one night next week? Art, you, me, and maybe Joe Damien, if he's up to it."

"Something wrong with Joe?"

Mark shook his head. "He's all right—a bit under the weather these days and he's working hard. But he's all right. Say Monday night for the game?"

"Monday's fine. Your place?"

"No, Art's. His wife will be away that week visiting her mother in Albany. See you then."

When he left Viola's, Mark made an abrupt decision and headed on to the Prescotts' house. In the three days since Julie had been with him, he had wrestled with himself. He knew enough about himself to realize that what he felt was not merely desire, although God knew what alone had made him lose his head completely when he saw her standing in his doorway last Saturday—vibrant, breasts heaving, and the silky black thickness of her hair swirling around her like a gypsy's. But there was something far more than that between them. The idea that he would leave her to the arms of some older man was unthinkable, and over the three days he had come to accept the fact that even marriage was preferable to that. Eighteen. Ten years younger than he was. A virgin when she had come to him. John's daughter. Three days ago he could have withstood the temptation to see her, to be alone with her. Three days ago he could have done just about anything to avoid the pitfall of holy matrimony. Now, as the result of one wild night, he was trapped.

Marry her he would. If she was twenty-one, there would be no problem. But he didn't imagine that the Prescotts were going to consent, and she would need Jason's consent. If he knew Jason at all, his consent would be won only with concessions. Jason had built the considerable fortune he had inherited into greater holdings. There was the bank, of course, and the land. Jason had bought up a lot of land, foreclosed on more. He had definitely set Viola up in business, although he had managed that transaction without appearing to be involved. He was part owner in half a dozen enterprises around town and down as far as Albany. It would not be surprising if Jason were a silent partner in the Steuben Wine Company. The amount of stock he held in Fontaine's wasn't large. Even if Jason bought out all the other small stockholders, it wouldn't help. His own, Joe Damien's, and Miranda's were the largest single amounts of shares aside from Julie's. Those four holdings made Fontaine's impregnable to a Prescott takeover—unless, of course, Julie ever elected to throw in with her uncle.

And that was one of the barriers to Jason's ready consent. Not that they couldn't elope and marry, or even marry outright in full view of the town. But then Julie would lose her control of Fontaine's and the bulk of everything would be held over until her thirtieth birthday. That was part of John Fontaine's will: "Should she marry without the consent of her guardian prior to the age of twenty-one, her estate is to continue in trust until her thirtieth birthday." This was John's way of protecting his daughter from fortune hunters. No, the interview with Jason was not one Mark looked forward to.

A subdued Amos opened the door to Mark and he asked for Julie. Amos showed him into the living room and in a moment he heard Julie skimming down the stairs and across the foyer before she paused outside the doors. He could imagine her smoothing her hair and trying to appear cool and collected. He smiled himself, and he was still smiling when she came into the room, drawing the doors closed as soon as she entered and walking sedately toward him.

Amused, Mark made her a low bow. "Miss Julie Fontaine, I believe," he said.

"Mark, don't tease," Julie answered, and a second later her arms were around his neck and she was reaching up on tiptoes to kiss him.

He held her off, regarding her with an attempt at seriousness. "Not now," he said. "You'll distract me. I came to say something, and I must say it first."

"Not something bad." Her voice was tremulous.

"As to that, it depends on your point of view. I came to ask you to marry me."

"Of course I'll marry you," she said in a practical voice. "I always meant to, anyway. Now, will you kiss me?" She went back to his arms, saying against his lips, "Oh, I missed you, Mark. When you didn't come, I thought . . ." And then she said nothing more.

Three days' separation had heightened his feelings, and for long minutes Mark forgot that they were in the Prescott house and that any family member could walk in on them.

Finally, and with no small effort, he put her away from him. "We have to talk," he said.

"All right. Then will you take me away from here for a while?"

"Julie," he groaned, "you aren't making this easier."

"I don't mean to. I told you I missed you, and, besides," she added candidly, "I like you to make love to me."

"Didn't anyone ever teach you the virtues of modesty and patience?"

"Oh, yes, tons of people. But it's such a waste of time. Shall I pretend that I am indifferent? After the other night? Would you like me to make you chase me and refuse you?"

"No," he said. "I like you as you are."

"Like me?" She raised her eyebrows and he laughed.

"Love you, then," he answered, and the words he had never said before sounded strange to his ears.

"I love you, too. And you know it. So why must we stand here? Why can't we go away and be alone?"

"We can. We will. But there are things I have to tell you, and then I have to see Jason. Now, sit down, Julie, and behave yourself."

"No." She was obstinate.

"Sit!" he ordered and propelled her firmly into an armchair, taking one opposite her. "And listen."

When he had finished explaining, she said, "First of all, you can't see Jason now because he's out. And something else—Aunt Millicent is ill. It's something to do with her heart, Dr. Vincent said, and she has to take pills and stay in bed for at least two weeks. I know it isn't a good time to see Uncle Jason. If you want anything from him, it's better to get Aunt Millicent on your side first. Even Holt pays attention to Aunt Millicent."

"Yes," he answered in a dry voice. "I've noticed that women seem to rule the house everywhere. It's . . ." His face darkened. "Never mind," he went on roughly. "That's one thing, Julie—you won't rule my house."

"I don't care. Mark, can't we go now?" She gave him a bright, ardent look.

"I'll take you for a walk," he compromised. "But when Jason comes in, I want to see him and I want to get this settled." He felt like a man who, having decided on a course he had never planned to take, was now desperate to complete it before doubts overcame him.

She agreed to the walk so equably that it surprised him. As they left the house they walked carefully apart, but when they had turned up toward Deer Hill Trail, following the old road that wound around past the park and out on River Road, she slipped her hand in his.

The early evening sky was a dusty blue and birds called sleepily as they settled down for the night to come. Wild roses growing along the banks of the old dry riverbed were misty in the twilight hush.

"Why do they call it River Road?" Julie asked idly. "There's never been any water there and, anyway, it's so narrow that even if it had water, it wouldn't be more than a creek."

"Years ago it was wider and it did have water. Then they built a dam some miles north that diverted the flow. I guess no one bothered to change the name. That's all. Didn't you know that?"

"No. I never thought about it before. But then I haven't walked here often. It's too lonely and the forest on the other side makes it lonelier. But I like it now that there are just the two of us."

"Not for long," he said as the faint chug of a motor came to his ears.

"Holt!" Julie exclaimed. "Oh, let's hide. I don't want him to see us."

He laughed out loud. "Julie, what a child you are. What difference does it make?"

"You don't know Holt," she said desperately. "He knows about the other night. I don't know how, but he does. And he can make trouble. He can. It'll go much harder with Uncle Jason." She was tugging at his arm, pulling him into the trees at the side. He followed her, holding aside the branches and letting her precede him.

Moments later Holt drove past. He slowed down a little, as if he were going to stop, and Mark felt Julie tense. He slipped his arm around her, waiting. The car picked up speed and they could hear it turn with a squeal of tires.

As the sound of the motor died out, Mark said lightly, "There, that's it." He felt her relax and turned her in his arms, pressing her face against his shoulder. "Someday," he said, "you must tell me just what it is that Holt does." He moved one hand along her soft cheek and turned her face up to his.

It was a mistake, he decided minutes later. Their feelings were too new and passion ran too close to the surface. One day in a future that he did not presently envisage, gentle affection might be possible between them. Not now. This girl roused him so quickly and so fiercely that the iron control he could bring to bear in almost any other situation slipped.

Her open response, her ardent nature, and the sensuality in her that he had perceived that first night of her return only increased his appetite. Another over-eager woman might cool his ardor. But Julie was different.

He was holding her now, her head once more pressed against his shoulder, holding her with hard arms, trying to quell the flames of desire that were engulfing them both. She stirred, pressing closer, as if the arms that embraced her were not holding her strongly enough.

"Not here," he said in a strangled voice. "I can't take you here." He wrenched himself away and pulled her blindly back out onto the road, striding swiftly so that she ran along after him. Sensing that she began to lag behind him, he slowed his pace a little.

At the corner of Seneca, he finally stopped and she

moved to stand beside him, her breath coming in labored gasps.

"Smooth your hair," Mark ordered curtly. "I'm taking you home."

Julie obeyed and after a moment or two they went on to the house.

Jason was home. They could hear him talking to Holt in the library. "Go upstairs," Mark whispered. And he went to knock on the library door.

Julie never knew all of the details of what transpired that night. She lingered at the head of the stairs, where after a time she heard voices raised, heard Jason bellow, "No, absolutely not!" and then quiet for several minutes.

If Uncle Jason means no, I'll do it in spite of him, she told herself, quelling the sense of uneasiness that had risen with that shouted refusal.

The voices began to rise again. She heard Holt's snarling tone, but the words were indistinguishable, and then came Uncle Jason's hoarse voice: "My God, Holt, apologize!" And a second later came the heavy crashing of furniture and Jason's shouting.

So intent had she been on the scene below that Julie forgot about Millicent. She was halfway down the stairs, fearful, but determined to intervene, when she heard her aunt gasp out her name. Julie spun around in time to see Millicent, hand clutched to her chest, staggering toward the head of the stairs.

My God, she'll fall! Fear flashed through Julie's brain and she was running back up the stairs in a desperate effort to catch Millicent. She reached the next to last stair as Millicent toppled forward, and for a few seconds they swayed there as Julie braced herself against the wall, fighting the force of Millicent's dead weight. With a Herculean burst of strength, she succeeded in getting them both back onto the landing, and with Millicent still hanging limply from her arms, she called for help.

It roused the household and reached the fighting men below. Jason was the first to reach them and he literally tore Millicent from Julie's grasp. Holt, coming behind him, grated out, "You little tramp! This is all your doing!" But Julie was too stricken by the events to pay any attention. She followed Jason to the door of Millicent's room.

"Call Dr. Vincent, son," he said to Holt. Then he said

to Julie, "Let Jenny come in, and get Margaret. You've done enough for one evening."

Before he closed the door, Julie saw Millicent, white and still, lying on the bed looking as close to death as she had ever seen anyone look.

She summoned Jenny and Margaret and then went in search of Mark, only to find that he had left the house. She went back to her room, listening to the household attempts to revive Millicent, then hearing Dr. Vincent's voice at last as he went past her room on the way to Millicent's. Millicent's door was opened and closed and then there was nothing but silence.

An hour later she heard Jason coming along the hall and Dr. Vincent saying, "She'll do. But this must not happen again. Absolute bed rest. Regular meals, medication. She has angina. She can live for years with it if she takes proper care of herself and avoids excitement."

Jason murmured something indistinguishable as they went down the stairs. Julie left her room then, following them down and nodding to Dr. Vincent in the hall before going into the library.

Jason found her there shortly afterward, picking up the fallen chairs and the overturned smoking stand and attempting to clear away some of the debris left from the room's disarrangement.

"You will never marry Mark Douglas," he began without preamble, "not with my consent."

"Then I'll marry him without it," she said steadily.

"Will you? I think you'll find that Mark isn't interested in marriage if he has to wait twelve years to get his hands on your trust."

"That's a lie," she said.

"Ask him yourself. Go on out to the winery tomorrow. I have forbidden him to come into this house again."

She did not answer but walked past him and up to her room. There she changed clothes and sat waiting until everyone was in bed and the house was still.

Shortly after midnight she went down the stairs and out the door.

Driving, the distance between the Prescotts' house and her old house took less than fifteen minutes. On horseback it was half an hour. Walking, it brought her to the back field after one o'clock. The house was dark and the back door was locked. She went around to the stable and saw that Rusty's stall was empty.

So sure had she been that Mark would be there that the letdown was unbearable. She leaned against the stable door and let the tears fall down her cheeks. Presently, she wiped her face with the edge of her riding skirt and went to sit on the kitchen porch. He would come home and she would be here when he did. She leaned back against the corner of the house where it joined the railing and closed her eyes.

Around her, the stillness of the warm night beat against her ears. The whirlwind of emotions that had bound her until now left her exhausted and her mind felt numb. The thoughts slipped in and around the edges of her brain, half formed. After a while she dozed off.

She awoke, instantly alert, sometime later, hearing Rusty's hooves coming down the front drive and around the side of the lawn. Sleepiness vanished. She watched as Mark reached the stable, dismounted, and led the horse in. She could hear him talking to the roan while he unsaddled him and his words were indistinct.

As he emerged from the stable, he put out one hand as if to steady himself. She rose then and went to meet him, calling his name.

If he was surprised that she was there, he didn't show it. He opened his arms and she ran into them. She could smell the whiskey on his breath and knew that if he wasn't drunk, he was close to it.

"Let's go inside," she urged, and they walked, his arms around her shoulders, to the door. He unlocked it and drew her inside, turning on the kitchen lamp.

His eyes were bloodshot and his voice was faintly blurred, but he showed no other effects from the whiskey.

"How is your aunt?" he asked.

"She's all right."

"And Jason?"

"He told me."

"And that's that." He waved a hand.

"It isn't true, is it? What Uncle Jason said?"

"What did he say?"

"That you . . . that you wouldn't marry me without his consent, because it would hold up my control of the stocks."

"Yes, he would say that. True enough, though. If I

marry you, you'll be at Jason's and Holt's mercy. They can do as they please, invest as they please, and probably vote your stock. You can see where that would leave you and me and the Damiens and the Fontaine Wine Company."

"I don't care," she cried. "It's you I want."

"I care," he said. "I have no intention of letting the Prescotts take over Fontaine's."

"Then it is true? It was the stock you wanted? Not me?" The enormity of it struck her and she flew at him, beating on his chest with her fists, crying, "You . . . you cad, you . . . oh!" She drew back. He was looking at her intently, his face impassive under her words. Maddened, she drew back and slapped him hard across the face. For a minute he didn't move, and then he moved so swiftly that she did not realize at first what was happening. She was up and down over his lap, her skirts above her head, her knickers on the floor, and he was slapping her with hard, deliberate slaps across her naked buttocks.

She cried in pain and humiliation, although the slaps were few, and she tried to wriggle upward. When he finished, he grasped her, turned her roughly around to face him, and then he kissed her with a hardness and a cruelty he had never shown.

She fought him, but he rose with her in his arms as she kicked and clawed at him. Then he threw her across the bed and flung himself down beside her.

He had pinioned her arms now and all her wild struggles were to no avail. His hands moved over her, beneath her clothing, with a sureness born of long practice, and even as she fought she could feel the wildness rising inside her. Then all at once she was returning those kisses, straining closer to him until everything melted away and his touch became the core of her being.

She did not return home that night. They slept past dawn and Julie, remembering how it had been through the long night, felt her body glow. She turned to face him and he kissed her, running his hand gently along the place where he had slapped the night before.

"It hurts," she said.

"Don't ever raise a hand to me again," Mark warned quietly. She did not answer him. Instead, with sure instincts, she set about taming him in the only ways open to her. She caressed his body, pulling at the chest hairs and snaking one hand down along his belly, stopping just past his navel and sliding her hand up again and down again, always barely grazing the pulsating tip of his organ until at last she let her hand close over it. She heard his quickly indrawn breath, and she slid her hand over the hardening mounds of his flesh.

She looked up at him, saw that he was lying there, his eyes slanted down at her. The fact of his immobility excited her and she began to kiss his body as he had kissed hers, opening her mouth to take his flesh in soft-lipped bites and finally engulfing his member with her moist lips. All at once he moved, seizing her, lifting her around so that she was up astride him, impaled. He held her firmly, moving her body rhythmically until she took the initiative. He lifted his head from the pillow then and bent her body down until his lips reached her breasts.

It had been thrilling to arouse him; it was more thrilling now as he sought to extract and prolong the increasing throbs of pleasure. One moment it was as if there was all the time in the world; and in the next, he had seized her again, moving her quickly, saying hoarsely, "Now, now!" And there was a mutual, electrifying explosion of feeling, and she was lying on his body still wriggling against him in the aftermath of passion.

It was close to nine before they left the house.

"I'd better drive you home," Mark said.

"No, please don't, Mark. It will be easier if someone else does."

In the end he agreed, and at the winery Avery Bertram obliged, helping her into his ancient electric motorcar as if she were royalty. On the road between the winery and house, he said nothing at all beyond "Yes, indeed" to her casual comments about the weather. When they arrived in front of her house, Avery again gave Julie regal treatment as he assisted her out of the motorcar.

As Julie entered the foyer, Jenny was just coming down the stairs bearing Aunt Millicent's breakfast tray.

"Good morning, Miss," she said. "My, you're out early this morning."

"Yes," Julie replied. So they hadn't missed her. She went into the dining room, ravenous for food, and found Holt gone, but Uncle Jason was still at the table having a second cup of coffee.

She filled her plate from the sideboard chafing dishes and sat down in her accustomed seat, saying, "Good morning, Uncle Jason. I want to talk to you."

"Where have you been?" he asked in reply. "Out," she told him. "And that doesn't even matter. What I want to say is that if I don't get your consent to marry Mark, I won't marry him."

"Ha! I thought not."

"No. And you were quite right. He won't marry me."

"I warned you . . ." he began.

"So," she said, "I will become his mistress. I will sleep with him and quite possibly get pregnant, and then, quite naturally, you'll look pretty silly withholding your consent, and everyone will think you're the one who wants control of my money."

Having delivered herself of this brazen proposal, she picked up her fork and attacked her scrambled eggs while beside her Jason sat, first mute with outrage, and then incoherent with fury.

He was handicapped by his inability to raise his voice for fear of rousing Millicent and precipitating another attack, remembering Dr. Vincent's stern warning. But his language was both forceful and abusive, and through it all Julie ate with a feigned calmness that she was far from feeling. What Mark would say when or if he found out, she didn't dare think about. For that matter, after the last week she might be pregnant already. She didn't care. Jason prided his name above all else. The disgrace would be unbearable for him, and even as he was threatening to lock her in her room until she came to her senses, to take a strap to her, which she knew he would never do, she thought to herself, I will win. If I just don't break in front of him, I will win.

"And your cousin Holt will think I've lost my mind," Jason said.

She knew she had won. She put down her fork and looked at him. "If you tell Holt what I've said, we'll have a scandal of a different sort. He might decide to take on Mark, and Mark's the one person Holt wouldn't stand a chance against. And if Holt does anything to hurt me, Mark will kill him. So if I were you, Uncle Jason, I wouldn't say anything about this to Holt. You'll just have to say you've changed your mind."

He looked at her for a long moment. "I was always

fond of you, Julie," he said at length, "but I see now that you are a scheming, willful, wanton girl. Very well, you'll have your way. But I will insist on a proper engagement period. Next summer, perhaps."

"This summer."

"Not before spring."

"This fall," she countered, "after the harvest."

He rose from the table, flinging down his napkin and saying, "Fall, then, provided your aunt is up to it. You've won, Julie, but mark my words, this is one victory you will live to regret for the rest of your life."

7

Julie rode high that summer of her engagement. She had triumphed over Jason and she had won the subdued approval of her aunt. In fact, it seemed to Julie that there was almost a look of relief on Millicent's face. Uncle Jason might not have had Millicent on his side, after all. Holt was furious, but he was unable to make his position known out loud due to Millicent's illness, and he was forced to content himself with the occasional snide remark to Julie when they were alone.

What Holt said bothered her not at all. Mark's sapphire ring with its softly gleaming star now reposed on her finger. The summer waxed lush and opulent and the grapes grew to a brilliant purple in the sun, weighing down the vines that gave them birth. The air was drenched with the perfume of flowers, and the heat of July and August was mitigated by the cooling breezes that swept from hill and lake. It was a perfect summer, people said. The most perfect I have known, Julie echoed.

If Jason had disapproved and if the town wondered at his sudden acquiescence to a marriage they would have wagered he'd oppose, there was no public evidence of it.

And for once he seemed to keep Holt in line so that when Art and Lillian Douglas gave a dinner dance for the engaged couple, Holt made his appearance with some show of family solidarity.

Julie liked Art Douglas. Older than Mark by fifteen years, he bore a strong resemblance to him. He was a bit shorter than Mark and his eyes were a clear blue rather than the tawny hazel of Mark's, but his hair was a dark red and his face still bore the traces of the same clean, hard lines Mark's had.

Lillian, his wife, was very different. Small, plump, and frankly forty-five, she lacked the Douglas geniality and was harder to know.

"Will any of Mark's family be coming for the wedding?" she asked Julie at the dinner dance.

"I think so," Julie answered. "His sisters and their husbands. His mother isn't really up to such a long journey."

"And his sister Valerie isn't well enough for it," Lillian added. "You do know about Valerie?"

"Mark told me," Julie said. "He's very fond of Valerie. In fact, she's his favorite."

"She would be," Lillian answered cryptically. "Mark likes his women weak and compliant."

It was a dreadful thing to say and Julie suddenly remembered that Lillian Douglas had been very fond of Miranda Latham as a prospective in-law, and she was, in fact, still very good friends with her.

"Then it's lucky that I'm not strong and willful," Julie said with a grin, thinking how Mark would laugh if he heard her.

Sam Howard came up just then and Lillian's answer died on her lips. "You're looking beautiful, Julie," he said. "You'll be a radiant bride. That's what all brides are supposed to be, if you read my accounts of local weddings. For once I'll be able to say 'beautiful' without exaggeration."

"Were you as surprised as we were?" Lillian asked before Julie could answer.

"Nope. Knew it all along. I'll bet I knew it before young Mark decided to propose. Part of my job is looking beneath what people say," he said, giving Lillian a keen look that made her flush a little and turn away.

Lillian said, "Oh, here come Miranda and Alec Fremont. Excuse me."

"Don't let the old cats worry you, Julie. Be happy and make Mark happy," Sam advised when Lillian was out of earshot.

She smiled at him gratefully. "I will," she promised.

"Your father would have been glad about this," he added. "John had Mark picked out for you from the first. Oh, he'd deny it when I'd tease him about it, but I knew. Then, before he died, he owned up. I guess he must have felt that something was going to happen. Don't see how he could, and I don't hold much with clairvoyance and premonitions, but we had a long, serious talk just a month before his accident."

"Tell me," Julie begged, sentimental tears misting her eyes.

"Not if you're going to puddle up like that and disgrace me," Sam said in alarm and made her laugh. "Nothing much to tell," Sam went on. "Just what I've told you and that he hoped you'd grow up the way you showed promise of growing. He was proud of you, Julie. He'd be prouder of you today. And that's a good man you've got—thorny, maybe, and stubborn, and not always diplomatic, but then you need a man who won't let you ride all over him."

"I like Mark just the way he is," Julie answered. "Oh, here comes Miranda. I don't really want to see her. She always coos over me as if I were a puppy."

"Run along, then." Sam smiled. "I'll fight a rear-guard action for you."

He wondered if Julie knew that town gossip still centered on how Miranda Latham was taking Mark's defection. From where he sat, she seemed to be taking it very well, but he knew better than to take the face value of things for the truth.

Sam Howard was more right than he knew. Publicly, Miranda had taken it remarkably well. Not even to Mark did she betray her chagrin. Privately, she raged, as Sam suspected. Her mind turned around and around, seeking some means to prevent the marriage. In Jason Prescott she had a willing ally, but barring some unforeseen event, there appeared little either could do to accomplish his separate and mutual ends.

Miranda found herself wishing the impossible and wishing she had the courage to eliminate her rival, but short of hoping that Julie would meet with some accident, her venom found no outlet.

In August, Millicent felt sufficiently recovered to plan a trip to New York with Julie to shop for her trousseau, but Dr. Vincent wouldn't hear of it, and in the end Julie was forced to go with Mrs. Bradford. While she was grateful for Mrs. Bradford's kind offer, her own spirits were curtailed by her chaperone's obvious fear and distrust of the huge "metropolis," as she persisted in calling it. Julie hastened back rather sooner than she might have otherwise.

The days drew closer and closer to the harvest and, as the crops gathered, Julie spent much of her time out in the vineyards, watching the pickers bring their full crates to the women who waited with their baskets before them with sharp pairs of scissors in their hands to cut out the grapes that were withered or unripened or unsound and to leave only the perfect purple clusters for the pressing to follow.

The days in the sun tanned Julie's face and arms and hands and cast a reddish glow to her black hair.

"I'll be marrying a gypsy if this keeps up," Mark teased one day.

"It will fade before the wedding," Julie said tranquilly. "I loved this summer," she added, "all of it. I love the parties and I love coming out here. I love the sun and I love . . . oh . . . everything."

"I take it I am included in everything?" he asked, smiling.

"You are the everything," she assured him.

He said, "Will you think so five years from now? Ten?"

She was disturbed by the seriousness in his voice. She did not pursue it, however, saying lightly, "Fifty, at least."

At home, she was a model of deportment and solicitude. Nothing could mar her good temper or cast a shadow on her happiness, and Jason, for all he had opposed them in the beginning, seemed to be taking it all as if he had always approved.

Privately, however, Jason, like Miranda, fumed. It was small consolation to him to realize that if he had not tried so hard to persuade his brother-in-law to sell out to

Steuben Wine the year before he died, John would not have barred him from voting Julie's stock during her minor years. Now it seemed impossible that he would ever be able to bring off the merger with Steuben, and with Julie firmly in Mark's pocket along with Joe Damien, only a miracle could either stop the marriage or remove Mark from control of Fontaine's.

And then the unlikely occurred. In the middle of September, with the wedding three weeks away, with the harvest in and the grapes in the first pressing, Mark's mother died. As one of the heirs and the executor of her estate, he was forced to go to California to take care of everything.

"A matter of two weeks," he told a tearful Julie. "I'll be back in plenty of time."

"Something will happen. I know it," she said. "Take me with you."

"Don't be foolish. Nothing is going to happen, and I am not going to take you with me. It would only delay things out there. Millicent would insist on a chaperone. There's no time to move up the wedding date. Be reasonable, Julie."

She could not sway him. Her pleas only annoyed him without budging him an inch. Finally she gave up. Millicent, to whom she complained, only said, "It's time you were curbed, Julie. You've had your own way for too long. Mark Douglas is a match for you, I'll say that. You'll never be able to threaten him into giving you your own way."

Julie was silent. So Jason had told her the method by which he had been forced to agree to the wedding.

"Yes, I know," Millicent said dryly, as if reading Julie's mind. "I also believe with your uncle that this is one time you'll regret your waywardness."

"There is nothing wrong with Mark," Julie answered. "You and Uncle Jason may not like him, but my father loved and trusted him."

"I know that. But then your father was always the sort of man to put his trust too easily in other people. Mark wormed his way into that position at the winery. He was unable to get along with his own family in California, unwilling to go into the dairy business here like his cousin Art, always in some kind of fight . . . well, there's no point in going into that now. What's done is done. You've

got your wedding, just the way you managed to get sent
away from the convent. You've been pretty full of yourself, Julie. I must say, it's not unpleasant to find you
balked for once. In fact, it raises my opinion of Mark.
A strong hand is what you need. And a strong hand is
what you'll . . ." Millicent gave a little gasp and reached
into her skirt pocket, withdrawing a vial of medicine that
Dr. Vincent had prescribed. Her face was very white and
Julie, stricken with remorse, went to help her aunt.

Moments after she had swallowed the medicine Millicent relaxed, some of the eerie, tight look gone from
her face. "I shouldn't let myself get excited," she said.
"It's bad for me. Go away, Julie. I need rest."

Mark left two days later and Julie felt that somehow
in the leaving she was alone and unprotected. It was a
feeling she could not shake—a strange sense of fore-
boding that remained with her despite the fact that her
reason told her it was baseless.

She haunted the winery those first few days, pelting the
Damiens with questions, standing absorbed by the old
oak presses from which the juices of the grapes were
seeping.

"I know so little about everything," she said one day
to Joe Damien.

"Ah, Julie, to know wine, to know champagne, that isn't
something you learn in a few hours or days, or even
years. I can show you how the grapes must be chosen,
I can demonstrate the way the juice runs from the press
down into the collecting station, and I can show you
many other things from the first pressing through to the
last, when we have the most inferior of the juice. Peter
can take you to the fermenting vats and show you the
must that collects. If we took you everywhere through
every step until the last when I choose the cuvées, which
is the best, and decide the blends, even then, as you
watched the bottling, you would only have a schoolgirl's
knowledge."

"You mean I will never really learn?" she asked,
dismayed.

"Of course, but only when you have come time and
time again, and only by example and by working yourself. Testing the wines! That is something that cannot be
learned overnight."

"But I know good wines," she protested. "I can tell a

good champagne from a bad one, and I can tell a Fontaine from a French champagne."

"I would hope so," Joe laughed. "They have a very different taste."

"I like the Fontaine taste," Julie said.

"That is good. So do I. So I had better, and so had you."

"I'm going to come out here every harvest and every pressing and all the time until I learn."

"Very well. Next year we will put you with the women who cut away the bad grapes, and then the next year we will let you help with the pressing—year after year until you are about forty, and then you will know all that I know."

"You are poking fun at me," she accused, looking up at him.

"Only gently. I was thinking how much like your father you are—how much he would love to see you as you are today, still brown like a gypsy and so full of confi——"

He broke off with a little gasp and Julie, alarmed, said, "What is it?"

He didn't speak for a moment, holding his side, then he said, "It's nothing—a muscle spasm. Hurts like the devil, but it isn't serious. Don't worry."

But shortly afterward, he sent her on her way, saying that he had work to do. Peter was busy somewhere in the vaults, and there was no one else around, so, reluctantly, Julie went to call Fancy from the field across from the winery. When she had mounted and was turning past the winery, she glanced through the big window of Mark's office, as was her custom, and saw Joe, sitting in Mark's chair, his head down on his crossed arms. It worried her, yet the next day Joe was back at work, looking fit and ready again to answer her endless questions.

Mark's absence weighed heavily upon her in spite of her efforts to keep busy. Several times she rode out to Douglas Farms, ostensibly to pay a family call and talk to Lillian, but more to see Art, whose resemblance to Mark both hurt and soothed her.

"He'll be back next week," Art said on her third visit. "Will we see as much of you then?" And she blushed, embarrassed that her intent was so apparent.

"Perhaps not quite so much," she answered, her spirit rising as it always did to a baiting. Art laughed.

"Mark will have his hands full with you, Julie. Won't he, Lil?"

"Indeed, yes," Lillian agreed sweetly.

Meeting her eyes, Julie flushed, again remembering Lillian's warning: "Mark likes his women weak and compliant."

The marriage was to take place at St. Stephen's, and Julie and Mark had already had their preliminary discussion with Father Gannett. She had found the priest rather orthodox in his views, but Mark said, "He's all right, better than most—not so nosy and not so full of general platitudes."

Julie had meant to go privately to see him. The nuptial Mass would mean confession, and she had not been to confession since the week she left St. Veronica's. She didn't relish the prospect and kept putting it off.

Now her wedding dress was finished and hung all alone in the sewing room; her trousseau was complete; the invitations had been mailed out and were now answered; all the wedding presents were suitably arrayed on the long library table with each giver thanked. There was nothing left to do except wait for Mark and see Father Gannett.

On the Sunday before Mark's return, hearing the banns read for the last time, Julie was uncomfortably reminded that she was overdue for that visit with Father Gannett and that she had put it off long enough.

She had tried to talk to Mark about it before he left, but he had laughed away her trepidations. "What can he do to you?" he asked. "You confess, admit you were wrong, and he absolves you. It's neat and tidy."

"He'll scold me," Julie said.

"It's part of his job."

"You'll have to go, too," she said.

"That doesn't bother me. Big wedding, nuptial Mass —that was all your idea. Can't have the bridal couple refusing to receive at their own wedding Mass. A bore, but it can be gotten over. You worry about too many unimportant things."

It did not comfort her and, even though she knew he was right, she still clung to the idea that the whole process would be humiliating.

"Anyway," she had added resentfully, "I don't think all that is a sin."

"All what?"

"Oh, love and things like that," she said evasively, and he shouted with laughter.

"A prude, after all," he teased " '. . . and things like that,' " he mimicked. "Well, neither do I, but the Church does, and Father Gannett definitely does, and I can't see the harm in leaving them to their fancies."

"Why, Mark, that's heresy. You mean you'll actually go into confession and not believe in any of it? I mean, communion or . . ."

"Exactly. Form, ritual. I don't normally bother with it, but now it's necessary."

"Aren't you afraid?" she asked.

"Of what?"

"Hell? The devil? God's wrath?"

"I don't believe in hell, first of all, and all the devils I've ever known were human. As for God's wrath, just what is that? Is that when he wipes out a whole city like San Francisco in one big earthquake? If so, his wrath is pretty indiscriminate. Innocent and saintly people suffered along with the sinners. We might as well sin, then, since the rewards appear equal."

"But . . . but that doesn't count. I mean about here on earth. It's for getting into heaven."

He smiled at her. "You look like a woman, God knows you act like one when it comes to 'things like that,' but you're still a baby. Heaven! As far as I can tell, a man can cheat, lie, steal, and commit adultery all his life, even do murder—then confess on his deathbed and receive pardon, right along with the daily communicant. They both go to heaven."

"But the sinner has to go to purgatory first."

Mark shrugged. "Nevertheless, they wind up in the same place."

"At least you believe in purgatory and heaven," Julie said, relieved.

"I never said that. In any case, I certainly don't believe in pearly gates and harps and wings."

"What do you believe?"

"I believe in myself. And that's enough religious discussion for one day. Marry in the rectory and skip the Mass or go to confession. But stop worrying about it.

It's a bit late to switch churches. The first banns were read at St. Stephen's this morning."

A nudge at her left startled Julie out of her musings and she realized that the Mass had ended. Filing out to the church entrance, she saw Father Gannett greeting parishioners and stood aside. Now or never, she thought, and when the last worshipper had left, she approached the priest to ask if he would hear her confession.

It went far more easily than she had expected. Stepping out into the sunshine on that crisp early October morning, Julie felt less sense of impending disaster. Later, she would remember that and wonder at her lack of perception. But at the moment the day was fine, the priest had been mild in his rebuke, and the penance was light enough. Mark would be home the following Friday.

The streets were deserted. All churches had emptied and their congregations were hurrying home to their big midday Sunday dinner. Julie walked slowly, savoring the day and her own well-being.

As she turned into Seneca Avenue, however, she saw several motorcars parked in the drive, and even as she identified them—Mayor Bradford's, Mr. van Houten's and Avery Bertram's—she felt a throb of nameless anxiety.

Still her feet lagged and she mounted the steps reluctantly. The foyer was empty. From the depths of the house she could hear the clink of china and silver being laid, and from behind the closed library door she heard the low murmur of men's voices.

She went directly to her room to remove her hat and freshen her appearance, still with a half-somnambulant feeling. Moments later a soft tap on the door and Aunt Millicent's voice saying "Julie" set her heat beating faster.

"Come in," she called, hardly recognizing her voice as her own.

Aunt Millicent's face as she entered the room only increased Julie's dread. "What is it?" she half whispered. "Is . . . is something . . . has something happened to Mark?"

"No." Millicent's voice was harsh. "I'm sorry to say that I wish it had. He will not be returning Friday. Your wedding is postponed indefinitely. We had a telegram from him this morning. There's one for you, too."

"I don't believe it." Julie's voice cracked sharply.

"Some business to take care of," Millicent went on, "but that isn't all. There is a third telegram to us." She handed all the yellow envelopes to Julie. "You'd better read them yourself."

"I don't want to," Julie answered.

"The third one is from Miranda Latham to me, asking me to break the news to you. It seems that she and Mark were married last week. She went with him to California. Did you know . . ." She broke off as Julie paled, her eyes growing large and then closing as she slid into a faint.

Julie regained consciousness to find the room still swimming and Aunt Millicent alternately slapping her wrists and waving a vial of spirits of ammonia under her nose.

"I've never known her to faint," she was saying to someone else in the room, and Julie perceived that Uncle Jason stood just behind her aunt.

"Didn't have breakfast this morning—that and the shock, I suppose."

"I'm all right," Julie said weakly. "I . . . let me see those telegrams. I don't believe any of this."

The sight of the written words made no more sense to her than the rest. Mark's telegram merely said:

URGENT BUSINESS. CANNOT RETURN AS PLANNED. LETTER FOLLOWS.

The one to Aunt Millicent was agonizingly plain:

MARK AND I MARRIED AT NOON. PLEASE BREAK NEWS GENTLY.

It was signed Miranda Latham Douglas, Fairmont Hotel, San Francisco.

No matter how often she reread it, Julie could not bring herself to accept it. "I don't believe it," she kept saying dazedly. "Miranda. Mark. I don't believe it."

"If you don't believe it," Jason said, "then call Mark and ask him yourself. Go on. He's at the Fairmont. You can telephone to California now, you know."

Julie shook her head mutely, and from behind her Holt said, "Yes, you would be afraid to call, because you know it's true. We told you all along about Mark Douglas, but . . ."

"I'll call!" Julie cut across his speech. "Please, will you get the Fairmont for me, Uncle Jason?"

She rose, over Millicent's protests, and led the way to the foyer.

Jason lifted the receiver and placed the call. When he finished, he turned to Julie and said, "I never liked Mark Douglas, but I didn't believe him capable of jilting a girl without so much as a note of apology. You're well rid of him."

"*If* it's true," Julie answered, white-lipped. "I wouldn't put anything past Miranda Latham."

"Oh, Julie, don't," Millicent said. "Come along upstairs. It will be a while before they get that cable connection through. You'll want to freshen up."

"Yes, I suppose so," Julie answered listlessly and followed her aunt upstairs.

When the two women were out of sight, Holt said to Jason, "Now, if Miranda has only gotten the thing straight, we'll be all right."

"Of course she has," his father said irritably. "I questioned her over and over. She checked into the Fairmont as 'Douglas.' Mark's still at the ranch and won't be down in San Francisco for a week. Lucky he was forced to move the wedding forward. It would have been too difficult otherwise."

"I don't see why. The delay worries me more," Holt said. "Too much of a chance that Mark might get in touch with Julie before we can get her out of town."

"Nonsense," Jason replied. "We can keep back her mail just as we did the telegram and the letter he's sent already. There's no phone on the ranch, and in any case, if he tries to ring her from San Francisco . . ."

"What, then?" Holt asked.

"That's more than a week away," his father said testily. "She'll be on her way to New Orleans with Millicent before that. It's a bit of luck that the doctor wants Millicent to get away for a rest. Julie can be persuaded to go with her."

"We'll see," Holt said. "Sometimes Julie is very hard to persuade."

"You stay out of that part, Holt," Jason warned. "If anyone can turn Julie stubborn, you can. All this business of getting Miranda out to the Coast the day before Mark arrived and her visiting the ranch . . . that was tricky enough. So far, so good. Now, don't meddle. We'd better go back to the meeting. I wish that call would come through. Julie isn't going to be persuaded to vote Mark out unless she's convinced he's married to Miranda."

Julie heard the telephone ring as she lay across her bed and jumped up to answer it, flying past Millicent in the hall, taking the stairs so quickly that she nearly fell. Jason and Holt were just emerging from the library by the time Julie lifted the receiver.

"When you're finished, Julie, come into the library," Jason said. "There is something else you should know."

She nodded, saying, "Hello, hello," into the mouthpiece.

Miranda's voice purred softly over the miles. "Oh, Julie. Why, I never thought that you would call. Poor dear. I know how upset you must be. But Julie . . ."

"Let me speak to Mark," Julie cut through.

"He isn't here right now. He went out early. Shall I have him call when he gets back? Julie, dear, he did write to you—at least he promised me that he would. Why don't you just wait for the letter?"

Numbed, Julie replaced the receiver without answering. She felt alien, unreal, as if all the familiar sights of the house existed in a dream. She walked into the library to find Mr. van Houten, Avery Bertram, and Mayor Bradford with her uncle.

She closed the door behind her, leaning back against it, her hands braced behind her. "You have something to tell me?" she asked.

"You'd better sit down, my dear," Mr. van Houten said kindly.

She shook her head. "Tell me," she demanded. She would not break down in front of them. Later, when she was alone. Not now.

Most of what they said made little sense. Mismanagement of the winery . . . her stocks in it virtually worthless . . . Mark not here. Uncle Jason would have to assume . . . something about lacking her consent. He would seek legal means to charge Mark with . . .

"Vote my stock?" she repeated. "Vote it, how?"

"Why, to sell, Julie. We've had an offer from Steuben. Of course, it won't be anything as big as it might have been if Fontaine's were in better shape," Uncle Jason explained.

"No," Julie said, "I won't agree to sell. You can vote any way you please, but I won't agree to that. I'll fight you on that."

Gone, she was thinking. Everything is gone. There isn't anything left now except the winery. That's all I have.

"We also want to replace Mark as manager. If we have your consent to that, Julie, it will be easier on Mark. Otherwise, we will have to bring charges. Very unpleasant for him. I expect he will be remaining in California, of course, but still . . ."

"Do as you like about that," Julie said. "Is there more?" Mark, she thought in agony. How could you do this? How could you?

"That's about it. Mr. Bertram will be in temporary charge." Julie focused on Bertram and his eyes slid away from her accusing stare.

"I see," she said. "You, too, Mr. Bertram. And what of Joe Damien?"

"Well, he . . . we don't really need his vote now," Jason answered. "I'm sorry, Julie. I tried to warn you," he added. Although his voice was sympathetic, she saw the poorly concealed satisfaction in his eyes, and with a stiff nod she left the room.

The following days passed like a hideous nightmare. Julie, torn between humiliation and heartbreak, kept to her room, tensing anxiously when the telephone rang, searching feverishly through the mail each morning and afternoon.

"It would be a difficult letter for any man to write," Aunt Millicent said, trying to console her.

"You're glad it all happened," Julie accused her in reply.

"I'm glad it happened now instead of later, yes. Mark is not like other men. He's wild and stubborn and godless."

And, Julie remembering, thought. So am I, then.

Each night she wept herself to sleep and in the morning she woke with a dull, leaden feeling. She had agreed to accompany Millicent to New Orleans, but she had no real interest in planning for it or packing. Three days before their departure Millicent said, "You'll make yourself ill."

"I don't care," Julie answered.

"You'll feel better once we're in New Orleans, and so will I," Millicent sighed. "I'm almost glad Dr. Vincent ordered me off on a trip. It will help you now, too. But you're young, Julie. You'll get over this, believe me. Why, there's a whole world ahead of you. And somewhere in it lies a good, decent man."

"No, thank you," Julie said again. "I don't care about that anymore. I don't intend to get married."

"Of course you do. Every girl gets married."

"You didn't," Julie pointed out, and her aunt blushed. "I . . . I lost the man I . . ."

"So did I," Julie replied. "So did I."

"Be sensible, Julie. You need some diversion. Call Alice . . . oh, no," Millicent interrupted herself. "I forgot, the telephone is out of order. Well, then," she continued briskly, "walk over to see the Bradfords. The walk will do you good."

"I don't want to see the Bradfords," Julie answered. "Mayor Bradford wasn't very pleasant about my refusal to sell Fontaine's."

"But Alice is your best friend," Millicent protested.

"*Was* my best friend," Julie replied. "It seems she thinks I'm foolish, too."

Alice, in whom she had tried to confide, had dismissed the whole episode with a breezy reply: "Oh, Julie, there are other fish in the sea. Anyway, you did pirate Mark from Miranda to begin with."

As if she enjoyed what had happened, Julie thought.

That evening Holt approached Julie. "You're making a fool of yourself, you know," he said without preamble. "Everyone in town must know now. And they know you're afraid to show your face."

"Go to hell!" Julie answered with the first sign of spirit she had shown. "You and your appearances. I don't care what anyone thinks."

"Come, come, Julie," he sneered. "There are other men around. And I know you. Once you get over these sulks, you'll be out running around like the . . ."

"At least I haven't eloped with a whiskey drummer!" she yelled at him, and he was across the room in one stride, grabbing her up from the chair, his face red with fury, his hand raised.

"I'll scream," she said calmly. "And if you hit me, you won't be able to explain it away."

He stood, frozen for a second, and then flung her back into the chair. "You'll live to see the day when you're sorry for that," he said between clenched teeth.

But the threat did not frighten her as Holt's threats once had. As the days had gone by, despondency had laid its grip upon her. Death seemed preferable to anything else, and even that was not a state to be tried for. Let it come or not, she thought. She felt cold inside and took to lighting the coals in her bedroom grate each evening, huddling near the warmth as if it might melt the ice within.

The following night the entire household went to the annual church social. She took pleasure in the solitude and spent the evening in the living room listening to records.

Shortly after nine she heard Holt drive in. Hastily she rose, switched off the Victrola, and left the living room. She was halfway up the stairs when Holt entered the foyer and she continued her ascent, a little more swiftly, so that she was actually running by the time she reached the upper hall. So intent was she on reaching her room that she did not hear him behind her, and as he reached out and grasped her around the waist she screamed in fright. He laughed hoarsely, saying in her ear, "I've got you this time, sweet cousin. And no one is around to hear you."

He half carried, half dragged her into her room and slammed the door. In the dimness of her bedside lamp, his eyes glittered madly. His face was flushed and he smelled strongly of brandy.

"Everyone will be home soon," she managed to say. "If you hurt me, they'll know it."

He laughed, an ugly low laugh. "There won't be a mark on you, Julie—unless, of course, you count the burns from falling accidentally into the embers." She drew back and he followed her, towering over her, forcing her to her knees.

"Not a bruise," he said softly. "When I'm finished with you, you'll wish *you* had eloped with a whiskey drummer."

He dragged her close enough to the fire grate so that

she could feel the heat, and he pushed her face perilously close to the flames.

Cowed, she stopped fighting him, saying, "Holt, for God's sake, let me go. What are you . . ." She stopped. He had pulled her up and was tearing the clothes from her body. She screamed once and he bent her backward toward the grate, twisting at her breasts as he did so. Terrified, she stifled her scream of pain.

"Are you going to be quiet?" he grated out. She nodded, numb with fear, and he let go of her. "Don't move!" he ordered. "Don't move!" He went on with his task more slowly now, taking pleasure from the sight of her fear. "It's so good to see you tamed, Julie," he laughed. "So good," he exulted.

"A whore's body," he said when she was finally standing shivering and naked before him. "Come here," he ordered, and she was too afraid to disobey. She began to pray that someone would come in—anyone. What time was it? How long had they been gone?

"Kneel down." Holt's voice broke through her mindless prayers.

Something in his voice jerked her back to action and she darted across the room to the door. He was on her before she could turn the handle, wrestling with her. His hands on her bare flesh awakened a deep revulsion and she fought harder and harder. He had her braced against the wall with one hand, his body pinioning hers. She could feel him moving about and all of a sudden he dragged her around to face him, forcing her to the floor. Still she struggled. He's mad, she thought, mad. And then she saw that while he had held her to the wall he had removed his trousers, and even as she tried to cry out she was on her knees and he was dragging her back to the fire. She twisted away and he knocked her to the floor. She was on her hands and knees again, trying to crawl away, when he shoved her so close to the blaze that the heat of it seared her face. He pushed himself upon her from behind, in a frenzy of excited rage. "This is what whores are good for," he said. "This is all they're good for." And he entered her body violently, tearing at the slender passage until the pain and the heat of the flames drove her to semi-consciousness.

It was no good. Whatever his desires, however his debasement of her aroused him, he achieved nothing from it, and with a last frantic burst he flung her away so that she fell, toward the fire, managing to save herself in the last split second by rolling to one side of it.

He left her lying there on the floor and went out. She heard him pounding down the stairs and slamming the front door. But even when his motorcar came to life and he wheeled down the drive, she lay there, too sick in mind and body to move. At long last she pulled herself erect and made her way slowly down to the bath, where she drew a cold tub and tried to wash away the brutal effects of Holt's depredation.

Shivering, she returned to her room and crouched in front of the fire. She heard the household return, heard them saying good night. Presently, Millicent came along the upper hall, checking to see that Holt was still out, pausing in front of Julie's door, tapping, and turning the knob quietly. Finding it locked, she moved on.

Jason's tread followed sometime later, and then at last the house was quiet. Julie opened her own door then. She wanted to talk to her aunt. She had to tell her about Holt—if not everything, at least enough to give herself some future protection against him.

Looking down the hall, she saw that Millicent's door was slightly ajar and went softly along to it, careful to make no noise that might arouse Jason.

She pushed the door open a bit wider, poking her head around it, intending to whisper her aunt's name. The word was formed on her lips but it never was uttered. Millicent sat up in bed, and leaning over her, his mouth pressed hard to hers, was Jason.

All the breath left Julie's body and her mind reeled even as she saw that Millicent's thin arms were around Jason's neck and that one of his hands caressed her back. A lover's kiss. They were so lost in it that they did not hear Julie's muffled gasp or her swift flight down the hall.

Incest—the word repeated itself over and over in her brain. Incest. Millicent and Jason. So sacrosanct. So high-minded. Such churchgoers. And Jason's son, Holt, had sexual appetites that were grossly unnatural, even as they were appetites he couldn't satisfy.

I've got to get away, she thought. Where can I go? She lay wide-eyed on her bed until dawn, when she rose, her mind made up. She dressed quietly in her riding clothes, packing what she could fit into an old carpetbag, stuffing her pieces of jewelry into her handbag. Her throat hurt as she put aside the pin and ring that Mark had given her and the necklace that she had worn on her birthday. She gazed at the hair ornaments, the tiny pearls from her childhood, and the heirloom lavaliere with the eighteenth-century miniature painted on it.

"I am going away," she wrote hastily to Jason, "far away. I'm never coming back to this house again. I know everything about you all now. If you sell Fontaine's, I will tell it all."

She put Mark's jewelry in a separate box together with a note to Joe Damien. She would leave these at his door on her way.

She propped the note to Jason on her pillow, and with infinite caution she tiptoed out of the house and around to the stable. She would ride Fancy as far as Elmira. There she could sell her. That, together with the four hundred twenty dollars left from her shopping expedition, would get her safely to a hotel in New York. What she would do there she did not know. But she could work, perhaps as a teacher or even a governess. She would change her name. And never, as long as she lived, would she set foot in Prescottville—at least not as long as any of the Prescotts were still around.

8

Riding back from the bank in Napa on his third Saturday in California, Mark was struck anew by the incredible deterioration of the Douglas ranch since his father's death. It didn't seem possible that one of the leading stock ranches in California could have been brought to near ruin in seven years.

In his father's day, selective breeding and improving the strain had gone on as a matter of course, and the

price for a Douglas bull or heifer was the highest anywhere. The ranch had lived on its stock sales, was nour-
ished by careful tree-cutting and replanting, and managed
to sustain both livestock and humans by its crops, its
milk cows, and its chickens.

Since his father's death the stock breeding had been
haphazard, less and less money was used to improve the
stock, and more and more stock was sold quickly at
lower prices. The dairy cows were fewer in number and
the crops themselves had dwindled.

The figures Mark had been able to get together from
his brother-in-law Harper King's accounts spelled disaster in a few years unless steps were taken immediately
to restore a smooth ranch operation.

In the weeks he had been home, the family arguments
alone had impeded progress. Valerie, always frightened
by loud voices, had taken to hiding in her room or down
by the riverbank, where she sometimes sat for hours
plaiting reeds into endless chains.

Grace wanted to sell and so did Carrie, and no matter
what he said they refused to believe that the ranch
wouldn't command a price that would enable them to
live in San Francisco amid luxury and in idleness. If it
weren't for Valerie and a need to conserve for her future
care, he'd be tempted to take the loss on his share if only
for the pleasure of watching their disappointment when
they learned just how expensive living in luxury in San
Francisco would be. But there was Valerie. And she had
to be protected.

Coming up to the crest of the hill just outside the ranch
proper, Mark reined his horse and let his eyes roam over
the land. The forests rose to the west, and to the north he
could see the hazy outline of Mount St. Helena. A winding river, so narrow that it might have been called a
stream, bisected the property. The grazing land lay to the
east as far as the broken foothills of the coastal range,
the crops and barns lay to the west against the forest
fence, and in the distance were the beginnings of the
Diablo Mountains, which stretched south.

Lying as it did in a small, fertile valley spanning the
borders of Sonomo and Napa counties, and blessed by
the streaming water, the ranch was a valuable piece of
property—or it had been a valuable piece of property
when it was flourishing. Now, as Mark surveyed it, only

the ranch house showed careful tending. Freshly painted white, with green lawns and flowers and trees surrounding it, its sprawling width was circled by new fencing—another of Grace's fancies: new fencing for the house when the grazing fences were in disrepair, the forage crops diminished, and the outbuildings shabby and ill kept.

Two weeks more, he had written Julie. A postponement of his wedding. And all because his family, whose livelihood depended on the ranch, was too eager for quick cash to reckon with a barren future.

He spurred the horse forward and dismounted at the gate of the house. One of the ranch hands came running up to meet him and lead the horse away.

"Give him a good rubdown, Sancho," Mark said.

"*Sí, señor,*" the man replied.

The family was gathered in the living room, enjoying after-luncheon coffee, when he entered. They scarcely paused in their conversation to greet him.

"I'm glad you're here, Carrie and Tom," he said without preamble. "This is the last family talk we're going to have. I'm wasting my time here. And I don't intend to waste any more time. First of all, we aren't going to sell this place until it's put back in shape."

There was a startled chorus of protest, and he turned first to his sister Grace. I've never really liked Grace, he thought. He eyed her now, seeing her sharply featured face coloring to an angry red and her eyes beginning to snap as she readied for battle.

Behind her, Valerie made a soft, whimpering sound and Mark said gently, "Val, why don't you go along to the kitchen and ask Mrs. Winters to make us some more coffee?" Valerie scurried away gratefully and Mark turned back to Grace again.

"I don't want to hear one word out of you," he said grimly, "not one. I mean to have my say first. I'm not beyond slapping you, Grace, or you, either, Carrie." He swung around to Carrie and she blinked her eyelids nervously, her long, narrow upper lip beginning to quiver.

"See here," Harper said uncomfortably.

Mark fixed cold eyes on his brother-in-law. "I mean it," he said, "if I have to take you all on."

"Oh, come on, Mark." Tom tried to joke. "We're all a

little unstrung, but I'm not going to sit here and let you insult my wife."

Mark looked from one man to the other. Harper's skinny frame seemed to shrink under his glance, but Tom, with the belligerence of a large, fat man, tried to bluster it through.

"You just calm down," Tom said angrily. "There's no call to talk to the girls this way."

"I'm calm," Mark said. "But I meant what I said. This is not going to be just another wrangle. Now, shut up, Tom, and let me get on with it."

"Coward," Grace hissed to her husband.

"Grace," Mark said with warning, and she subsided with a venomous glance at him.

"I've thought it all out and I'm going to outline what I want. There's to be no more money for luxuries—at least not until that stock is built up and the outbuildings are repaired and the land is yielding full again. No more cutting trees on the west slope until there's some new growth, and no cutting at all without replanting.

"I intend to go into San Francisco this week and set up an arrangement with Wells Fargo to put all this in trust. I'm going to draw up a budget, and the only money available, aside from what you need for necessities, will be for improving the stock or the land or the forest."

He paused and looked around the big, low-ceilinged living room. "You've bought enough rugs and furnishings and whatnots to last this ranch a generation," he said to Grace. "You've robbed the place to put clothes on your back and give yourself and Carrie all kinds of extras."

"Not I," Carrie said quickly. "Every time Tom or I wanted anything, Grace would be in there telling Mama that the ranch was going broke and that we shouldn't get anything at all."

"That's not true!" Grace broke in heatedly. "Didn't you talk Mama into putting up all that money to expand the lumberyard?"

"That was nothing compared to you. Why, look at this place." She flung out an arm, catching Tom just below the chin. He grunted.

"That's enough!" Mark's voice cracked like a whip. "Between you, you've nearly ruined the place. And what about Valerie?"

"Valerie?" Grace said. "Why, the same as Mama, I expect, dear Mark. You weren't around after Papa died. Mama just got worse and worse. It got so she wasn't lucid. And then she had that stroke, and after that she was simply foolish. You criticize *us!* Where were you when we were taking care of the ranch and of Mama and of Valerie?"

"Earning my own living," Mark returned, "not sponging off a foolish old woman."

"Maybe not, but you'll be pretty glad to see your share of this ranch," Grace sneered.

"That's right, I will. But I want to see a *full* share. Seven years ago this place was worth twice what it is now, and you know it, don't you, Harper?"

"I know it," Harper said, sitting forward eagerly. "But you can't tell Grace what you're going to do with her property. Funny thing is," he added with the first spirit Mark had ever seen him show, "the ranch is always 'my ranch' to Grace, but the money I get from the mine out in Nevada, small as it is, is 'our money' to her." Grace glared at him, but Harper went on: "'Fact is, Mark, I agree with you. You give me final say and set it up so Grace can't nag me out of it, and I think we might get the place really working again."

"Tom?" Mark looked at his other brother-in-law.

"Well, I suppose it does make more sense to wait for a good price," Tom said reluctantly. "Thing is, I do need some cash for the mill."

"You can get a loan from me," Mark said. "But I'll want it paid back. How much were you thinking of?" He whistled as Tom mentioned the amount and said, "I couldn't come close to that. Why don't you borrow from the bank?"

"I'm loaned out," Tom admitted unhappily.

Mark sighed involuntarily and Carrie flushed. "It isn't easy starting a business and running it yourself," she said. "You've always had things fall into your lap, Mark. Why, if Mr. Fontaine hadn't taken a liking to you when you went east to visit Cousin Art, where would you be?"

"I wouldn't be running down a ranch or loaned out at a bank," he said. "For that matter, John Fontaine wouldn't have offered me that job if I hadn't worked two years for Lodi Winery after I left the Point. Tom, I'm sorry for you. I'll see what can be spared from the ranch and what I can spare. But if I do that, then I want the mill and the lumberyard to be part of the whole thing. And there's Valerie. I said it before. I want to see that she's settled. If you'll go along with what I've outlined, then when the ranch is worth something again, I'll consider selling—if that's what you all want then."

"Fair enough," Tom said first.

"They may not want to sell then," Harper said with a grin. "It's a lot different being a Douglas from the Douglas ranch . . . or a King"—He bowed to Grace, who kept her face stony—"than it is to be someone living on a fixed income in town. You see, Grace, here, thinks that her share would set us up on Nob Hill. I can't make her listen to reason. I hope you can."

"I don't care whether she listens or not," Mark answered in a lazy voice. "You can't sell without me. So take it or leave it."

They took it, of course, but with a sullen antagonism they could not conceal. Carrie and Tom left almost at once, and Harper followed Grace out with a half-apologetic look at Mark.

Valerie, coming in a few minutes later bearing the coffee tray, stopped in bewilderment. "Where did they go?" she asked.

"Carrie and Tom had to leave," Mark said, coming to her and taking the tray from her hand. "Grace and Harper went for a walk. They'll be back." He set the tray down on the table and said, "Now, Val, don't worry. It's all settled. You're staying here at the ranch. Everyone is—for a good, long time."

"Does that mean you're going away again?" she asked, crestfallen.

He looked at her and for a moment remembered how she had been before the illness: bright; eager; full of mischief. As smart as the rest, anyway—perhaps smarter than her two older sisters. But the disease that had ravaged her body, leaving it frail and delicate, had also dulled her once inquisitive mind and rendered her timid. He reached out and gave her a hug, saying, "You know I'll see you're happy, don't you, Val?"

She nodded. "I'm glad we're staying here, but I miss you when you're away, Mark. I wish I could go back with you and see your wedding."

"I couldn't take you back. Grace and Carrie aren't

coming east, and there wouldn't be anyone to travel
back with you."

"Is Julie pretty?"

"Beautiful," Mark assured her.

"Is she like that lady who came out to see you last
week?"

"Miranda?" He laughed. "Julie's much more beautiful."

"Will you ever bring Julie here to meet us?"

"Next spring," he promised.

"That's something to look forward to. It isn't very
cheerful here." She paused, frowning. "Grace and Carrie are so mean these days, Mark. They keep quarreling
and Harper . . . well, I love Harper," she said innocently,
"but I don't think Grace does at all."

Mark felt a pang of guilt. It was probably wrong to
leave Val here. But he couldn't bring her to Prescottville with him. Not now. Not just marrying Julie. Later,
he thought, soothing his conscience. Later, when Julie
and I have been married for a while. It would be all
right then. Valerie wasn't a bother to anyone. All she
ever wanted was kindness and affection and gentle days
of dreaming and busying herself about the house. Julie
would love her, too. Val was easy to love. Thinking of
Julie, he was stricken with an impatience to be finished
and back in Prescottville. A few days in San Francisco
and then he would be gone. One more week was not a
lifetime.

"And will Miranda come back to see us?" Valerie
asked.

"Miranda? No, no, I don't think so. She's only visiting
in California for a little while."

He had been surprised to find Miranda in California,
even more surprised that she had come out to the ranch
to pay a condolence call, complete with French maid.
He grinned suddenly. That was definitely Miranda's style.
It would be amusing to see her when he was in San
Francisco. She'd been a good sport about his breaking
off with her, and there was nothing in her manner since
to suggest anything but a pleasant friendship. It piqued
his curiosity. He had expected a scene when he announced his engagement to Julie, and for a moment he
had expected one when she appeared at the ranch. Instead, she had been gracious, charming, and helpful, even

booking a suite for him at the Palace, where she was staying. That wasn't really Miranda's style at all. He frowned, feeling oddly uneasy.

"What's wrong, Mark?" Valerie asked, and he erased the frown with a smile. "Nothing, Val, just thinking. And Val, one of these days I'll be bringing you east to live with Julie and me. Would you like that?"

"Oh, yes," she replied fervently. "There's always more to do with you around."

"Come on, then. Let's go down to the stream. Maybe we'll catch a fish for dinner."

"Grace doesn't like the smell of fish cooking," Valerie said doubtfully.

"Don't worry about Grace," Mark said. "Don't worry about anything, Val."

The following Monday Mark checked into the Palace to begin negotiations for a transfer in the administration of the estate. It was an annoyingly time-consuming business, and he had difficulty controlling his mounting impatience as the endless forms and papers were held up, delaying the necessary court approval of his actions.

It was Wednesday afternoon before the bulk of the business was finished and he began to see the possibility of returning to Prescottville a few days sooner than planned.

Coming into the hotel that evening, he paused at the desk to arrange a telephone call to Julie and he received a packet of mail forwarded to him from the ranch.

He opened it quickly, hoping there was a letter from Julie, but there was only a telegram and a letter from Fontaine Wine Company. He opened the telegram first and the words leaped up at him with the force of a physical blow. Julie had canceled the wedding and had left Prescottville. Her whereabouts were unknown. It was signed Millicent Prescott.

Dazed, he tore open the other envelope and extracted a brief, formal letter signed by Jason Prescott that stated that he was no longer manager of Fontaine Wine Company by virtue of a majority vote of stockholders. Majority? Joe Damien? Julie? Julie? Was that why she had run away? Majority. Julie, Jason, probably Bradford, and van Houten. Not enough. Joe . . . or Miranda!

Light broke through the haze. Miranda. In California.

Coming out to the ranch. Bored. Bored, hell! He swore softly under his breath.

"Do you wish to place that call, sir?" the clerk was asking.

"Huh? Call? No, no. Cancel it for now, please. I'd like to have a note delivered to a Mrs. Latham. I believe she's staying here."

"Yes, sir, she is." The clerk handed him paper and pen. Mark scribbled a hasty note to Miranda, inviting her to dine with him that evening, and he gave it to the clerk for delivery.

He had not been in his room ten minutes when the bellboy knocked with Miranda's acceptance. He smiled thinly. Like a trout jumping to a fly, he thought.

Somehow, someone had gotten to Julie. His own telegram to her had been clear enough and the letter that followed had made plain the problem. He could imagine that Julie was disappointed. He could not imagine her throwing everything to the winds over a two-week postponement that simply could not be avoided.

The Prescotts had to be involved. But how had they managed to convince Julie? Miranda—she was the only link. There was the coincidence of her being here, and her seemingly innocent remarks out at the ranch: "Oh, and postponing the wedding? How worrisome for Julie." He could still hear her. And what else had she said? Some excuse about not wanting to be in Prescottville for the big day as another reason for taking "an extended trip west." What a fool he had been, what a fatuous fool.

He knew Miranda, and if he hadn't been such a fool he'd have known she wouldn't take defeat with anything approaching the kindly and cheerful resignation she had affected back in Prescottville.

How everything had been accomplished remained to be seen. He clenched his fists until the knuckles turned blue-white, fighting down the overpowering rage that rose within him. It would afford him only a momentary satisfaction to give Miranda the beating she deserved. There were better ways of dealing with her, better ways of getting at the truth. As he began to plan coolly, his rage abated and presently he smoothed the crumpled telegram and went down to the desk to write answers to them and to wire Joe Damien.

Mark and Miranda dined in the Palm Court and Mark insisted on keeping Miranda's wine glass filled. "It's a celebration of sorts," he told her, letting a note of intimacy creep into his eyes and his voice. "Old friends," he added, his tone conveying more than that. He was amused to see her respond in kind.

When dinner had ended and he was escorting her back to her room, he suggested his own suite for the champagne he had ordered sent up. "I don't know," she parried, "an engaged man?"

"Yes, well, that's one of the reasons for a celebration," he answered.

"Now, tell me about this celebration," she purred when they were sipping their champagne. Her voice was blurred and her eyes moist from an unaccustomed surplus of wine.

"Can't you guess? Why do you suppose I'm still in California? I could have returned as planned and then brought Julie out on our honeymoon trip."

Her mouth formed a startled "O" and something flickered in her eyes. Disappointment? Dismay? He couldn't tell.

"Exactly," he went on. "I was bored. Young girls have their charms but . . . I feel like a heel," he confessed. "However, Julie's young. She'll get over it, and in spite of my summer madness I am not, as I have repeatedly stated, the marrying kind."

"Poor Julie." Miranda managed to cover her delight under a voice filled with sweet commiseration.

"Poor me," Mark said. "I imagine it will be a bit difficult going back. After all, Julie does have a vote at Fontaine's now, although, of course, she can't do anything too drastic without other votes. She'd need mine and Joe Damien's, and possibly yours. Or mine and Jason's, and again yours. All very unlikely—unless, of course, it becomes a question of mismanagement, gross mismanagement. Then Joe and I would be in trouble without Julie—or you."

He heard her quick intake of breath and went on smoothly: "Let's forget all that. If I delay long enough, Julie will have one of her temper tantrums and break the engagement all by herself. And then . . ." He leaned forward and pulled her into his arms, upsetting the champagne so that it spilled over her silk gown. "I've missed you, Miranda," he whispered.

It was almost too easy, he thought, his mind coldly apart from his actions. Deliberately he seduced her, removing piece after piece of her clothing while he remained fully dressed, until at last she lay across his lap, naked and panting and moaning, and then he stood up so abruptly that she fell to the floor with a cry.

"How did you manage it?" he said, towering over her. "Just how did you and the Prescotts manage it?"

"Mark!" she pleaded. "You must be crazy! Manage what?"

He jerked her to her feet, holding her arm in a tight, cruel grasp. "I got the telegram this morning. Just how did you manage it? What did you tell Julie? What made her run away?"

She cowered, trying to cover her body, reaching for the garments that she had shed so eagerly moments before. She was gasping and weeping and trembling from shock.

"Tell me," he grated, "or I'll beat you until there isn't anything left of your face."

"Please. I . . . nothing . . . I did nothing. . . ." He slapped her face with his open palm and she cried out in terror.

"The truth," he said. "It's your only chance, Miranda."

Between sobs, she poured out the story, trying to minimize her own part in it, not daring to tell him about Julie's phone call and her own deception at the Fairmont. He couldn't know about that. She kept that much to herself, improvising her lies at random.

"Why?" Mark asked. "Why? What's your gain out of all this revenge?"

"You," she said. "Jason wanted control of Fontaine's, and I wanted you."

"You're the loser, Miranda. Jason has control of Fontaine's, but you have nothing. Put on your clothes," he snarled, gathering them up in a bundle and flinging them at her. "You aren't at your best naked."

She clutched them to her, unwilling to dress herself under his contemptuous gaze.

"You, you used me!" she accused.

"I know you, Miranda. I told you that before. Put

your clothes on. I want more information. Was Joe Damien in on this?"

"No." She pulled her dress on hastily, no longer caring how she looked or what he thought, feeling dull and abased, with a flash of sullen anger boiling up under it all.

"Who, then?"

"Jason, me, Willis Bradford, Ned van Houten, and . . . and Avery Bertram helped. Julie wouldn't vote to sell and neither would Joe. They couldn't move them on that, and they had to have one of them, at least. So they'll have to keep Fontaine's going somehow until they can bring Julie around."

There was a small silence and then Mark said, "Quite a crowd you run with, Miranda: telegrams under false names; letters that don't reach their destinations; lies; theft; false charges. Well, tell your little crowd, for me, that first I mean to find Julie, and second, I mean to move back into control of Fontaine's. When I do, Miranda, I suggest that you arrange to move elsewhere. Not here, of course. This is my territory, too. I suggest you make arrangements to leave here in the morning. I won't be responsible for what I might do if we happen to run into each other again. Now, get out!"

"I . . . I can't leave the room like this," she said.

"Why not? Surely the hotel has seen more disreputable women. Get out, Miranda!" In a moment he was at the door, flinging it open violently, holding it wide open while she scurried out beneath his arm, clutching her undergarments and shoes.

She reached her room, without meeting anyone. To her French maid's scandalized *"Madame!"* she uttered a stream of abuse that only partially satisfied her rage.

In the morning, Miranda awoke with a germ of an idea that, carried out, might somehow repay Mark and rescue the situation. She tried it out on her maid, talking in a soft, conciliatory, embarrassed way to the white and silent Carmen.

"I must apologize," Miranda said. "It was thoughtlessly cruel of me to take out my humiliation on you. I . . . I don't know how to excuse myself without telling you the truth. But that is very painful for me to do. You

see, the gentleman from Prescottville, Mr. Douglas . . .
you remember him?"

Carmen nodded, her dignity slightly restored by the
apology and her curiosity aroused. She had expected that
there had been some kind of disgraceful behavior, but
she had not imagined that it included rape and brutality
or that such acts had been committed in Prescottville
and that the Mr. Douglas who seemed such a gentleman
had been suspected of them. Thank heaven that Mr.
Douglas would not be returning there, for she, Carmen,
had no wish to live in a place where such atrocities
were allowed to go unpunished. Poor *madame*. Carmen
felt forgiveness and compassion flood her and, making
soothing sounds, hurried away to bring *madame* a
tray in her bedroom.

Miranda sank back on the pillow, smiling a grim
little smile. When Carmen told her story on the servants' grapevine and Jason Prescott let it be known
around town, Mark Douglas would be lucky not to be
stoned when he returned to Prescottville.

Mark witnessed Miranda's hasty departure the next
morning. He leaned against a pillar in the lobby while
she darted nervous little glances at him as she organized
the procession of bellboys handling her mountains of
luggage. She had apparently come for a long stay. She
must have imagined that the news from Prescottville
would give him no alternative but to bow out gracefully.
If any of them had thought that, they were more
stupid than he had imagined them to be.

On Friday, his business concluded, Mark began to
make arrangements for the trip back. Now that the ranch
affairs were settled, he was free to pursue what line of
action he could take in Prescottville. He thought briefly
of calling Joe Damien and then of calling his cousin Art,
but he discarded both ideas. It would be better if he
arrived unannounced.

By the following Friday he was stepping off the
train in Bath, where he hired a car to take him out to
his house over the less-traveled roads that skirted
Hammondsport and Prescottville, taking back country
lanes to the old Fontaine place, where he dumped his
luggage.

He paused there only long enough to change his clothes and saddle his horse.

He rode swiftly across the fields leading to the winery, but at the edge of the fields he tethered Rusty to a young sapling and made the rest of his way on foot.

The late sun cast a medieval glow over the old stone buildings, and the vineyards stretching behind them lifted their newly pruned branches in stark supplication to the heavens. A mist rising from the lake promised an early frost. Summer, with its ceaseless activity, was over. A hush lay over the spent land now that the harvest was in.

Mark trod softly across the road and the lawns, entering the winery with the same silent tread. Avery's door stood open and behind his desk sat a young man Mark recognized as a former employee at the Prescott Bank. His own door was closed. He walked toward it and opened it soundlessly. He closed it with a sudden bang that made Avery Bertram jump in his seat, his face turning ashen when he recognized Mark.

"You . . . you . . . I thought you were in California," Avery muttered.

"I was. All right, you miserable little bastard, what are you doing at that desk?" Mark had moved swiftly as he spoke so that he had reached Avery and jerked him up by his lapels by the time he finished speaking.

"T-take y-y-your h-hands off me . . ." Avery's stuttering worsened with each word. "I-I . . . we'll . . . you . . ."

"Tell me!" Mark commanded, throwing Avery back into the chair. "Just what were you up to? All of you! I want the truth, Avery, or so help me God I'll kill you where you sit!"

"Please," Avery began, "I didn't plan to do anything. Mr. Prescott just asked to see an accounting. The others—Mayor Bradford, Mrs. Latham, Miss Fontaine —they voted to-to . . ." He broke off. "Please, Mark, I can't . . . that is, if you stand over me like that . . ."

"All right." Mark moved away and pulled up a chair, straddling it so that the back was between his hands. "Take it slow, Avery, and don't lie to me. I want the whole truth."

It was not long in the telling. Avery apparently knew nothing about the involvement with Julie, nor was he aware that she was no longer in Prescottville.

"Where is Joe Damien?" Mark asked when Avery had finished.

"Down in Elmira Hospital. He had a gallbladder operation. He was very sick, let me tell you. No one can see him except his family."

"Where is young Peter?"

Avery shifted uncomfortably in his seat. "Ah, you see, with things the way they are now . . . Peter . . . that is to say, Peter hasn't been working here since, oh, last Wednesday."

"I see. Fired him?"

"Er, no, that is, you see, with Joe sick and the harvest . . . well, we sold a lot of the . . . that is, rising costs . . ."

"What happened to the wine?" Mark asked in a dangerously quiet voice.

"We . . . er . . . when Joe got sick we thought it would be best to sell most of the barrels to . . . er . . . to . . . other wine companies. I mean, you can see that with Joe gone and no one to replace him, there wouldn't be any way to really supervise the racking, the blending. I mean, we couldn't tell how long Joe would be laid up, or if, that is, if he'd even come back."

Mark rested his head briefly on his arms. That beautiful harvest, a vintage year—all gone. Julie might have refused to sell out, but this kind of thing would force a sale sooner or later, with or without her consent. Fontaine's would be finished.

He lifted his head. "How many barrels are left?" he asked, and then took some hope from Avery's answer. Nothing compared with what it could have been, but still something to salvage. He rose.

"Don't call Jason Prescott," Mark warned. "I'll know if you do. And don't tell anyone else I'm here, Avery. I wouldn't put myself out to step on a worm unless the worm acts up. Do you understand?"

Avery nodded and Mark left the office, closing the door behind him. He stood a moment outside listening, and when he heard Avery murmuring he flung the door open again. Avery sat petrified, the telephone receiver still at his ear. "Number, please?" Mark could hear the operator saying. "Number, please?" He strode across the room and yanked the cord from the wall, cutting off her voice.

"The next time I'll be throwing you against the wall," Mark said as he left.

He did not bother to approach the Prescott house quietly. He galloped the distance from the winery and flung himself off the horse just in front of the Prescott lawn. He knew he had been heard. He could see the hastily dropped curtain in an upper window as he came up the steps. He did not knock, but flung open the front door as hard as he could.

"All right, Jason!" he yelled. "I'm back! And I've heard Miranda's story! Now, let's hear yours!"

Jason appeared almost instantaneously on the upper landing, hastily buttoning his jacket.

"See here, Mark. My sister is ill. Please lower your voice."

"I'll yell as loud as I damned please! As for your sister, she wasn't too sick to connive with you. Get down here before I come up after you."

Jason's gaze shifted and fear swept his face. Mark turned around as he heard Jason's shout of, "Holt, don't! Let the police handle this!"

Holt was advancing from the living room, a poker in his hand. Mark lunged for him, wrestling the poker away and flinging it with all his strength through the open door. And then he hit Holt, one short, sharp uppercut that connected, and Holt slid into a heap on the floor.

Mark turned back to Jason. "One of these days they're going to lock up that son of yours," he said in a quieter voice. "Now, get down here, Jason. I want some answers."

"You're out of Fontaine's. That's your answer. You can hold your stock. But we've got Julie's vote. And Julie's gone. There isn't anything you can do."

"Where is Julie?" Mark asked.

"We don't know. She ran away. I . . . I have her note."

"Show it to me," Mark commanded.

Jason turned and went down the hall. Mark heard him speaking to Millicent. "It's nothing. You know Mark. No, Holt's fine. For heaven's sake, don't excite yourself. Stay here until that ruffian leaves the house."

Jason was back presently, and he came slowly down the stairs, the paper held stiffly in front of him.

Seeing Jason's apparent fear, Mark's lips drew back in a contemptuous grin. "Don't be afraid, Jason. I never hit fat old men—not unless they hit me first."

Mark took the proffered paper and read the contents. "What does this mean?" he asked Jason. "She says 'I'll tell all.' To whom?"

Jason shook his head. "An idle threat. Anyway, we can't sell without her signature. There aren't enough votes. But one day they'll foreclose on Fontaine's, and then it won't matter how she votes."

"So that's your game. Just how much of Steuben's stock do you own, Jason? How long do you think it will take for Fontaine's to go bankrupt? Well, let me tell you something. Joe Damien is alive, and before I let you get away with this . . ." He stopped. "Never mind. Where is Julie?"

"I tell you I don't know. I don't know why she ran off, either." Behind them Holt was making feeble efforts to rise, and Jason hurried to his aid, only to have his arm pushed back.

"I'll get you for this," Holt said thickly to Mark.

"You better pull yourself together first," Mark answered evenly. Without saying more, he left the house, Julie's note clutched in his fingers.

That night Mark took the Buick and drove down to Elmira Hospital. It took every ounce of persuasion he had to convince the nurse to take Joe a message. It became easier after that. Joe was anxious to see him and alarmed the nurse so much with his agitation over her refusal that she reluctantly agreed to let Mark in.

"You don't look as bad as I thought you would," Mark said, lying, when Joe grasped his hand. Joe's hair, that black curly shock of hair that had been only lightly laced with gray, was now white at the temples and noticeably grayer elsewhere. He had lost a lot of weight. It made the lines in his face seem deeper. Joe's brown eyes looked back at Mark, clear and unwavering, and he took heart from that.

"I'm better, a lot better," Joe said. "I'll be going home next week. Two weeks in bed then, they say. But"—he lifted his hands expressively—"it could have been worse. What a pain it was. I thought it was my heart."

"Lucky for you it wasn't," Mark said. "Can you talk?"

"About Fontaine's? Sure. Listen, I know what they've

done. Peter told me. All that wine gone. The bastards! But don't worry, Mark. They can't fire me. I'll be back there before Christmas. Between us . . ."

"I have to find Julie," Mark said. "Do you know where she's gone?"

"New York. She left a package at our house the night she went away—your . . . your ring, the pin you gave her. There was a note saying that she was going to New York and asking me to give you . . ." He stopped. "You didn't marry Miranda, did you?" he asked.

"No."

Joe sighed. "If only Julie had talked to me first. I could have told her. I figured something was wrong. It wasn't . . . well, I just couldn't figure why you'd do something like that. Miranda!"

"Don't worry about it," Mark said. "Listen, Joe, I want you to do me a favor. I'm going to leave my proxy with Art Douglas, just in case you need it while I'm down in New York. I should be back again before you're out of the hospital. But whatever you do, Joe, don't leave Fontaine's. We'll get this straightened out. I promise you that." He patted Joe's arm and stood up.

"I'm going now before that nurse comes back and throws me out."

"I feel better," Joe told him. "Now I'm not so worried."

"See you," Mark said.

He was bone weary when he arrived back at the Fontaine place. He parked the car outside the front door and went around to the back. All he wanted was sleep, and yet, even in his exhaustion, a prickling alertness along his nerve endings told him something was wrong. Without breaking his stride, he circled wide, coming around the corner of the house, and caught Holt Prescott's blow against his arm. A second later Holt had flung himself on him and he was down, rolling over and over until he was finally astride Holt, pinioning him to the ground, slapping his head from side to side.

"Haven't had enough?" Mark panted, his fist raised. "Will you tell me now where Julie is?"

Holt cringed. "I've had enough," he said sullenly, and Mark got up, standing back warily as Holt rose to his feet.

"Just why did Julie run away?" Mark asked.

"Don't you know? Surely Miranda told you. She seems to have told you everything."

"She told me that you lied to Julie, told her I had married Miranda, convinced her I had ruined the winery, and got her to vote with you."

Holt snickered. "Didn't you wonder why Julie didn't answer your letter or why she believed you married Miranda?"

"Yes. I mean to ask her when I find her."

Holt laughed. "*If* you find her. Even we don't know where she is. And that's the truth. But I can tell you why she believed us."

"And why would you do me that favor?"

Holt rubbed his face. "To get it over with. Let the rest of them take their beatings. I've had mine. Miranda sent the telegram; you know that. What you don't know is that she sent it from the Fairmont and signed it 'Miranda Latham Douglas.' We showed it to Julie, and when she wouldn't believe the telegram we persuaded her to telephone. Miranda answered as Mrs. Mark Douglas. *Then* Julie believed us."

Mark said nothing.

"In fact," Holt went on, "Miranda is probably the only one who knows just where Julie is. She says she doesn't, but her maid let something slip one day that makes us think Miranda does know. If we cared, of course, we'd make Miranda tell."

He was backing toward his car and Mark said suddenly, "Go on, get out of here!"

He waited until Holt had driven off and then he went to get his own car. His fatigue had vanished. If Miranda knew where Julie was, he had no doubt that he would be able to get it out of her.

Miranda's house was dark as Mark drove up, but the door opened to his knock very quickly. Miranda stood there in a flowing robe. She gave a muffled gasp when she saw him and Mark stepped over the threshold, following her as she retreated before him.

"Sorry to disappoint you," he said. He eyed her casual attire and added, "I guess you were expecting someone else. I won't keep you a minute, Miranda. Suppose we go into the living room and talk. Light the lights. This isn't a social call."

"Please," she began to whimper.

"Please what? Don't be a fool, Miranda. Go in and light the lamps." She moved ahead of him, and as she stepped into the room she stopped to pull the light cord.

"What do you want?" she asked fearfully.

"I want to know where Julie is." he said coldly. "And don't lie to me."

"I don't know. What makes you think I know? Even her family . . ."

"You know, Miranda. I just beat that much out of Holt Prescott. Now, tell me. Where is Julie?"

He moved toward her and all at once she began to scream and tear at her robe, crying, "Help, oh, help, he's trying to murder me!"

The transition was so abrupt that it took Mark totally by surprise, and for a split second he couldn't react. "What the devil are you doing?" he exclaimed at last.

She screamed again and the scream was echoed by Carmen out in the hall, and above it all rose the sound of the police siren.

Mark, in the act of catching hold of Miranda, dropped her arm. His eyes narrowed thoughtfully. "It won't work," he said. "It just won't work." Hearing the police at the door, he went swiftly to a chair on the other side of the room and sat down calmly.

Miranda was still screaming when the sergeant and another police officer entered. Her robe was torn down the front and she sobbed out as she clutched it to her with one hand, "Oh, it's the same thing he tried to do in California! He's crazy. He tried to kill me!"

The policemen looked in the direction of Miranda's dramatic gesture and saw Mark sitting quietly, a look of amusement on his face.

"I don't know what this is all about," he began pleasantly. "But Mrs. Latham invited me in and then proceeded to rip her robe and scream."

The sergeant looked bewildered. "Don't look as if he was doing you any harm," he said.

"He was, he was! He heard you and he let me go! But he was! Oh, ask my maid. Carmen!" she called out.

The maid entered timidly from the hall, her face white. "It's true, messieurs," she quavered. "Oh, mon Dieu! I am so frightened. It was the same in San Francisco. He had torn away madame's clothes and she had to fight to free herself, and now . . . oh, when I hear her scream . . ."

"Very good, Carmen." Mark applauded.

"All right, that's enough," the sergeant said. "Look here, Mr. Douglas. I don't know what you're doing in this lady's house. But we had a call not ten minutes ago saying someone was going to kill Mrs. Latham."

"Look at her," Mark answered. "Does she look as if she's been touched?"

"Well, her robe's torn. Of course, we got here in time. Fact is, our warning said you were headed this way . . . well, not you, but whoever's been beating up the girls out at Viola's. So we came along. Caught you in the act. You'll have to come with me."

Mark rose. Everything depended on just how cool he could maintain his manner and voice. He looked full at Miranda, who lowered her eyes hastily, uttering a whimper of fear.

"It won't work, Miranda," he said quietly. "I told you that. Now you tell the Prescotts that for me."

He turned to the sergeant. "I'm quite willing to go along," he said. "But I'll want to call my cousin Art Douglas from the station."

"One call. You can have one call," the sergeant said. "And you'll need it. Fact is that Holt Prescott was in the station as we left. Beaten up pretty bad. Says you did it."

"I did," Mark replied. "I did not touch Mrs. Latham."

"Fact is, there are gonna be charges laid against you."

"Fact is, you'll have to make them stick. Good night, Miranda. I'm sure we'll meet again."

"You'll meet again, all right—in court," the sergeant said with a heavy attempt at humor.

"Mark the Avenger," his cousin Art said the next day. "What the hell possessed you to break into Miranda's house that way?"

"I didn't break in. She opened the door. All that was a lie," Mark said wearily. "She must have called the police when I drove up . . . or before," he said suddenly. "What a fool I was. Holt and the rest planned the whole thing. She's been lying through her teeth ever since she got back. That maid swearing I attacked Miranda in the Palace. Of course! That's why the police were there minutes after I got to the place. Jesus, I can still hear her screaming and see her tearing her dressing gown."

"I'll buy it," Art told him, "and so will Sam Howard. Damn it, Mark, you've got to get out of here, though. They're after you. It's going to take everything Sam and I have to talk reason into the police. They want to make you the lunatic who's been going around beating up Viola's girls. And it doesn't help matters that no one was robbed or hurt out there while you were in California."

"It's a bluff, Art—Prescott's way of keeping me away from Prescottville. They didn't arrest me last night, did they? I'm not running," he said stubbornly.

"I didn't ask you to run," Art told him. "Hell, I can't even reason with Lillian. Miranda's about convinced her that you're some kind of Jack the Ripper."

"I'd like to strangle Miranda," Mark said.

"That's fine talk!" Art exclaimed. "Look, get out of town. There aren't any charges against you at present. Go find Julie. Give Sam and me a chance here."

"I suppose you're right," Mark agreed finally. "Once I find Julie, the whole story will come out, anyway."

"Good thinking," Art said approvingly. "You can't take on the town singlehanded. The banker, the mayor, and the police are against you. You're fighting in a mist. Wait until it clears."

"All right. But there are a few things you have to do for me, Art. I don't know how long I'll be gone. I'm leaving you my Fontaine vote proxy. Just vote it whichever way Joe wants to vote it. Oh, and Joe has some things of mine—at least his wife has them at the house. Pick them up for me and put them in your safe."

He and Art had talked the rest of the morning away and at noon they parted—Art to drive back to the dairy and placate Lillian, and Mark to turn his Buick onto the road toward New York City.

PART TWO

9

In March of 1917 New York City ran high with war fever, its expanding network of political and financial power pulsing with each new headline from Europe. The tide of battle turned increasingly in the Central Powers' favor, and the new German submarine offensive swept the Atlantic, coming close to American shores, sinking neutral as well as enemy ships.

With the report of each new shipping loss, the pressure to retaliate was growing, and where once President Wilson's cautious policy of neutrality and of trying to effect a peaceful settlement was tolerated, he was now reviled almost everywhere.

Yet the city was filled with gaiety. There were few serious dramas on Broadway; revues, comedies, and farces grew in number side by side with the mounting tensions that were building inevitably toward war.

Flo Ziegfeld's Follies led the parade of musical extravaganzas, but the Scandals and other lesser revues crowded close on their heels, with Lewis Belmont's Parade of 1917 their acknowledged leader.

Marilyn Miller and Fanny Brice topped the Follies, and the new Irving Berlin hits were on everyone's lips. "Whose Little Heart Are You Breaking Now?" overtook the previous year's "When I'm Out with You."

At Fortieth Street, the Belmont Theater headlined Madeline James and Thirty Beautiful Show Girls, including "the incomparable Angela Grant."

Julie Fontaine, walking south along Broadway, looked up at the Belmont marquee with a feeling of awed wonder that the sight never failed to arouse in her.

In those first gloomy winter weeks in New York, trudging from employment agency to employment agency during the day and counting her dwindling supply of

134

money each night in the small residence club for women, her highest ambition was to obtain a position as a governess.

Although her qualifications had been good, she lacked any character references under her assumed name, and while once or twice she had come close to being hired, that lack remained an impediment to her employment.

It had never occurred to her that she would one day become involved in the world of the theater. On the day that she had been interviewed by Madeline James, she was too nervous to make the connection between the Mrs. James who had a young daughter named Cecelia and the glamorous star of the Lew Belmont productions.

"You don't look much like a governess," Madeline James had said doubtfully. "We'll give you a try, though. Cecelia will be going to boarding school next fall, but she needs tutoring, especially in French."

There had been that awkward moment when no immediate references beyond that of the agency had been forthcoming. And then it passed. As Madeline James said later, "I knew you were all right. And don't ask me how, because I can't explain it."

My one and only governess job, she thought now with a smile. Cecelia was a charming little girl, but not much of a student, although she was willing and obedient. Julie had hardly settled into the routine when the job disappeared almost overnight. And that she owed as much to Madeline James' wariness about her arrival in the house as she did to Lew Belmont himself.

He had been out of town during the first two weeks of her employment, but during the third week, coming into the living room with Cecelia after an afternoon spent ice skating, Julie found a tall, heavyset man with a look of ruddy good health about him standing near the window talking with Madeline James.

Cecelia had bounded across the room, saying, "Oh, Uncle Lew, you're back!" And she gave him a hug, which he returned affectionately.

Madeline was making the introductions, and as she did, Lew Belmont had said, "Governess? But you don't look the part." And his eyes had raked her with more than casual interest.

There was an air of successful confidence about him that gave him an indefinable charm, and Julie had felt her cheeks grow warm under his frankly admiring appraisal. She had sensed almost at once that Madeline was equally aware of it and that she wasn't too pleased.

During the following days, Julie learned that Lew Belmont was a frequent visitor at the house and that his presence there seemed to disrupt the pleasant relationship between herself and her employer.

Once, finding Julie alone in the house waiting for Cecelia to return from a walk with her mother, Lew had said, "You are far too beautiful to waste yourself at a job like this." Then he had moved toward her, putting one hand on her shoulder to turn her around.

Madeline had come in at that moment with Cecelia, and Lew, not bothering to remove his hold on Julie, said, "Well, what do you think? She's the right height and weight. I think she'd be sensational. And no one would have to teach her how to walk."

"I say yes," Madeline had answered with a smile, but Julie had seen the wary look in her eyes.

She wished she could have said, "Look, you needn't worry about me. I don't like Mr. Belmont."

"We'll try it, then," Lew said. "Laurel leaves the show next month, and I want the prettiest face I can find to replace her."

"Try what?" Julie had managed to ask, conscious that his hand still rested on her shoulder and that Madeline, for all her seeming casualness, had her eyes riveted on the two of them.

"Try being a show girl," Madeline had said.

Julie hadn't believed it at first. Show girl? She had rejected the idea out of hand, but they persuaded her. Madeline, in fact, had been the most persuasive of the two.

"Do you know how many girls would jump at this chance?" she had said. "Why, now that the word is out that Laurel is leaving, girls are lining up outside Lew's office daily."

"But suppose I can't do it. Suppose I . . ."

Madeline shrugged. "Try it," she advised. "You won't be losing anything."

But I will, Julie had thought. I'll be losing this position, in any case. In the end she had agreed to it, dazed by the swift turn of events.

Madeline had taken charge after that, and within

a week Julie found herself sharing an apartment with three other girls from the show and going to daily rehearsals. Her position as governess was taken over by a thin, colorless girl with a poor complexion and a hopelessly diffident manner.

"I can't keep losing governesses," Madeline had said by way of explanation, but Julie had an idea that Lew was not deceived by that any more than she was.

Now as Julie stood looking up at the marquee that spelled out "Angela Grant," she thought that it would have been more of a thrill to see her real name in lights, but the miracle of her success after eighteen months in New York never failed to amaze her.

She was about to enter the theater when Madeline, stepping from her chauffeured motorcar, hailed her.

"Still like to make sure you're up there?" Madeline said, coming to a halt beside Julie.

"I still can't take it for granted, I guess. If anyone had told me I'd meet Madeline James on my first interview for governess and lose the position only to go into the theater, I'd have thought they were crazy."

"Honey, with that face and body, you'd have been wasted as Cecelia's governess. And, anyway, I can do without that kind of competition in my own house. Lucky for me that Lew saw you as a show girl the first day he met you. At least I can keep an eye on you here." She laughed as she said it. It was a variation of her theme about Julie and Lew. But there was more than a grain of truth in the teasing, and Julie wasn't unaware of the fact that without Madeline riding herd, Lew would have insisted on an intimate relationship.

Julie had often wondered if there had ever really been a Mr. Stanley James who had died of pneumonia shortly after Cecelia had been born. A dozen years ago Madeline had been Julie's age, singing with a traveling light opera company. Cecelia, eleven now and in boarding school, had Madeline's curly red hair and bright green eyes and the same sprinkle of freckles across her nose. It was never easy to see a resemblance between Lew Belmont, a man nearly fifty, and the young Cecelia, but backstage gossip hinted that Cecelia was his natural child.

It was an open secret that Madeline was Belmont's mistress. Julie used to wonder why they hadn't married and then later learned that Belmont had a wife tucked away in Virginia and a grown daughter. There would never be a divorce. Mrs. Belmont wouldn't hear of it. From a wealthy merchant family herself, it was not money or fame she craved.

"She wants to be married, that's all," Madeline once told Julie. "She hates Lew. But she'll never let him go. Mrs. Schoenberg she is, and Mrs. Schoenberg she'll stay. And that's that."

Once Julie had asked Lew what made him pick Belmont as a name, and he had said, "It's a French version of Schoenberg. It means the same thing— 'beautiful mountain.' I figure if a nice Jewish boy from Austria named Augustus Schoenberg could become August Belmont, Protestant, and grow rich, why shouldn't a nice Jewish boy from Delancey Street at least pick the name and hope to get rich?"

Madeline and Lew had been good to Julie. They accepted her story that she had no family and the name she had chosen for herself. Every so often, especially as the friendship grew, guilt tempted her to say, "Look, I'm not Angela Grant, I'm Julie Fontaine, and I do have a family." But she was afraid that once the secret was told, somehow they would get wind of it back in Prescottville. So she remained silent, consoling herself with the thought that one day she would be free to tell them and one day they would understand.

They had done so much for her. Her featured role and salary increase had allowed her to rent a little apartment of her own and to hire a maid.

The apartment was in a town house and had a small living room, kitchen, a large bedroom, and a small bedroom, which her maid, Elsie, occupied. The address was good and the landlords, who occupied the two upper floors, were pleasant. Cozy in winter, it was desperately hot in the summer, and Madeline had said, "Well, never mind that. You can always come up to the Rye house with us on weekends if it gets too hot, and, of course, you're welcome in August, when the show is closed."

"Good evening, Miss Grant." It was Fred, the stage door man. She had passed him without really seeing him.

"Oh," she said. "Sorry, Fred. How are you?"

"Fine, fine. I suppose we'll be taking baskets of flowers

up to your dressing room again tonight. Fifteen last night. You've got a lot up there already."

"Well, just put them anywhere, Fred, and save the notes for me." She smiled.

Madeline's dressing room was on the first landing along with the other stars' rooms. Julie's was on the second, down the hall from the two big dressing rooms that accommodated the show girls. She passed those, giving a friendly wave through the first door, which was opened. It had been fun being in with the other girls, but it was better to have her own little place.

How much of her success depended on Madeline's friendship and how much on actual talent bothered her from time to time, despite the fact that it was Lew and his director, Roy Arlen, who had discovered her gift for mimickry. Lew might like her, but his show came first with him. Madeline didn't begin as a star. She worked for it in spite of her relationship with Lew.

Still, Julie knew, there had been some backbiting when she was featured. "Nothing like being in the family business," one girl had said snidely. In a way it was true. Madeline and Lew had treated her more like family than any of the Prescotts ever had.

When she thought of Jason and Millicent and Holt these days, it was all like a bad dream from which she had awakened. Prescottville itself had dimmed in the excitement of her new life. She had had no contact with anyone from home since the morning she ran away. In fact, of all her old life, only Eileen Butler, from her convent school days, knew that she was still alive and well, and Eileen would never break that confidence.

When Julie thought of home at all it was synonymous with Mark, and so she tried to push it from her mind. In the beginning she had dreamed of him, had awakened morning after dreary morning with his face before her, and with his name trembling on her lips. Now those times were rare. She had flung herself into her new role, working, practicing, learning, taking singing lessons and dancing lessons, filling all her waking hours with so much activity that the memories receded and began to lose some of their power to hurt her. However, every once in a while, a word, a turn of phrase, a place name would bring Mark vividly before her, and for an instant she would experience a throb of the old anguish.

She would never be able to think of him with Miranda Latham. It would never be real to her. It, too, would remain part of the bad dream from which she had mercifully awakened.

One day she would go back. One day, after she turned twenty-one and Jason had no control over her, she would go back, if only to claim what was hers. In little more than a year she would be free to make her whereabouts known without fear.

No, Prescottville was behind her, Mark was behind her, and the future stretched ahead. The past couldn't touch that. Yet, she acknowledged to herself that in ways it still touched her. Mark's defection and Holt's terrible abuse of her had smothered the fire in her blood. All the show girls in almost all the revues were sought after, flattered, proposed to, propositioned, and she had been one of the most popular.

Julie had not kept to herself. She accepted the invitations to dinners, to champagne suppers, to balls, and to parties. But not one man had been able to coax more than a chaste kiss from her.

Sometimes she would remember how she had been. She had hazy memories of those few nights among the willows, and she still had vivid memories of her time with Mark. She knew that there had been a passionate fever in her then and knew that she had gloried in the lovemaking. Now, though, she cringed from the idea of a man's touch.

The other show girls called her "Saint Angela," and she would smile grimly at that, remembering Eileen's nickname at St. Veronica's.

"One day you'll choose some man and heaven help you then, Angela," Madeline would say, knowing nothing of Julie's real previous life. Or she'd say, "You could do a lot worse than Steven Randall, honey. He's rich and good looking, and he's crazy enough about you to put up with that pure-as-the-driven-snow performance."

Donning her first-act costume for the show that night, Julie remembered the words and frowned into the dressing room mirror. She was fond of Steven but unwilling to move out of this world and into his. She never would become his mistress. She had told him that from the beginning, but lately he had pressed her for marriage. And marriage to Steven would mean an end to the shows. Marriage. A faint revulsion stirred in her. Not now. Perhaps never. She was still young; there were many years left. She knew she would never make it as a star. She was not like Madeline. She didn't have the drive or the ambition. Her present position pleased her for the moment. And when her looks or figure began to fade, then it would be time to think of something else. She peered into the mirror, seeing the image of a glamorously beautiful young woman, her figure svelte and provocative in the tightly fitted, sequined, turn-of-the-century gown. Feathery red plumes on a glittering band curled above her dark hair—a dramatic sweep of color that emphasized her flawless complexion.

There was a sharp rap on the door and Bert, the callboy, said, "Five minutes, Miss Grant."

Julie called an answer as she touched her nose with a final dusting of powder. Her dressing room was filled with the mingled odors of greasepaint and the variety of flowers that crowded all available space. Steven's nightly basket of red roses had been joined by other offerings accompanied by notes inviting her to supper or asking to see her after the show. Tonight Steven had asked her to see the midnight supper show at Tony Pastor's.

She sighed. What was wrong with her? She had some small success—a featured role in this new Belmont revue and her own dressing room for the first time, tiny and tucked away, though it was. She had admirers and one devoted swain proposing marriage; she was young; she was termed beautiful; her name was up in lights. She should be ecstatic with excitement. "The way I used to be," she said aloud. Hearing the muffled sound of the orchestra tuning up, she quickly stifled that memory and hurried below.

Exiting from the second of her two skits, "Parisian Lovers," in which she and Jimmy Harrigan, the comedy lead, played an updated Harlequin and Columbine, she found Steven waiting in the wings.

"Steven, what are you doing here? I can't talk to you now," she said, trying to brush past him.

"I have friends waiting to meet you tonight," he said, "and I want to know whether or not you're coming to Pastor's."

"Yes, yes, I'll come. Please, Steven, I have only five minutes to change." She heard the impatience in her voice and wondered why he put up with her. The fact that he did increased her annoyance, and while she changed with the help of Jeanine, the dresser, she began to regret having said yes. "Marry a man like that," she muttered aloud.

Then Jeanine said, "I beg your pardon?"

"Nothing. I'm just tired of . . . oh . . . I don't know."

"Trouble is, there's too much when you're young and too little when you're old," Jeanine answered.

Looking down at the bent, graying head and the roughened hands as Jeanine stitched a slight rip in her gown, Julie thought, yes, it's true—at least in this business. Jeanine long ago had been an actress, singing second leads in operettas, touring with some of the top stars. Once she had been sought after and flattered and important. She had played before King Edward when he was still Prince of Wales, and she had actually been invited to supper with the royal party. Once Jeanine had had youth and hope and excitement. But that ended twenty years ago, and now she was a little sparrow of a woman who came to the theater each night to watch others climb or try to climb to the top.

"Were you ever married, Jeanine?" Julie asked curiously.

"Once," Jeanine answered. "Once, when my name was still Janet Landon. But that's a long time ago and a long story, and you are due onstage in a few minutes. There," she said, patting the skirt into place and rising heavily. "Take my advice, Angela. Marry someone. This life" —she waved her hands—"this life doesn't last for most of us."

As Julie rode downtown with Steven after the show, Jeanine's words returned almost as an echo of the comments made by the crowd around the stage door as she and Steven hurried to the car. "Ooh, such a handsome couple. Are they going to get married?"

They were a good-looking couple, Julie thought, as they drove through the congestion of carriages and motorcars on their way downtown. Steven was indecently handsome, his sleek hair as dark as her own, his eyes nearly black above a straight Roman profile. He looked especially well in his white tie and was one of the few men she had ever seen who didn't look a bit ridiculous in an opera hat.

He never appeared to worry about anything and he never was too busy to play. Steven Randall III—heir to a fortune and possessor of a fortune himself from his grandparents' wills. Scion of an old North Carolina family, he had been educated in the North, graduating from Yale. He had lived most of his adult life right here in New York, making visits home from time to time and never staying very long.

"Very dull down on de ole plantation," he responded to Julie's remarks about how seldom he went down to North Carolina. New York was home to him, he preferred the North, and yet he had never completely lost his Carolinian accent. She half suspected he didn't want to because it added to his glamour. She knew she was the envy of half the women in the city. Steven was in constant attendance and seldom to be seen with anyone else.

He had everything, as Madeline pointed out. Yet Julie couldn't summon up enough response to him. But, then, I can't to anyone, she thought and sighed, snuggling down into the fur collar of her evening wrap.

Steven said, "Are you chilly? Will you have the lap robe?"

"No, I'm fine, Steven. Steven?"

"Yes?"

"What do you do all day? Do you just do things for fun? Do you work at anything?"

He turned to her, surprised. "That's the first time you've asked me anything serious. Dare I hope this means an awakened interest?" he asked in a mock serious voice.

"Don't be silly. I want to know. I've never really seen you except in the evenings or perhaps at the odd luncheon. In fact, when I think of you . . ."

"Which is often, I hope," he interposed.

"I always see you dressed just as you are. I can't really imagine you, oh, I don't know, in an office, or . . . or even walking through the park."

"You mean you imagine that I am something like the fairy prince who spends his days croaking on a lily pad and then is transformed at dusk?"

"Oh, do be serious."

"I'm a ne'er-do-well," he said. "Anyway, I am not gainfully employed. I do whatever pleases me. I play tennis and polo and I ride. I collect things. I take ladies to luncheon and supper and dinner. I go to the races, the theater, and the opera, and every so often I have meetings with lawyers and accountants and bankers and brokers. But I much prefer squiring the ladies, especially one lady. You're sure you wouldn't like to marry me and reform me? We could settle down and do good works. Or we might fulfill my father's dearest wish and retire to the endless rows of tobacco in North Carolina. You'd love my home, Angela."

"You're a wastrel," she said lightly. "But, then, I'm not at all who I pretend to be."

"Ah, sweet mystery," he rejoined. "You must tell me who you really are."

"Not now," she said. "We're at Pastor's already, and I expect your friends are waiting."

Heads turned as they followed the maître d' to the table where Steven's friends were already seated. "Angela Grant" Julie heard a woman whisper and thought, No, I'm Julie Fontaine, and one of these days I'm going to have to tell that much to Steven, at least—and to Madeline and to Lew Belmont.

Steven was making the introductions: a Mr. and Mrs. Tyler from North Carolina, friends of Steven's from childhood; a Miss Eleanor Marriot, also an old friend of Steven's; and Count René de Brugarde, a tall, older man of dark good looks.

"Brugarde," Julie said. "There is a beautiful French champagne called Château de Brugarde."

"I am the villain who produces it, *mademoiselle*. I should say *tries* to produce it. The Germans occupy most of the Champagne province," he replied with a smile. "But how do you know Château de Brugarde? It is not as famous as many of the others."

"So my uncle told me, but he finds it superior. And so do I."

"You are very kind. But surely you would not prefer it, for example, to Mumm's or Bollinger?"

"I find it more to my taste, although I do like Bollinger's quite as much."

"You are very young to be so familiar with wines."

"I grew up in . . . that is, I spent a lot of my childhood near wineries—in New York, not France."

"French wines are more exciting," he said.

"They have a different taste," she replied, "different grapes. The vinifera is not suitable to our shorter summers."

"Why, I never knew there were different kinds of grapes," Miss Marriot said animatedly. "You must tell me about that, René. I mean, are European grapes really different from ours?"

"Perhaps we should let Miss Grant explain," he said, stroking his mustache. "She's clearly patriotic about wines."

"No, not really," Julie demurred. "And I'm afraid I don't know as much as all that. In fact," she finished lightly, "I think I have used up all my knowledge in one sentence. Tell me," she said, changing the subject, "are you living here in America now?"

"No, I came on business, urgent business, and I must return."

"With all those submarines chasing merchant ships?" Steven asked.

René de Brugarde shrugged. "One takes one's chances in everything. I leave tomorrow. I must hurry back now. I do not think America will remain neutral much longer."

"I don't see how she can," Mr. Tyler said, joining the conversation. "Germany has not respected our neutrality. I must say, I think it brave of you to manage to get in and out of France and risk the Atlantic under these circumstances."

"Foolhardy, perhaps." René turned the compliment aside and then said, "Since this is my last evening in New York, you must honor me by being my guests. I shall not have another opportunity to repay your hospitality. This war"—he shook his head and a cloud of sadness passed briefly over his face—"this war does not show the promise of ending soon."

There was a murmur of agreement and the conversation continued. Mrs. Tyler remained silent throughout, and it seemed to Julie that she was observing her discreetly. Looking me over, she thought, and her chin lifted a little. Look away, she said silently, look to your heart's content, report back home on Steven's "show

girl." Wouldn't you be surprised to know that I keep
turning him down?

Julie turned to speak to René de Brugarde and, meeting his glance, felt a quick rush of excitement, as if they
had passed some invisible barrier and were . . . were
what? Flustered, she turned away without speaking, laying light fingers on Steven's arm, as if seeking reassur-
ance.

On the drive back to her apartment, Steven plied
Julie with questions, but she was not ready to confide
in him and turned him aside, saying, "Please, it's late,
and my story will keep. I'm very tired tonight."

At the door she presented her cheek for his kiss, but
he turned her face forcefully and kissed her on the
lips, drawing away for a moment, saying with a rueful
smile, "You madden me, Angela Grant. You look so
warm and passionate, and yet you're very cool under it
all. I don't know why I keep making a fool of myself.
Good night," he said.

"Good night, Steven," she returned imperturbably.

Elsie opened the door almost as soon as Steven closed
the outside one.

"I heard you coming in," she explained to Julie. "I
was up having a cup of tea. Can I get you some?"

"No, thanks, Elsie. I've had too much of everything
tonight, a bit too much champagne, too. I'm feeling
a little giddy. You go on to bed." She patted Elsie's arm
affectionately.

It had been a piece of good luck finding Elsie—or,
rather, Madeline finding Elsie. Madeline had good instincts. And she could never resist a sad story. Elsie had
been one of the girls who worked for Madame Roland,
Madeline's favorite modiste. At twenty-eight, she had
just lost her elderly mother, whose sole support she had
been for years.

"On slave wages, too," Madeline had said at the time.
"Madame Roland doesn't pay well at all. I talked to
Elsie. She's alone. She's living in a room in a boardinghouse. She's thrilled about the idea of working for
someone 'on the stage.' She'd have room and board with
you, and you could afford to pay her enough each week
to put something away."

Six months ago Elsie had been as light as a bird. Now

her small figure had filled out. She kept the apartment immaculate, cooked well, and, in fact, there was little she didn't do well. In the hours while Julie was at the theater, Elsie would sew for other people and was slowly hoarding money.

"She spends nothing on herself," Julie once said to Madeline. "I think she'll have more money than I do one day."

Madeline had given her a sharp look and said, "If you've been poor and if you've ever wondered when you would eat again, you become a squirrel with money once you have some."

Julie had said nothing in reply, embarrassed by the faint disapproval in Madeline's voice. It would have been nice to say, "But I've been poor and hungry." But this was something she couldn't do. Luck had been with her all the way.

But would it always be? Would she still have something left when she turned twenty-one? Was there anything left of Fontaine's? She had saved very little of her salary, spending it freely. She realized that she had never given any thought to a future in which she might be old and poor and have to rely on other people's kindness by giving her work or their charity.

Steven did offer security. He offered marriage and all the money she would ever need—more than she would ever need. He offered a permanent escape from Prescottville and insurance against a future like Jeanine's.

But I don't care for him, she thought. And he wouldn't care this much for me if I hadn't been so cool. She tried to envisage a life with Steven, she suffering his embraces, he always importuning. It was not a promising situation.

Someday it would change. Someday she would love someone again the way she had loved Mark. The thought made her sad and the memory made her ache again. Don't think about it, she told herself, trying to use her old charm against pain. Tonight it had less effect, and no matter how hard she tried to think of other things, Mark slipped in and out of her thoughts until she fell asleep. And when she awoke in the morning, he was still with her.

10

March blew itself out over the Atlantic and April teemed in its aftermath. On the third day of the new month, Congress declared war on Germany and Austria-Hungary. AMERICA AT ARMAGEDDON was the headline of the New York *Herald-Tribune*. Almost overnight troops were pouring into the city. Training camps began mushrooming in and around New York as America attempted to mobilize the five hundred thousand troops General Pershing stated were an absolute requirement by the end of the year. This figure was doomed to rise with each new report of German victories. Somehow, the one hundred thousand combined officers and men in all branches of the military service must grow to reach a major military force of one and a half million Americans.

Russia, in the throes of civil revolution, had collapsed and was rumored to be pursuing a separate peace with Germany, and Italy was considerably weakened. The result meant that Germany, however debilitated by her own war losses, would be able to withdraw troops from the Eastern Front and turn the bulk of the Central Powers' armies to the West.

With only token American forces available, with estimations of the numbers of men needed rising daily, Congress passed its subscription act, and by June General John Pershing arrived in Europe.

Trees budded in Central Park and the lake, which a few short weeks before had been thronged with skaters, now teemed with boats. There was a spirit of irrepressible optimism in the air. The Yanks were going over, and no matter what the doomsday prophets said, that would end the war.

The addition of the military in New York increased the number of productions on Broadway. Irving Berlin was already composing songs for a new patriotic revue to open that fall, "Yip Yip Yaphank."

Belmont's "Parade of 1917" had thrown out Angela Grant's "Parisian Lovers" skit and substituted one called "My Soldier Boy."

Steven Randall received a commission and was billeted as staff aide to the New York provost marshal.

"Comfortably settled in New York for the war," Madeline said to Julie. "I must say, he looks divine in his uniform. Now's the time to say yes, Angela."

"He hasn't asked me recently." Julie smiled. "Perhaps he's tired of the whole thing."

"You're a fool to let that one slip through your net."

But Julie did not reply. All spring she had toyed with the idea of marrying Steven without coming to any conclusion.

And then, one day, coming into the apartment after an afternoon of fittings for her new costumes, she found Eileen Butler waiting for her. She hardly recognized Eileen. She had grown heavier, her complexion was bad, and her normally tidy hair looked terribly unkempt.

"Julie," Eileen said, "I . . . I couldn't think of anyone else . . ." She stopped, laboring under some terrible emotion.

"Eileen, what is it? You look so . . . so different."

"I'm pregnant . . . and I am not married," Eileen said humbly, and then she began to cry with deep, heaving sobs that welled up from the depths of her being.

"Eileen, you can't be, not you. How can you be sure? How did it happen?" Julie began in a rush of questions as she put her arms around Eileen and tried to stem the flow of anguish.

Bit by bit, the story came out—such a pitiful little story, so trite in its outlines of the innocent girl betrayed, as if it were a melodrama and not real at all.

The man who had swept the shy and plain little Eileen off her feet had disappeared as soon as he knew she was pregnant.

"Only once," Eileen gulped in answer to Julie's question. "And he said he . . . he was going to marry me . . . and then when I wouldn't . . . that is, when I refused to see him until . . . until . . . he asked Father, he stopped calling. I went to him when I knew I was going to have a baby and he told me not to worry, and I went home.

The very next day he was gone. I don't know where. I told my mother you'd invited me to visit—and here I am."

"Why didn't you tell your mother the truth?"

"Tell her? Oh, Julie, you know her. And my father. It would kill them. They would kill me. What am I going to do?"

"We'll think of something," Julie said absently. Eileen, of all people! It should have happened to her, but it hadn't. Mark had been prudent enough there. And at least he had offered marriage, she thought, and then remembered that the offer had been brutally withdrawn. Men, she thought. All the women who'd ever warned her were correct in saying that the only way to marry a man was to hold out the prize until the return trip from the altar had been completed. She said as much aloud and sent Eileen into fresh sobs of guilt and fear and regret.

"I know what to do," Julie said, suddenly inspired. "I'll telephone a friend of mine. She'll know the answers. Madeline James, I've written you about . . ."

"Oh no, Julie, don't tell anyone!"

"I've got to tell someone. I can't take care of this alone. I wouldn't know where to begin. You can trust Madeline. Believe me."

Madeline wasted almost no time on tactful questions and delicate suggestions.

"I've been there, honey," she said candidly to the dazed Eileen. "I'm not going to tell your secret, and you aren't going to tell mine, right?"

Eileen nodded, dumbfounded before this self-assured, elegantly dressed redhead, who exuded both glamour and practicality, as if those two things went together normally.

"The rat I got involved with did pretty much the same thing. He was with the show I was in. He ran and I had to leave. I found myself at eighteen out of a job, pregnant, no family, and not even a friend like Angela. I went it alone. Got a job in Biloxi working for a lady who had a dressmaking business. Told her I was widowed and pregnant. I had a picture of Cecelia's father and me, taken in some little town where the show had played. Funny thing is, the friend who took it had made us move over in front of the church so he could get a decent light.

Anyway, if Mrs. Larrimer believed me or not, I don't know. She let me work until Cecelia was born and she helped me afterward. She was good. And then one day I was delivering some clothes to the star of another show that was in town. And I met Lew Belmont. He'd only come down to see this woman. He was there when I walked in, and the next thing I knew he came around to Mrs. Larrimer's asking for me. He liked me—loved me, I guess. He offered me nothing but the truth, and he got the whole truth out of me. Brought us both—Cecelia and me—up to New York, got me working again, and made me what I am today." Madeline finished her story with an impish grin.

"I don't say that all this is going to work out for you. But you're too far gone to think of anything but having the baby. You could give it away, of course, but I think you ought to wait to decide that. You can stay at my place and I'll help you. We'll fake a wedding if you like. I can get one of the boys down at the theater to pose, I guess. Pick a name, buy a wedding ring, and write and tell your family you've eloped."

Eileen, like Julie, had sat in amazed silence during the speech, but now, at the mention of her family, Eileen became voluble, repeating that they'd never believe her and they'd never forgive her.

"You can't just disappear, Eileen," Julie said.

"Why not? You did."

"That's different."

"Julie Fontaine, it's not different," Eileen answered, and in the confusion neither of them noticed that she had spoken Julie's real name. Madeline picked up on it at once, but she delayed saying anything until they had settled Eileen into Julie's bedroom.

Returning to the living room, Madeline said, "Okay, Angela Grant, what does the 'Julie Fontaine' stand for?"

Julie had always meant to tell Madeline, but she hadn't imagined having to do it under such circumstances. Madeline's eyes plainly said, Look, we trusted you, and you know our secrets.

Julie told her story haltingly, skimming over Holt's assault and not mentioning her uncle's and aunt's involvement.

"And where is he now, our hero?" Madeline asked when Julie had finished.

"Do you mean Holt?"

"Holt's the villain. What's the matter with you? I said *hero*—Mark . . . the used-to-be hero, I mean."

Julie shrugged. "I don't know. I don't care."

"You care, all right. I hear it in your voice. Men. They can be beasts. Not Lew. He's one in a million. Oh, I know he takes the odd fling. Sometimes a girl catches his fancy and he gives in, as he would have with you if I hadn't been on the watch and you weren't such an ice maiden. But I don't mind. Well, I don't mind so much. I know that whore he married. No," she interjected at Julie's gasp, "not a real whore, the married kind—the one who gives in only when she wants something, and gets headaches the rest of the time, or makes scenes, or has backaches. And then she tells her friends how clever she is at fooling the idiot she gets her keep from.

"Lew got out. A lot of men don't. A lot more play around for just that reason. That kind of woman is the worst kind of woman. By the time she's finished with a man, he's lucky if he has any manhood left. So I know that Lew played around before, and I know he still gets the urge to reassure himself—less and less, though." Madeline grinned. "He's wearing down a little, and then I don't say no to him. I wasn't mad about him when we first got together. Grateful. Affectionate. But he did so much for me. Well, I love him now, all right. Not that giddy feeling. But who needs that? Be smart, Angela/Julie, marry Steve Randall. He's crazy about you and he'll be good to you, and if you're good to him . . . well, you'll be happier than most."

Madeline stood up and stretched. "Listen to me. I feel like a teacher—talking myself blue. You won't take my advice, anyway, you and your little friend—sheltered, spoiled, and when trouble hits, you run. I was luckier. I didn't start out with anything. I just learned to survive."

"I'm surviving," Julie said stiffly.

Madeline eyed her appraisingly. "Yes, you are. I suspect there's a whole lot more fire under that don't-touch-me act than even you know. Don't throw it away like your friend in there, or like me." She smiled. "Protect yourself, honey. That's the first thing a girl has to learn. I'd have married Lew if I could have. But, as it is, he's taken care of me. No matter what happens now, I won't have to look forward to the poorhouse or to a job like

Jeanine's when my looks go and my voice flies south. You do the same, kid. Don't count on your family. From what you've told me, you'll be lucky if you have six dollars by the time your uncle is finished. See you later. Want me to send the car around and you can swing back for me?"

Julie shook her head. "No thanks, Madeline. One more thing, Madeline."

"Yes?"

"You're not as practical underneath as you pretend. You've just saddled yourself with a real problem."

"I'm paying back Mrs. Larrimer's favor," Madeline said quietly. "Not everybody gets his payback-day chance."

Eileen moved into Madeline's apartment the following day, and two nights later Julie told Steven Randall she would marry him.

To her confession about her real name and her life before she came to New York, he said with satisfaction, "I knew perfectly well you weren't the average actress-show girl type."

And Julie said, "What a snobbish remark, Steven."

"I am a snob," he replied calmly. "I've never pretended to be anything else. I like the fine, the interesting, and the elegant. Anything other than that bores me." He put his arms around her, saying, "Now that we're engaged to be married, I think some token of affection is warranted."

With his lips hungry and warm on hers, she tried to respond. It had been such a long time since she had been in a man's arms, and for a few minutes she yielded to the comfort of it, but no matter how she returned his kisses, none of the old passion was aroused. He didn't seem to notice, not even when his kisses grew more demanding and she put him off.

He won't know, Julie thought, and I'll learn to love him. She couldn't live in the present forever, not any more than she had been able to dwell mournfully in the past. Live or die. That's what it was all about. The weak died; the strong survived. No matter what happened to Eileen, she was finished. That talk of killing herself. It was something Julie herself had never considered, not even in the depths of her earlier misery. Like Madeline—

that's how she would be, doing what had to be done to protect herself and her future. There would be no illegitimate babies; there would never be another episode like Mark; and she would not wind up like Jeanine—on her knees sewing rips in young girls' costumes. She would control her own destiny, at least so far as that was humanly possible.

"I'd like to have the wedding at Thanksgiving," Julie said to Steven, "right here in New York. I'll write to my family when it's over."

He protested that. He wanted a splashy affair; he wanted his family to come north. He said his mother would think it odd if she weren't married at her own family's home.

"I don't care," Julie said stubbornly. "I don't want all that. Anyway, the war is on, and you can tell your mother it isn't being done so much now. We can go to The Little Church Around the Corner."

"It's Protestant," he said, "and you're Catholic."

"I'm nothing anymore. It doesn't matter to me where I'm married. We can elope to Gretna Green, if you'd rather."

She knew she would have her way. He wanted her. Marriage was the only way he could get her. It had been different with Mark. Then she had complied with everything. But then she had been besotted. Mark hadn't. She wondered why he had bothered to propose at all. She had been his for the taking. Some spark of decency. Or, maybe once he was away from her, she no longer meant anything to him. She could think about that now almost dispassionately. Maybe I am over it at last, she thought, but the idea, while awakening no pangs of sorrow, did not gleam with the brightness of truth.

The show was closing in August, and in September the new rehearsals would begin. Meanwhile, the Belmont girls, along with all the other show girls and actresses in town, were making appearances at Liberty Bond rallies, being photographed with soldiers, and posing under army recruiting posters. It was a gay and glamorous war. "Lafayette, we are here!" said General Pershing on his arrival in Paris with the first small American expeditionary force, and it was the banner headline in all the dailies across the country.

Join the army and see Paris. Show the Kaiser how

strong a Yank can be. "K-K-K-Katie, beautiful Katie," the country sang, and "Over there, over there, the Yanks are coming." Flags unfurled, banners waved, drums rolled, and trumpets sounded. The Sixty-ninth Regiment marched out of the armory to the strains of the Garryowen. Irving Berlin had written "It Takes an Irishman to Make Love" and "The Fighting Irish." These brave Irishmen, who had won their name and distinguished themselves at Gettysburg, now stood on the decks of a troop ship waving to the girls they were leaving behind.

"Keep your head down, Fritzie, boy . . . if you want to see your father in the fatherland," people sang gaily. And in the streets of New York's Yorkville section, German-American shopkeepers had their windows broken and their children were stoned by young American patriots.

It was the war to end all wars, and America was going to win it for the Allies. Raw recruits poured into the hastily built training centers and were churned out to New York to await sailings.

Broadway gleamed with lights; supper clubs and theaters and restaurants were filled nightly. In the factories across the nation, overworked women and children spent long hours alongside the men to grind out the assembly of materials needed to equip the soldiers.

Julie, learning lines for the new revue, playing eight shows a week, and selling bonds, felt that the world was moving too fast and that she herself was on a feverish ride from which there was no turning back. Steven demanded more and more of the precious little time she had left to herself.

News of her forthcoming marriage was greeted with cries of delight from Madeline and a wistful expression for her happiness from Eileen, who was growing heavier in her body and thinner in her face as the weeks progressed.

Lew Belmont had reservations. "You haven't told Steven that you're doing the new revue?" he questioned one day.

"I didn't think it was necessary. Steven knows I've signed for this new revue. I just assumed . . ."

Lew shook his head. "Steven was in to see me today. He expects that once you're married, that's it. And, Angela . . . er . . . Julie, that's the way it will have to be. I've agreed to let you out of the contract."

"I don't want to be let out!" Julie cried. "How dare Steven do that without saying anything to me!"

"Steven is an investor in these shows. You must know that."

She shook her head.

"It's true. I don't rely only on Steven's money, but at this late date . . . I mean, we get along, Steven and I. He puts in the money, and I give him his profits. He doesn't run the show. Still . . ."

"I won't marry him then," Julie said. "At least I won't marry him until the next show closes. I'll tell him so."

Lew eyed her speculatively. "Do you love this man? Or are you marrying him to have security? Somehow, I didn't take you for that kind of person."

"It's . . . it's hard to explain. I'm . . . well . . . I'm not going to be a great star."

Lew nodded in agreement.

"So what will I do? Steven . . . I'm very fond of Steven. I'll be a good wife to him. Anyway, there is no one else."

"I see. He's the best of a bad lot, hmm?"

Julie flushed.

"Listen to me, and then make up your mind. Madeline is thrilled over what she thinks is her matchmaking. I know. I know how she talks and what she says and what she thinks. But you aren't Madeline. You're different. You come from different worlds." Lew held up his hand as Julie started to speak. "No, that's something I knew before we heard the whole story. I didn't know why. I didn't care why, but I knew you had run away from something—the way you talk, walk, carry yourself, and many other little things. Yes, you'll fit right into the Randalls' life . . . at least on the surface. But if you don't bring something more than a fondness to this marriage . . . well . . . look, I'm talking to you as I'd talk to my own daughter. Randall's world is different from yours, too. Think about what you're doing."

"Will you fire me if I marry Steven this fall?" Julie asked.

"Fire you? No. You have a contract, and there isn't anything in it that says you can't marry. All I told Steven was that I'd let you out of it. It's up to you from there."

"I'm staying with the show," Julie said. "I'll take care of Steven."

11

July smothered New York in a heat wave. Still the places of amusement were jammed. The prohibitionists had succeeded in getting a wartime prohibition bill before Congress, and between its introduction and passage, people drank as if each drink would be their last.

Sweaty, half drunk crowds poured into the theaters, adding to the suffocating heat. Electric fans whirled with little effectiveness, and onstage at the Belmont the cast melted under the lights.

Still the shows went on and more and more of the audiences were filled with soldiers in uniform. They clapped loudly, they called out, and they jammed the stage door entrance. This was a far more demanding group than those who sent discreet invitations in bouquets. They wanted to see, to touch, to be able to write back home and say: "I talked to Marilyn Miller or Madeline James or Olive Thomas. I touched Elsie Janis. I've got Will Rogers' autograph."

The last month of the show dragged on interminably. Even Madeline, normally bright and cheerful, began snapping at the rest of the cast, at the stage crew, even at Jeanine, whom she had always treated with affectionate respect.

Going to the James' house these days became more and more depressing for Eileen. Her legs were swollen, and she moved ponderously around the apartment, lending herself to whatever task presented itself or sitting in her own room sewing, mending, and darning.

"Like a poor relative," Madeline said. "But when I try to get her out, to make her join us for a little fun, she says the work helps her."

When Julie tried to talk to Eileen, she met with no greater success. Eileen simply turned a sweet, sad smile on her and said gently, "You're all very kind, but keeping busy helps me. It really does."

Eileen's face had acquired a certain unearthly beauty, a radiance that shimmered in spite of the sadness in her eyes.

"Let her be" became the motto. The baby was due the first of October. After that things would be better. Only three months away . . . less than three months. Eileen had been persuaded at last to wire her parents and tell them of her "marriage" to a fictitious Peter Wilson, who was in training camp. The Butlers had reacted with disappointment and anger. For the moment the estrangement helped.

"When you finally get through this," Madeline told her, "you can be widowed and go home. Once they see their grandchild, all will be forgiven."

To this Eileen would say, "I don't know that I can live a lie like that."

Late one Sunday afternoon near the middle of July, Madeline and Julie persuaded Eileen to come into the living room for tea.

Eileen must have felt some relief that her ordeal was nearing its end because she smiled and talked in a way she had not done since her arrival in New York. She was softer, too, less tense, and her inner radiance grew until it seemed that she was bathed in a glowing rosy health.

And then all at once, in the middle of a sentence, she went very white and clutched at her belly. "The pain!" she cried out. "It's awful!" And she doubled over, gasping.

"Take her to bed," Madeline ordered Julie. "I'll telephone Dr. Johnson."

It was a struggle to get Eileen out of the chair and to help her walk the long hallway to her bedroom. Her knees kept buckling and she sagged against Julie's supporting arms. Once on the bed, she began to writhe and moan and finally to scream.

Dr. Johnson, hurrying from his house around the corner, took one look at her and ordered Madeline to call for an ambulance. Julie, standing near the bed, watching the agonizing convolutions of Eileen's body, bit her own lip so savagely she drew blood.

"I didn't know it would hurt like this," Eileen sobbed.

"Dear Mother of heaven, help me. Dear God, forgive me." Then she began to scream again. The baby arrived minutes later, dark and limp and malodorous.

"Dead," Dr. Johnson said grimly and reached for the bottle of chloroform. "Here," he said brusquely to Julie, "put this cloth over her nose and hold it there. I'll tell you when to take it away."

Julie obeyed, her eyes riveted on Eileen's face. She saw the lines begin to relax and heard the cries and supplications fade away to incoherence.

"Take it away," Dr. Johnson said, and she was conscious that he was working frantically just below her—shoving pillows and blankets under Eileen's buttocks to stem the flow of blood.

"Get me more clean towels," he said to Julie, and she went away to obey him, hardly conscious of what she was doing.

Madeline, always cool and collected, stood outside the bedroom door unable to enter. "I can't," she said sickly. "I can't stand the sight of blood. Isn't that funny? I . . . I think I'm going to be ill."

Julie went back with a load of towels and sheets. In a dream, she stood by helping the doctor pack Eileen's body, but the blood kept seeping through.

"So much blood," Julie whispered.

"I can't save her," Dr. Johnson said and swore violently.

Eileen stirred and moaned weakly, calling Julie's name, and Julie ran to her side, taking Eileen's thin, cold hand in hers and pressing her own warm flesh against Eileen's, as if by the pressing of that boneless hand she could somehow stem the life force that flowed away, soaking the packing, the sheets, and the mattress.

"I'm dying," Eileen whispered. "Julie, please. A priest. Please."

"A priest," Julie said to Dr. Johnson. "I don't know any priests."

"St. Ignatius is around the corner," Dr. Johnson answered tersely. "Hurry."

Afterward, Julie would not remember running through the hot, airless street. She never remembered leaving the house. One minute she had been beside her dying friend, trying to press life back into her body, and the next she was saying frantically to the startled young priest on duty, "Please, Eileen is dying, come quickly." She waited dumbly while he packed his case and went into the sacristy to get the host. His movements were swift and economical, and yet it seemed that everything was in slow motion, like the separate cards of the animated, disconnected figures on drawings.

She led him back to the apartment without speaking. He walked silently behind her, carrying the host. Madeline met them at the door. "I think she's gone," she said in a shaken voice, but the priest brushed past her, following the still silent Julie to Eileen's bedroom.

He approached the waxy white figure on the bed. Seeing Eileen's face with its look of unearthly peace, Julie thought, Too late. But as the priest bent over the bed, Eileen's eyes fluttered open and she said, "Bless me, Father, for I have sinned. Oh, Father, I have sinned so grievously."

Dr. Johnson turned away, facing Julie, and she saw that tears lay on his lined face. "Come outside," she whispered to him. "Confession is private."

"I can't stop the bleeding. It's less now, but she's lost too much. She can't live."

"How long?" Julie asked.

"I don't know. A few minutes . . . not more than a few hours. She's a healthy girl, strong. But the baby— that baby was dead inside her for a long time. The infection . . ." From outside the apartment they heard the wail of the ambulance and Dr. Johnson said tiredly, "Too late. It was always too late." It was less than half an hour since he had arrived.

"She was good, you know," Julie said to the doctor, "really good and innocent. Dumb. She was dumb. Why, when we were in school together, she really thought you could have a baby if you kissed a boy. I should have told her the truth then. 'Saint Eileen' was what the girls used to call her behind her back." Julie began to cry. "I have to call her family," she said. "I can't tell them the truth. It would kill them. Please, Doctor, if they ask you, could you say she was only just . . . well . . . that she was only three months gone? To spare them? Eileen didn't like to lie. But I don't mind."

"Neither do I," he answered shortly, just as the ambulance attendants came hurrying down the hall.

Eileen lingered the night, surviving the transfer into

the hospital, where nothing they did could save her. Julie sat by her bed, holding her hand, making soothing sounds whenever Eileen swam back to consciousness. Toward early morning she seemed brighter, as if she might rally. "It's all right, Julie," she said. "I don't mind dying, you know. You mustn't cry. Help my mother and father. Tell them . . . tell them I love them."

I can't bear it, Julie thought, her throat thick with sternly repressed tears. "I will," she managed.

"I feel so strange," Eileen said, "light and . . . I can't breathe very well. Could you lift me up, Julie?"

Julie lifted Eileen's weightless body, supporting her shoulders and propping her head up higher.

"That's better. Thank you, Julie." Eileen's head fell back against Julie's arm and, with a long, whistling sigh, she was gone.

The days following Eileen's death held the same dreamlike quality of that terrible day. The Butlers, arriving to claim the body and to arrange for burial, were like two walking corpses, as if by their only child's death their own spirits had been permanently diminished. The floridly expansive Mr. Butler of a few short years ago was an old, quiet man, and his wife's face bore a look of such utter despair that it was painful to look at her.

They accepted the explanations that Madeline and Julie gave them about the boy Eileen married being somewhere in France and that she had looked forward to going home after her baby was born. They took some comfort from Dr. Johnson's kindly lie that Eileen was too frail ever to have borne a child.

"So it really didn't matter, after all," Mrs. Butler said pathetically. "It would have happened, anyway, no matter whom she married. I'm . . . I'm glad at least she had some happiness."

Julie, thinking of the pitiful, woebegone Eileen of the past few months, murmured agreement. Forgive me, Eileen, she said silently. But I can't hurt them with the truth. You can tell them yourself when you all meet in heaven—if there is a heaven.

The show went on each night and Julie played it, wondering how she managed. But it was separate and apart from the rest of her life. No matter that the tragedy haunted her daily and every night before she went to sleep. Real life was the play and the revue was the living reality.

She was dimly grateful that Steven had been ordered to Washington for a few weeks. She couldn't have dealt with Steven now, and it occurred to her that his very presence had never held much reality for her. She grew thinner and more introspective, and on the day before the show closed, Lew Belmont called her aside and said, "I'll expect a little more weight by the time we go into rehearsals. You're losing your figure, Julie. Snap out of it."

"I'll be all right." She smiled at him. "I will, really. I'm going up to Rye with Madeline when the show closes. We both need to get away and we need a rest."

"And when are you getting married?"

"Married?" she repeated gravely. "At Thanksgiving, I think."

He raised his eyebrows. "You think? Did you think about what I said to you?"

"Yes. I thought about it. It'll be all right, Lew. Steven isn't going to make me quit, not until after the new show closes."

"I see. Well," he said, giving her arm a heavy pat, "take care of yourself, Julie. Like I said, we can't use skinny show girls."

During the intermission that night, Bert knocked on her door with a note. "Soldier says he's an old friend of yours," he told her. He winked. "They all say that, don't they?"

Julie, reading the note, scarcely heard him.

Andrew Clay. Andrew, of all people.

"You want me to wait for an answer?" Bert asked when she didn't speak.

"Yes, yes," Julie said eagerly. "He's from my hometown." She scribbled a hasty reply and handed the folded paper to Bert. "Tell Joe to let him up afterward, will you?"

"Sure thing."

Andrew Clay in New York. The secret she had kept for so long wouldn't be a secret much longer unless she could persuade Andrew to keep silent about her.

She managed to put it out of her mind during the last act of the show, but coming down close to the apron during the finale, she was greeted by a roar of applause

from the audience and could hear her name being called
—"Angela Grant! Angela Grant!"

She would need all her powers of persuasion to obtain
Andrew's silence. He would find this too good a story
to keep. She took the curtain calls, smiling with artificial
gaiety, and as soon as they were over she hurried quickly
up to her dressing room, trying to think of what kind of
argument might win Andrew's silence. The truth might
help, but she didn't want to tell him the truth about her
family if she could help it.

She worried about it as she removed her makeup and
changed her clothes. She was putting the finishing touches
on her hair when he knocked, and she called out with
a brightness she was far from feeling: "Come in, Andrew."

The door opened and, looking up in the dressing mirror, she saw Holt Prescott framed in the doorway.

The shock of it was so great that for minutes she
could not find her tongue.

"Come in, Andrew," Holt mimicked with a sneer.
"Yes, dear cousin, it is I, not Andrew. But, then, I
didn't imagine you would want to see me. Andrew, of
course, is different. One of your lovers, isn't he?"

I mustn't let him see that I'm afraid, she thought rapidly. He can't harm me here. Her head went up and her
eyes narrowed. Without turning around, she said, "Get
out of here, Holt. You aren't welcome."

"Indeed, not?" he inquired coolly and, stepping inside,
he closed and locked the door.

Julie turned then, forcing herself to move slowly.

"This isn't Prescottville," she said quietly. "One
scream and every man in the theater will be breaking
that door down. You beast," she said clearly and distinctly, "you filthy, insane beast."

She saw his face mottle and he made a quick move toward her. She felt behind her, and her hands closed on her
nail scissors. The cool steel against her palm lent her
fresh courage.

"Get out!" she repeated.

He gave a slight bow and moved back, taking a chair
near the dressing screen.

"Won't Father be surprised when I tell him? Surely
you don't imagine you'll be allowed to remain here? How
did you find your way into the theater? Oh, I guess we

could say that any place that caters to harlots and . . ."

"I'm going to ask you one more time," Julie said evenly. "Leave my dressing room."

"I could scarcely believe my eyes when I saw you on-stage." Holt went on as if she hadn't spoken. "Just think, if I hadn't gotten this army commission and hadn't been on my way to Washington, I'd never have found you. Odd how these things work out, isn't it? We'd been hoping to receive word of you—preferably that you were no longer among the living. It would solve so many problems at Fontaine's. The tedious business of waiting seven years to have you declared legally dead was very trying. But that's over now."

He rose and came to stand in front of her. "Which will it be, Julie? Will you sign proxies over to us, or shall I try to find other means of persuasion?"

"Don't," she said, trying not to let panic creep into her voice. "Don't lay a hand on me, Holt. I'm not the frightened girl I was. I'm not afraid of telling everything I know about you, describing what you . . . what disgusting . . . things you did to me. I'll tell the police. I think they do things to men like you."

"You'll tell the police," he said sardonically. "And just whom do you think it will harm? Who will they believe —some runaway girl with a bad reputation, or me? If you try that . . ." He raised one hand and slapped her across the face.

She screamed then, screamed and screamed until she heard people pounding on her door.

Holt drew back. "Now we'll see," he said grimly. He strode to the door, opened it, and began: "My cousin has become slightly hysterical."

Cousin. Fred and Bert looked at her. Behind them the show girls were crowding together, craning their necks to see into the room.

Julie pulled herself erect. "This man is not Andrew Clay," she said in a shaking voice. "He . . . please, get him out of here."

Both men seized Holt, who was saying angrily, "I am her cousin. She ran away from home. My father sent me to bring her back."

"It's a lie," Julie said. "Please take him out of here."

"Come along now, Lieutenant," Bert said. "We don't

care who you are. No one comes into Miss Grant's dressing room unless she says so."

"Very well." Holt sought to regain his composure. "I'll leave, only take your hands off me."

Bert looked at Julie and she nodded. He and Fred released their hold but remained next to Holt.

"We'll see about this, dear cousin," Holt said. "I won't make the mistake of visiting you here again." He laid the slightest emphasis on the word "here," and he saw his shaft strike home. He smiled. "Think over what I said," he added.

The girls were dispersing with murmured conversation among themselves. Bert and Fred were moving out with Holt when Julie heard Steven's voice saying, "What on earth is going on here?" She slumped back against the dressing table, feeling her legs go weak now that it was over.

"Darling," Steven said at the door, "what is happening?"

"It's all right now," Julie answered, coming forward to meet him. "I . . . I'll explain later. Steven, I'm so glad you're back. Don't ask me questions now. Please, take me home."

He was puzzled and curious, but solicitous, and he made no attempt to question her further.

Steven, always the gentleman, she thought, in a rush of affection. Mark had left her and Holt . . . She gave an involuntary shudder.

Once they were at Julie's apartment, Steven said, "Can you tell me now? I can see how this has upset you."

"It's such a long story," Julie answered, "and not a very nice one. You see, there was more to my leaving home than a madcap urge to have fun."

He started to say something and she interrupted him. "No, Steven, let me tell you about it and you can question me later. That was my cousin Holt Prescott you saw being hustled out of my dressing room. The Prescotts aren't exactly what you might have thought—what anyone thinks, for that matter."

Haltingly, she recited the essential facts, unable to bring herself to tell him about Millicent's and Jason's relationship or the worst of Holt's behavior, but giving him enough so that her very real fear of Holt and what he might do came through to him.

When she had finished, he came to take her in his arms, saying, "Poor darling. Don't you know that there are ways of handling a man like your cousin? You leave all that to me. I can see that he never comes near you again. Put him out of your mind."

"But . . ." she began.

Steven said, "Trust me, Julie. I can see to it that he gets fair warning, and after that . . . well, I don't think we need to worry about him anymore."

"It was the one thing I was always afraid of. You don't know him. He . . ."

"Shhh," he soothed. "I'm taking care of you now. Here." He drew her down to the couch and put her head against his shoulder. "I love you," he said, "and we're going to be married. I think I can handle the Prescotts—father and son and any assorted other little Prescotts who pop up."

He bent his head and kissed her gently. His lips were warm and comforting, and stirred, Julie returned his kiss with an ardor that she had not shown him before. They stayed that way for a while, just kissing each other, and then, quite without warning, Julie felt a trembling start deep within her. Steven sensed it and his kisses became more ardent, his mouth parting her lips, moving downward, kissing her throat and the low décolletage of her gown. For the first time since that last night long ago with Mark, desire welled up in her. Steven shifted her in his arm and drew her across his lap. She pressed herself to him, uttering soft sounds of pleasure as his hands, seeking her body, reached down through her bodice and cupped her straining breasts. She gave herself up to the feelings, not stopping him as she had so many times before. Dimly, she thought of Eileen, of what Madeline had said about holding out for the ultimate prize, but it no longer seemed to matter.

Her gown lay discarded and his hands, moving up beneath the thin silk petticoat, fell upon her thighs. She pressed them closed, gasping at the thrill it evoked.

"Not here," he was saying, "not here. Come." He moved her away so that she was half-sitting, her head leaning against the back of the couch. He stood up and, bending down, he gathered her up in his arms and carried her into her bedroom, kicking the door closed behind them, leaving them in darkness.

He leaned his back to the door, lowering her so that he was holding her while he removed the rest of her clothes. She felt the hardness of his belt pressing into her flesh and the buttons of his uniform were like small, cold circles upon her breasts. Slowly, she began to unbutton those buttons until her hands could reach inside his shirt and feel the warmth of his chest. She longed to feel that flesh against her own and moved closer. She was dizzy as he released her to take off his own clothes. In the darkness she saw the blurred whiteness of his naked body coming back to her.

For an instant he clasped her so that their flesh melded and slowly, inexorably, he forced her toward the bed. She lay across it, her arms held up until she felt his weight upon her, and then with a sigh of pleasure she felt him enter her and they were moving slowly, rhythmically, and then with desperate haste, rolling together like puppies until her body arched and waves of ecstasy engulfed her.

Steven was asleep almost at once and Julie, lying half awake, thought that now he will know he's not the first. She wondered if it would matter to him, but the contentment that spread through her body left no room for worry, and she was soon sleeping beside him.

Madeline had counseled waiting for the wedding ring to ensure marriage, but she was wrong. If anything, that night together made Steven all the more determined to have Julie for himself. Content at first to wait until Thanksgiving, he now began to want the date moved forward, and Julie, finding it difficult to resist the newly awakened responses of her body and vaguely fearful that no matter how Steven reassured her she would become pregnant, agreed to consider it.

Spending August in Rye with Madeline while Steven was in Washington, Julie found herself seized with the same feverish desires that had left her sleepless in those old days before Mark. Sometimes she would dream of making love, but never with Steven, always with a faceless man who evoked such intense feelings that she would awake trembling, thinking that she must be with Steven soon again.

Coming back to New York in September, she found a letter from Jason and knew that Steven had been successful in frightening Holt away.

"To have your new fiancé, as I believe he calls himself, daring to threaten Holt with actions taken through the army, is the ultimate insult," his letter ran in part. But he made no mention of trying to interfere with her plans.

He urged her again to reconsider selling Fontaine's and said that her accumulated allowance would be forwarded. "Next summer your trust will be turned over to you. Please make the necessary banking arrangements." He went on to tell her that the trust was affected by the "fluctuating market one can expect in times of war."

Other than that, she was requested not to contact her aunt, who was still not well and who had been distraught to learn that her niece had entered the vulgar world of theatrics.

As if they were really what they pretended to be, Julie thought with contempt, tossing the letter aside and writing a quick note in reply, reaffirming her intention not to sell Fontaine's.

Jason's letter put the period to her fears. The week before the show opened, Julie agreed to Steven's pleas and moved the wedding date up to mid-October. With Holt no longer a threat to her, and in her present relationship with Steven, a new sense of well-being overcame her. Life was now the way she had ordered it. Steven's long absences in Washington made their lovemaking something she looked forward to eagerly, and once he said to her, "Who ever would have believed that you were like this?"

"Like what?" she asked.

For an answer he reached out, touching her body, smiling at her quick involuntary response. "Like that," he said with satisfaction, "cool on the outside and a fire within. And all mine," he added.

She did not answer him directly, but propelled herself into his arms with a little sigh. "I was told men liked this more than women," she said. "I don't think it's true."

"Not of you, anyway," he answered. "Julie, don't change your mind about us."

"I won't," she promised.

As their wedding date drew nearer, Madeline said to Julie, "Aren't you glad now that you followed my advice? There's a difference in you. . . ." She paused. "I almost envy you," she added lightly. "You're at the peak, everything going your way and a very rich husband coming up to frost the cake. Well, I told you if you dangle the prize . . ."

Julie laughed. "If that were all," she said enigmatically.

"Is there more?" Madeline asked.

"No, not really. I'm not sure what my philosophy is, except to take what you can get and be pleased with it."

"My very own sentiments," Madeline answered. "Well, kid, in two weeks you'll be Julie Randall. Just think of the publicity that will bring the show."

"Oh, yes." Julie agreed tranquilly, but privately she wondered what the effect would be on those friends back in Prescottville who had yet to learn of her new life. Thinking of Prescottville, she was suddenly reminded of it as it had been when she was happy there. A time like this. A full, lush summer, followed by that beautiful harvest when she had haunted the vineyards and plied Joe Damien with a hundred questions. That lovely year, whose loveliness had been torn away so abruptly with the news of Mark's marriage to Miranda. She experienced a swift throb of pain at the memory and her face clouded over.

"What is it?" Madeline asked. "You look as if you'd just had bad news."

"It's nothing," Julie said hastily. "I . . . I just thought of something I . . . er . . . had to do."

Well, I won't think of it again, she told herself. I've got what I want and I intend to keep it and not let anything or anyone from the old days spoil things for me now.

12

The long troop train wound through the Delaware Valley, slowing at each village and town through which it passed. Groups of people gathered to wave, to throw flowers, and to cheer.

At the beginning of the trip the doughboys had lined the windows, waving back and shouting in reply to the cheering. Now they had tired of the sport, and as the convoy neared its terminal it passed like a ghost train, leaving the cheering crowds without as dispirited as the troops within.

In one of the forward cars, Private Lindstrom, Company B, Third Battalion, Second Division, California, moved down the swaying aisle of the train, lost his balance momentarily, and fell sideways, jarring his company commander.

"Excuse me, Captain," he mumbled as he regained his footing.

"Easy, soldier," Mark Douglas replied.

Lindstrom went toward the latrine and Mark shook his head. "They're all so damned young," he said to his lieutenant, Dan Sebastian.

"Aren't we all?" Dan answered, his quiet face lighting in a broad grin. "In an army where thirty is a ripe old age, to make captain in one year you can't expect to find a lot of elderly privates. Whatever made you enlist before war was declared?"

"Oh, I don't know. Figured I might get a head start."

"I see. Hoped to make general and stay well behind the lines for the duration, right?"

"Colonel, anyway." Mark smiled absently. He thought of the events that had led up to his decision. The sudden reversal of his life two years ago had started it, he supposed. In a few short weeks he had lost both job and girl. It was still hard to believe that Julie would pick up and go off like that. From what he knew of her, she would have been more likely to stand her ground. But what had he really known, when all was said and done? There had been that overwhelming feeling between them, sweeping and primitive. No other woman had had that effect on him before or, for that matter, since. He hadn't brooded about it too long. He was too pragmatic for that. In the two weeks that had passed, there had been other women. The need for that was as much a fact of his life as the thunder and lightning of his few months with Julie. He accepted both and let neither interfere with the course of his life.

Losing out at Fontaine's had been different, that and the kind of vicious lies that Miranda had spread. He flexed his fingers unconsciously, remembering how close he had come to strangling her before she fled to her cousin's house upstate. Idly, he wondered if he ever would have done her real harm. At the time his rage had been nearly uncontrollable. Now when he thought of her or of the Prescotts, it was with a deep disgust.

In his early passion, he had tried to locate Julie—weeks in New York, checking hotels and walking the streets, trying to remember that old address of Sara Prescott's without success. He supposed Sara had finally succumbed to the effects of alcohol, which had become a way of life with her, from what John Fontaine had told him. It was a dim hope that Julie might have gone there. She had once told him she knew her father had sent money to Sara. She was clearly unaware of the rest of Sara's story. Just as well. Julie, with her outspokenness, might have let Holt know, and the already volatile situation in that household would have exploded.

Mark moved impatiently. No use going over a dead past. What had followed hadn't been all bad. At least the ranch was in decent shape. If Harper didn't let it run down again, Valerie would have a secure home.

Even the time he had spent at Bianco's Winery had been all to the good, however it ended up. He would have left eventually, anyway. As it was, the Bianco brothers, using his knowhow to build up the business for their sons, just precipitated his departure. No, he wasn't meant to work for someone else for any length of time. At Fontaine's he had been in control.

Join the army and see France, he smiled wryly to himself. Well, it was one way. If he lived through the war, he might even stay on in France. He wondered what the vineyards of Champagne were like now with the Germans holding the Marne and battles raging across the valleys and plains of the old province.

There would be a lot of rebuilding to do once this war was over—if this war ever ended, and if the Allies won. In spite of the patriotic fervor that swept the country and the high, optimistic belief that once the Yanks were there, the Germans would turn tail and run, his own hopes were not so sanguine.

Mark was too aware of the inexperience of all the troops, not to mention his own lack of it. Captain! He was about as ready to be a captain as young Lindstrom, who had fallen against him a few minutes ago. Two years at West Point before he resigned may have given him an edge over the young soldier as far as understanding logistics were concerned, but that was about all. His lieutenant, Dan Sebastian, was as good as they came, but he, too, lacked any real experience. Mark sighed. Here they were, Company B, and nothing between them and annihilation but the old sergeant, Jim Malone—a twenty-year man, reenlisted after ten years of ranching, but he had the experience of the Spanish American War behind him.

"You look like you expect to lose the war before we get there," Dan said.

"I'm getting back into familiar territory," Mark answered. "I was thinking about things I haven't thought of in quite a while."

"We're billeted into Fort Dix," Dan said. "Any idea how long we'll be there?"

"A few weeks, anyway. I understand the Seventh is shipping with us, and they're still down in Georgia. We're coming into Newark," he added. "Be off this prairie wagon pretty soon. Better have Malone alert the troops. I want them debarking in order. If the girls are out with flowers and doughnuts, there's to be no breaking ranks like they did in Chicago. I don't want to spend an hour looking for that kid Lindstrom again. Maybe he's not very bright, like Malone says, but I have an idea he's getting lost on purpose."

"Yes, sir, Captain, sir," Dan kidded.

"Easy, Lieutenant," Dan answered in the same voice he had used on Lindstrom.

He began to pull his own gear together. New York again for a few weeks. He wondered if Julie was still there or if she had gone back to Prescottville. It had been a long time since he'd heard from anyone in Prescottville. Valerie, who was the best in a barrel of bad correspondents, managed a letter every few months. Since he'd been in the army, she had the habit of baking him cookies and cakes and wrapping them in her haphazard fashion so that they generally arrived in pieces with the enclosed letters covered in crumbs and blurred by bits of icing. He hadn't the heart to tell her.

The train slowed and halted. He heard Malone give his orders. The company lined up and departed, Dan in the lead, Malone bringing up the rear. "They'll do," Mark said to himself. "Young, green, and only half trained. But they will do. Keep it up," he jeered at himself. "Next thing you know you'll be singing 'Over There' and promising the ladies to win a war for them."

"Lindstrom!" Malone barked. "Eyes front!" Moments later the cheering and squealing began.

The truck convoy to Fort Dix was slow, and by the time the men had been billeted and Mark reached his own quarters, the bright October day had faded into evening. His mail, forwarded after he left Kansas, waited for him along with one of Valerie's offerings. The wrappings were half torn and the fragile box was crushed. He looked through the letters first: one from his San Francisco bank; one from a girl in San Francisco he had only a hazy memory of. He opened Valerie's package, fishing through the thoroughly mixed crumbs of a chocolate layer cake and corn bread to extract her undecipherable note along with a letter she had forwarded from his cousin Art.

He opened Art's letter first, expecting the usual report on the Prescotts' ongoing attempts to sell the winery. He smiled at the opening: "Dear Soldier Laddie, the Prescotts are at it again." And then his smile faded. They had found Julie! Julie. "I wouldn't know all this," the letter went on, "but Miranda Latham had it in confidence from Jason, and Miranda can't keep a secret from Lillian, and Lillian can't keep one from me. Imagine, Little Julie Fontaine, an actress. She calls herself

Angela Grant. She's one of the Belmont girls. Of course, the Prescotts are keeping it a secret. An actress in Jason's sacred family almost drove the man to apoplexy. I hear it was Holt Prescott who found her. Holt got himself one of those easy commissions and will be stationed in Washington for the remainder of the war. You might like to know that Julie hasn't changed. She still won't sell Fontaine's. So for now everything is as it was. Joe Damien is still running the operation as if there wasn't a wartime prohibition, and Avery Bertram scuttles around after the Prescotts like the meek mouse he is."

Mark put the letter down. Julie. She was alive and in New York and . . . He looked at the date on the letter, July 31, and swore softly. Nearly three months since the letter had been written. Valerie, with her squirrel instincts, hiding his mail to send in her package—that is, if she didn't forget where she had the mail. He must write to Grace about Valerie, he thought irrationally, and then it struck him again. Julie. She was only a few miles away from him. He read the letter again, carefully this time. No mention of why she had fled Prescottville or of any marriage.

He looked at his watch. Nearly nine. If he hurried, he could be in the city before the show ended. And if she wasn't still with the show, someone would be able to tell him where she lived.

Less than half an hour later, shaved and bathed and in fresh uniform, he was on his way into Manhattan.

Fred, at the stage entrance, eyed Mark's captain's bars with as much disfavor as he viewed the stripe of a private first class.

"Nobody goes up without Miss Grant saying so," Fred said. "If I let everybody up who says they know her, the place would be jammed every night." His lined face was impassive. "Send up a note or go away, sonny."

Mark looked past him, a smile lighting his face. "Never mind. There she is now," he said, and as Fred turned, Mark went past him, taking the stairs two at a time.

Below, Fred called out, "Here, fella, you get back here or I'll call the police!"

On the second landing Mark poked his head around a partially opened door and was greeted with squeals of dismay as girls in various stages of undress grabbed for covering.

"Sorry, ladies," he said. "I'm looking for Angela Grant."

"End of the hall," someone answered.

Someone else said, "For pity's sake, close that door."

He went along the corridor until he found the small sign saying MISS ANGELA GRANT.

He tapped on the door and turned the knob at the same time. The door opened and he saw her at once. She was standing in the circle of a soldier's arms and had just turned her head at the sound of his entrance.

For a moment the tableau froze and the picture was burned into his mind—the man's possessive hold on her, her face pale with shock.

"Mark!" she said faintly. "It's Mark."

"Ah, it's Mark," the soldier said, "whomever Mark may be. I say, don't you believe in knocking?"

"Everything all right in here?" Fred was at the door.

"Fine," Julie answered, disengaging herself from Steven's arms. Fred nodded and shut the door.

"This is Mark Douglas . . . a . . . an old friend," she said steadily enough, but Mark saw her lips shake. "Mark, this is my fiancé, Captain Steven Randall."

"Fiancé?" he repeated stupidly.

"Yes, that's right. We're going to be married in a few days."

"Congratulations," Mark answered, his throat dry. "I heard from Art that you were in New York and in the theater. Quite a surprise."

"And how is Miranda?" Julie asked.

"Miranda? Why, I . . ." He stopped. He was damned if he was going to stand in front of this Captain Randall and explain the hoax of Miranda.

"I have no idea how Miranda is or where she is," he replied. "Julie, I'd like to talk to you."

"There is nothing I care to discuss, past or present," Julie answered. She was in control again. He could see it in the way her eyes darkened. As she spoke, she reached for Randall's hand.

"Steven and I were just on our way to supper," she said. "I'd ask you to join us, but I promised Steven we'd have this evening alone."

"I want to talk to you," Mark repeated in a very quiet voice. "I'm sure you can spare a minute or two."

"You heard Miss Grant," Randall spoke up, "Now, be a good chap and run along."

"I'll run along when and if I please," Mark said. "Julie, there is something that needs clearing up."

"If it's about Fontaine's," Julie said, "my vote stands . . . as far as you're concerned. And I won't agree to sell. It surprises me that you'd expect me to change my mind."

"I didn't ask you to change your mind," Mark said. "I asked you to talk to me for a few minutes to clear up . . ."

"And I told you I haven't the time right now. If you'll drop me a note, I'll try to arrange something later, next week, perhaps." She had moved away from Randall and was drawing on her gloves, smoothing each finger carefully, her pose as arrogant as the tone of her voice.

"Now, see here," Mark said, his temper beginning to flare, "don't put me off with that cool little performance. I'm not some stage-door Johnny hanging around for a smile." He whirled on Randall. "If you'd be good enough to leave us alone for a few minutes . . ." he began.

Randall interrupted. "Will *you* be good enough to leave *us* alone?" he answered pointedly. "Miss Grant has asked you to excuse her. I ask you to excuse us." He moved forward confidently and caught Mark's arm, as if to urge him from the room.

"Take your hands off me," Mark said evenly. But Steven ignored him. As he reached out to open the door and propel Mark through it, Mark's right arm shot out and he caught Steven neatly at the point of his jaw.

Steven had not seen the punch coming and he was unconscious almost as soon as it made contact, sliding slowly into a half-sitting position against the wall.

Julie gave a little scream and then said furiously, "Look what you've done. Who do you think you are, coming in here like this after two years and ordering us around? You got what you wanted. You got Miranda . . ."

"Miranda is not . . ."

"I don't care about Miranda," she raged on. "I suppose you got bored with her, too. Well, you needn't think you can come back and ruin my life again. I'm going to marry Steven Randall." Saying it, she suddenly realized that Steven was hurt and started to go to him.

Mark seized her as she passed him and said, "Shut up, Julie, and listen. I'm not married to Miranda. I never was."

"Oh, no? Well, what were you doing with her at the hotel? Why was she in your room?"

He stopped a minute, shaking his head in bewilderment. "What are you talking about? If you'd only listen to me!"

"I won't. I won't. You left me. I begged you not to, but you left, anyway. Of course you couldn't take me with you. That would have interfered with your plans for Miranda. You . . . you're what everyone said. Well, I'm glad you're out of Fontaine's, and as far as I'm concerned, you'll stay out. And I don't care whom you're married to." She glared at him, her eyes stormy. "You used me. All you ever wanted was the winery."

In one swift movement he grasped her with hard hands and pressed his mouth against hers brutally. She struggled with him, trying ineffectively to turn away, and finally, beyond the rage and the humiliation long remembered, she heard the old thumping in her ears, felt herself go limp, and in spite of everything, she was kissing him back.

A sound from Steven brought her to her senses and she wrenched her mouth away, saying, "Stop it! Stop it!"

Mark released her then, stepping back with a small, knowing smile. "As you wish," he said. "I'll be seeing you, Julie . . . sooner than you think."

He looked down at the slowly recovering Randall and said, with supreme irony, "Forgive the intrusion, Captain. I leave you to your fiancée."

There was a dreadful silence when the door had closed behind Mark. Steven pulled himself to his feet, nursing his jaw gingerly and throwing off Julie's belated effort to help him.

"Very pretty," he said coldly. "Quite something to be knocked out and come to, only to find your wife-to-be in a passionate embrace with a . . . what did you call him? . . . 'an old friend.' "

"He means nothing to me," Julie said.

"Oh, I would like to believe that. You see, I knew I wasn't the first man in your life. I was willing to overlook that. Still, I hardly expected that I would become just *one* of the men in your life."

"You aren't just one of the men in my life," Julie said, "and as for 'willing to overlook it,' just whom do you think you are? You've been chasing me since we met. Am I to assume that I'm the only woman in your life?"

"Of course not," he said distantly. "That's quite a bit different."

"Different be damned!" she cried out. "If you don't like it, you can have your ring and give it to some pure and worthy girl. Try a convent school." She was stripping the left glove from her hand and pulling at the sapphire on her finger as she spoke. As he made a move to stop her, the door opened and Madeline and Lew Belmont stood there with Fred behind them.

"What's happening here?" Lew Belmont demanded. "Fred tells me some soldier came up here and when he followed you, you told him it was all right. The next thing we hear is that there's a fight going . . ." He broke off, staring at Randall. "So there was a fight, I see. Just what is going on?"

"Nothing," Steven said. "The man was abusive and I tried to eject him. Julie's annoyed with me for creating a fuss."

"That was some fuss," Madeline said practically. She looked at Julie. "Who was that red-haired fury of a giant who tore past my room, Julie?"

"Mark Douglas," Steven volunteered before Julie could speak, and Madeline's eyes widened, although she said nothing.

"You better come along to my office and take care of that jaw," Lew Belmont said quickly. "We'll meet you there when you've gotten settled," he said to Madeline.

"So he's back again," Madeline said when the men had gone. "How much does Steven know about him?"

"Nothing," Julie said. "Nothing at all."

"Well, don't tell him, then. You . . . what are you doing with your engagement ring in your hand?"

"I was giving it back," Julie said numbly.

"Don't be a fool. Mark Douglases come and go in a girl's life. Steven Randalls are forever."

"I know," Julie whispered, turning away to hide the tears that were forming under her lids.

"Don't ruin your life," Madeline said. "Oh, I admit he's some man, from what I saw. But he's married . . ."

"He says he isn't," Julie told her.

"Well, what was he doing with the other woman? No, don't tell me. It was all a joke?"

"I don't know," Julie answered. "And I don't care," she said suddenly. "And I don't care about Steven Randall, either. I don't have to get married to anyone. Talking to me as if . . ."

"Steven?" Madeline asked.

"Yes. Mark knocked him out and then . . . well . . . he was . . ."

"Don't tell me," Madeline interjected. "Steven came to and found you in the old beau's arms. Am I right?"

Julie nodded.

"Very unwise," Madeline said dryly.

"Look, Madeline, if you don't mind, I don't want to talk about it anymore." Julie slipped the ring into her bag and reached for her wrap. "I'm going straight home," she said. "Will you tell Steven I'm too tired to see him tonight?"

"I think you're making a mistake," Madeline said.

"I make a lot of them," Julie answered. "But I need to be alone and I need to think. Thanks for everything, Madeline. You really are the best friend I ever had. And I won't do anything rash." She managed a smile. "I promise that, all right?"

Julie managed to slip away from the theater without encountering Steven again. Yet when she got home, lying in her own bed, she began to regret her decision.

Mark. Her feelings about him were terribly mixed now. For too long had she borne the ache of losing him and for too long had she struggled to put him out of her mind and heart. That he should come back now just as she had settled her life—it wasn't fair.

The memory of his kisses burned on her mouth, and no matter how she tried to erase them, they clung, blurring all else so that even those nights with Steven were fading as the old memories of Mark poured into her brain to torment her once more.

It was a long while before she slept, but she arose in the morning resolved to heal the breach with Steven and leave Mark in the dead past. Not married to Miranda, but keeping her in his suite at the Fairmont, registering as Mr. and Mrs. Mark Douglas. No, if he could do that, he was capable of coming back only to leave her again. "I won't go through it twice," she said aloud.

Steven rang shortly before one o'clock, and from his tone Julie knew that, while last night still rankled, he was not going to let it change his plans. We've come to the same conclusion, she thought, relieved and yet depressed.

Still, she refused his invitation to luncheon, pleading a headache.

"Douglas hasn't been around, has he?" Steven asked.

"No, and he won't be," Julie answered steadily. Mark wouldn't plead or beg or importune, and he wouldn't apologize, either. She knew him too well for that. He would walk away first.

Steven ended the conversation on a conciliatory note, saying he would call for her and take her to the theater.

The days went on as they had before Mark had come back and Steven spent every waking hour with Julie, as if fearful she would escape before the marriage took place. Mark's reappearance began to take on the quality of a dream.

Still, she was refusing Steven's demands now, finally saying, "After the wedding, Steven. There's been too much said. I don't like to be treated as if I . . . well . . . after the wedding."

"Aren't you going to forget all that? I don't care if there have been other men in the past. I only care about the future."

"The future is five days away," she told him, Saturday, after the show, and a trip to Gretna Green. And then that would be the end of worrying about anyone from the past who might come back into her life. It was Steven who had saved her from Holt and thus stopped Jason from attempting to coerce her into returning home. Steven, not Mark. The night that Holt had attacked her, Mark had been with Miranda Latham. No, Steven was the one for her. And if she wasn't desperately excited over the marriage, once it took place everything would be all right.

On Friday evening after the show, Madeline threw a spinster's party for Julie at her home, inviting all the girls from the show. Lew had hosted a bachelor dinner for Steven that evening, and as the party was breaking up at Madeline's, Steven called, his voice blurry from drinking, but his spirits high.

"I'll come around and fetch you." he said.

"You can't," she told him. "It's bad luck for the groom to see the bride on her wedding day. You must stay away until we leave for Maryland. Steven, it's nearly three A.M."

"I'm afraid to let you out of my sight," he admitted.

She laughed. "I'm fine. Madeline's sending me home in her motorcar. I'll see you later."

The chauffeur waited while Julie fished for her key. As she entered the darkened apartment, she heard the motorcar drive off. She switched on the living room lights, unaccountably lonely in the aftermath of the party's gaiety. Her ears still rang with the sounds of revelry, and the silence of the empty apartment was unnatural by contrast.

Now she would love to have someone to talk to and wished she had not given Elsie the two weeks' vacation so that she and Steven would be alone the first weeks together. The apartment felt cold and she went into the living room to light the fire, fanning it until flames caught. When she had changed into her nightclothes, she went back to the living room to put a guard in front of the fire and turn off the lights. The doorbell rang just as she was settling into bed.

"Steven?" she said aloud. He was impossible! She really ought not to answer him. The bell pealed again and, resigned, she pulled on her robe and went to the door.

"You'll be sorry," she said as she slipped the bolt. "It's bad luck to . . . oh!" Her hand flew to her mouth. "Mark!" she exclaimed. "You . . . what are you doing here?"

He pushed her back into the apartment and closed the door. Then, taking her arm, he led her through the arch of the living room.

"I told you that I wanted to talk to you," he said. "I've been waiting for the opportunity. I don't intend to be shoved out of a room again." His face was stiff, his eyes smoldering.

"Mark," she began, "I don't want . . ."

"I don't care what you want," he answered roughly. "I found out from your maid that you were getting married later today, and I also found out about your 'spinster's' party. Very chatty, your maid. I decided the best thing was to wait and catch you alone."

"Do you mean you've been watching my apartment all night?" she asked.

"Hardly. It was easy enough to give you an hour or two at the party and then come around. It must have been quite a party," he added. "I was here earlier, but you hadn't come in. I've been waiting an hour."

"Just standing in the street?"

"I told you I wanted to talk to you, and I don't like being dismissed. Now, shall we talk?"

"Mark," she said, beginning to feel frightened, "I . . . there's nothing to talk about. It was all so long ago. I've decided to marry Steven, and that's that. I love him." Her eyes fell before his penetrating stare.

"Love him?" he repeated.

"Yes," she said defiantly, "love him. And he loves me. He stands by me. He doesn't run off and sleep with other women and . . ."

He had put rough arms around her as she spoke, and his mouth found hers, cutting off the flow of words. She made one brief effort to stop him and then it was too late. It was always too late, she thought. Suddenly it didn't matter what Mark was, what he had done or not done. And Steven . . . his face rose hazily in her mind and as quickly faded away.

She felt her lips trembling beneath Mark's kisses, felt a weakness spread through her body, and then a surge of wildness so that even the harshness of his caresses fired her to the core.

A madness seized her and her responses became as fierce as his. She bit his lip and tasted the salt of his blood in her mouth. He wrapped one hand in her hair, pulling her back with it until she cried out. His mouth covered hers again as he tore at her gown. She heard the silk rip. He began to press her flesh slowly, voluptuously. She broke away, standing naked and panting in the center of the room. His face in the firelight was pagan-like. Swiftly he removed his clothing while she stood there. His eyes never left hers, and then when he would have caught her to him once more, she evaded him, slipping through his hands, twisting and turning as he sought to hold her, until at last he had her, forcing her to her knees and down, down, while the leaping flames cast a reddish glow over them.

He took her hard and she cried out again, twisting beneath him, until he laid the full weight of his body on hers, mastering her so completely that her arms were up and around his neck once more, her lips eager beneath his own, her body loving him as if it had a will beyond her control. It was all beyond her control. The climax was as sharply fierce as their lovemaking had been, and a wild, primitive scream escaped from her.

There was no wish in her to end it, and even as Mark left her, she went back to him, burrowing against him, wanting him still. It was a long time before her trembling ceased. The arms that held her were shaking, and Mark's breath was hoarsely uneven.

"You're mine," he said as he had said it on their first night together.

Now, as then, she whispered, "Yes."

After a while the fire began to die in the grate and he rose, pulling her up beside him, saying, "We'll go to bed now."

Beneath the blankets, close together, they slept for a time, and when next he made love to her it was the love that she remembered, that love that left her always with a heart that felt too full of him, a heart made vulnerable and open, a heart spreading wide enough to encompass the universe.

There had been no need for words. Between the night and the day, Julie knew that whatever happened, there could never be anyone else. If he left or if he stayed, no matter how she tried, he would always be first. There was no question at all of going through with the marriage to Steven, and when at last she and Mark began to talk together, she told him so.

"I would have stayed with you, anyway," she confessed in her newly awakened vulnerability, "even if it hadn't all been a lie, even if you had had Miranda with you in San Francisco."

"Don't say things like that," he said in a constricted voice.

"Why?" she asked.

"I . . . nothing. It undoes me because I love you so much. I never wanted to," he said. "I never wanted to be caught."

She laid a hand on his. "I know. I like to be caught, though."

"You would," he said.

"About Steven . . ." she began.

"I don't want to hear about Steven—or anyone else," he answered brusquely. "Don't confess to me. Let it go. It's over. The past is over."

"When must you go back to camp?"

"This evening. But I have three day' leave next week. We'll have to make some plans. I can't leave you again unless I know you're legally mine, all tied up with a ribbon." He laughed. "Imagine that—me running to the altar."

"I can't really imagine it," Julie said fearfully. "What if . . ."

"Nothing will happen. Look, you'll have to tell Randall today, of course. Shall I meet him with you?"

"No. I owe Steven that much—to see him alone and try to explain. It would be terrible for him to hear it with you there. He's . . . Steven is a gentleman. There isn't anything to worry about."

"If you're sure."

"I'm sure," she told him steadily.

She was not so sure after Mark left to go back to camp as she phoned Steven's apartment. His voice was jubilant over the wire, and even more jubilant when she asked to see him at the theater before the show.

"But I thought you said it was unlucky for a groom to see a bride . . ."

"That was last night," she cut across his words. "This is today. I'll meet you there at seven. Is that all right?"

"Nothing's wrong, is it?" He sounded anxious and her heart sank. She couldn't tell him over the phone.

"I must see you, that's all," she temporized. "And I've got to hang up now, Steven, or I'll be late."

She had imagined the scene would be painful, but she had not imagined the aftermath. In the end, Steven took it well enough. "I think I knew it that night when I saw you kissing him," he said with some bitterness. "It was a way you had never kissed me, not even in the few nights you permitted us to spend together."

She winced at that, and he said lightly, "Well, you must allow me some bad feeling. I'm not the perfect sport, you know. As a matter of fact, I hate losing. Did I ever tell you that? One doesn't show it, of course, but only a fool really believes it's how you play the game. Frankly, if I thought I had any chance at all, I'd do just about anything to keep you. But," he said as he picked up his cap, "I wouldn't care to have a wife who would rather have someone else. Good-bye, Julie. Good luck."

Steven's acceptance of the situation had not erased Julie's remorse for having hurt him, but as she readied herself for the performance, the glow of knowing that she and Mark were together again enveloped her and nothing else really mattered, after all.

She was sitting in front of the makeup mirror, staring into space, waiting for the knock that would announce the first call, when Madeline and Lew came in. One look at their faces told her that Steven had already apprised them of the facts.

"You must be insane," Madeline began without hesitation. "And not only have you given Steven up for that disappearing lover of yours, but Steven has left."

"Please, Madeline." Lew raised a hand. "Look, Julie, as far as I'm concerned, your life is your own. But Madeline thinks you're throwing away a big chance. I am not so sure. Randall was in to see me right after you canceled the wedding. He's withdrawing from our partnership. Frankly, it doesn't come at the best time but," he paused and shrugged, "if our partnership depended on which girl would marry him, it wasn't much of a partnership."

"Now, see here," Madeline interrupted. "It was a darned good partnership—for years. Julie, if you weren't going to marry him, you shouldn't have let it go so far. After all, Steven's taken other girls out. He hasn't won them all. But you, you simply made a fool of him. No man can stand that."

"I didn't mean to make a fool of Steven," Julie said. "It . . . it was just something . . . oh, I can't explain it. Mark . . . Mark is the man I love. That's all. It wasn't true . . ."

She broke off as Bert knocked and called out, "Five minutes, Miss Grant."

"I can't tell you now," she resumed. "But I can explain. Wait until you know Mark. You'll see why I . . . or maybe you won't. But don't jump to conclusions," Julie pleaded.

"The trouble with you is that you're spoiled, Julie," Madeline said. "As for your friend, I don't care about meeting him." She swept out of the dressing room.

Lew said, "Don't let it worry you, Julie. She's disappointed. She's upset because Steven quit on us. But, mark my words, she'll be fine. As for meeting this man, you know Madeline—curiosity alone will kill her if she doesn't meet him. You'll bring him around one evening. We'll have supper together, and once Madeline gets used to the idea, she'll think she planned it herself." He patted her. "He's a lucky man," he added.

In spite of Madeline's coolness, nothing dimmed Julie's happiness or stilled her desire to have Mark back with her once more.

She didn't want to share him with anyone and was, for a time, just as glad that Madeline had no wish to meet him. However, when Mark called for her the following Saturday, Madeline had already issued an invitation. "We may as well get a good look at this paragon of yours," she said.

The supper went off smoothly. Mark was at his best—attentive and interested in what Lew had to say, and charming to Madeline, who was plainly fascinated. In the powder room, Madeline said bluntly, "I really envy you this time, Julie. He may not have the money Steven has, but he's certainly got everything else and more. If we weren't friends, I don't know that I wouldn't try to catch him myself."

"But there's Lew," Julie reminded her.

"Of course there's Lew, and I love him for everything he's done. But romance—that's different. Even wise women like me can't help wishing for a little romance. And no matter how I tell myself I've got everything I want, I'll tell you the truth, Julie. I'd like to be married."

"Maybe one day . . ."

"No." Madeline closed her compact with a little snap. "No, I don't mind a wish now and again, but I'm not such a fool as to believe it will come true. There. I've been silly enough as it is. All this romantic drama you've been playing in real life went to my head."

"How did you like them?" Julie asked Mark when they were alone.

"Fine. He's the kind of man I can talk to, and she's quite the glamorous lady. Shrewd, though. Very definitely shrewd."

"They've both been very good to me," Julie said. "I

often wonder what I would have done, where I'd be . . . Oh, Mark, you might never have found me."

"That's enough of that," he said firmly. "Have you any more social engagements for us?"

"No. I want you all to myself," she said.

"I'm yours for three days," he answered. "Well, until Monday, to be exact. Julie, we have to talk about us."

"Not now," she said. "We can be serious later. Plan a future. Decide when to get married. We can do all that later."

That night, waking in the dark, frosty chill, she murmured, "Don't ever leave me again, Mark."

He said against her lips, "No, never," stilling the impulse to bring the truth before her. Soon he would be leaving her, for all he knew, forever. He had assessed the situation coldly and unemotionally during the few days they were apart, but here, with Julie soft and warm and yielding in his arms, it was nearly impossible to imagine leaving her.

The next day he told her the truth and suggested that they plan to marry before that happened. "I don't want you alone and unprotected again," he said, frowning.

She told him about Eileen then, and when she finished he said, "It isn't going to happen to you, baby. We'll get a license before I go back to Dix. It's a three-day wait, but I'll get leave."

He did not tell her that all leaves had been canceled and that one more day would be all he could manage. Thursday or Friday. There was no need to worry her before it was necessary.

"It's a funny thing," Julie told him while they waited to fill out the license on Monday morning, "but I never get tired of you. I wish we were alone this minute."

He gave a mock groan. "Incorrigible," he murmured. "What on earth will you do when I'm . . ." He stopped himself.

"When you're overseas?" she finished calmly. "I've been thinking about that. Mark, why can't you do what Steven Randall did? Get attached to the staff of some nice general, one that has to stay here and do things."

"Ride out the war safely, do you mean?"

She nodded.

"Julie, you don't know me at all."

She said nothing, her eyes falling beneath his fierce look. But back at the apartment she took it up again.

"No," he said. "Don't make it more difficult for me, Julie. It's not that I'm some half-assed hero who imagines war is all glory. I know better. But this is my company. I've watched those boys train. I know how much more training they need. Most of them are barely old enough to shave. They . . . well, if they have any chance at all, it's going to be with a solid company, the officers they began with and good old Sergeant Malone. I knew what I was getting into when I enlisted."

"But it was different then," she protested. "Everything was different. Would . . . would you have enlisted if . . . if things hadn't gone wrong? Would you if we'd been married and I was . . ."

"Those are all 'what ifs,' Julie. The fact is, I did enlist. I'm not a hero. But, then, I'm not a coward. I won't run because life is suddenly precious to me again. It's precious to that ragtail, bobtail company I've been nursing along. God knows, it's precious to Malone. He left a family back there in Richmond. Dan Sebastian's got a fiancée waiting, and Dan's only twenty-four himself. We can't all sit safely at desk jobs. Who the hell would go to France?"

"I could understand it if you were . . . oh . . . like one soldier I met. He was so full of the idea of fighting the Germans, and he was glad to have a war to be a hero in."

"He was an ass," Mark said succinctly.

"It isn't as if you were patriotic."

"What makes you think I'm unpatriotic? The fact that I don't swallow all the stuff about this war ending any chance of another? Whichever side wins, Allies or Central Powers, they'll be back at it, given a generation or two. Julie, do you know how many wars we've been involved with in the last sixty-odd years? Mexican, Civil, Spanish-American, and this one. I'm not even counting the Mexican border skirmishes or the Indian wars. And that's only America."

"I can't think of life without you again," she said, "and when I think that you might . . . It was different before. I knew you were alive. Even when I thought you were married to Miranda, even though I hurt, still it wasn't the end. Oh, Mark, when you left the first time, I knew something would happen, and this time . . ."

He laid gentle fingers over her mouth. "Hush," he said. "Don't bury me before I have a chance to shoot my rifle. I'm not going to die in France. If you go on like this, you'll tear us both up. I could be killed on a New York street tomorrow. Once you start thinking that way, danger and death are always just around the corner. Believe in me. Believe I'll come back to you."

She swallowed back her desire to cry and managed to say in only a slightly tremulous voice, "I will. I do, Mark."

"That's my girl." He smiled and held her close, burying his face in her hair, saying, "I love you, Julie Fontaine. God, how I love you!"

She did not mention her fears again, but in those last hours together, even as they were making love, she could not rid herself of the feeling that this time, too, some terrible fate would intervene to deprive them of their happiness. She felt unaccountably that this might be the last time she brought all of her heart and soul into their exchange of love. It seemed to her that Mark felt something of the same thing, and in their passion he sought to lay his own fears to rest.

"Thursday," he said when he dropped her off at the theater. "See if you can't get that one day off. I don't fancy waiting around the stage door on my wedding night, although," he added in a whisper, "we can't complain about the honeymoon we had before the ceremony, can we?"

She smiled up at him blindly, not letting him see the sense of loss she felt at this particular parting. "Thursday," she whispered back. "I love you, Mark. I'll always love you."

Julie busied herself over the next few days, trying to push back the idea that somehow something would keep them apart. It was silly, anyway, she told herself. For all she knew, his old regiment might be around New York all winter, or the war might end tomorrow. It was better to believe that than to dwell on fancied doom.

Wednesday she went shopping with Madeline for the brief ceremony at City Hall. "Just you and Lew and Dan Sebastian, Mark's friend. That's all. I don't care about

anything now except marrying that man before . . .
well, never mind," she told Madeline.

"This must be true love," Madeline teased. "I can
see now that it would have been a mistake to marry
Steven, although I was pretty annoyed with you about
that, and with Lew. I am annoyed with Lew right now.
He's so smug about it all. 'I told you so,' he keeps saying."

"Madeline, help me pick a really beautiful dress."

"And a beautiful negligée and nightgown. That's even
more important, wouldn't you say?"

"Yes, of course," Julie replied demurely. Maybe ten
years from now, she thought to herself, but not now.
Mark didn't need to see her in fetching nightclothes. She
thought suddenly of the first night they had been together, when she had come to him out of the rain, her
riding clothes soaked, her hair flying every way, and
the physical memory was so acute that she felt weak with
desire, in the middle of Fifth Avenue, too. She thought
to herself, I wonder if it will always be this way.

They shopped until the stores closed and then stopped
at the St. Regis for something to eat before going back
to her apartment.

"I'll make you a bet," Madeline said. "I'll bet you this
is your last Belmont show. I can see you settled down
somewhere in one of those little white cottages for two
with roses and children climbing all over the place."

"Don't say that," Julie said sharply.

"Why? What on earth is the matter?"

"Nothing," Julie mumbled. "It's just me. I've got a bad
case of nerves. I'm so afraid something will go wrong,
that . . . oh, never mind me. Lord," she said, "look at
the time. We'd better hurry."

Lew Belmont was waiting for them in front of the
building, and the moment Julie saw him her heart leaped
in her chest like a frightened rabbit. She threw up one
hand in protest, as if to ward off whatever was coming.

"He was looking for you," Lew said. "Mark. He had
only a few minutes. Look, his ship is at Pier Fifty-four.
If you hurry, you can get there. I got a friend of mine,
a police captain, to give you an escort."

"No," she insisted. "He can't be going now."

"You want to see him, Julie? If you do, come now."

Dazed, she let herself be led to the waiting motorcar.

It's come true, she kept thinking. "That which I greatly feared has come to pass," Julie said aloud, quoting a line from the Bible. She believed in the worst, and the worst had happened. Oh, God, she prayed, if you let him come back alive, I'll never believe anything bad is going to happen again. The police sirens screamed into the traffic and Lew's car sped in their wake. Julie saw horses shy at their approach, and startled wagon and private coach drivers struggled to pull their animals to the curb.

Lew and the captain helped her through the crowds massed at the dock. Bands were playing and soldiers lined the rail and waved. Everywhere faces were upturned in good-byes, some the mindless, silly faces of girls who loved the uniform but not the man inside, and some faces bore the tear-wet smiles of wives and sweethearts and mothers.

Mark stood at the gangway and, seeing him, Julie rushed forward, stumbling in her blind haste. He caught her in one mighty hug of farewell, pressing a kiss on her mouth, smoothing her hair.

"I'll be back, darling. Believe that. We didn't find each other again only to lose each other. Believe in me, Julie." His voice was low and urgent.

"I do," she whispered, her throat aching. "I'll always believe. I will. Oh, Mark, I love you."

"Love you, too," he whispered. The ship's whistle sounded its lonely, long farewell and he tore himself from her, running up the gangway as a mighty cheer went up.

She followed along as he turned onto the deck. Then for several minutes she lost sight of him before he reappeared, standing at the rail, his eyes on hers, face sober.

The ship's whistle sounded again and there was another cheer as the gangway was removed and Mark stood, holding her with his eyes. The bands played louder and louder, the cheers came faster and faster, and suddenly the ship was sliding away from the pier, moving out into the harbor, nudged by its fat tugboats. Still Julie waited, her eyes on Mark until she could no longer see him. Lew Belmont's arm came around her shoulders.

"Now, Julie, it's time to come away. I'll take you home," he said in a kinder voice than she had ever heard him use.

She shook her head. "No," she said steadily. "I want to work, Lew. I can make it."

"Good girl." He patted her shoulder. "But I'll tell you, it's going to be a real disappointment to your understudy."

"Mark will be back," she said. "He will, won't he?"

"Of course he will," he answered heartily.

I hurt all over now, she thought. Before, when he was gone before, I didn't feel anything, except misery, in my heart. Now, it's as if everything in my body pains, as if I had just taken a terrible fall.

"Talk to me," she said to Lew abruptly. "Tell me something, anything. Tell me how you began in show business."

"Julie, you know that story by heart."

"Tell me, anyway," she insisted. "Tell me something with a happy ending. It helps to hear stories with happy endings." She did not realize that tears were raining silently down her cheeks until Lew handed her his handkerchief, talking to her quietly while she mopped her face.

13

Mark left on a Wednesday, and within the first two weeks Julie threw herself into activity the way she had right after Eileen's death. Action, any kind of action, was her panacea, and she used it instinctively to calm her fears, to cure a heartache, to erase from her mind that which she could not bear to face.

She redoubled her volunteer efforts, appearing willingly at any rally. Finally she joined the Red Cross volunteers, where she learned to roll bandages, serve doughnuts and coffee to incoming troop trains, and where she began a course in first aid.

Her activities and her popularity in "Star-Spangled Beauties" led to an increase in publicity. At the end of the month her photograph was appearing regularly in the rotogravure sections of the papers, and one enterprising reporter, learning her true identity and background, did a story on "Heiress of Wine Company, One of the Belmont Girls."

The piece brought another cool note from Jason, mentioning that her notoriety was especially upsetting to Millicent. She did not bother to reply.

That was that, she thought, amused—years of hiding and changing her name, only to have it emblazoned across a newspaper. If she had used her own name to begin with, Mark . . . no, she wouldn't go back to regrets, those futile "what ifs," as Mark had called them. It was hard enough to live with the fact that he was somewhere in Europe now. There had been no news of sinkings or of ships lost in convoy. He wasn't in any real danger yet, she tried to tell herself. The regiment was still training in France. There were to be two months of that, anyway. Next month she would begin to worry, next month, when the green troops joined the decimated ranks of the British and French veterans of the past three years' fighting in Flanders.

He would be safe, he would come back, the war would soon be over. She recited it to herself nightly like a litany, intermingled with fearful exhortations to the Lord not to let her disbelieve and not to let anything happen to Mark. The idea that other women all over the world were believing, praying, doing everything to hold back the fear of losing men they loved was never far from her mind. God didn't save them all. Men were dying daily. Some prayers went unanswered. Thinking that, she would fall to praying feverishly again.

On a Sunday afternoon, two weeks after the new article had appeared, Julie received a visitor. She had risen late and was alone in the apartment when the bell rang. Expecting Madeline, she went to answer it and opened the door on a small, slight woman with hennaed hair framing a white, lined face. She was cheaply dressed and reeked of a strong perfume that barely covered the stale whiskey smell of a confirmed drinker.

"I'm Sara Prescott," the woman said. "May I come in?"

"Sara," Julie said. "I . . . we . . . thought . . ."

"That I was dead. Yes. Once your father was gone,

there was no one left to write to. May I come in?" she asked again.

"Yes, yes, of course." Julie opened the door and ushered her in. Sara looked like one of the women that walked the streets near amusement centers, and there was nothing but that low, cultivated voice to distinguish her from them.

"Can I get you some coffee? Sandwiches?" Julie asked, feeling hopelessly inadequate.

"I'd rather have wine or . . . I don't suppose you have anything else in the house?"

Julie nodded her head. "Some brandy," she said, remembering the bottle that Lew had sent over to celebrate the wedding. "Some brandy," she said again. "Or I also have wine."

"Yes, thank you. I'd rather have the brandy, but it doesn't matter," Sara said. "You must see that it doesn't matter."

When she had poured out the first glass, Julie said, "I never thought I'd meet you." She watched Sara pick up the snifter with shaking hands, spilling a few drops as she brought it to her heavily rouged lips.

"No, no, I can see that," Sara said. "I came because . . . because . . ."

"Yes," Julie prodded.

"This wartime prohibition law," Sara said, "makes it so much harder." Her glass was empty and Julie refilled it.

"Do you know why I left Jason Prescott?" Sara asked abruptly.

"Mark told me. I forgot; you don't know Mark. It doesn't matter. My father confided in him a great deal. Anyway, I know Holt is really Millicent's son."

"Yes. Poor little . . ." She stopped. "I adopted him—Jason and I. It was all managed so cleverly. We were taking a honeymoon trip to France. Millicent was going to visit an old school friend in Virginia, only, of course, Millicent joined us in France. The honeymoon extended for a year." Sara laughed, a low, ugly sound, and held out her glass again. "I was the envy of all my friends. When we got back we had Holt—with the proper birth certificate and the registration of birth at the American embassy. You see, Millicent went into the hospital as Mrs.

Jason Prescott. So there was never any chance that anyone would find out."

"Why are you telling me this story?" Julie asked.

"I . . . I have to tell you this story. Jason . . . Jason was not a real husband to me. He hardly touched me, not even in the beginning; later, not at all. I wanted a child of my own." Her mouth trembled and tears filled her dark eyes.

Julie thought of Jason and Millicent together as she had seen them last and wondered if it had always been so. Unbidden, the thought occurred that . . . it couldn't be. "Who is Holt's real father?" she heard herself ask, her mouth dry.

Sara looked away. "Holt was everything to Millicent. I think it used to drive her crazy to hear him call me 'Mother.' She spoiled him, catered to him. He was a difficult baby, a more difficult child. Temper tantrums— I still remember the temper tantrums. But I was never allowed to discipline him. Millicent always had the last word, and Jason would say, 'He's her boy, after all.' I should have known. It couldn't have worked, not with Millicent in the house. But when Jason asked me to marry him . . . I thought I was in love. You know how it is when you're young?" She looked at Julie, who nodded in pity.

"I was nineteen. Jason was twelve years older, a confirmed bachelor, everyone said. He was . . . he was handsome then. Not fat. He got very fat that first year we were married and then . . . I don't know . . . I don't know when I realized. I was so lonely. I was living in that house. I was the envy of many women—a rich and successful husband; a beautiful baby; plenty of clothes. Oh, Jason was never stingy about giving me things. That was his conscience money for what he did to me. And then"—her voice dropped and Julie had to strain to hear —"and then I found them, Millicent and Jason. You see, I had awakened and Jason wasn't in his room next to mine. I was nervous. I had terrible nerves those years. I went down to the dining room to take the brandy bottle. You see, brandy and wine, they helped me to sleep. They still help me," she said and reached for the bottle herself this time, pouring the liquor with steadier hands.

"Anyway, I came back upstairs. I was creeping for fear that someone would awake and find me. I heard them then. I heard them. I went to Millicent's door and I heard them. You know, you don't have to see. You can hear! I went mad then. I began to scream and beat on the door."

Julie stared at her, thinking, I will never be the same after this. I will never be the same. I wish she had never come. What I knew and what I saw was bad enough.

"I woke up the household," Sara went on. "Holt began to scream for Millicent. The servants were calling, hurrying from their rooms. Jason came out of Millicent's room in a fury. He hit me, knocked me nearly unconscious, and dragged me back to my room. He told everyone I was hysterical, said I hadn't been right since the boy was born. He sent them back to their rooms and Holt was quiet at last. Then he told me what he would do to me. He would have me committed. If I said anything he would have me committed, and all the time Millicent stood in the doorway, smiling—actually smiling. I thought I wouldn't be able to keep still. I thought I would lose my mind altogether. But I managed. I managed to keep quiet. I managed . . . dear God . . . I even managed to apologize." Telling the story, Sara's body had begun to shake, and Julie poured out a full glass of brandy, taking it to her, holding it between her lips until she had drunk a goodly quantity and her body began to grow slacker.

"You're like your father," Sara said, "very much like your father. He was good to me. I never told him about . . . about Jason and Millicent, only that Holt wasn't mine. I was afraid. I was afraid John would face Jason with it and somehow Jason would find me. I had some money. Your father . . . when I wrote to him . . . when the money was gone . . . he came to see me in New York. He tried to help me. I worked for a while then. He found me a position in a little French import shop, mending laces and embroidering. I was always very skillful at that sort of thing. It didn't last. I could never do without this." She lifted her glass and drained it.

"You ran away from them," Julie said. "I did, too. I knew about them, you see. I didn't know Holt was Millicent's son. Holt hates you for running away. Holt is . . . Holt is different, strange . . . it's more than his temper."

As if she hadn't heard Julie, Sara said, "They used me.

Jason only married me because Millicent got pregnant. Holt was born six months after we were married, and we brought him home when he was six months old and we said he was only three months old. Everyone said what a big baby he was." She laughed. "Oh, if they knew better. They only thought that Jason had married me in a hurry because I was the one who . . . but I was never the one.

"There was never any room between Jason and Millicent for anyone except Holt. Holt is Jason's son, too, you see."

I suppose I knew it all along, Julie thought over the rising revulsion within her. I didn't need to hear it said.

"Why did you come? Why did you tell me?"

"I needed money," Sara answered. "I thought . . . well, it would be better if you knew why I'm like this. Once I was pretty. After I left the shop and when I couldn't write to your father anymore for money, I . . . well, there were . . . men. Now, now I'm old and I look . . . I look like what I am and . . . what I have become . . . what Jason made me."

Julie made a sound as if she were going to speak, but Sara went on: "What I made myself then," she said, as if reading Julie's mind. "You see, I didn't have the courage to kill myself. I thought about it—the shame, the degradation of what I had been through. But I didn't have the courage for anything. If my parents had been alive, if I had had a brother, anyone to turn to . . . but I didn't."

"I'll give you some money," Julie said. "My father would have wanted that. I haven't a lot to give."

"Anything," Sara said eagerly, "anything at all. With the new law, brandy has gone sky high. I can't . . . I . . ." She broke off. "Anything at all," she repeated, drawing herself a little more erect, trying to reassemble some half-forgotten dignity.

"If you had told my father the truth," Julie said, as Sara was finally leaving, "he would never have left me in Jason's and Millicent's care. And he would have helped you. My father was strong. He wouldn't have let Jason get away with anything like that."

"I was afraid," Sara said. "I was always afraid. Now, now I don't care anymore." She stuffed the bills Julie had given her into her bag.

"I can send you something each month," Julie offered, "if you tell me where to send it."

"There isn't any one place anymore. There is a candy store, though. I'll ask the owners. Maybe they'll let me pick up a letter there. I'll . . . I'll write to you." She was painfully desperate to leave now. "I'll write to you. Thank you, Julie."

Sara was gone, weaving from the effects of the brandy and trying to smile brightly as she turned at the stairway and waved. From that distance she looked garish, unreal, like a painted marionette from a Grand Guignol.

Julie did not expect to hear from Sara again, but on the following Tuesday a brief note of thanks arrived together with the address of the candy store.

Tuesday was Julie's regular day at the Red Cross, and on her way down she stopped at her bank to arrange for a small monthly sum to be sent to Sara in care of the store.

Somewhere in the long hours after Sara Prescott had left, she had come to a decision about herself and about Mark. Life was short and love was too rare to lose. She wouldn't stay in America while Mark was in France. "I'll follow him," she promised herself aloud. "If I'm there, I can see him. Surely some of the time I can see him, be with him. If he knows I'm there, he'll come to me."

The formalities attendant on her volunteering for overseas duty with the American Red Cross were long and difficult. The fact that she was completely fluent in French gave her the chance to be accepted. She was grateful that she had gotten that much out of St. Veronica's and the odious Camp Joy. Her schoolgirl French had been refined and extended during those three years so that very little practice brought it readily to her tongue.

She had applied at the beginning of November, and it was February before the orders came through. In the interim she had increased her volunteer time, learning all she could about the various Red Cross functions, visiting hospitals, and taking advanced first aid courses.

Her first letter from Mark arrived at the beginning of January and she answered it at once. Now that she had his army address, she wrote nearly daily, but in all the letters she refrained from mentioning that she would be going overseas. She was afraid he would write back and tell her she couldn't do that.

While awaiting the final order, Julie set about arranging for her bank to send on a monthly check. She also signed over her proxy vote at Fontaine's to Joe Damien. The attorney suggested she also draw up a will.

During the summer when she and Mark had first become engaged, they had made a mutual will so that whatever one had went to the other. It was curious that neither of them had even thought to change it. There was still no need.

"I have one," she said.

Wills. Wills were for old people. Nothing would happen to Mark or to her, anyway.

With her goal nearly in sight, Julie thrived on work. The long days followed by the nightly show curtailed her social life, and in spite of the short time she had left for sleeping, she felt elated and buoyant. It showed in her face.

"I don't know where you get the energy," Madeline sighed. "I must be feeling my age."

But Julie had not revealed her plans, and until the orders came through for her departure, she said nothing, not even to Elsie. She would have to help Elsie get a new job, of course. That was one more item to take care of before she could leave.

Breaking the news to Lew Belmont was easier than she thought. "Madeline may be fooled, but I'm not," he told her. "I knew you had something like this in mind. Go. I'll break the contract for you. Besides," he said, smiling, "it wouldn't look patriotic, would it? Hard-hearted producer standing in the way of a young girl ready to serve our boys in France."

Madeline was less enthusiastic. "I know you're crazy about that man. I even understand why. But being a Red Cross girl in France isn't exactly like it is here. And that voyage across the ocean, all those German U-boats. You'll be terrified, and seasick," Madeline said.

Julie laughed. "Is seasick worse than sinking?"

"Believe me," Madeline answered feelingly, "I've been seasick going and coming from Europe back in '13. You'll wish you could sink if it happens to you. First you think you're dying, and then you are afraid you won't."

"I'll chance it all," Julie said. "I want to be where Mark is. I know what I was like when he was away last time when I thought . . . never mind. I'm not going to sit home and worry and wait. I'm going. Somehow it won't be so bad if we're both in thee same country."

"You know, kid, I envy you, even now. No man ever meant that much to me. I don't think any man ever will."

"You never know," Julie said. "It comes when you least expect it. I was fresh from a first boyfriend, out to flirt and play games, not quite eighteen when I fell in love with Mark, and I didn't even try to do it. All I was going to do was . . . well, I think about it now and I see how foolish I was. But afterward there just couldn't really be anyone else."

A shadow passed over Madeline's face and she turned away quickly.

"I know what you're thinking," Julie said calmly. "If something happens to him, then what? Nothing will happen to Mark. I know that. Because if it did, there wouldn't be anyplace I wanted to go or anything I wanted to do. So, you see, I'm not afraid of U-boats . . . or seasickness," she ended lightly.

The day Julie sailed for France aboard the merchant ship *Patrick Henry*, a blizzardy snowstorm swept in from the northwest. As the ship moved out of the harbor, the waters of the bay were already churning furiously, and by the time they hit the open sea the gale-force winds at their back propelled them faster through the gray-black waters of the Atlantic.

The ship rolled and pitched in the agitated swells. The American coast fell behind them, hidden in an ever-encroaching mist that muffled the foghorn's warning. The troopship rode deep in the convoy, not far from the *Henry*. In front and behind them, the rest of the convoy were all darker gray shapes in the dwindling light.

There were twelve Red Cross volunteers aboard and twenty-five nurses. They were billeted in an off-limits section of the ship, with a gate barring passage to the outside deck.

"As if any of us wanted to go out on deck in this weather," said Kitty Behrens, Julie's cabin mate.

Kitty was sitting glumly on the edge of the lower bunk of an inboard cabin. She was twenty-five, looked eighteen, and had a soft, candy-box prettiness. Small and well proportioned, she was like a Dresden doll. If she were in one of Lew's shows, Julie thought, they'd put her in a shepherdess costume to match that pink-and-white skin and those pale blue eyes.

"Where are you from?" Julie asked.

"Cleveland, Ohio. I've been living with my older sister and her husband in New York for the past two years, though. I was studying nursing, but I gave up after a year. Can't stand the sight of blood."

"Does the Red Cross know that?" Julie asked, amused.

"Certainly not. No one does. Don't tell. How do you think I wangled this overseas trip?"

"What made you volunteer?" Julie asked her.

"I don't know. Sounded glamorous, I guess. But you had a glamorous life all fixed up. I saw all that hoopla on the pier and I saw your pictures in the paper: 'Miss Angela Grant, Julie Fontaine in private life,' etc. A big plug for the Red Cross. 'Glamorous show-girl-actress sails to do her bit for our gallant infantrymen.' "

"I'm not here for the glamour. It's . . . it's something I have to do, that's all," Julie said decisively.

"I'll bet there's a man somewhere in the picture," Kitty said wisely. She settled her slender body on the bed and shivered. "I must be crazy," she said. "Glamour. I think I'm going to be sick." Julie took one look at Kitty's green face and raced for a wastebasket. She steadied it beside Kitty, bracing herself against the roll of the ship.

"I'm not going to be sick," Julie said determinedly as the rank and sour odors rose in the room and Kitty, moaning, fell back against her bunk.

"I think I'm going to die," Kitty said.

"No, you're not. I understand that's the worst part of it—you don't die." Kitty moaned again.

The crossing took nearly two weeks, most of it in heavy seas that kept Kitty in a fluctuating state of misery. Coming far north on the great circle route, the skies cleared to a brilliant blue and the sun shone so strongly that its reflection on the water was blinding. Julie, along with all the others who were ambulatory, spent as much time as possible in the cold air, pacing the deck space, exercising whenever possible, letting the freezing Arctic wind clear her of the musty odors and stifling heat of the cabin below.

She ate with fair appetite, did her best to make the still-suffering Kitty comfortable, and at night she went to bed, clutching Mark's letter in her hand beneath her pillow. She had written him the week before she sailed. She would see him once they reached France. Soon, she promised herself, soon.

On the thirteenth day, Julie rose to find the morning shrouded in a fine mist of rain. Peering through her porthole, she saw the outlines of the French coast. They had made it. They were through. She dressed hastily, waking the still-sleeping Kitty to tell her that the voyage was nearly over.

They were at breakfast when the alarm bell rang. Secure in knowing they were only an hour or two from docking, the alarm took them totally by surprise. The daily drills had prepared them, however, and even in their shocked state they went mechanically through the procedures.

Assembled on the boat deck, weighted down with heavy clothing beneath their life preservers, the women were unnaturally calm and quiet. A few minutes later the first mate's voice came over the ship's speaker with the information that it had been a false alert and that they would be landing within the hour. Danger past, thirty-seven women ranging in age from twenty to forty burst into tears, clutching each other until their tears finally gave way to laughter while two harried sailors tried to disperse them.

"Women," Julie heard one of them say. "What are women doing in a war, anyway?"

She turned to face the speaker. "Whatever we can," she said to him. "You'd be glad enough to have us if you were lying wounded in some hospital and swearing the pain away. You swear. We cry." She walked off, still seething inside, conscious that her voice had carried from the sudden silence behind her. A man's whistle broke it, and when she recognized the tune, an old burlesque number, "Take it off, take it off . . ." her cheeks flushed, but she did not turn around.

14

Julie wrote to Madeline the week before Easter: "France may be at war, but it is not as dangerous in Paris as you thought. We came up here through beautiful country outside the war zone. Paris itself is very gay, not, perhaps, as gay as New York, but still it is hard to believe that fighting is only seventy miles away." She paused and nibbled her pen. It would be as well to avoid mentioning the air bombings. They were sporadic and so far the casualties to civilians had not been severe. She reread the letter. It sounded as if she were having a quiet vacation. "There has been no word from Mark this month," she went on. "His company is attached to the British forces along the Somme. I don't know when I will see him. Our Red Cross headquarters is in the heart of the city. I share a room with a girl from Ohio, Kitty Brehrens. We are only a few blocks from the office, and from our window we can see the spire of the Church of St. Gervais.

"The head of the office is Mrs. Jones. She must be fifty but she's very tall and very strong and has us all cowed.

"Life here is not much different—that is, we feed doughnuts and coffee to the soldiers, and we still roll bandages and pack medical supplies and we do clerical work. So far, I have seen no American casualties, except for a field ambulance driver who broke his leg when his motorcar ran into a stone wall outside the city."

She paused, trying to think of what to say next. Somehow, she did not think that a description of the house they lived in or of the large, happy family of Gautiers who owned it and the bakery shop beneath it would really interest Madeline or Lew. Monique Gautier might. At fifteen, she showed every promise of becoming a great beauty.

When Julie and Kitty had first moved into the room

below the eaves, Monique had come around nearly every evening, sitting shyly at the edge of the bed and asking Kitty or Julie questions about America. Her large, expressive eyes would glow with wonder and delight when Julie told her stories of New York, of the theater, and of her own life in it.

"You can't escape it even here," Kitty once said. "Theater is glamour, and even if Monique is slated to be a quiet little French housewife like her mother, she's still star-struck."

Julie smiled to herself now. Star-struck wasn't really a description of Monique Gautier. She was curious, intelligent, and interested in a life besides the one she knew —a life of school and helping her mother care for the younger children and of relieving her parents in the shop.

There was a soft rap on the door and Julie called, "*Entrez.*" Monique poked her head around the corner and Julie said, "Well, thinking of the devil."

"*Pardon?*" Monique said.

"It's nothing. I was thinking of you. Come in, Monique."

"No, thank you. My mother has sent me to ask if you will please have chocolate with us."

"With pleasure." Julie put aside her half-finished letter and followed Monique downstairs to the Gautiers' apartment.

Small and cluttered with the belongings of the six children, it was a homey place. The smaller children were already in bed, and the table was set with the large flowered chocolate pot and matching cups and saucers. In the center there was a freshly cut loaf of bread and pots of butter and jam.

Madame Gautier greeted Julie with a smile, and Monsieur Gautier rose from his chair near the stove to offer her a seat.

"It is cold tonight, so I make the chocolate," Madame Gautier said. "Outside it is cold. Inside, with the curtains drawn against the airplanes, it becomes close, no?"

Whenever Julie saw Monique and her parents together it was hard to see any family resemblance. Madame Gautier was nearly as tall as Julie, wide of frame, and well fleshed, with a plain lined face whose chief beauty was her snapping black eyes. Her husband, as thin as his wife was plump, but an inch shorter, had a rather long face with very light brown eyes. Older than his wife by fifteen years, his hair was already white. They were undistinguished people who had created the beauty that was young Monique.

The little ones looked rather more like the parents, but sometimes one could see a resemblance between them and Monique in a fleeting expression or in the flash of a smile.

"If it were not for my sister," Madame Gautier said as she poured the chocolate, "there would be very little butter and jam and cheese in this house. She has a farm in the south and each week she sends up to us what she can spare."

Monsieur Gautier cleared his throat. "It has gone on too long, this war," he said. "It is not like the last one. One year, a little more, and it was over."

"And what of that?" said his wife. "We lost that war. This time we will not lose it."

"One hopes," he replied. "With the Americans in, perhaps we will win?" He smiled at Julie. "The first reports say that the American troops are helping and that they fight well."

She thanked him, knowing that much of what he said was out of courtesy and that many of the French were not so generous. It was, in its way, strange that at home everyone imagined the Americans were being welcomed like saviors of the Allied cause, while in Europe it was quite the opposite. The general reaction seemed to be: *Alors,* they are in, well and good. Now, let us see if it makes any difference.

"And you, Julie," said Madame Gautier, "you will be glad to have this war over and have your young man back again. You are very brave to come here to France. You American women are much freer in your spirit than we French."

"I don't know if that is true," Julie answered. "More foolhardy, perhaps."

"I think you are very brave, *mademoiselle,*" Monique said shyly. "I would not like to go so far away from my home. I think I would be very lonely and very frightened." She blushed as she spoke, and her lids lowered over her eyes.

"Well, what is this talk?" her father said. "You are too young to think of leaving home."

"Yes, Papa," Monique replied.

"Listen to that man." Madame Gautier laughed. "Fifteen is young, yes. But one day Monique will marry, and she will not wait until she is an old woman of twenty-eight, the way I did."

"*Alors,*" Monsieur Gautier said to Julie, "there was nothing to do but wait. First of all, there was the fact that I was not rich enough to please her father. I must pay off this house and the shop and be all ready before he would let her marry me. Seven years we must wait. And I was not such a young man then, either."

"Tell what Grandfather said, Papa," Monique urged, her face alight.

"*Alors,* he was a farmer, you see. And here is me, this wicked baker come south on a holiday from the fleshpots of Paris. On the top of that, I was also not a rich baker, which could be forgiven. Therefore, I must also be a fool. And he tells my bride on her wedding day: 'So, marry that idiot if you must, but do not be surprised if one day he puts you into the oven and brings the bread to bed.'"

They all laughed as if the story was new to them. "But that he has not done," said Madame Gautier complacently. "I always knew. In the beginning I said, 'Very well, I will wait, then.' My father thought once we did not see each other that I would be interested in someone else. But never did that happen. I had confidence and faith, and soon it was all finished and we were married."

"Did you stay down in the country while Monsieur Gautier was up in Paris?" Julie asked.

"But of course. Sometimes I did not see him for months . . . once over a year. But"—she shrugged expressively—"if it is right, you will have each other no matter what the father says."

She exchanged a glance with her husband, and in the moment before they looked away Julie saw the flicker of feeling between them. It made her nostalgic and she thought, I am getting stupidly sentimental.

"Yes," Monsieur Gautier said, echoing his wife, "no matter what the father says."

"Well, remember that when it comes Monique's time," his wife laughed.

"But I will not be married," Monique said suddenly.

"Oh, that is what I said. When the man comes along, you will change your mind," her mother answered complacently.

Monique did not reply. Politeness forbade her arguing with her mother, but Julie saw the almost imperceptible shake of her head.

Julie left the gathering reluctantly. She enjoyed these evenings with the Gautiers. They were simple, uncomplicated people with a love of talk and food and a practical view of what life could offer them.

Kitty enjoyed them somewhat less. "They always talk of the same things, always the war and prices, and they tell old family stories about people I never heard of."

"I like that," Julie had answered. "It makes me feel . . . oh, I don't know . . . as if all good things are possible."

Back in her room she picked up the letter she had been writing to Madeline and reread it.

There was really not much more to say. She added a few general inquiries and expressions of affection and enclosed the letter in the envelope she had already addressed. She laid it on top of the letter she had just written Mark and rose, stretching and flexing her fingers.

Mark's company had been in the war zone for three months now, and from what she had been able to gather, they might be rotated into Paris on short leave in the next few weeks. Might. Again, they might be held until fall. Julie walked over to the open window and lifted an edge of the blackout curtain to look down on the rooftops and the spire of St. Gervais, which gleamed softly in the moonlight. Kitty was still out and she began to regret that she had not gone along with her and that friend of Michel's, one of Kitty's many soldier friends. The room was stifling.

Julie put out the lamp by which she had been writing and drew back the curtains to open the window and let the night breezes blow through. She leaned over, with her hands on the windowsill, taking deep breaths. As always when she was free of pressing duties, or between tasks, her mind wandered back to Mark. No matter how she longed to see him, no matter how frustrating it was to realize that he was so close and yet so far away, she was still comforted by the knowledge that the distance between them was little enough, and thus she could hope to see him. If she had stayed in New York, she could not take even that poor comfort from their separation.

There was a dull roar to the north and she withdrew her head quickly, closing the window and the curtains and relighting the lamp. Another German plane raid. She crossed herself automatically, something she had taken to doing of late, and muttered a wordless prayer in the hope no one had been hurt.

The tiny room she shared with Kitty had no area to pace. Two cots, one wardrobe, and a desk that served also as bureau and dressing table left little more than three square feet of standing space.

Sighing, Julie began to disrobe, unknotting her uniform tie slowly. Suddenly the room shook slightly and light flashed through the heavy curtains. A louder explosion followed immediately. Seconds later, Kitty burst into the room, looking wild-eyed and scared.

"Something bad is happening," she said. "There aren't any planes up there, but we're being bombed. Did you hear that last one?"

"Yes. But there must be planes. The Germans are too far south and east of us for it to be cannon fire."

"Are they?" Kitty's teeth were chattering. "Michel thought something was wrong. He's gone back to his barracks."

"We'll know soon enough," Julie answered and continued to undress. "I'm sure there was a plane up there. There isn't any way the Germans can send a shell sixty or seventy miles."

She got into bed and Kitty, still uncertain, sat on the edge of her own. "It isn't really glamorous, is it?" she said wistfully.

"Oh, I don't know." Julie smiled. Here you are, the toast of the French Army, wining and dining every free night, seeing Paris iike an American on vacation. On the other hand, I am generally to be found sitting here writing letters and reading."

"I'm not in love," Kitty answered. "So far I can't think of anyone who would make me all moony and distracted the way you are half the time. Mark Douglas must be some man to make you quit the theater and come all the way to France."

"He is," Julie said shortly. "Come to bed, Kitty. You see, there isn't anything going on. There hasn't been another explosion." She turned over, burying her head into her pillow and drawing the coverlet up to shield her eyes.

"I'll say this for you, you're very nerveless," Kitty complained. "You'd probably sit in the trenches and tell everyone the firing was due to stop any second."

"That nerveless I'm not," Julie said dryly. "But I can't see any reason to get excited about something I don't think can happen. Come on, Kitty, let me go to sleep."

Coming into headquarters the next afternoon, however, they found the place in a turmoil. German guns some sixty-five miles away had clearly managed to fire a long-range shell into Paris, not once, but twice. The citizens could now expect bombardment and panic to run high. Already many Parisians were fleeing south into the countryside despite efforts of the authorities to reassure them.

"Eight people killed in that second bomb last night and dozens hurt," Kitty said to Julie. "You said it wasn't possible. I should have listened to Michel."

"And done what? Sat up all night? Nothing is going to happen to me," Julie said. "I'm sure of that."

"I wish I were," Kitty answered nervously. "Look at me. I'm all thumbs today. My hands are shaking."

Julie made no response, thinking if Kitty were this frantic over that one bombardment, she would never last out the war. Uppermost in her own mind was that if the Germans did succeed in taking Paris, and they had to get out, where would Mark find her? Somehow, her fear that the months of separation from Mark would extend into years again was greater than any other fear.

The week passed with the dull bombardment continuing sporadically but without any serious results, and some of the panic in the city ebbed. People called it "an unlucky strike," and the social life of the city picked up in spite of the approaching holy days.

On Good Friday, Paris was quieter than usual. The bombardment had continued only intermittently since French artillery now engaged the gun crews and forced them to seek shelter until their own artillery could bring a counter offensive. Bombing had ceased for the

past two days, and on the somber note of the anniversary
of the crucifixion the churches were filled with the faith-
ful following the ritual of Christ's agony on the cross.

Coming out of the pension that morning, Julie met
Madame Gautier, who was with the two youngest of her
five daughters.

"Bonjour," Madame Gautier said. "I . . . come . . . ah
. . ." She broke off, smiling, then continued: "I think
with all the Americans and British in Paris and all those
who have stayed here with us, that I will surely learn
English. But it comes very hard. The brain is old." She
tapped her forehead.

"It takes daily conversation," Julie said, "and people
who won't let you speak any other language."

"That I have not the time for. Zut . . . with five
girls and two boys and my husband, I am cooking all
day. It is a beautiful morning, isn't it?"

"Lovely. And quiet for a change. You're out early
this morning," Julie said, smiling at the rosy-cheeked
little girls.

"I took them to church with me. Monique makes the
breakfast. I will send the others after breakfast and
Monique, well, when I can spare her. What I would do
without Monique, I don't know."

"She's a lovely girl." Julie said, "very mature for fifteen."

"Yes, I have given her too much responsibility," Madame Gautier sighed. "But the others came so quickly
when they came. Five years Monique had me all to herself, and then, pouf! One, two, three, four, five, six. No
wonder she wants to become a nun. That is what she
has told us."

"Monique?" Julie thought, Monique, with her lovely
oval face and dark, expressive eyes and a way of walking that makes all the young boys around watch her
pass?

"Very religious, Monique. This afternoon she will go
for the stations of the cross and the last service before
evening. She is too good, my first one. The rest, ah, they
are imps." She shooed the small girls in front of her and
mounted the steps.

"A bientôt," she called back to Julie.

"A bientôt," Julie replied and waved her hand. It
was a lovely day and the quiet was lovelier. On a day

such as this she could live in Paris forever and believe that no harm would befall anyone.

At four-thirty that afternoon Julie was packing cartons of supplies to be deployed to the forward field hospitals. Kitty was chatting brightly beside her as she handed the proper items into Julie's busy, efficient hands.

Julie was lifting one filled carton aside to make room for a new one when the explosion came. It was deafeningly close, and almost as they heard it one of the windows of their building shattered, sending flying glass everywhere.

Before they had had time to recover from the shock, the door to the main office burst open and a man catapulted through, calling in French, *"M'aidez, m'aidez!* St. Gervais, *elle est détruite . . . des bombes . . . mon Dieu, les femmes, les petits . . . beaucoup de petits enfants . . ."* He paused, tears pouring down his face.

"Dear God," Julie said "They've blown up St. Gervais, and there are women and children there. *S'il vous plaît,"* she said to the weeping man, *"est-ce qu'il y a beaucoup de blessés, ou . . . ou plus de morts?"*

"La même chose. La même chose," he wept. *"Dépêchez-vous, mademoiselle."*

"What is he saying?" Kitty begged.

"There are as many injured as dead in the church. Kitty, stay here and wait for Mrs. Jones to come back. Tell her what happened. Call the ambulance brigades and the fire brigades. Someone come with me and help me carry the first-aid kits."

The scene that met their eyes as they came into the street was devastating beyond belief. The church itself, packed with women and children, had been hit. Dozens of injured streamed from the wrecked edifice, some too dazed to speak, others weeping noisily, some screaming in an echo of the calls from the dying.

One woman seized Julie's arm in her blood-stained hands, crying, "My little son. Oh, please, I can't move him."

Julie followed her into what remained of the church. The nave was a mass of rubble. Everywhere lay bodies and pieces of bodies. She stumbled over something and, looking down, she saw that it was the severed limb of a man, its blue woolen trousers leg still whole.

"Here, here!" the woman cried, and Julie followed her

to a pile of smoking rubble where the white figure of a small boy lay motionless beneath a splintered pew. Bending down, she felt for his pulse and laid her head against his chest. There was no sign of life. His eyes were closed; there wasn't a mark on him. Shock, she thought. He simply died of shock. She tried to resuscitate him, but even as she breathed into the cold mouth she knew it was hopeless.

"Get him out!" the mother cried. "Get him out!"

Julie began to dig around the debris, lifting the wood and the plaster from around the still form. At last she lifted him in her arms.

"Give him to me!" the woman cried.

"Please," Julie said gently. "He's . . . he . . ." She couldn't say the words, and there was no need to find them, for the mother, comprehending the meaning, tore the child from Julie's arms, calling to him, begging him to speak to her, shaking him, as if somehow that would make him respond. When the tiny arms fell limply and the head rolled back, she screamed.

If Julie lived to be a hundred years old, she would hear that mother's scream re-echoing down the corridors of all her days. All around them were the sobs and prayers and shrieks of despair, but all the misery in the world lay in that high, long, feral sound of a woman bereft of her young. When it ended the woman seemed drained of life. Her face was an open wound of tragedy, and Julie lowered her eyes from the sight.

"Let me help you," she whispered.

The woman said dully, "No one can help me now." With wooden, jerky steps, she bore her burden out of the church.

Julie stood for seconds, lost, unable to move to help the rest, and then she heard her name called. Mrs. Jones had arrived from headquarters. Seeing that tall, commanding figure, hearing that quiet, authoritative voice, Julie felt her energy flow back.

"Here," she called back steadily, and Mrs. Jones was beside her.

They worked for hours, helping the ambulance crews and the doctors who arrived to treat the wounded. Cots were set up in the street and blankets brought from nearby homes. Mrs. Jones organized and mobilized all the efforts of her office, dispatching teams to bring hot soup and coffee, to find relatives of the wounded, to take names and addresses of those borne away to the hospital, to man the barriers of the cordoned-off street, and to answer the questions of anxious relatives.

Darkness fell and crews trying to sift through the rubble for still more bodies worked in flaring torchlight that intensified the already macabre scene.

Julie saw the endless bodies on stretchers, some dead, some still alive. One stretcher carried young Monique Gautier, her eyes closed, the sweet oval face covered in blood and dirt, the long masses of dark curls matted with more blood and dirt.

"Monique," Julie whispered, bending over her.

"She is unconscious," a voice said. Looking up, Julie saw the Gautiers, their faces a mixture of terrible fear and desperate hope.

"My angel," Mrs. Gautier said, "my first baby."

Julie felt the woman's agony as if it had been her own. "She's alive," Julie said quickly. "She's alive. She'll be all right."

It was nearly midnight before it was over, and Julie, dragging her aching body up the long, narrow stairs to their little attic room, was too sick with sorrow, too fatigued emotionally, spiritually, and physically, to think of food. Hours before Kitty had seized the first opportunity to leave the hideous nightmare and was somewhere in the city bringing comfort to the bereaved . . . or possibly telling the story to whichever soldier she had planned to dine with tonight, Julie thought. Well, she was better off that way.

Lying across her bed, too weary to change, Julie closed her eyes in the dark room and suffered the figures that floated still before her: the maimed; the desolate; the dead. She slept after a while, the sleep of utter exhaustion, and awoke to the first light, sore of body, heavy of mind.

Mass funerals for the nearly ninety victims of the assault took place the following Tuesday, a soft April day marked by a cessation of bombardment on the orders of General Ludendorff, who had silenced the long guns out of respect for the tragedy.

"It was decent of that German general," Kitty remarked.

"Decent!" Julie looked at her angrily. "It would have been decent to bar the shelling during holy week. It would have been even more decent not to shell civilians. Decent! There is no decency in war."

Kitty shrank back, bewildered by Julie's sudden rage.

"I'm sorry, Kitty," Julie said after a moment. "I didn't mean to berate you. Will you take over for me in the morning? I am going to the funeral mass for Mrs. Gautier's sake. Monique died in the hospital on Saturday."

The church was crowded, overflowing with mourners. The list of the dead seemed endless—Mathilde Thibault, Renée Dupres, and Monique Gautier among them. Julie felt her throat contract in pity and sorrow.

"May their souls rest in peace," the priest intoned.

"And may perpetual light shine upon them," Julie murmured with the rest of the mourners.

The enormity of this mass for fifteen of the victims, all children, turned individual sorrow into congregational bereavement. Fifteen white coffins, some so small the sight of them tore at the heart, lined the aisle. The soft sound of continuous weeping blanketed the church, and all the priest's talk of heaven and all of the comfort of the litany for the dead could not erase the desolation.

What did it all mean, anyway? You were born, you lived a while, and then sooner or later something took you away, leaving behind broken hearts and aching minds. Fifteen young children here, more in other churches, and fathers, mothers, sisters, brothers. What had any one of them done to deserve this catastrophe? Miranda Latham sat snug and comfortable in her home. Holt Prescott was as safely billeted as Steven Randall or Kenneth Bradford. And Mark was fighting with poor, dumb Andrew Clay along with him. Eileen was dead at twenty-one.

And somewhere there was a German general who had carelessly ordered the death of the innocents and then played the gentleman by giving his death guns a holiday during the funeral of his victims.

There were Jason and Millicent, hypocrites before God, growing old comfortably, and there was Sara Prescott, their victim, living out her days in degradation and despair. There was no justice and there was no mercy.

And even I, Julie thought, even I can only be glad that this is not my personal tragedy.

The mass was ended and the congregation rose, silently facing the aisle through which the coffins were carried, followed by grieving relatives. At last, moving out of their pews to the end of the procession, they came into the bright spring sunshine where birds sang in the quiet air.

The attack upon St. Gervais marked the beginning of a long, treacherous period of bombardment. In the first few weeks the city began to accept it as another fact of life. If you were lucky you were not in the place where the shells struck. If you were unlucky . . . *zut, alors,* you were unlucky.

By mid-April the tragedy of St. Gervais was all but forgotten. Only in the streets around the church, which served as a mournful reminder, did people still speak of it. And in the pension the subdued faces of the other Gautier children and the sorrow of their parents' eyes were daily reminders to Julie and to Kitty, who finally said, "I wish we could live somewhere else. It's terrible to see this day after day."

"Move if you like," Julie replied, and Kitty flushed.

"I know that's selfish. I wouldn't, anyway, unless you were moving, too. Forget I said anything. It's just that . . . well . . . I see them and I remember, and then I feel so darned guilty whenever I have a good time."

"Don't be a fool, Kitty. We're alive. Going around with a long face wouldn't help anything."

Near the end of the month some American soldiers, back from their first battles on the front, began trickling into Paris. The hospitals were receiving American casualties from the field stations, and the work at the Red Cross office increased. Often, after a day of alternating between the office and the canteen and then evenings at the hospital, it would be nearly midnight before Julie got home. Kitty, too, had begun to give more conscious effort to work and less and less to the rounds of parties that had been her real interest in the earlier days.

For Julie, life had become a methodical routine in which she had temporarily given up hope of hearing from Mark. Thus, when she finally walked into the canteen to see him standing at the counter in the act of accepting a cup of coffee from Kitty, she could not quite credit her senses. It took her several minutes to propel herself forward and touch him on the sleeve.

"Mark?" she said on a high, questioning note, and he turned so swiftly he nearly upset the coffee cup.

"Julie," he answered. "I went around to your room and to the office. I've been looking for you. We just got in this morning." He was still holding the coffee; she still had her hand on his arm.

"I'm glad you're here," she said. They were talking in quiet, almost formal voices, but their eyes spoke another language altogether.

"When are you finished?" he asked.

"I can leave in about an hour," she said.

He put his coffee down, still untasted, and moved her away from the line of soldiers jostling at the counter.

"Meet me at my hotel," he said in a low voice. "I'm not sure how long we'll be here. I'll know more about that soon. I've got a room at a little hotel off the Boulevard Montparnasse—the Picardy. Know it?"

She nodded.

He covered the hand on his arm with one of his own, pressing it firmly, and she curled hers around to meet his, stroking the back of his hand with her thumb.

"I missed you," he said. "I could have beaten you when I found out you were in Paris. Now I'm so damned glad you're here."

"I'd almost given up," she said in an unsteady voice. "I haven't heard from you in so long, and . . ."

"Big German offensive—the Somme and then at Lys. We've been shuffled around. We're joining the French soon."

"Is your whole company here?" she asked.

"Yes. We were luckier than most. I even managed to keep an eye on Lindstrom." He grinned.

"Who's Lindstrom?"

"'What is Lindstrom?' would be a better question," Mark said. "If something is going to go wrong, Lindstrom will be the one to get caught in the middle. He's probably going to be the only soldier in the army who winds up private second class after four years. But we can talk later." He looked at his watch. "It's five now. Say seven at the Picardy. I'm in Room Fourteen, third floor."

TASTE 'EM!

KENT GOLDEN LIGHTS
ONLY 8 MG TAR
YET TASTES SO GOOD, YOU
WON'T BELIEVE THE NUMBERS.
(See other side for your brand's tar numbers.)

Kent Golden Lights
Regular & Menthol:
8 mg. "tar," 0.7 mg.
nicotine av. per
cigarette by FTC Method.

COMPARE YOUR NUMBERS TO KENT GOLDEN LIGHTS

FTC Report Dec. 1976

Filter Brands (Regulars)	MG TAR	MG NIC	Filter Brands (Menthols)	MG TAR	MG NIC
Kent Golden Lights*— King Size	**8**	**0.7**	**Kent Golden Lights* Menthol— Kings**	**8**	**0.7**
Lucky 100's — 100mm	9	0.6	Iceberg — 100mm	9	0.6
Pall Mall Extra Mild — King Size	10	0.7	Vantage — King Size	11	0.7
Vantage — King Size	10	0.7	Multifilter — King Size	11	0.7
Parliament* — King Size	10	0.8	Doral — King Size	11	0.8
Doral — King Size	13	0.9	Salem Lights — King Size	11	0.8
Multifilter — King Size	13	0.8	Fact — King Size	13	0.9
Marlboro Lights — King Size	13	0.8	Kool Milds — King Size	14	0.9
Winston Lights — King Size	13	0.9	Marlboro — King Size	14	0.8
Raleigh Extra Mild — King Size	14	1.0	Belair — King Size	15	1.0
Viceroy Extra Mild — King Size	14	1.0	Alpine — King Size	15	0.8
Fact — King Size	14	1.0	Virginia Slims — 100mm	16	0.9
Viceroy — King Size	16	1.0	Saratoga — 120mm	16	1.0
Virginia Slims — 100mm	16	0.9	Silva Thins — 100mm	16	1.1
L&M — 100mm	17	1.1	Pall Mall — 100mm	16	1.2
Benson & Hedges — 100mm	18	1.0	Eve — 100mm	17	1.1
Pall Mall — King Size	18	1.2	Kool — King Size	17	1.4
Lark — King Size	18	1.1	Benson & Hedges — 100mm	18	1.0
Marlboro — King Size	18	1.1	Salem — King Size	18	1.2
Winston — King Size	19	1.2	Winston — 100mm	19	1.2
Tareyton — King Size	20	1.3	More — 120mm	21	1.6
Lowest of All Brands Sold	0.5	0.05	Lowest of All Brands Sold	0.5	0.05

*FTC Method

*FTC Method

KENT GOLDEN LIGHTS ONLY 8 MG TAR

AS LOW AS YOU CAN GO AND STILL GET GOOD TASTE AND SMOKING SATISFACTION.

Kent Golden Lights Regular & Menthol: 8 mg. "tar," 0.7 mg. nicotine av. per cigarette by FTC Method.

He was still holding her hand and they were standing very close. She could feel him more than she could see him, as if waves flowed between them, although, save for their linked hands, they had not touched each other.

"See you tonight."

A curious calm settled over Julie after Mark left. She relieved Kitty behind the service counter and dispatched coffee and doughnuts and American cigarettes with an efficiency that amazed her. At six Kitty came back and Julie slipped away to go home and change.

Julie arrived at the Picardy shortly after seven and, without pausing at the desk in the lobby, went straight into the ornate elevator cage. She was still possessed of a detached poise, and when Mark opened the door to her knock and drew her inside, she did not, as had been her custom in the past, fling herself into his arms.

Instead, she put down her bag and wrap and surveyed the room. It was three times the size of the one she shared with Kitty. A large four-poster canopied bed occupied the center wall opposite the fireplace. The carpeting was soft and thick and the massive carved provincial armoire and dresser did not dwarf the room's proportions. Windows overlooked a small, well-planted garden, peaceful in the fading light.

She turned back to Mark, who had not moved from the door, and said, "It's a lovely room, Mark—the loveliest we've ever been in together."

"The best is none too good for you," he answered, looking at her questioningly.

She turned back to the window, saying, "It's got a lovely view, too." She heard him crossing the room to come and stand behind her, but she did not move.

Presently, he put his arms around her, crossing them under her breasts and putting his face into the side of her neck where he began to kiss her softly, saying between kisses, "What is it, Julie?"

"I don't know. It's silly, but I feel . . ." She was going to say, "I feel shy with you," with Mark, of all people.

"Feel what?" he persisted, turning her in his arms so that she had her face against his chest. "Look at me," he said.

She raised her eyes and felt the old electricity crackle

in her ears, saw his face dark and unreadable, his eyes velvety brown in their deepened emotion.

"Julie," he breathed against her mouth. The room spun around then and emotions tore through her body. "I dreamed about you at night. I wanted you so badly sometimes that . . ."

"Shhh!" she said. "I'm here." And all the fears and longing and love so long denied fused inside her. How I love him, she thought wonderingly, everything about him: his skin; the way his hair grows; the broad firmness of his hands; the dark hairs on his chest; and the way his body smells. These were all food for her delight.

Later she lay awake as he slept, his head against her shoulder, and she put her arms around him, holding him as she might have held a child. Each time they were together her love seemed to grow, to change, to deepen, as if she were on a voyage of infinite discovery, uncovering newer and better treasures. He stirred a little and, reaching down, she drew the coverlet over them both, tucking it tenderly around him, keeping him cradled in her arms. His head dropped farther down and she felt his hair against her mouth. She bent then to kiss his head and finally slept, her lips buried in his hair.

15

That week in Paris was the happiest Julie had known in years. In spite of the bombing, in spite of the increasing press of work at the office, she was gay and laughing, feeling the way she had three summers before. She asked for and got three days' leave of absence.

"You've earned it," Mrs. Jones said in one of her rare compliments.

"Mrs. Jones wouldn't give me the time," Kitty said that night as they dressed. "I suppose she thinks I take enough as it is. And I do," she added before Julie could answer. "And she is right. You do deserve it."

"You're sure you don't mind coming along with a man you've never met?" Julie asked. "Mark wants me to meet some of his friends. Dan is his lieutenant. Jim Malone is his sergeant."

"I thought officers don't fraternize with the men," Kitty said.

"Mark does as he pleases. If he thinks a rule is silly, he breaks it or ignores it or gets around it somehow."

"What's Dan Sebastian like?"

"Search me. I've never met him. Don't fall in love, though. I understand he has a fiancée back home."

"Thank goodness that Michel is not in Paris this week," Kitty said. "That man is becoming very possessive. You'd think I was his fiancée. Do you like Michel, Julie?"

Michel? Julie paused to consider. She'd only seen him two or three times. He was medium in height, slender of build, and he had a long, rather sad face with a heavy beard that always looked as if he needed a shave. He was soft-spoken and rather shy, but clearly mad about Kitty.

"I don't really know him," she said aloud.

"I knew it. You don't like him."

"Oh, Kitty, of course I do. I just don't know him at all. He seems nice and he's good looking." Julie lied without a qualm.

"Yes, he is. I like him better than anyone else. So don't ever let on that I went out with Dan while he was away."

"Wouldn't dream of it," Julie assured her. "You may not like Dan at all, of course."

She couldn't have been more wrong, Julie told Mark later. "Look at them," she said, nodding to the dance floor, where Kitty was wrapped in Dan's arms.

"Wartime romance." Mark grinned. Across from them Jim Malone grunted and stood up.

"Nice to have met you," he said to Julie. "I'm going along now. Thanks, Captain." A smile split his truculent face and he was gone.

"That's the most he's said in over three hours," Julie remarked.

"Jim's the best," Mark answered. "Without him half of us wouldn't be in Paris at all."

"Don't say that."

"All right, I won't." He smiled at her and caught her hand. "Had enough night life?" She nodded and he pressed the hand he held. "We'll give Romeo and Juliet a chance to come back to the table and then we'll go home, all right?"

"Here they come," she said as a flushed Kitty slid into her seat.

"Would you like to dance, Julie?" Dan Sebastian asked politely.

"No, thank you. I'm getting very sleepy. I think Mark is, too. He said something about taking me home."

Dan slipped into his own chair, leaning over to talk to Mark, and under cover of their conversation, Kitty whispered, "You don't mean back home to our room, do you?" Julie shook her head. "Good," Kitty answered.

"Careful, Kitty. He belongs to someone else, and there is Michel."

"I know, I know. But don't spoil it for me, Julie."

"Warning withdrawn," Julie answered lightly. A few minutes later she and Mark left.

Mark returned to the front on a day when the April rains fell steadily across Paris. Julie, imbued with her belief that nothing would go wrong for them now, was able to accept this parting with some equanimity. Each time they had found each other again, and there was little doubt in her mind that they would finally be together again after the war.

"Do you think," Mark had said on that last day, "do you think we will ever make it down the aisle?"

And Julie had laid firm fingers across his mouth. "Shhh! It's the only superstition I have. When it's all over, when we know we're together for good, then we can talk about that. But I promise you the next time the date is set, I won't let you out of my sight."

There was a different feeling in Paris that summer, an anxious waiting, as if anticipating some final blow. Morale among Parisians soared or fell depending on the news from the front, but in July, in spite of the steady shelling from the German long guns, news that the American troops had distinguished themselves well in battle and had added the much-needed bolster to the war-weary French armies gave Paris fresh hope for peace.

"At least the Germans have been held at Château Thierry," Mark wrote, "although they still hold the Marne bridgehead, but not for long."

In August Julie applied for transfer to a forward field hospital, and with the increasing need for hospital personnel, and especially bilinguists, behind the lines, it was granted to her.

She embarked with the new contingent of Red Cross aides and nurses on a truck convoy that followed the American-French forces. They set up hospital and cooking and sleeping tents, and as the American First Army advanced they dismantled and followed.

Close to the battle lines, the constant fire and shelling that had been so random, so far away in Paris, became part of each day, and after the initial recoil from the steady pressure it ceased to affect Julie.

Since the field hospital moved as the troops moved in continuing battle, the stream of litters bearing the wounded and the dying increased. Days melted into nights and sleep was something to be caught for a few hours whenever possible.

In September they were behind the Argonne-Meuse offensive. The fact that Amiens had been won and that the Germans were driven back from the Marne caused rejoicing in Paris, but here, among the increasing number of casualties, elation was muted.

The ones who died did not move Julie as much as the ones who lived maimed. The sight of a young boy from Texas waking from the anesthesia to find his left arm gone pierced her heart. The shell-shocked, the deaf, and the blind—she never got used to it. Each new casualty was the first.

Early in October, bringing fresh bandages to Dr. Gilbert, who was leaning over the cot of a badly wounded blond private, she had her first news of Mark in months.

"Lindstrom, B Company, Second Battalion, American First Army," the soldier was mumbling. "I can't see, Doc," he said. "I can't see anything."

"It's all right," the doctor soothed. "You're wounded and I've bandaged your eyes." But he shook his head at Julie as she bent over Lindstrom.

"Private Lindstrom," she said, "from Captain Douglas' company, right?"

Lindstrom smiled below his bandaged head and eyes. "Right, Captain Douglas' company."

"And how is Captain Douglas?"

"Mad as hell at me. Said I had no business gettin' hit. Said I wasn't deep enough in the trench. I was, though. I swear to you, Nurse, we dig those trenches so deep I keep thinkin' we'll hit water any day."

"I'm Julie Fontaine," she said. "I'm not a nurse. I'm a Red Cross worker."

"Any coffee?"

"Sorry, soldier. You'll have to wait until you're up and around." She looked at Dr. Gilbert questioningly, and again he shook his head.

"Could use the coffee. It's damned cold in here."

Julie, covered with perspiration from an unseasonably hot day, was suddenly transported to Eileen's deathbed. A hot day like today, and Eileen whispering, "I'm so cold."

"Got a sweetheart you'd like me to write to?" she asked.

Again the smile tugged at the pale and weary mouth below the bandages. "Too many sweethearts," he said. "You might write my mother for me, though. Fightin's been so heavy, I haven't had a chance."

Julie took the notebook from her pocket and wrote down the address. It was worse, somehow, to have known who Lindstrom was. She wondered if that fact would be any consolation to his mother.

"You'll be all right," she said as the doctor injected him with morphine. "You'll rest now." She patted his one unbandaged arm.

As she moved away to follow the doctor to the newly arrived litters, he said, "When you write his mother, tell her that he died peacefully. He'll be gone before the morphine wears off." He said it brusquely, and she forebore asking him any questions, but he went on as if talking to himself. "Shell. Blinded him, cut his head. I thought he was all right, but when I took off the blanket . . ." He stopped and cleared his throat, ". . . couldn't even sew him up," he finished. Then, once more in command, he said, "The boys on either side of him—they can be transported back by next convoy. They'll make it. This one won't," he said grimly, looking down at the unconscious form of a lieutenant on whose face the gray-blue signal of impending death was slowly deepening.

Late in October even the field hospital personnel began to sense the coming of the end. The American First Army was rolling across the open countryside and the Germans fell back before their advance. By November 5, word from the front brought through from field ambulance drivers, from field medics, and even from the wounded was that the war was nearly over.

Julie had had no direct word from Mark since Lindstrom's death, but one of the ambulance drivers managed to bring her the news that he was still among the living, and she took refuge in that. If he had made it this far, he would surely make it to the end—which was only days away.

"C'est fini," a French corporal told her on the morning of the tenth. "Et moi, je vive. Un peu blessé mais vivant."

Living, but a little wounded. So am I, she thought. So is Mark. It's over. Somewhere a few miles ahead Mark would soon be returning to Paris. And then? It didn't matter. Then, wherever he went she would go. There would be no more partings. She wondered suddenly what he would be doing at this particular moment, and how long it would be before the rest of the wounded could be sent back, how soon she herself would be on the way to Paris to meet Mark.

It was over. But it was not over. The treaty had been agreed to: the Germans would withdraw west of the Rhine; they would surrender equipment; they would give up all territory presently gained. It was total surrender, and yet on the Western Front the battle-fatigued troops of the German Army continued their fight as the American First Army pushed on.

"Over, my ass!" Mark said to Dan Sebastian in the trenches outside Sedan. "If it's over, why the hell are we still fighting?"

"Not official." Dan smiled. "You know armies and governments. Everything goes by timetable. Jesus!" he breathed as a bullet flew low overhead. He returned the fire, and suddenly ahead of them a dozen German troops appeared, firing as they rushed the entrenched American position. "A couple of heroes," Dan said even as the order came to move over the top.

It was a sudden, bitter skirmish, the last offensive the Germans would ever take. Yet in the death and destruction it brought, it was the Battle of Argonne Forest, it was Somme and Lys and Amiens and the taking of Sedan. It was the Marne and Château Thierry.

To his right Mark heard Dan Sebastian call out, and then the call ended abruptly in a gasp. Bending low, he zigzagged across the open space between them, crouching over Dan's prostrate body, and pulled him back to the trenches. There was a brief cessation of fire. Malone was moving the men out cautiously. "Leg," Dan said to Mark. "Caught a rifle bullet. For Christ's sake, get down, Mark!" But even as he said it, a grenade burst near them and they saw Malone spin away, his body arched and then suddenly limp and falling. Like a rag doll that had been tossed into the air, it came to rest drunkenly.

"Baker!" Mark shouted. "Pull the men back! Regroup! Concentrate your fire!"

Then Mark was down, zigzagging once more across the field to where Malone had fallen. "Malone?" he said. "Malone?"

And Malone stirred and opened his eyes. "Shoulder and back," he grunted. "Didn't get it full. That kid Fallon over there . . ." He nodded painfully.

Mark said, "Take it easy. The litters are coming up."

"You better get the hell to cover," Malone said. "They got the lieutenant and me. That leaves Corporal Baker as company commander if you go. And Christ Almighty knows what Baker will do to them. He's a brassbound hero-type."

"I'm pulling you over to the trenches," Mark said, and bending low, he half dragged, half carried Malone to lie beside Dan Sebastian.

"You two boys have a nice chat." He grinned. "Soldier!" he yelled. "Get those litters up here." And he was gone, running low and zigzagging again to catch up with Baker and the troops ahead.

"He made it," Dan said quietly to Malone. Suddenly there was a blast that rose above the rifle fire. A white cloud of smoke obscured the landscape, and when it cleared, Mark Douglas was no longer visible.

Hours later, lying on his litter, waiting to be put into the field ambulance, Dan said, "The captain, Captain Douglas?" And Corporal Baker stepped forward.

"Dead, Lieutenant. I saw him fall. He and Berger and Fallon. Fallon's bad. Berger's injured. But the captain, sir, he . . . he was dead. I thought the war was over," Baker added.

"The captain knew better," Dan answered. "It could have been me or Malone," he added. "The captain saved us." Silent tears made paths along the dusty grime of his face.

"We'll get you to the field hospital, Lieutenant," the soldier said. "Take it easy."

The armistice went into effect at eleven o'clock the next morning, and everywhere people poured into the streets to celebrate—everywhere except in the field hospital, which still ministered to the last casualties, and in the city hospitals, where some would never walk again.

That morning Julie, on coming into the hospital tent, found Dan Sebastian among the newly arrived wounded and hurried eagerly toward him. "You look all right," she said, greeting him. "You're the second of your company I've seen." Something in his face sent a thrill of anxiety along her nerves and she rushed on, suddenly afraid that he would speak. "You heard about that poor boy, Lindstrom. I remember Mark telling me about him. I wrote to his mother. So sad to lose a son, to lose anyone. Well, at least you're all right, and I can see you'll be up and about."

"Julie," he interrupted quietly, and she fell silent, her eyes downcast.

"It's Mark," she said dully. "I knew when I saw you. I can't bear it. Don't tell me," she begged. "It isn't really true. It can't be true. I'd know. I would know if . . . I'd know," she finished.

"He saved my life," Dan said. "I told him to get down. I . . . I saw him fall, Julie."

"Don't," she moaned.

"I sent the soldiers for him, but they said . . ."

She turned abruptly and began to walk away. The doctor called to her, and she heard Dan's voice saying, "I'm sorry." Still she went on past the rows of cots, past the litters, past the people who sought to stop her, throwing off the arm of a nurse who hurried up. She walked blindly, heedless of her direction, knowing only that she had to get away. She was well down the road, headed toward the open fields, when one of the ambulances came along beside her, moving to cut her off before it stopped.

The driver leaned out. "I wouldn't go that way, Miss," he said. "There was a battle yesterday and there are a lot of . . ." He broke off and peered at her. "Are you all right?" he asked.

"I'm all right," she said. "I have to find someone."

"Not that way. The army is well ahead now, and we've cleared out the wounded. There isn't any . . . that is . . ."

"I have to find him," she said. "I have to find him."

"Here, Miss, you don't look so good." He got out of the ambulance and caught hold of her arm.

At his touch she began to cry and then sob. "Let me go. I will find him. I will find him. Let me go."

He had trouble subduing her, but at last she stopped struggling. "Look, you tell me who and what, and I'll go look for you. But that battlefield . . . there isn't anything left except . . . except some dead Germans. We cleared out our dead early this morning. Buried them. Look, you go on back. We took in all the I.D. tags and personal things. Ask the commandant. He'll be able to tell you what you want to know."

The battle scene was no place for her to go. If she saw some of the German corpses, stripped of shoes and clothing, some without any identification . . . Battlefield scavengers. They ranged France, looting the dead. Thank God it was over.

"Look," he said more quietly, "I'm going back there now. I'll check. I promise if you'll go see the commandant. Tell me the man's name."

"Mark," she said, "Mark Douglas. Captain . . . he's a captain."

"Okay. Now if he isn't on our list and he isn't out there, then maybe he's up ahead with his outfit. Did you think about that?"

"They saw him fall," she said. Her tears had stopped and her face was now expressionless.

"Might have gotten up again. Look, don't bury the man until you know something more. Now, do me a favor and go back to the hospital."

"Thank you," she said, but there was no light of hope in her face. She turned obediently and walked back the way she had come.

Julie returned alone to Paris the week before Christmas to find a jubilant Kitty on the verge of marriage to Michel. "It worked for me, after all," Kitty bubbled over while Julie set her bags down and began to change her battle- and travel-stained uniform. "Remember I said that I wanted glamour? Well, Michel is glamorous enough for me. He has a house down in Provence, and he really isn't poor or anything. I met his parents last week and they actually like me. We're getting married on January 10, and I'm so glad you're back because you're really the best friend I have, and I want you to be my witness.

"I'm happy for you, Kitty," Julie answered, summoning a smile.

"What's wrong?" Kitty asked. "You . . . you look so different . . . older, I don't know."

"Mark is missing in action," Julie said flatly. "They believe he's dead. He . . ." She paused. "They're still looking for him, for his body. You see, he was hit and then, well, he just wasn't seen again."

"Oh, Julie." Kitty came forward, contrite and sympathetic, to put an affectionate arm around Julie's shoulder, a shoulder that stiffened at her touch.

"Don't," Julie said. "I know you mean well, but don't. I can't stand sympathy. It . . . it tears me apart."

Kitty drew back awkwardly. "I'm so sorry," she said.

"Yes. Everyone is sorry. It's funny. This was the time I believed, and now . . ." She shrugged. "Here," she said, reaching into her bag. "I brought us a bottle of wine. Open it, will you? At least we can celebrate your good news."

"Not now. How can I?" Kitty protested.

"How can you not? Anyway, I want some wine. It helps." She unpacked her robe and toilet articles as Kitty poured the wine into water glasses.

"Not very elegant," Kitty said, handing one to Julie. "Mmm, this wine is good."

"It's a wine from Burgundy, a Beaujolais. There's more in my case."

"More? Are we having a party?"

"No. It helps me to sleep. I don't sleep otherwise," Julie said. "Don't look so shocked. It isn't spirits. A little wine never hurt anyone. It takes a lot of wine to get drunk."

Kitty sipped from her own glass, saying nothing.

"Go on, Kitty. Tell me all your plans, all about how Michel finally proposed. I don't want silence any more than I want sympathy. Besides, good news always makes me feel better. In fact, you could say it makes me feel hopeful. Anyway, you look very strange bottling up your natural flow of conversation. Depressing." Julie finished her wine and poured another glass. This she took to her bed, setting it on the little table and stretching out with her robe wrapped around her. "Talk away," she commanded again. "How was it here during the summer?"

"Awful. There was so much bombing. But, then, after a while, when we knew the Germans were on the run, it was . . . oh . . . as if the war was over long before the armistice. You'd hardly know there'd been a war now, except, of course, for all the American soldiers getting ready to ship home . . . and some are . . ." She trailed off and added, on a wailing note, "Julie, everything I say reminds me of . . ."

"I know about the American soldiers," Julie said. "In fact, I'm seeing one tonight—Dan Sebastian. Do you remember him?"

Kitty blushed and said nervously, "You won't tell Michel about Dan, will you?"

"Of course not. Don't be worried. You weren't engaged to Michel then."

"No, but he has a terribly jealous streak. Why, I got a letter from a man I used to see back home and you'd think I'd been cheating, the way Michel acted. The poor fellow heard from his sister that I was in Paris and wrote me from the front lines, saying he hoped we'd meet before he was shipped home. I had to write back and tell him my fiancé wouldn't allow it. He'll think I'm crazy." Kitty looked injured. "That's one thing that worries me."

"What?" Julie asked, amused.

"Well, you know how friendly I am. I mean, I just naturally like to talk and smile and, well, you know. . . ."

Julie nodded. "If Michel goes mad now every time I say hello, what will he be like after we're married?"

"It's something to think about," Julie agreed. She sipped slowly on her wine, beginning to feel the warm relaxation creep over her. Kitty was five years older than she was, but for all of that she was still like a child. I, Julie thought, feel ancient.

"I have thought about it," Kitty said. "I think maybe I can manage him better once we're married, don't you?"

I don't think so, Julie said to herself, but who am I to give advice. Then she said aloud, "If you love him, you'll have to put up with his ways—that's all."

Kitty smiled, the temporary shadow of doubt lifted. "I don't mind that, really. Anyway, it is kind of flattering. Just think, in a month I am going to be Mrs. Michel Delibes. And I'm going to have my own beautiful house. Michel is going back into the building business with his father. There is a lot of building to do right now. We'll probably get rich, and then Michel says he will get me a little place in Paris so that we can stay in it whenever we want to come up here."

There was more, but Julie's mind had slid away from the conversation. It was nearly five and she wanted a nap before she met Dan at eight. Hopefully, he would have some news. There had to be an explanation. Mark had to be somewhere, whether he was alive or . . . or not.

". . . but you probably ought to rest," Kitty was saying. "Michel and I are motoring to his aunt's in St. Cloud for the weekend."

"I will sleep for a bit now, I think," Julie said, setting down her empty glass. "I'll see you on Monday."

She heard Kitty moving silently about the room as she dressed and packed, and then the wine and the fatigue overcame her and she drifted off to sleep.

It felt strange to be in ordinary clothes again after the months in uniform. Her red velvet Poiret gown, bought when she first came to Paris, made her face look very white, and she added a bit of Kitty's rouge to her cheeks, blending it in an effort to simulate natural glow, with only moderate success.

There was a leaden feeling inside, one that she had carried for the past six weeks, one that no amount of prayer or adherence to her belief that Mark still lived had been able to lift. Perhaps tonight, she thought, on her way downstairs, where Dan waited—tonight Dan might have some news. But the charm did not work.

"You look ravishing," Dan said when they were seated at the restaurant off the Champs Elysées. All the way there they had talked of inconsequential things, and now Dan appeared to be staving off the final answers. She had known from the first that there was really nothing he could tell her. His face looked calm enough, but his eyes did not quite meet hers.

Now she leaned forward and said, "Tell me, Dan, is it just no news, or is it . . . is it worse?"

He reached out and took one of her hands across the table. They might have been lovers, and other diners, noticing the beautiful dark young woman and the handsome blond American soldier, smiled.

"Worse," she repeated steadily.

"There isn't any doubt, Julie. God, I wish I didn't have to tell you this. You'll have official word in the morning. There isn't any chance that he's one of those who just were not identified properly. Julie, listen. I was there. I saw. When the battle was over, we knew. There was . . . that is, I believed, along with you, wanted to believe, I guess, that somehow he had been alive, that the soldiers were wrong, that Mark simply came to and moved up with the rest of the army. But it just isn't so."

She disengaged her hand and picked up her wine glass, drinking quickly. He hoped she would believe him. He didn't want to have to tell her about the stripped bodies that led to unmarked graves. But the graves matched the losses, as far as the army knew. Any hope that Mark was alive was too slim to hold out to her.

"That's that, then," Julie said as the hovering waiter came forward to refill her glass.

"You'll be going home soon, I expect," Dan said uncomfortably. He had been afraid she would cry, and now he wished she would. It was infinitely more painful to watch her white face and those enormous despairing eyes.

"Yes," she said. "I suppose so." Then she said, "Talk about something else, Dan. Tonight I would welcome talk and quite a lot of wine."

"Be careful. Too much can make you sick," he warned.

"Don't worry about me. I learned to drink wine when I was a child. I have a very good head." She smiled at him, almost provocatively. "And you," she said, "will go back to San Francisco and marry that girl?"

"Yes, no, I don't know. I haven't thought past getting out of the army. We ship for home at the end of the week. When will you go back?"

"I don't know, either. There are still all the soldiers in the hospitals. I've become very good at visiting soldiers and helping nurses and writing letters. Somehow, that's more meaningful than going back to the Belmont Theater—that is, if Lew Belmont would have me back. By his standards I am woefully thin. In the spring, perhaps."

But she knew it was not so. Mark was gone. Intellectually she could accept that. But, quite irrationally, she felt that to leave France would be to admit it fully. Someday. Not now.

They both drank far more than they needed. Taking her home in the fiacre, Dan found himself forgetting that she was Mark's girl and that Mark had been his friend. Julie leaned against him, languorous and seductive, her hair brushing against his face. Without meaning to, he kissed her and she moved against him, kissing him back.

When they reached her pension, she said, "Come up. Kitty is away."

He was sorely tempted, but something in her manner made him draw back. She was looking at him, her parted lips soft and blurry from his kisses, her eyes half veiled. He still held her at the waist and could feel the yielding in her body, and suddenly he knew what was wrong. Indifference, he thought. Not just to me. To any man. I could be any man. Not that it mattered to him. Hell, he was no plaster saint, and it had been a long time between women. He could forget that Mark's ghost lay between them, even forget that he had once spent the night in that very pension with Kitty Behrens. But he knew that Julie was well the worse from the wine, and his own private code wouldn't allow him to take advantage of her, even if he could believe she would not regret it in the morning. And he didn't believe that, either.

"You're very tempting, Julie, but I think we'd better

say good night here. Tomorrow . . . you'd . . . well . . . there is Mark."

"Mark is dead," she said thickly, "and we're alive. And tomorrow, what does tomorrow matter?"

"It will," he assured her. He ushered her to the door. "Good night," he said and kissed her gently on the forehead. "Go home, Julie. You'll be better off at home."

But she only answered, "Good night, Dan. Good luck."

He did not see her again.

PART THREE

16

In the late afternoon on the last day in June, Julie sat sipping her aperitif in the Café des Deux Magots on the Boulevard St. Germain. Opposite her, talking earnestly, was an American soldier recently discharged from the hospital. She had met him after the armistice was signed, and now, seven months later, his wounds healed, he was returning home. He was one of the luckiest ones, she thought idly. He was alive with all his senses intact, and despite the severity of his wounds and the long mending of broken limbs, he was now as good as new.

". . . staying here. Come back to America," he was saying, and she focused on him again. For a moment his name escaped her, and she experienced the little thrill of anxiety these brief lapses brought. Alexander Rollins. Called Sandy because he had reddish-blond hair. Twenty-four. From . . . where was he from again? Oh, yes, Paris, Texas. That had been quite a little joke among the other convalescent soldiers. And he was worried about her.

"I'll be going home any day now," she said to avoid argument. "You're one of the last American soldiers. I scarcely have any duties these days. No, I'll be going home, perhaps in July. It's dreadfully hot here in August. I remember that."

"Why not come with me? I'm sailing in a few days. Come with me to Texas. You'd love Texas."

She smiled at him automatically. "You're very kind, Sandy. But my family is really expecting me in August. Suppose I write to you, and perhaps after I'm settled back in America, you can come and visit me."

She didn't mean it, of course, but he seized eagerly at

234

the straw, beginning at once to describe his Texas home
again, as if she had not heard about it over and over.

In an effort to change the subject, she said, "What
do you think of the Versailles Treaty?"

"The what?" His round, boyish face was startled. "You
mean the terms of surrender?"

"Yes. I have heard nothing else for two days now
except how disappointing the terms are. What do you
think?"

"Why, I don't know," he answered. "I hadn't thought
too much about it. After all, we licked the Germans and
moved them back from the Rhine, and France got some
coal mines. I don't see anything disappointing about it.
And what is a pretty girl like you doing bothering your
head about such things? That's for men to worry about."

Julie drained her glass and indicated she would like
to have another.

"Don't you think you might get just a bit dizzy?"
Sandy asked when the next round arrived.

"I don't think so," Julie said. "After that, I'll have to
be getting along. I have several things to do."

"But you'll have dinner with me?" he pressed.

"I'm sorry, I can't. This is our little farewell."

He raised his glass and she touched it briefly with her
own.

"Until we meet again in America," he toasted, and
she murmured agreement.

Paris was nearly empty of servicemen now. All but
a skeleton crew of the American Red Cross had returned
to the States, and the rest were leaving in a few weeks.
She wondered what she would do with her time now
that even the light demands at the hospital were ending.

In the first months after Mark was declared officially
dead, Julie had moved in a nightmare of disbelief, aided
only partly by work and more by the increasing doses
of wine and aperitifs. Sometimes she would still wake
up in the small hours of the morning with his name on
her lips, and for a minute she would feel a flood of
happiness. Often she dreamed that the news of his death
was an error, and she would see him coming toward her
in her dream and would reach out for him only to
awaken, knowing he was gone.

Desperate, she began to wait until bedtime to drink
the wine so that she would be too numbed to remember

dreams, but even then she often woke up in the morning with sadness so heavy upon her body that, while the memory of the dream vanished on awakening, she knew its general content.

If she had been chaste in the days when she and Mark had been separated and she believed him married to Miranda, his death would have had the opposite effect. Yet no man pleased her, and for the past weeks she had contented herself with casual meetings, such as the one with Sandy, and flirtations that died aborning.

Lately the old thrust to break through the foggy numbness that enveloped her had reappeared. Now, as she sat listening to Sandy, still extolling the beauties of Texas and the thrill it would be to have her meet his family, she thought, but not you, Sandy, and not tonight.

She began to gather her things together while he tried to persuade her to stay.

"I beg your pardon," a man said just at her elbow, and Julie looked up to see a familiar face she couldn't quite place.

"You are Miss Grant, is it not?" he said. "I am Count René de Brugarde. We met in New York some years ago . . . with Monsieur Randall."

"This is Miss Julie Fontaine," Sandy bristled, rising.

"Forgive the intrusion. I was so certain . . ."

"I *was* Miss Grant." Julie smiled and then said to Sandy, "It's all right. It's a very long story, but the gentleman is right." She made introductions and saw Sandy's awe at the mention of René's title.

"I had never expected to see you in Paris," René went on. "You must permit me to call on you. Perhaps we can have dinner one evening. In fact, my daughter and her husband are here in Paris with me. They would be delighted to meet you."

Sandy, who had subsided, was beginning to glower again, and Julie rose, saying, "I am at Number Seven, rue de Genet. I am engaged this evening, but if you will call on me, I shall be very pleased to see you."

He bowed. "I shall call you tomorrow, if that will be convenient, or may we say dinner tomorrow evening at seven?"

"Lovely." Julie smiled, holding out her hand, which he promptly raised to his lips. *"A demain soir,"* he said.

"A bientôt," she replied.

"But I was going to ask you to have dinner with me," Sandy complained when they had left the café and turned up the boulevard toward the Seine. "It's my last evening in Paris."

"I'm sorry, but that is someone I met through friends at home. I really must have a chance to talk to him. Do forgive me."

He would not forgive her, and he sulked as he walked her back toward her house, so intent upon his injury that he narrowly missed being struck by a motorcar as they crossed the Boulevard St. Michel.

At the door of Number Seven, Sandy attempted once more to change her mind. When she remained adamant, he stalked off in a huff.

As she started up the stoop, Madame Gautier hailed her from the shop entrance.

"You are early this evening," Madame said, clambering up the stairs and pausing on the stoop for breath. She was easily tired now. In the time before Monique's death, Madame Gautier had been quick and tireless. Now there were lines on her face that had not been there before and streaks of gray in the dark hair so like Monique's.

"I needed a rest," Julie answered.

"You have been too much at work, too much at play. Always running, running."

"My candle burns at both ends," Julie said.

"It is not good. You are young, but if you will go on like this, you will be very old at thirty."

"I will sleep tonight," Julie promised. "How are the little ones?"

"Well, thank the good God." As she spoke, Madame Gautier's eyes looked up to the spire of St. Gervais, rising over the rooftops. "So, the war is over and the nave is almost rebuilt, and now we have no more worries."

"We had enough," Julie said.

Madame Gautier gave her a dim smile of comradeship. They stood silent, each intent on personal sorrow, and then, as if she could not bear to dwell on it, Madame Gautier said, "Life goes on, doesn't it? But with that treaty, zut, I don't know. My husband says it is no good. That Clemenceau—the tiger of France has become the little pussycat for Mr. Wilson and Mr. Lloyd George to play with." She spat briefly.

"Mr. Wilson didn't want to impose too harsh a peace on the Germans for fear it would make another war."

"That one—he is crazy," Madame Gautier said. "Excuse me. He is your President, but he is crazy."

"That's what my uncle used to say." Julie laughed.

"You will see. Germany will try once again—at least once again. My grandchildren will be fighting, if not my sons."

"That is a long time away. I'll worry then . . . if it comes." Julie mounted the steps and Madame Gautier followed her.

As Julie turned up the long flights to her room under the eaves, Madame Gautier exclaimed, "Zut! I nearly forgot! You have a letter from America." She fished inside her apron pocket and pulled out an envelope. "Maybe an old friend, yes?"

Julie looked at it, seeing Jason's cramped hand, and shook her head. "More like an old enemy," she replied.

Jason's letter was another of his pleas to dissolve Fontaine's by selling to Steuben, which, now that the Volstead Act had passed, was busy converting to the sale of juice grapes and medicinal champagne. Julie made a moue of disgust. Medicinal champagne, indeed, and cooking wine, with salt added to render it unfit for drinking. The trust turned over to her last year on her majority, while it enabled her to live moderately, had dwindled far below her earlier expectations. There had been nothing in the way of dividends from Fontaine's, and she had foregone her salary as a nominal board member in an effort to keep Fontaine's afloat. Mark's shares had come to her on his death, according to the wills they had made the summer before they were to be married. Consequently, Jason's tone had taken on a certain air of conciliation.

"Your Aunt Millicent had the flu and it was a miracle that she survived. So many died last year—twenty million, I believe the figure was. A soldier fighting in France was safer. She is still very weak and wonders when you will come home."

Julie tossed the letter on the dresser without finishing it. The mention of the flu epidemic brought back more painful memories. So many people had died in those few winter months following the armistice, millions more, in fact, than had been killed during the war. Several people she had known back in New York had succumbed, and several here in France. But, of all of them, Lew Belmont's death had been the greatest shock to her.

It was impossible to imagine Madeline without Lew or New York without the Belmont Girls, for that matter. Before Lew's illness, Madeline had written that so numerous were the daily deaths in the crowded tenement sections of the Lower East Side that private burial became impossible and the wagons rolled each day through the streets with the draymen calling, "Bring out your dead. Bring out your dead."

The poor always suffered swiftly and horribly during any disaster, but this time the virulence had reached far uptown, into the homes of the affluent. Before it was over, it had claimed half a million Americans and millions of others throughout the world.

Millicent, already ill, had survived. Lew Belmont, vigorous and healthy and in his prime, had died. Mark had been right. It mattered not at all whether you were good or bad, puritan or sinner. No wonder the ancient Greeks had conceived of the Three Fates. It described the cycle of life ending in Atropos' arbitrary snipping of life's threads.

Julie threw herself across the bed, feeling unutterably depressed. "There is a void in my days," she said aloud. And I am beginning to talk to myself, she added silently. Kitty, now married and living happily in Provence, had been a welcome relief from her dreary thoughts. In the four months Kitty had been gone, Julie had begun to feel her own isolation more keenly.

She had no plans this evening. She would arrange for a bath and to wash her hair. When she summoned the necessary will to do it, she would dine on the bread and cheese she had bought earlier and write to Uncle Jason with one more refusal. And she would write to Joe Damien. If Steuben's was selling juice grapes and medicinal champagne, why not Fontaine's?

Tomorrow. Tomorrow there was the afternoon at the hospital. And tomorrow evening . . . She sat up. Tomorrow evening she was dining with Count René de Brugarde—something different. It gave her a lift and she went below to arrange for her bath.

The following evening Julie dressed with care, something she had not done for many months. It was a new gown, one she had bought on a shopping expedition to fill an afternoon between luncheon and what might be considered a reasonably appropriate hour to have an aperitif. Of white peau de soie, it was the latest fashion. The arms were bare, the neckline low, and it was delicately beaded with iridescent crystals. Paris might be torn between the exhaustion of the war and relief that it was over, but it had not lost its incredible gay optimism, which even the current raging over France's forced settlement could not extinguish.

Rebuilding the city had commenced almost at once, and many couturiers had rallied in time for the spring showings. Goods were dearer, the price of food was rising, and entertainment grew more and more expensive. Yet there did not seem to be any lack of money to spend in spite of the inflation, at least not in Paris, where American civilians were settling in large numbers almost as quickly as the town emptied of American servicemen.

You are very chic, she told her mirrored reflection, except that you need to cut your hair. She had wound it tightly around her scalp, repressing the waves and effecting a bobbed image. She secured it with the old *brillante* hair clips. If only the bodices of the new clothes were not designed to eliminate the bosom, she sighed. The modiste had tried to persuade her to buy one of the new flat bandeaus that bound the bosom, leaving a flattish look, but Julie had demurred. It was too reminiscent of those convent corsets—restricting and uncomfortable. What fashion relieved you of on the one hand, it bound you in on the other. Gone forever were corsets, and she loved the new suspender belts that freed her waist and hips. She would not suffer herself to be confined anywhere else, either.

One of the Gautier children came to tap on her door and say that a gentleman waited below. There was a repressed excitement in the child's voice that piqued Julie's curiosity. Surely René could not arouse that kind of interest. She caught up her gold silk-fringed capelet and her beaded bag and hurried down the stairs.

René stood in the small foyer, elegant in his evening clothes, good looking in his middle-aged, distinguished

way, but not so very different from other men. Yet, from
the Gautiers' rooms on her left, she could hear the
suppressed giggling of the children and the whispered
admonishments of their parents.

Coming out into the street, she realized that what excited the Gautiers was not René so much as the sleekly
polished Rolls-Royce with its chauffeur standing at attention near the rear door.

"Hélène and Guy are at Maxim's waiting for us. I
think you will enjoy my son-in-law. He spent some time
in your country and likes Americans very much."

"And you?" she asked, smiling.

"But of course I like Americans," he replied with an
exaggerated gallantry as he assisted her into the car.

René had not said she would like his daughter, and
early in the evening Julie decided she did not like Hélène
de Perrier. Hélène was inclined to pout, to demand, and,
otherwise, to retreat into silence. Julie judged her to be
in her late twenties. Her sleek, dark hair, cut in the
latest fashion, framed a lovely slender face; her eyes
were large and deeply brown; her flame-colored crepe de
Chine gown clung to her slim, almost boyish, figure.
Hélène looked, in fact, like the height of sophisticated
chic.

Her husband, Guy, was quite her opposite. Inclined
to be a bit plump, fair-haired, good natured, with rather
protuberant light blue eyes, he was the soul of affability.
He spoke nearly fluent English, and the conversation continued that way for some time.

Then Hélène, in her rather heavily accented English,
said to Julie, "You are to go soon home?"

"I haven't decided," Julie replied. "I like Paris. I'm
used to it. Perhaps I will stay on. Perhaps not."

"It must to be, how do you say, *difficile* not to have
someone of others of Americans," she floundered, and
Julie answered her in French.

"But that is amazing!" Guy exclaimed, giving Julie a
look of admiration.

"Not at all. I've been taught French since childhood.
I was schooled by French nuns and, of course, I have
been living in Paris for almost two years now." She
turned an amiable glance on Hélène. "If you were to
spend a year or so in New York, for example, you would
speak better English than I speak French."

"Very tactful, Mademoiselle Fontaine," Hélène said with a trace of rancor in her voice. "But I assure you, English is a language that bores me."

"Hélène!" This came sharply from her father.

She shrugged. "I apologize," she said. "It was thoughtless of me."

"You must tell us the mystery," René interposed. "I met you as Angela Grant, the toast of Broadway, and I find you again as Miss Julie Fontaine, a dedicated Red Cross volunteer. Which is really you?"

"This is really me." Julie smiled slightly. "At least, I am really Julie Fontaine. I . . . er . . . took the other name so that my family would not come running to New York to remove me from the theater." She dissembled with only slight hesitation.

"My father would have killed me," Hélène said flatly.

"My father is dead," Julie answered, "and my mother," she added.

"An orphan, then?" René commented. "Many orphans do not do so well in life."

"I come from sturdy stock." Julie laughed. "And, of course, I did have guardians."

"An actress," Hélène murmured in a voice that just missed being insulting.

René gave her a sharp glance and said, "You must forgive my daughter. She is missing her home, I think, and is very bored to be visiting Paris with her father." Hélène flushed, but there was an undeniable steeliness in both her father's voice and the look that apparently subdued her.

The rest of the meal was less difficult, as Hélène made an effort to restore herself to her father's good graces.

"I remember," Julie said at one point, "how brave we all thought you were to risk crossing the Atlantic during the German submarine offensive."

"I? Not at all," René said modestly.

"He is too modest," Guy interposed. "My father-in-law was on a mission then. You see how quiet he is? How modest? Ah, but that is one of the reasons he was a good agent. Not myself. I am too noisy and I am not so modest."

"Don't pay any attention to him," René said. "It is my son-in-law who was the agent. His mother's people are from Alsace, and Guy is very good at languages. He is more fluent in German than he is in English, for example. I, I made one little trip. But, Guy, he was active all during the war on many dangerous missions. It is he who is modest. I, I stayed home and tended my vineyards against the German foxes, and Guy went out to shoot the foxes for me and save my vineyards." He said it lightly and with a laugh, but beneath the joking Julie saw the mutual admiration René and Guy shared. She saw also from the tightening of Hélène's mouth that she resented their friendship.

"It was not easy tending the vineyards—I should say *defending* the vineyards—either," Guy remarked.

"Were they badly damaged?" Julie asked René.

"I was luckier than most," René said. The château vineyards escaped the worst of it. A few of the vignerons from which we buy grapes did, also. But for many it was nearly ruination. And, of course, during the long occupation of Champagne it was very hard to check the vine diseases."

"Yes, I understand that the Phylloxera damaged nearly fifty percent of the acreage, especially around Rheims," Julie said.

"How do you know about wines?" Hélène asked.

"My father had a winery. In fact, it is still there—Fontaine Wines Company, in New York State. We, too, make champagne. Or we did until recently. Our winemaker, Joe Damien, came from Villedommange as a little boy. His father left France during the time of the big Phylloxera epidemic in 1865 to work for my grandfather."

"Formidable!" René breathed. "A beauty who used to be an actress, who speaks flawless French, and who also comes from a wine family. And she is intelligent, is she not?" He appealed to the table at large, and Guy smiled broadly in agreement. "Now, tell me more about this," René demanded. The conversation centered entirely on wine, Julie's background, and also on Château de Brugarde and the lovely countryside around the village of Lacon and Hautvilliers, the closest large town to it.

Julie talked animatedly, carried away from her troubles for the first time in many months. The men entered eagerly into the discussion and suddenly the atmosphere was light and gay, as if a bubble from one of the champagne glasses had escaped into the room and, growing bigger and bigger, had enveloped them all—all save Hélène, whose smiles were forced and who scarcely contributed more than a murmured word of agreement.

In the week that followed that first dinner at Maxim's, René's Rolls-Royce appeared nightly at Number Seven, rue de Genet. It never failed to awe the Gautier children. In fact, the more it appeared, the more excited they grew.

Although Guy and Hélène joined René and Julie from time to time, they gradually stepped into the background. Finally, at Hélène's insistence, she and Guy returned home. She had, she said, enough of the theater and of concerts and of dinners and quite enough conversation about wine.

"Hélène is temperamental," René explained to Julie. "I have spoiled her."

During the days and nights they were in each other's company, Julie learned everything about René's life. He had been widowed for many years. Hélène had been six when her mother died, a few short weeks after delivering a stillborn son. There previously had been two other stillbirths, both boys. "I was destined never to have a son," René said. "Perhaps that is why I spoiled my daughter. It was all very sad for Hélène—her mother's illnesses, the grieving for the babies, and then that final illness."

Julie found herself drawn to René, partly in sympathy, partly for the humor he brought to their times together. Unlike the men she had always known, he did not importune her, nor did he make any effort to bridge the gap between friendship and love. For, as much as he talked about himself, he made her talk, too. She told him about Mark and about all the separations until the last permanent separation. Telling him, she wept for the first time since that day outside Sedan and was comforted by her tears.

Only on one of the last evenings before he was due to leave Paris did they approach the reality of their mutual attraction. They had dined at the Ritz and gone afterward to a little café in Montmartre where they consumed more champagne.

Driving home, Julie leaned back against the upholstery,

and when her head touched René's arm as it lay along the back of the seat, he slipped the arm around her and drew her over to him for a kiss. It was a light kiss, but feeling sensual and slightly dizzy, Julie returned it warmly, until his kiss became deep and searching. She settled closer and closer against him, and as she did, desire flamed up along her nerves. Moments later he drew away, eyeing the chauffeur's ramrod back and saying in a soft whisper, "I think I may fall in love with you." For an answer, she leaned back to him and kissed him. It was a brief kiss.

"I must return to Lacon in a few days," he said, pulling away.

"I know," she replied. It was a phrase men had used with her over and over in the months after Mark's death, and too often, lonely and desperate to feel love again, she had made that last night more than it ever needed to be. Soon René would be gone. Well, why not René?

Yet, when they drew up in front of her house, he escorted her to the door, pressed a light kiss on her forehead, and said, "Until tomorrow night, chérie."

"And what will we do tomorrow night?" Julie asked.

"Perhaps you will dine with me at my cousin's house, where I am staying. My cousins are due back this evening from Monte Carlo and I want to introduce you before I return to Lacon."

"I'd like that," she said.

"Good. I will send the car for you at eight, if that is agreeable."

"It is agreeable." Julie smiled and once again he leaned down and pressed a chaste kiss on her forehead. "Until tomorrow," he murmured.

Julie was apprehensive the next evening. The invitation to dine at his relatives' home was a clear indication of his interest, but that had not disturbed her. It was that, for some reason, despite the title and the chauffeur and the Rolls, she had imagined nothing so grand as the Delon mansion off the Champs Elysées.

Ascending the steps, her knees felt a bit wobbly, and as she entered the vast reception hall, with its glittering chandelier and elegant furnishings, she began to hope that she was not too much of a disappointment to these cousins, whoever they were.

A silent maid took her light wrap and ushered her through a door about halfway down the hall. René was standing near the fireplace of a dimly lit salon. He broke into a smile at her entrance and came forward to greet her eagerly, taking both her hands and kissing first one and then the other.

"I am so glad you have come, but I am afraid I have some disappointing news. My cousins are unavoidably detained in the south. Naturally, I suspect that they are not yet ready to leave the gaming tables. Still, I have gone to so much trouble."

"Trouble?" she echoed.

"Yes. I have ordered a beautiful dinner. But their telegram arrived too late to halt preparations. Will you mind dining alone with me? Then, perhaps, we can go on to some amusement later."

"Whatever you like, René," Julie said.

"Ah, good. See, I have had a table set here in the small salon. It will be less formal that way since we dine à deux. Come, let me pour you some champagne. Alain will be along to serve us presently."

It seemed to Julie that presently took rather a long time, and she grew desperately hungry as she waited. The champagne went to her head and she found she was having difficulty following what René was saying about his family, save that it was a long history. She was immensely grateful when the door opened and Alain entered bearing the first course.

A delicious pâté began the meal and was followed by a cold soup, some fish in wine sauce, and orange duck. There was a memorable salad dressing over watercress, and at the end of the meal the light, creamy cheese nipped at the ripe sweetness of the strawberries.

They drank champagne throughout, but now that the food had been consumed, Julie felt only pleasantly warm and gay.

"It was a lovely dinner," she sighed as she moved to the couch while Alain silently and efficiently whisked away the dishes.

"I'm glad you enjoyed it. We'll have some coffee and brandy, and then I must see to providing you with entertainment. It is too late for concerts, of course. But would you like to go to a lovely little café I know where there is a marvelous chanteuse?"

"Yes, I'd like to hear some music," she answered equably.

Alain returned just then, bearing a coffee service and brandy. When he had poured, René dismissed him for the rest of the evening and then excused himself for a few minutes.

When he returned, he came to sit beside her. "It will be easier to talk without Alain popping in and out," he said, reaching for her hand.

She smiled hazily at him. "I don't think I need brandy," she murmured as he handed her a glass.

"A little cognac. Very good. It's Hennessy's. I have a horse trainer who is Irish. He persuaded me that it is the best. I suspect that was only his patriotism, because the Hennessys are of Irish descent. Still, it has become my favorite cognac. Try it."

She lifted the glass obediently, feeling the warmth and sweetness of the liquor in her throat. "It's nice," she said.

"I want you to come down to Lacon," René went on. "You must see the château and the vineyards, and you must meet my mother, who is very old and very difficult, but at the same time quite charming."

"I mean to leave Paris soon," Julie murmured, sipping at her brandy.

"Not back to America?" he asked, alarmed. She shook her head. "No, at least not for a while. I want to get out of the city in August, though. It gets so desperately hot here. I like to be near the water."

"Then you must come to Lacon. There we are surfeited with streams and brooks and ponds and waterfalls . . . well, at least one waterfall from spring water in the hills that feeds the brook running through our fields."

"It sounds lovely and cool. Yes, I will visit you." She turned her face to him and smiled again. He took the glass from her hand, set it down, and bent his head to kiss her. It was a slow, sensual kiss. His mustache tickled her lips pleasantly, arousing her. He held her easily in his arms but made no move to touch her otherwise, just that kiss and then a brief lessening of the pressure as the tip of his tongue traced the outline of her mouth before his own closed over hers again.

All at once, she was weak with desire, and yet the kisses went on and on. When she thought she could bear it no longer, his hands began to touch her body lightly, knowingly. With the same infinite delay, be began to remove her gown so that it whispered away from her before she realized what he was doing. And now his mouth moved downward, placing small, light kisses along the edge of her slip. His hands were on her back and her breasts were bared. His mouth moved over them with the same light lack of emphasis.

The gentler he was, the more passionate she became, and then all at once he placed her back against the cushions and rose. Swiftly, he gathered the discarded garments and held out his hand to her. "Come," he whispered. His eyes moved from her face to the fullness of her exposed breasts and he said softly, "Beautiful." He drew her up and, walking ahead of her, led her out through the vast, darkened reception hall and up the broad stairwell, up, up through darkness and then into another room lit with candles that glimmered softly and multiplied their light in the dressing table and triple pierglass mirrors.

Dimly, Julie saw her multiplied reflection. She was bare from the waist up and her hair was still bound. She stood that way for a moment as René moved away from her, and then he was behind her, his bare chest pressing into her back, his arms around her waist, his head next to hers so that they were reflected together. Her eyes met his in the mirror and he held her glance as his hands moved up to loosen her hair and send it cascading over her.

His arms went around her again, his hands cupping her breasts. She leaned back against him, breathing in quick little breaths. After a long moment he turned her away from the mirror and stepped a little way from her. His hands came out again and the last undergarment rustled to the floor, leaving her naked, save for her stockings and suspender belt.

"Beautiful," he said again, running his eyes over her body. She swayed toward him and he caught her, drawing her to the bed, reaching one arm out to pull aside the covers before he set her gently down.

He stood for several minutes then, looking at her as she lay there. She felt strange. Her body was flushed with longing, but her mind was detached. I want him, she thought. I want him to make love to me desperately, and yet . . . The thought remained unfinished because he had thrown himself quickly beside her, and now all at once he was touching her everywhere, over and over, with his hands, his mouth, moving from one part of her body to another even as she began to quiver. Sensation piled on sensation until it seemed she was clinging to the edge of a high precipice and then falling, falling and crying out. As she lay trembling in the aftermath he said, "It was good for you? You liked that?"

"Yes," she said.

"You are wonderful," he told her. "Be quiet for a moment now." He got up and went across the room through a doorway, reappearing sometime later. She roused herself from half-somnolence as he came back to the bed.

"This is what I like," he said. Julie thought, Yes, of course, and followed his wishes obediently. He moaned once and then, even as she began to go on more quickly, he drew her away. "Not yet," he said, "not yet." She felt him reach a hand out to the table beside him and then the hand was back, massaging her body. A fiery-cold glow enveloped her wherever his hands touched, a wild desire seized her, and she was suddenly writhing on the bed, unable to stop. His body, pressed to hers, was hot.

Never had she been so deliriously desperate for someone. Yet he still made no move to take her fully, bringing her relief in a variety of ways until she cried out feebly, "No more, please, no more."

She slept then, waking sometime later to the realization that he had aroused fresh fires in her as she lay sleeping. "Again," he said, whispering his demands, and she bent her body obediently until he moved her sharply away, pulling her back up beside him, flinging his body on top of hers, and when at last it was over she slept the sleep of utter exhaustion.

In the morning Julie awoke to find that René was no longer beside her. The candles had burned down and out and their waxy odor hung over the room.

She pulled the covers up around her neck and lay thinking about the night. He had unlimited patience. She was expert enough to know that not all men were that capable. With Mark it had been different. They were as one and together always. But the others that had followed had been for the most part unsatisfactory beyond the occasional release her body had demanded. She had thought it was owing to the fact that she had mourned Mark, but if that were so, then surely last night could never have happened. She yawned and stretched, feeling her body ache as if she were still tired. There was a discreet tap on the door and she sat up, clutching the covers around her and looking wildly about the room for her clothes. They appeared to have disappeared, but across the cream Empire chaise longue to her left, both a nightgown and dressing robe were draped. She darted out of bed and grabbed at the clothes, pulling them on hastily as the tap sounded again.

"*Entrez,*" she said, keeping her back to the door as she drew the sash around her waist and knotted it.

"You wish breakfast, *mademoiselle*?"

Julie turned to see the maid who had admitted her last evening. She was carrying a tray on which reposed a white porcelain breakfast service decorated with delicate pink rosebuds.

"Please," Julie said, suddenly famished.

"Will *mademoiselle* prefer the breakfast at the table?" the maid inquired.

"Please," Julie said again and followed the maid to the small round table in front of the windows.

When she had finished setting the food on the table, the maid opened the heavy damask portieres to reveal tall windows overlooking a garden. The sight of the garden reminded Julie of that week in the Picardy with Mark, and for a moment the day darkened and the night before became a dream. The moment passed and Julie sat down to her breakfast, attacking the croissants and jam and fruit as if she had not eaten in days. She drank two steaming cups of *café au lait,* and as she finished the last drop it occurred to her that she had not eaten breakfast with such relish in a long time. Too many mornings had found her headachy and slightly liverish from too much to drink the night before. Yet last night she had drunk an enormous amount of champagne and followed it with the cognac. But last night there had been René.

Where was he and what was he doing? He surely didn't expect her to dress and leave? And in her evening gown? She groaned. Impossible. She looked down at the light peach silk robe she wore and the soft matching gown. How had René come by these? His cousin's?

She stood up in agitation. Those cousins! What if they were to return and find her here with no luggage, no clothing beyond her evening dress? And where was her clothing? She went across to the wardrobe and looked in. Her dress hung neatly there, and beside it was a very pretty afternoon frock in lavender Georgette, and next to that were three daytime frocks. Her evening slippers were on the shoe rack, and next to them were two pair of ordinary shoes. He had provided everything. The armoire would be sure to reveal her underclothes, perhaps even more. Of that she was sure. And the dressing table? She opened the drawers to find all the necessary toiletry articles—brand-new ones. He had planned it. There were never any cousins to come to dinner. Or at least the cousins had not planned to be here.

Julie had hardly assimilated that thought when there was again a discreet tap on the door and the maid entered on her invitation.

"*Pardon, mademoiselle*, but Monsieur le Comte asks if you will be kind enough to join him and his aunt, Madame Delon, at your convenience."

"Say that I will be down presently," Julie murmured. His aunt? A real aunt. More real than his cousins, she devoutly hoped.

"*Mademoiselle* requires assistance with her dressing?" the maid asked. At Julie's sedate glance she said, "Very good, *mademoiselle*. If you will ring when you are ready, I will return to show you the way."

As Julie dressed, choosing a simple muslin frock from the clothes rack, she marveled at René's cool assumption. He surely had purchased these things ahead of time: they were new and unworn. How did he know everything? Slowly, bits of remembered conversation came back to her. "Your dress is lovely. Did you bring it from America?" And she had told him the name of the dressmaker that she used. "Perhaps I shall drink my champagne from your slipper as they used to do in the old days. But perhaps not; it is such a tiny foot."

And she had told him her shoe size. She even remembered saying, "Six is not tiny."

How long had she known him? Ten days. Yet the clothes were made and ready. How could he have been so sure? There had been nothing between them at all until the night before last. Well, she would go down and meet this aunt if, indeed, there was an aunt, and then once she had him alone she would demand answers.

Half an hour later, sitting in the boudoir of Madame Delon, assuring that ancient lady that she had not in the least minded dining without her last night, Julie felt her confusion mount.

"You are very French for an American girl," Madame Delon said in a reedy voice.

Julie turned to look at René, saying, "But surely you know that I am of French descent. René has thought of so many things, I am surprised he didn't tell you that, Madame Delon." Julie turned back to Madame Delon, who was looking at her with a puzzled glance.

From his position just outside his aunt's line of vision, René said quietly, "My aunt is quite deaf, *chérie*. She reads your lips. Her eyesight is remarkable, but then she cannot get about the house without assistance." Julie looked over at him and he smiled with meaning, adding, "Otherwise, I should not have dared."

Julie felt the blood come up in her face as she remembered the way he had seduced her and how she had reveled in it. Desire quivered in her body again. He saw it in her eyes and said warningly, "Careful, *chérie*. She is deaf but well sighted; feeble but not at all stupid."

He moved his chair so that he faced his aunt and said, "I was explaining to Mademoiselle Fontaine that the house goes back to Napoleon's time. She is fascinated by old houses. Last night, she insisted on a tour, but, alas, it grew too late, so I have promised her one this morning."

"You are very kind to have me, Madame Delon," Julie added. "This is a side of Paris I have not seen. It will be very difficult to enjoy my little pension again."

"But, of course, you will remain until you leave for the country? René tells me that you have arrangements to visit friends tomorrow. It is very convenient for us to have you, with my son and daughter-in-law away and my grandchildren, too. It has been so nice to have René here with me. I will miss him when he leaves. How fortunate that he is able to drive you to your friends. Of course, you must stay."

Julie murmured her thanks, her mind racing furiously.

What had he told the old woman? How had he explained? Madame Delon's next words dispelled her concern.

"So nice that an old friend of your father's should chance upon you here. In my day young ladies did not travel without their families or chaperones. Ah, but the war has changed that, and you young Americans, you are very brave to come all the way to France to help your soldiers when they are wounded."

"Very brave," René agreed. "But now, Aunt Clothilde, we have kept you too long." He rose and signaled to Julie. He made a great fuss over his aunt, promising to take tea with her that afternoon, promising to bring Julie back.

When at last they were in the corridor outside the room, Julie whispered, "You've been telling terrible lies to us. Why?"

"Come, come, *chérie*. Surely last night tells you why." He took her elbow in his hand and moved her down the corridor, talking easily as he went, explaining the different paintings, the period of the tapestries and of the furnishings, and opening doors and showing her various chambers until they were descending to the reception area again. She had followed him mutely for the most part, still dazed by the events. Now, as he ushered her into the salon where they had dined the night before, she turned to him inside the room and said, "How did you manage to find clothes for me?"

He laughed. "That is my secret."

"But you were so sure of me." She frowned.

"Not perfectly sure," he said. "But one must be prepared. And one must be discreet. Your luggage was delivered to the servants while you were dining with me. *Voilà!* The young *mademoiselle* is the daughter of old friends. My aunt has invited *mademoiselle* to spend a few days before she leaves for the country."

"And suppose I had said I would go home last night?" she challenged.

"Well, then, the young *mademoiselle* was called away hurriedly and we send on the luggage. But, *chérie*, you did not refuse," he said, looking down at her, his dark eyes flickering over her body. "You aren't sorry?"

"No," Julie said boldly. "I'm not in the least sorry."

For answer he drew her into his arms. She raised her

face, expecting to feel his mouth on hers, but instead he grazed down her cheek to her neck and behind her ear, nibbling softly. She arched against him voluptuously and then the moment was gone. He moved away, leaving her disappointed.

"I have business today. Tonight I will take you to that little café I spoke of. We will be Apaches tonight. At least we will not dress. We will go like the poor people of Paris. And then we shall see."

She felt vaguely resentful. "I am going to headquarters. I don't know how long I will be gone," she said.

"Shall we say eight, then? Will that give you enough time?"

She nodded, irked with herself for agreeing, annoyed that he was able to exercise so much control over himself and over her.

They parted coolly and all day Julie half-believed that she would remain at home that evening and let him invent whatever insane excuses he liked. Yet, evening found her back in the bedroom at the Delon mansion, dressing herself with care.

The closer it had come to evening, the greater her desire grew. He waited for her in the reception hall, so they were in the Rolls, sitting carefully apart, before she realized that they had exchanged only a brief word of greeting. Wanting to move closer to him, Julie perversely edged away instead.

"You are annoyed with me," he said.

"Yes."

He laughed. "Then I must beg your pardon, I see."

"Don't play with me, René," she said angrily.

"Ah, but that is what I enjoy most," he returned. "Your eyes grow so stormy, and your mouth becomes pushed out like a mutinous child's." He reached for her hand, running his thumb lightly over her wrist. "It is our last night for a while, chérie. Don't spoil it," he whispered quietly, and her annoyance melted away.

They left the café and wandered through Montmartre, down dark little streets where he would stop and draw her fiercely into his arms, crushing her mouth until she could feel the salty sting of blood on her lips. "I am mad about you," he whispered. He brought her to a little park and drew her deep into its shadows. Around them, she was aware of other lovers, hidden in a niches of their choosing. She lay in his arms, a dark, spreading chestnut tree above them, the bushes screening them from passersby. It reminded her of the long-ago night at the willow grove, only, for all of his kisses, for all his ardent caresses, there was no release of the tensions building within her. Coming out of the park, walking back to the car, she felt dazed with the same desperate longing to be taken.

They sat apart in the car, and back in the house he brought her to her room and said a quiet good night. She could not believe it. She stood there, watching him go down the hall to his door, saw him enter his room and close the door, and still she did not believe that he had left her.

Trembling, Julie went into her own room and undressed feverishly. The effects of the wine had worn off and she wished now that she had drunk more. How would she sleep with this passion raging through her body? She stood in the center of the room, her nightgown in her hands. She was in the act of drawing it over her head when suddenly she threw it aside and put out the lights, running to open the draperies and windows, shivering as the cool breeze caressed her fevered flesh.

A sudden gust of air billowing the curtains alerted her to the soundless opening of the door. She whirled about, outlined against the pale curtains.

"You," Julie whispered, "why do you torment me?"

René made no answer, coming to her, gathering her up and bringing her to the bed. She wanted to fight him, but he had brought her too close to fruition, and she hadn't the will. When this is over, she told herself, I will not see him again.

He was like a demon now, using all his expertise to bring her again and again to the moment she longed for, only to stop and wait even as she moaned, "Don't, don't stop."

"It is better this way," he answered, "slowly, slowly, to the right moment." And when the moment finally came, her body felt as if it were being torn apart by the force of the reaction.

"You see?" he said, stroking her quivering limbs. "You see?"

It was a long time before she was quiet, but then that, too, was better, for with it came a profoundly peaceful sleep. He did not disturb her again and, in the morning, when she awoke, he was gone once more.

This morning the maid came to bring her luggage and to assist with the packing of it. "Monsieur le Comte waits below," the maid said.

They were in the car and driving toward the Gautiers' house when René asked Julie to marry him. She had not expected that, and at first she did not know how to answer him.

"I love you," he said. "Surely you must feel something of the same. These past nights . . ."

"I . . . I'm not ready to marry just yet," Julie begged. "I . . . I care for you, of course. But marriage?"

"You wish to continue as we are, then? Indefinitely?"

"Well, no, it's just . . . I'm not ready to . . . René, I need time. We need to see more of each other. I haven't known you two weeks. Stay in Paris, or . . ."

"I can't stay in Paris. If it is no, it is no. Then I must say good-bye."

He changed the subject at once, entering into a frivolous recital of some comedy he had once enjoyed.

At the door of the pension, he lifted her hand to his lips. "Good-bye, Julie. Thank you for these beautiful days and nights. I will treasure the memory." And he was gone. Just like that. Gone.

She was alone again. She spent the day in desultory pursuits and that night finished nearly a whole bottle of wine before she slept. In the morning she awoke with the old familiar dullness.

It went that way for the next few days and she began drinking earlier and longer, knowing it was not going to help; she was still unable to make decisions. Mark was dead. René was alive, but he was gone. She should leave Paris, but there was no place she really wanted to be. There was no one she really wanted to be with . . . not for long—not even René, if it came to that, although she liked him better than she had anyone else.

The despair made her neglect her appearance; it kept her from the few duties remaining for her. She grew thin from disinterest in food and awoke each morning lethargic from the effects of too much wine the evening before.

Once, sitting in a café, waiting for a newly met friend to appear, the waiter approached her with the discreet inquiry as to whether or not she would compliment an old patron of the café by joining him.

She said no, and all at once a vision of Sara Prescott rose before her. Appalled, she left the café, forgetting altogether about the man she was to meet and walking for miles, up through the streets of Montparnasse, stopping to look at the Hotel Picardy, where she and Mark had stayed, heedless of the tears running down her cheeks.

At dusk she turned back toward home, her head clearer, her thoughts slowly marshaling. Self-pity. Sara's disease. Self-pity and rage at a fate that had taken her love. What had Madame Gautier said? She had told Julie that she was young, but at thirty she would be an old woman. Sara, not more than forty-eight, looked sixty. She was raddled and made up and puffy—an alcoholic. That's what I am or will soon become, Julie thought, whipping herself relentlessly. That's what happened when life had no purpose. Well, she must find a purpose —back in New York. Would she find work there? Lew Belmont was gone, dead in the flu epidemic that had nearly killed Millicent. Madeline was starring in another producer's show. "But my days are numbered," she had written Julie. "In another year or two I'm going to retire, while I'm still young enough to marry and have another baby. Cecelia is nearly grown now and I am not yet thirty-four."

No, there was nothing there anymore for Angela Grant or Julie Fontaine, not in New York and not in Prescottville.

But I must make a new beginning, she thought. I must. First she would change her habits. Exercise. No more wine. Get herself into some semblance of routine and then . . . then? Never mind "then." She would think about "then" later.

Lacking daily routine, she walked. At first she lay awake at night, her nerves tingling with unaccustomed alertness. But, gradually, as the endless walks around Paris started to take effect, she began to sleep naturally and awaken in the morning feeling the way she used to feel—alive and able to see the day with something approaching optimism. There is a time to grieve and a time to leave off grieving. Renewed by the return of physical well-being, Julie faced the future more hopefully. And she faced, too, Mark's place in her heart. For-

ever. She knew that. But surely the years would dim
the memory. She would marry and have children. If she
couldn't replace the love she lost, she would fill her heart
with other loves, but no more casual encounters and no
more throwing herself away.

If she steered a better course one day, Mark's memory
would be like the faded flowers pressed in Aunt Millicent's albums—faint reminders, faded with time, their
scent gone.

July was over and the heavy, exhausting heat of an
inland city in August smothered Paris. The Gautiers
had closed their shop and gone to a little village near
Marseilles for their summer holiday with Madame
Gautier's relatives. Soon the Paris streets would be empty
of all the inhabitants who could afford to flee and filled
instead with English and American visitors.

Julie, seeing her reflection in the mirror on one still,
muggy day that promised showers by evening, was struck
by the difference in her appearance. Gone was the look
of languor and boredom. Her cheeks glowed and her
eyes were bright, and some of the sadness in them had
gone, too.

All at once she thought, I needn't stay here. I can go
down to visit Kitty in Provence. Heaven knew Kitty invited her often enough. And then? And then I will sail
for New York, she decided abruptly. It didn't matter
that she couldn't really imagine herself in New York
again. It was time to move on. She would advise the
Gautiers by letter.

She was in the midst of sorting through her clothes,
putting those she would give away to Madame Gautier
in one pile, when a loud ringing of the bell below interrupted her. She peered out the window and saw the
familiar outlines of the Rolls.

René! She flew to the mirror to make herself present-
able and then went skimming lightly down the stairs.

René looked younger to her somehow. His face was
tanned and his eyes sparkled. "You are ravishing," he
said, taking both her hands and pirouetting her before
him. "And if you are not busy all the day, will you come
for a picnic with me in St. Cloud? It is a picnic feast I
cannot eat all by myself. It is too hot to remain in Paris

today. And I know a beautiful spot near a cold, cold stream. Doesn't that sound enticing?"

"I'm not busy." She laughed. "I'd love to go with you."

On the drive to St. Cloud they talked eagerly, as if the three-week separation had been longer than that. "I was afraid you would have left Paris," he confessed.

"If you had waited one more week, I would have been gone," she told him.

"*Tiens!* I have been very lucky." He reached for her hand and pressed it lightly.

The chauffeur carried the blanket and the large picnic hampers to a spot that René had chosen and then left them, with instructions from René to return at five.

"Did you mean to ask more than two of us?" Julie asked, eyeing the baskets.

"No. But there is wine and cold duck and cheese and rolls and pastries and . . . many other things. Fruit—the pears are delicious and the peaches are beautiful."

They ate and drank, talking between bites, leaning back against the mammoth old oak tree and letting the soft breeze drift over them. Below the bank where they sat, the cold stream René had promised sparkled in the sunlight.

"I thought about you all the time," René said when they had repacked the hampers. "And I spoke of you to my mother and to my daughter. You are very young," he added in an apparent non sequitur, but she knew what he meant.

"Time will cure that," Julie answered.

"I am old enough to be your father."

"I know," she answered tranquilly. "It doesn't matter."

"Would you be happy to live at the château? The village is very small, and Hautvilliers is not Paris, after all."

"Hélène doesn't like me," Julie said.

"Hélène likes very few people."

"And your mother?"

"My mother is old," he answered. "She is over eighty and she lives for the past, and for her food and for her games. She will beg endlessly for someone to play monte with her or écarté or backgammon. She is very bad at chess, but she likes to play. If you oblige her with a game now and again, she will adore you. And if you buy her little pastries when you go into town, she will be your slave."

Julie laughed. "That sounds easy."

"Will you, then?" he asked.

"Will I what?" she asked in turn, her face innocent.

"Marry me, Julie? Will you?"

"I will, René," she said gravely, and it was as if they had made a contract, a contract he sealed at once with an ardent kiss.

Lying in his arms, Julie's face flushed with his caresses, and a sense of safety enveloped her. It was all solved then, all that blank gray future, and without her volition.

"It is like it was before," she murmured. "You are so sure of me."

"Not at all. I am sure of what I want, and I try to get it."

She stirred in his arms, saying, "I missed you."

"Very much, or only a little?" he teased.

"Very much, especially at night," she answered.

"Well, now we will have many nights. And, meanwhile, we have now. I like to make love to you in the light. Your body is so beautiful." He was slowly unbuttoning her clothing, making soft, satisfied sounds as he proceeded.

This is what I have needed, Julie thought. It's what I always have needed. She tried to hold back, to match his control, but it was impossible. Even as he caressed her, his eyes never left her face, and she closed her own eyes against that black, impenetrable stare. She heard her involuntary cry of pleasure, and above it his voice was saying, "And now you are especially beautiful."

Later, as they sat talking, waiting for François to reappear, she said, "But how can you do it?"

"Do what?"

"Oh, make love to me like that, but . . ."

"But wait for my own pleasure?" he finished.

"Yes."

"I like it that way. I like to watch you, to make you happy, and then afterward for me it is so much better."

"But we are leaving here now," she said.

"Yes, but we have tonight, after the marriage."

"After the marriage?" Julie echoed. "But, René, how can we possibly . . ."

"You will say again I was too sure. But I have arranged for the license, and tonight we will be married. My friend, the mayor of St. Cloud, awaits us at the inn. In France the civil marriage is absolutely necessary. If one wishes yet another with a priest, *voilà!* It can be arranged."

"You will never cease to amaze me," Julie answered. "I should be annoyed with your presumption, but I'm only astounded."

"And happy, I hope?"

A strange little tremor shot through her. "Yes," she answered automatically, thinking happiness was different. What she had in its place was pleasure and contentment. The combination, while very satisfying, did not produce the elation of true happiness. But, perhaps, in time, that, too, would come.

The wedding ceremony was performed in the private salon of the inn, with the round, fat little mayor beaming throughout the ceremony. There were small cakes and wine afterward, and then it was over.

"I feel very well married," Julie commented as they returned to their suite.

"You are very well married," René replied. "The Countess de Brugarde. I wonder, shall you enjoy making love so much now that it is required?"

"I look forward to it," Julie said in a prim little voice, as if he had been talking of a play or an opera they were about to see.

He laughed. "You are quite out of the ordinary, my little bride—very sensual and very frank and altogether maddening. That is why I enjoy taming you so much."

"Is that what you call it?" she asked, eyeing him curiously.

"It's what I am doing, is it not?" He looked sleek and well pleased with himself as he moved toward her.

On impulse, Julie avoided his embrace, saying calmly, "Perhaps I won't care to be tamed this evening."

"Very well, my child. I shall leave you to your own pursuits," he rejoined. Then, lifting her hand, he kissed it formally, smiling at her without a trace of rancor. A moment later he had stepped through to his own room, leaving her staring at the door now closed between them.

Julie smiled to herself, thinking that, of course, he

would return as he had the last time. She made a
leisurely toilette and got into bed, putting out the light.
She lay in the dark for a long time, expecting every
minute to hear René at the door. Gradually, it occurred
to her that he had taken her seriously; otherwise, he
would not play such a childish game. Nettled, she rose
and went into his room without knocking. He was sitting
up in bed, reading, and he looked up as she came in.

"Ah, you are ready for bed, I see," he said pleasantly.
"And am I to receive a dutiful peck on the cheek as a
good night?"

"René!" Julie exploded. "How can you do this on our
wedding night?"

"I? But, my dear, I understand that it is you who wish
to be alone."

"I was teasing."

"Ah. Is that what they call American humor?" he inquired.

"Don't be cruel, René," she said.

"Come here," he ordered, and she moved forward.
"Take off that robe and gown."

"No." She retreated a little.

"Very well," he answered, then rose leisurely from the
bed. "If you wish me to prove my point, I will." He
picked her up in his arms and laid her upon his bed.
"Now, we shall see," he said. "You are such a child,
Julie." He sat on the side of the bed and began stroking
her head, smoothing the hair from her temples, drawing
his fingers along the side of her face and her neck,
smoothing her shoulders with gentle hands. His fingers
ran lightly down her arms and she shivered involuntarily.
He laughed softly and, reaching over, put out the light.
Presently, he got into bed beside her and, with a murmured endearment, kissed her gently on the lips. He
slipped one arm underneath her shoulders and drew her
head down on his shoulder. "Good night, little one," he
whispered, and presently she heard the sound of his
deep and even breathing.

"Are you asleep?" she asked incredulously.

"No. Would you like to talk?"

"No," she replied.

There was another long silence during which she
moved closer to him, and in answer he pressed his hand
into the soft flesh of her upper arm. She put an arm

across his body and raised her lips to kiss him at the side of his neck. Almost at once, he began to caress her gently and undemandingly, but the effect was electrifying. Without thinking of what she was doing, she broke away and struggled erect, trying to remove the robe.

"Stand up," he whispered, and she obeyed. She heard him fumbling, and then the room sprang back into light. She removed the robe and, as he lay watching her, she pulled the gown over her head. "Lovely," he said, swinging himself up so that he was sitting on the side of the bed. "Now," he said, reaching his arms out to enclose her waist and putting his face into the softness of her belly, "this is so much better, is it not?" He raised his face to look up at her before his hands came down to cup her buttocks and raise her body to his lips.

"You're a devil, you know," Julie accused. A moment later she cried out sharply, "Don't, you're hurting me!" But René ignored her cries and after a while the pain became part of her intense sensual pleasure.

Later, lying awake with René sleeping beside her, she thought with a growing sense of fear and bewilderment that it was not the taming of her that bespoke her future so much as it was the fact that he had enslaved her physically. Even now, despite the flavor of cruelty in his lovemaking, her body glowed and tingled. "I am satiated at last," she half murmured aloud and, turning her back to him, curled herself into a ball and fell asleep.

17

Along the road from the small village of Les Deux Croix, which was situated several kilometers from Sedan, a narrow lane reached upward to a small plateau, hidden from view by the bushes and trees that lined its twisting path.

To the casual passerby, it was only one more lane up

a hill covered with scrub oak and brush whose roots went deep and clung tenaciously in their ageless effort to hold back the rocks and soil of the hillside. There was seldom any sign of life, save when smoke curled up above the trees, as if some hardy picnicker were cooking his meal over an open fire.

Inhabitants of the village of Les Deux Croix could tell you it was the home of Raoul Couline and that his son's widow also lived there along with her five-year-old son. That is, they could tell it if they would. The villagers were close-mouthed with strangers. They divulged little information beyond the fact that the village got its name from the two ancient stone crosses that marked its entrance and that the crosses were the site of an old graveyard attached to an abbey that was sacked and burned by the vandals centuries ago.

If they found nothing unpleasant about the stranger, they might advise him that the widow Duchamps took travelers in the rooms above the inn that her husband left to her and that she would sell them a meal.

They were seldom asked for such information. Les Deux Croix was not on a well-traveled road. The main road lay over two kilometers west, not far from the site of the last battle fought outside Sedan. The road leading through Les Deux Croix wandered off from the main road, passed through quiet, lovely countryside to the village where, some distance beyond the Coulines' small farm, it came to an end against a forest where yet a smaller road led off to the right and brought one back to the main artery along the banks of the Meuse.

On a Sunday late in August of 1919, Giselle Couline, Raoul's daughter-in-law, walked slowly home from the village, her market basket on her arm and a frown creasing her smooth forehead.

In the beginning when Raoul had brought the American, Mark Douglas, to the house, she had thought little beyond helping to tend his wounds and to bring him back to consciousness. For weeks he had lain in the little loft at the top of the winding stone steps, delirious first from infection, and then from what the village midwife had said was pneumonia. The midwife herself contracted it shortly afterward and had not survived.

During the long freezing nights of December and January, Giselle had been hard put to keep Mark warm. She

had piled the bed with goose-feather quilts as he lay
burning with fever in the beginning, and later as he
shivered damply with cold. Often she had climbed into
the bed beside him, trying to warm him with her body,
and then he would mumble a name. "Julie," he would
say, "Julie." But he did not awaken.

It was nearly the end of February before he was well
enough to remain awake for longer than a few minutes.
He spoke then——English. Giselle knew it was English, but
she could not make out the words. She answered in
French, but he didn't seem to understand at first. Then
as the days went by and he grew stronger, he began to
speak in French. It was difficult to understand that, too.
The accent was strange and the words were twisted,
but over the weeks he spoke with increasing fluency.

Papa Raoul would seldom go up to see him. "He will
ask me what brought him here. I am afraid he will
know I lie," Papa Raoul would say. Even now he avoided
talking to Mark.

Coward, Giselle thought, such a coward. Yet he had
been brave enough to bring the nearly dead soldier back
with him, brave enough to risk being caught and arrested
for battlefield looting.

It had been a bad thing to do. She knew that. If it
had not been for the terrible Boches who had killed
Jacques in the beginning at the Battle of Verdun. But
at least Jacques was lying in the graveyard at home. Papa
Raoul had spent much money to bring him back from
the Paris hospital where he had died of his wounds. She
shuddered when she thought that he might have been
buried in a nameless grave, as so many were.

"Or stripped by vandals," she used to accuse Raoul in
the early days of his scavenging. He and the rest had
ranged far from Les Deux Croix in those days. Old men,
past serving, but strong of muscle and hard of bone, they
had searched each battlefield, bringing boots and helmets
and clothing and watches and guns to a man in Sedan
who paid good prices for them.

What would they have done without the money? The
crops were poor, the village poorer, as the Germans
swarmed over everything, taking food and materials and
the women, as well.

Giselle and Papa Raoul had lied to Mark. They had
told him the war had turned, that the armistice was a

false one, and that the Germans had taken Paris and gone beyond that. Because he was ill so long and they thought he would die, they had neglected to report his presence to the authorities. When he was well, it was too late. They must lie.

He would have left, otherwise. In the end, the others, even Raoul, might have killed the American rather than let him go back and learn the truth and perhaps bring the gendarmerie. It was Giselle who feared the killing. In the many months that she had cared for Mark, during those nights, lying beside him, he had become her dream of a lover.

Then, when spring was over and summer upon them, her dream had become a reality. It had been five years since she had had a man, but now, such a man.

Her face lightened briefly and then settled back into a frown. She thought of the trickery she had resorted to, how she had nearly bribed the others to accomplish it. "I will not have blood on my hands," she had said. "Was it for this that Papa Raoul brought him here? He would better have been left on the battlefield."

So far, she had won. They had long since—in those first days, on her instructions—taken his identification all the way back to the battlefield and scattered it.

But the endless lies went on. Yes, they had tried to get a message to the American forces now fighting in Normandy. No, there were no Americans in Paris. They were dead or imprisoned or they had fled before the invasion.

Always when they made love—afterward, sometimes before—he would question her, and she grew weary of the same old lies and fearful that he did not quite accept her story, but he was simply unable to find a flaw in it.

It happened even that first night they had lain together, that night not two months ago, when he had left the house to walk and she had thrown her shawl over her nightdress and followed him, finding him in the field behind the barn, just leaning against a tree and staring at the moon.

"It is cold," she had said, "very cold for June. You are just strong again. You mustn't catch a chill."

He had looked at her, silently, unsmilingly for a long

minute, and some trick of moonlight laying a blue glint
over her eyes made her lower her own.

"And then you will have to pile the quilts high and get
into bed beside me," he said at length. He had known.

"It was the only way," she murmured in confusion.
"Some nights were so bitter and you were so ill."

"The Germans must be running out of men," he said
then. "They have so many losses, and then they must
have troops behind to guard what they have gained. If
they take all of France, will the French settle down and
say, 'All right, now we are good Germàns'?"

She did not quite understand the meaning then. But it
was a question he had rephrased many times since. Then
she had said only, "I don't know what will happen. Perhaps, after all, the Germans will be beaten again and
then it will not matter. You will go away."

"I will go away sooner than that," he said.

Startled, she grasped his arm, clutching it to her breast,
saying, "No, no, you mustn't. They will kill you!"

"They nearly killed me the last time," he answered, but
he did not throw off her hands or move his arm, and she
leaned against him more firmly until his hands came up
to encircle her waist, and the shawl slipped from her
shoulders as he bent his head into the hollow of her neck
and pressed her body against his. He had taken her
very quickly, in the furrow between the newly sprung
wheat. He had taken her hard and sharp, as if he were
angry, and yet she had thrilled to the experience. They
were like animals, she thought later, remembering that
there had been no kisses and that he had done nothing
more than disarrange their clothes to accommodate their
pleasure.

But after that, as the days went by, some of the anger
left Mark. It was difficult to keep the affair secret, but not
for the world would Giselle let Papa suspect. When he
went down to the village for the evening to have a glass
of wine, she would put Pierre to bed and slip upstairs to
the loft. And when Raoul was in the fields and the child
was at play, Mark would sometimes come to her as she
stood cooking over the coal range and slip his hands
beneath her apron, pressing her belly and saying, "Now,
before the old one comes for his dinner," and she would
follow him obediently up to the loft.

Of late, there had been less and less of that. Mark was

growing very restless, and even Papa Raoul noticed it. "He
will go away one day, no matter what we tell him," he
had said the night before.

"Let him, then," Giselle had retorted. "If you or the
rest do anything to him, I will tell the gendarmerie myself." But it was an empty threat, and they both knew it.
Armand and Raoul and Henri, the butcher, were the
only ones who knew Mark was still at the house. Henri
was afraid to come out there. "I don't want to see him,"
he said. "If I know nothing, I can tell nothing."

Today in the village Armand had spoken to her and
there was an oblique threat in his words: "Surely you
would not see us all in prison to save the American.
Surely the American means nothing to you."

"It is wrong to kill him only to save yourself. In a little
while it won't matter. He is strong now and well. If we
keep him at least a few months, then the Americans will
wonder why he did not come back sooner. They will
think he deserted them and that he is telling lies to save
himself."

"Why a few months?" Armand inquired. "If you
think we can lie and be believed, why not let him go
now? Tell him. *Eh, voilà!* Imagine, the war is suddenly
over." He laughed at her and she felt he guessed her
secret. Armand was the one who would have left Mark
there to die. Armand did not care at all. It was whispered
that Armand had stabbed more than one German lying
wounded on the field of battle, even that he had stabbed
other wounded soldiers, regardless of nationality. She
herself could believe that. Armand was sly, mean, like a
rat with his pointed chin, thin whiskers, his small body,
and baleful eyes. Like a rat, he scurried from noise or
light or danger, and like a rat, when cornered, he struck.

Giselle turned up the lane leading to the farm. The
basket seemed harder to carry these days. Everything
seemed more difficult, as if she stood on a narrow bridge
over a chasm, cajoling Raoul into lying to Mark while she
lied to Raoul and the other men. She knew in her bones
that it was coming to an end, that someone would make
a move. Mark would slip away one night as the men
feared and make his way to Sedan. There he would
learn the truth! She shuddered. He would be vengeful; of
that she was certain. So, soon she must tell him. Soon—
before he left or before Armand persuaded the rest to

kill Mark and bury him deep in a field where no one
would ever discover the grave.

Giselle admitted to herself that the fault was hers.
Long ago, as soon as Mark was well, she should have
thrown herself on his mercy and told him the truth. But
she had wanted him so much. *Mon Dieu!* She was not
yet thirty. And there was no one in the village who stirred
the fire within her. Oh, there were those who tried. There
was young Marcel, the baker's son, and there was Henri,
the butcher, widowed himself three years ago. But Marcel
was a foolish boy, six years younger than she, who would
be of no help to her. And Henri, while he was not so old
at thirty-eight, was very fat, although he had not always
been. Invalided home after Verdun, he had sat around
for a year, his bones healing. He had grown fat then . . .
and fatter as he took the salvaged articles from the
battlefield to Sedan for the others, gaining commissions
at both ends.

Still, she must think of something to do. Beyond everything was the fact that she was with child—Mark
Douglas' child. In her daydreams she imagined that he
would marry her and stay on to work the farm. Even
now, since his strength had come back, he did twice the
work in a few hours that Papa Raoul did all day. But it
was a foolish dream, and in her rational moments she did
not believe it could come true.

Giselle raised her face, looking upward through the
trees to the beginnings of the flatland, where the edges
of the farm began and stretched backward to the base
of the hill. She could not see the old stone house from her
vantage point, but she knew another turn would bring it
into view. Papa Raoul would be sitting at the doorstoop,
smoking his long clay pipe while Pierre played in the
grass before him. Mark would be in the barn, perhaps,
seeing to the two cows, or he would be in the fields beyond, leaning on his hoe, staring into space, delaying
the moment when he would return to the house for the
evening meal, always silent now, save for the chattering
of the child. She drew a deep breath and continued her
climb.

Above the lane that Giselle climbed, Mark Douglas
stood at the edge of the property, hidden from her view
by an outcropping of brush, and watched her ascend.
She looked tired and older than she had in the begin-

ning. She had been a beautiful girl, of that he was sure. Her bones were delicately fine and her large eyes a deep pansy brown, flecked with gold. Sometimes, in the light of the candle or under the night sky, they would glow like amber and remind him of a cat's eyes. At such times her beauty was there. But too much had happened to her—too much sorrow and too much hard work. Her skin had roughened from the weather and the washing and the scrubbing; there were deepening lines around her eyes from years of helping in the fields. Her body, maternally voluptuous, still bore evidence of its earlier symmetry in the slenderness of her waist and in the small bones of her wrists and ankles. She was a warm woman, passionate and giving. She had cured him and tended him and given him the comfort of her body. He knew he had given nothing in return. He had nothing to give.

At first Mark had accepted the fact that the war still raged, incredible as it had seemed. He had accepted, too, the idea that Paris had fallen, and for weeks he had been torn with worry for Julie's safety. Had she been killed? He could not accept that. Had she been captured? But she was a civilian. Had she fled with the other Americans who ran before the advancing Germans? He had finally come to believe that, and he held to the belief; otherwise, he would have driven himself mad. She had escaped, had probably been returned by convoy to America, and was probably even now back in New York, Angela Grant once more, and all the more famous for her service in France.

Slowly, over the past two months, he had come to doubt everything. If the Germans held Sedan, then why the appearance of the young men along the road below? Some of them should have been conscripted by either the French or German armies. It was the sight of over a dozen of them cycling along the road last evening that convinced him he was being lied to.

There were other things, such as Giselle's trips to the village to shop for provisions and to sell eggs and plums from the trees near the house and to sell butter from the churning and sometimes her homemade cheese. There were goods in the house and flour that had been milled in French mills. Last week she had bought Pierre a top and some sweets. France, overrun and devastated; the American, British, and French armies driven nearly to the sea in Normandy, and yet there was an abundance of purchasable items. It did not make sense. But the boys cycling was his final proof.

Mark remembered the way Giselle's eyes flickered when he asked idle questions pertaining to the German occupation, and he knew that she was deceiving him. Papa Raoul hardly spoke to him at all. Occasionally he would look up from his plate to find Raoul staring at him with a look of sadness in his eyes. It was a look that changed and became frightened on meeting Mark's glance.

It was just as well that he had not openly accused them of lying. Tomorrow night when Raoul went to his Saturday social in the village, when Giselle and Pierre slept, he would leave and make his way to Les Deux Croix and see the German soldiers for himself.

If he was wrong, and his instincts cried out that he was not, there would still be a way out. His French had improved to the point where he didn't think a German would notice his accent in brief and casual speech. He had the trousers, the work jersey, and the boots that Giselle had managed to get for him. He would take Raoul's old beret.

If he was right! He swore softly under his breath. He could not fathom why they had lied, unless they themselves were the scavengers who had taken his watch, his boots, his helmet, and all of his personal identification. That thought evoked a deep, cold anger, one he was familiar with because it was the precursor to a deadly, killing rage. That rage of his had broken one man's arm and had come close to killing others, one of whom still bore a long, livid scar down the side of his face where the force of the blow had split the man's cheek. His fist punched slowly into his other hand. He stood there, still staring at the lane below, yet not seeing it.

After supper that night, Raoul, departing from custom, announced that he was going to the village. To Giselle's questions he said, "I feel like going tonight. Perhaps tomorrow I will not feel like it. In any case," he added, cutting his eyes to Mark without actually meeting Mark's full gaze, "there may be news of the Allies. On Wednesday, you remember, I told you there had been a small victory in battle."

Mark pretended interest, rather successfully, he

thought, until he realized that Giselle was unusually agitated and he saw the faintest suggestion of a sneer hovering about Raoul's lips. Tonight, then. He would have to leave tonight.

He tried to keep himself occupied in the waning hours of light, cleaning out the barn, forking new hay down to the donkey's stall, and all the while his nerves tightened and his muscles ached with the mounting tension.

When he came back to the house, Giselle was in the bedroom with Pierre, telling him an old story about a shepherd boy who fell asleep and lost his flock to the wolves. If I were Pierre, Mark thought, that story would keep me awake all night. A few moments later, hearing the child say, "Mama, I am afraid," Mark smiled grimly to himself.

Giselle hushed and soothed Pierre and began to sing a cradle song filled with images of angels and a good God and Christ the shepherd, who kept all little children from harm.

She would be occupied for some time yet. Mark went into the tiny room that served Raoul as a bedroom to look for Raoul's old work hat. He found it on a hook behind an old sweater. It was stretched and sweaty, but, pulled out a bit farther, it would fit him. He paused in the main room on his return, listening. The pot-au-feu for tomorrow's dinner stewed slowly over the glowing embers of the open hearth. Giselle's voice had gone low and soft in a tuneless crooning, which meant that the child was nearly asleep. Breezes stirring the trees outside whispered about the house. The rest was silence.

Mark crossed the flagstone floor softly, treading like a wary jungle animal, and made for the loft. Fully clothed, he lay down on his cot and tucked Raoul's beret beneath the coverlet. When Giselle came to him tonight, he would feign sleep.

Presently he heard her tread on the stairs and he closed his eyes. She came to the side of the bed, whispering his name, but he lay there, unmoving. "Wake up, Mark." The whisper became urgent. "Please wake up." He stirred and mumbled, and she said frantically, "Hush. Please wake up. You are in danger!"

His eyes opened and he half rose on the bed. "What danger?"

"You must get away from here. They will come for

you tomorrow; I know. Tonight they will plan. Tomorrow they will come."

He reached out and took her arm in a tight grip, forcing her to sit on the bed beside him. "Tell me," he commanded. "Tell me everything. Don't lie to me, Giselle." He made no threats such as her father used to do, such as even Jacques had done, and such as old Papa Raoul would sometimes bluster about. But she feared Mark as she had feared none of the others. Slowly, haltingly, unable in the end to hold back her tears, she told him.

When she had finished, he said nothing for several moments, his mind racing to sort the rush of facts and their attendant results. The war was over, had been over for nine months. Julie was not dead or captured. She was either home or still in Paris waiting for him. He realized suddenly that Julie must believe him dead, and in one violent movement he was off the bed, standing and reaching under the covers for the beret, before it dawned on him that he no longer needed it. He flung the beret across the room.

"Please!" Giselle said. "Please, I love you!"

"So you said," Mark replied. "I'm sorry for you, sorry for everything that has happened to you. But I must go, and now."

"Be careful," she pleaded. "You can't go through the village. They will see you, follow you. Listen to me. Turn left when you come to the bottom of the lane. It is a bit over one kilometer to the forest. There, just beside it on your right, there is a very narrow path. It leads straight enough, though, and you will come out to the main road. There my cousin lives and he will take you in his cart to St. Mihiel. From there you can get to Paris."

Mark made her repeat the instructions three or four times, and when she had finished, she said, "Go now to the door and I will get you some money. You will have to pay my cousin and you will have to pay the railway."

Giselle crept down the stairs after him. While he waited by the door, she went into Raoul's room, emerging a few minutes later with a handful of gold coins.

"Papa Raoul's?" he questioned. "Won't he miss it?"

"He has much more," she said bitterly. "He thinks I don't know, but I do. He keeps it in a bag under the loose

bricks behind his bed. Like this one, see?" She darted to
the hearth and pulled out a brick from the side and,
reaching in, drew forth a sheaf of paper money and a
small pouch of clinking coins. "This, he tells me where
it is. He counts it each Saturday. The other?" She
shrugged. "I don't know when he counts it. Once I took a
few francs and he said nothing, so perhaps he does not
count it often and forgets in between how much there
is." She thrust the money back. "That money in his room
—one day my husband would have had it, and now one
day the old one will tell Pierre where it is hidden, but
not me."

She faced him, a strange defiance on her face, and he
was moved to a tenderness she had not precipitated in
him before. "I will remember you," Mark said gruffly,
"first for nursing me to health, and for the rest, you understand."

She nodded. "Go now," she said. Leaning over the
lamp, she turned down the wick and the room was in
complete darkness. He could feel her standing in the
room, but he could no longer see her. He opened the door
quietly and he was just about to step over the threshold
when a sudden noise stopped him and he withdrew behind
the door.

Giselle was beside him in a flash. "Now," she whispered. "They are coming up the lane. Quick, go to the
barn through the back window."

But he shook his head. "No. I will meet them here.
Go into the room with Pierre."

"They will kill you! I tell you, they will kill you!"
Her voice rose a little in her terror, and he placed a
hand over her lips.

"Go into the room," he said softly, "and whatever
happens, don't come out."

Giselle melted away from his side with a stifled moan.
He flattened his body against the wall and waited. There
were several footsteps. He counted more than two men,
but not more than four.

The door was pushed open very slowly. They did not
speak among themselves, but he could hear their hoarse,
uneven breathing. Still he waited, and when the door was
nearly open, Mark moved with the litheness and swiftness of a panther around the frame, his fist raised. The
first man never knew what had happened. Something con-

nected with his stomach, and before the gasp left his throat, a searing pain along his neck turned to flame and then darkness. He fell soundlessly, save for a short grunt. The man behind him stumbled and was caught upright in both of Mark's hands, turned swiftly with his hands pinioned behind him. Even as he cried out, something flashed in the pale starlight. A knife pierced Raoul's heart and blood spurted from the severed artery and bubbled on his lips as he catapulted forward, Mark still holding him, into his murderer's arms.

The force of the blow drove them backward so that the fourth man was flung to the ground. Like stacked dominoes, they went, the fourth man beneath, the third caught in his unintended victim's macabre embrace, and Raoul bleeding profusely over all.

For a second they lay that way. Then as Mark swayed to regain his own balance, Raoul was flung aside and the small, agile figure of the third man leaped up and landed on his feet, bent low, knife in his hand. He circled Mark warily. Behind him the fourth figure rose unsteadily and he, too, rushed at Mark, his own knife drawn. The small man, making weird, snarling noises, suddenly lunged and Mark caught him by the arm, twisting it behind him so that the man's back was presented to the high, stabbing arc of the last one's weapon.

Mark flung him back then, catching the boy as he tried frantically to regain the knife from its resting place. Mark circled him even as the boy struggled over the body and finally caught him on the side of the head, spinning him around. The body fell away and Mark's right hand connected on the point of the boy's chin.

Mark stood breathing heavily for long moments. Two dead. Blood still gushed in ever-widening circles over the dirt, turning it winy. The boy lay spread-eagled at the edge of the grass, and the first man, the fat one with the soft belly, was still draped on the threshold.

Mark stepped over the prostrate body and went to Giselle's bedroom door. He tapped softly and she opened the door at once. "Light a candle," he said. "It's over."

She obeyed him in a dazed fashion, her hands shaking as she struck the lucifer. The flame wavered a little and then caught and the room lightened.

She gasped when she saw the figure at the door. "Henri!" she said. She turned to Mark. "Is that all?"

He shook his head. "Don't go out there," he said. "They . . . two are dead . . . a small man with a pointed face."

"Armand—that's Armand."

Mark took the candle from her, setting it on the table, and put an arm around her shoulders. "Raoul is dead," he said flatly.

Giselle shivered but was silent. After a moment she said, "And that was all?"

"All but one. I knocked him out. It was a boy with very curly black hair, taller than the rest, and slim."

"Marcel," she said. "But why Marcel? He was not one of them."

"I don't know. He had a knife. They all had knives. They killed each other in the confusion. Armand killed Raoul, and when Marcel went for me, Armand was between us and Marcel's knife went into him instead of me."

At the doorstep, Henri began to moan and Giselle was suddenly galvanized. "Go now," she said, "before they are awake. No more killing. Please, no more killing."

Suddenly she began to shake. "I heard nothing," she gasped. "Grunts, breathing. I heard nothing else. They died so quietly." The tears started down her cheeks. Mark tried to comfort her, but she shook him off. "Hurry," she said. "I will tell the village men they killed each other. I will fix it up. Please, just go, go." From the bedroom, Pierre called in his sleep and she pushed at Mark. "Go," she said again.

He looked at her, nodding, and then very slowly he took her face between his hands, smoothing the silent tears away. Bending, he kissed her softly and with infinite tenderness on the lips. "And I will fix it, too," he said. "Tell them you"—he jerked his head in Henri's direction —"you are safe." He whispered his intentions to her and a moment later he was gone.

Giselle waited almost twenty minutes before she went to rouse Henri and Marcel. "My father-in-law and Armand have killed each other over the American. You are lucky to be alive. That beast! I curse the day Raoul saved his life! What happened here? When were you at the house?"

She streamed questions at them and slowly, despite

their befuddlement, they began to see the clear path she pointed out to them.

"I must rouse the village," Marcel said excitedly. "I must fetch men. They must see for themselves. We were coming for a friendly glass of wine and Armand attacked Raoul."

"Hurry, Marcel. You go to the village. It will take nearly an hour to bring someone back, and poor Henri is bleeding. Go quickly now."

As the boy hurried away, Giselle helped Henri into Raoul's bedroom. "Lie here," she said, guiding him to the bed. "I will fetch water and clean cloths."

She went swiftly into the main room and to the brick at the hearth, where she quickly withdrew the money and stuffed it in her apron pocket, then replaced the brick. She went then to her own room and, first checking the sleeping child, she put the money beneath her own mattress. Tomorrow she would take all the money and find a safe place for it. Only then did she go back to fetch the water and clean cloths.

There was very little time. She had perhaps forty-five minutes or a little longer. It must be tonight. Then Henri would marry her, and the baby would have a father. Back in the bedroom she made soothing sounds to Henri as she bathed his head and face and hands.

She sat at the side of the narrow cot, knowing his eyes wandered over the outlines of her body. She bent closer, leaning over him so her body grazed his chin while she pretended to examine him for other cuts and bruises. She could feel his heart beating faster and she moved back and smiled at him. "Poor Henri," she said. "Why did they let you go first?"

He goggled at her. "You knew?" he said.

"Of course I knew. Do you think I am an idiot? Oh, I didn't want it to happen. I didn't want any killing. But now, now I wish I had killed him myself, the pig!" She made a gesture as if she would spit.

"He will turn us all in," Henri said.

"He will not. And if he does, I will say that he killed everyone. I told him so. He would have struck me, but just then you began to moan and he thought you were coming to, and he ran like the rabbit he is." Again she made the gesture as if she would spit.

"We were lucky, Marcel and I," Henri confessed.

"And why Marcel?" she asked. He looked away from her. "Tell me, Henri."

"He heard us talking," Henri mumbled. "He was crazy to come with us. He was jealous of the American, afraid that you . . ."

She laughed. "The American! The trouble is that you never *saw* the American—a face like a monkey, he had, and so skinny, like a skinny monkey. I don't like skinny men."

"You don't?"

"No, I don't," Giselle said briskly. "Oh, Henri, there is also blood on your shoes, so I must take them off." She set about her task, removing his boots and hose and reaching her hand up his trousers legs to feel for cuts.

"And now the arms," she said, pushing her hands inside his jersey. "*Ah, bien.* And now for the chest." She rolled the jersey up and unbuttoned his undergarment, exposing his fat chest, well matted with hair.

"Good." She looked at him, smiling. "You are perfect." She leaned over, as if to button him up again, and her breast pushed against his hand. She gave a little gasp and moved a bit closer. For a moment she thought he would resist the open invitation. If so, it would have to be Marcel. But Marcel had no money and no prospects, and he was too young. She might well be accused of seducing him. She waited another imperceptible second and then began to move away. His hands closed over her breasts then, squeezing them tightly.

"Oh," she murmured, swaying above him, letting her eyes meet his, "you . . . you mustn't," she said, then made a gesture as if she would push him away.

But he released his hold only to pull her up over his body, shoving her around clumsily so that at last she was next to him and he was kissing her mouth, throat, and body, his hands groping to remove her clothing.

"They will be back soon," she murmured.

"We have time. I want you," he answered thickly, and after a moment she began to help him.

When it was over he fell asleep, as if drugged, and she got up and dressed. So, it was done. He would marry her. Of that she was certain, because he would want her again and again and she would say no, no more, and then he would marry her—and soon. By her reckoning she was nearly a month gone. A baby could not be premature by more than two months, and even then the old women would count and make snide remarks. It didn't matter. They would think it was Henri's child. Thank God that no one now alive had ever seen Mark Douglas. And thank God that Henri was not dark the way she was, so that if the child should be born with that red hair . . . well . . . there had been such a child in the village of such a combination of parents. And she had Raoul's money. She was safe.

Giselle went into her room and took her hairbrush and tidied herself. Then she closed the door and sat waiting for the men to come from the village.

It was dawn before it was over. The bodies had been cleared away and the men had all left satisfied. Even the priest did not ask too many questions.

Henri was the last to leave. She waited by the doorway until he came from Raoul's room. Pierre was sitting quietly at the table and having warm milk. The noise had awakened him and he was too frightened, even by what little he knew, to go back to his bed.

"The child is up, I see," Henri said significantly, and she lowered her eyes.

"I will come tonight," he said in a low voice, but she shook her head. "Tomorrow, then?" Again she shook her head. "Why? After last night . . ."

"That was . . . I was carried away. But I am not the woman who will have a man without marriage. Suppose I am . . ." She paused and shot a quick look at the child.

"Then I will marry you," he whispered.

"And suppose the baby comes early and the old ones talk?"

"So we will go to the bureau tomorrow."

"*Eh, bien.* Tomorrow, then." She gave him a wide smile. "*Chéri,*" she added.

She stood at the doorway a long time after he left, staring down the lane. Henri had done as she knew he would. He was too desperate for a woman, but if he ever had been expert in bed, he had forgotten it now. She looked down the gray years to come with pain in her heart. It would be a long time of tolerating Henri before she could put him off. Last night she had tried to pretend that it was Mark and then that it was Jacques, and finally both faces intermingled, but it had brought little relief.

Suddenly she remembered that before he left last night Mark had kissed her on the mouth, kissed her truly and tenderly for the first time. Thinking of it and of what lay before her, she allowed herself a brief moment of sorrow before she wiped away the single tear that rolled down her cheek.

"I will go to milk the cow now," she said to her little son, "and to gather the eggs. I will make you a fine omelet when I come back if you are a good boy."

"Has the American gentleman gone along with Papa Raoul?"

"Yes," she said. Then taking her basket, she went out to the barn.

18

Paris looked different to Mark from the moment he stepped off the train from St. Mihiel. There was none of the frenzied gaiety and taut anxiety that had marked his leave during the war. Paris was quieter and more tame.

The rebuilding of the city from the bombing was still going on, and everywhere there were houses and stores that bore new brick and stone and wood on some part of their façades.

He had expected difficulty from the American liaison officer. However, aside from an initial inclination to disbelieve his story, the major had expedited Mark's return to the land of the living.

He was billeted into a French officers' barracks and given a decent, if ill-fitting, uniform and a loan from a captain attached to the embassy who was his height and about ten pounds larger around the middle.

It was early afternoon by the time he had been processed through the medical check-up, which, more than

anything, allayed any doubts the army may have had
about his story. The old midwife who had taken the
shrapnel from his legs and scalp must have gouged it
out with a penknife. "This," grunted the doctor at headquarters, "accounted for the ravages of infection."

He had been pummeled, X-rayed, and had given sam-
ples from every orifice of his body, up to and including
a throat culture. In a few days, barring any accident, he
would be shipped home.

The details of notifying his family by wire and of
arrranging to extract money from the Paris bank, which
was fortunately unaware of his supposed demise, took
another hour. Showering, shaving, and changing into
the clean uniform, he was finally able to make his way
to the old Red Cross office, only to discover both office
and canteen were closed. While he had little hope of
finding Julie at the Gautiers' pension, he went there,
hoping to learn what forwarding address she had left.

The street was empty in the early evening quiet. Coming to Number Seven, he saw that the Gautier shop had
been closed. A placard in the window announced it
would reopen in September. He mounted the stairs of
the pension with a slight sense of expectancy, as if Julie
might answer his knock, after all. But the bell, echoing and
re-echoing through the silent house, brought no response.

As he turned to go back down the stairs, he saw that
a child had appeared in the doorway of the house next
door and was regarding him silently.

"Good evening," Mark said to him. "Do you know
when the Gautiers will return?"

The child disappeared without answering, and a moment later a plump, flurried-looking woman appeared in
his place.

"The Gautiers are in Marseilles," she offered, "on
holiday. They come back in September."

"And the American *mademoiselles?*"

"Gone," said the woman. "The blonde girl was married months ago. The tall, black-haired girl"—the woman
paused and shrugged—"I don't know. She was here until
the weekend. All at once, pouf! She is gone. I have not
seen her for two days. Madame Gautier was telling me
that she would go back to America soon, so perhaps she
has gone there now. She stayed on a long time, working
at the hospital for the American soldiers who were still

wounded. But then that was finished, and so she must go home."

"Yes, I see. Well, thank you, *madame*. You don't know where in America?"

"New York, at least so Madame Gautier said. She was an actress before the war, you know—the beautiful one with black hair."

Mark nodded. "Thank you again, *madame*," he said and walked slowly away. It was incredible bad luck that he had missed Julie by just a few days. If he had only listened to his own inner convictions, he would have left the Coulines weeks ago, certainly a week ago. He would have found Julie then. They would be on their way home together at this moment. Suddenly he was swept by an intense longing for her, a longing that he could not shrug away. It came from somewhere deep inside him, as if there was no chance of ever seeing her again. He knew that was ridiculous. He would arrive in New York only a week or so after she did. Yet at this moment reason could not assuage his mental and physical misery. He felt the pain gather in his throat and sting his eyes. Jesus! He would be crying in the streets next. He swore under his breath for several minutes and strode rapidly through the humid city until he was sweating. Having gained a modicum of control, he began to search for a café.

Just off the Quai d'Orsay he finally spied a small establishment and went inside. An ancient ceiling fan whirled slowly and several flies buzzed around it, undisturbed by the slight air current it stirred. There were three other customers, all workmen, who sipped wine and talked in low voices to each other.

Mark ordered a double whiskey and the waiter unearthed a partially filled bottle of J&B Scotch. He poured out a double measure and set it before Mark, saying in English, "Ten francs, Monsieur le Capitaine."

Mark paid him and downed the glass, holding it out for a refill.

Half an hour later the tightness in his chest eased. With his earlier torment blurred by the effects of the alcohol, he got up and went back out into the street.

"*Les Américains*," he heard one of the workmen say, "*ils ont les foies de fer*."

Mark laughed as the meaning struck him: "Americans

have iron livers." And addled brains, he added to himself. Julie was either on a boat to America or ready to sail. It wouldn't take much to find that out. Moving more easily now, he went on to the cable office to wire his cousin Art and Joe Damien. Art could break the news to the family at the ranch. The ranch. He swore again. He'd been officially dead for months. For all he knew, Grace had prevailed and the ranch was gone. His Fontaine stock and his Prescottville property had always been Julie's, should anything happen to him. No worries there. And Joe still had both proxies.

Leaving the cable office, he went along to the Medici Hotel, where he used the stationery in the writing room to send a brief letter to Giselle Couline in which he thanked her for taking care of him, and he also enclosed some money. He wanted to say something better to her, offer some word of affection, but he was afraid that the note might reach other eyes, so he kept it formally polite.

He was hesitant about sending cash, but he was afraid she would not know what to do with a bank draft. He could still see the brick lying on the floor below the aperture from which she had withdrawn money. No, banks were not in Giselle's sphere. Better to find a post office and register the letter. He addressed an envelope, crossing out Medici and adding his army postal address, then took some wax from the middle drawer of the writing desk. He sealed the envelope and then he lit a match, watching the red drops splotch across the envelope flap. It reminded him of the night he left . . . was it only last night? He was haunted by the memory of the blood that had seeped over the yard in front of Giselle's house. Another reason to regret the fact that he had not slipped away sooner. He stood up abruptly and left the hotel.

By the following afternoon, Mark had exhausted all efforts to find Julie's name on a ship's manifest. It was possible that she had gone on to England or that she was visiting someone first before leaving, or possibly she had moved and was somewhere else in Paris.

It was like those weeks in New York when he had looked fruitlessly for her. Of course! The ads in the personal columns. In New York they had been ineffective. Here, in Paris, an ad in English in a French newspaper would stand out.

It took him hours to place the ad in all the dailies,

finding he was hampered by the fact that nothing in his experience of learning or speaking French had provided for the idea of placing an advertisement.

He spent the rest of the afternoon going from newspaper office to newspaper office, paying for boxed ads that said simply:

> JULIE, LEAVE A MESSAGE FOR ME AT THE AMERICAN EMBASSY.
>
> MARK.

It gave him a brief hope. However, at week's end, when there had been no reply, he made up his mind that she had indeed left France and had elected to return to America via England.

The following Monday Mark boarded a train to go to Le Havre and meet the ship that would take him home. He had convinced himself that Julie would be in New York or, if not, that Lew Belmont or Madeline James would know of her whereabouts. Yet, as he stood aboard the *Ile de la Cité* and heard the ship sound its final farewell to the pilot boat, he was seized once more with the old longing that now aroused in him so many doubts. He would have stepped ashore again, had that been possible. He watched the French coastline recede, the hills misty and distant, enshrouded in oncoming fog. All his logic told him he was going to meet Julie. Why, then, did he feel so strongly that it was not so, and that in leaving France he was leaving her behind? The long illness had made him womanish. What he needed was work, movement, exercise—and a bloody drink to start. It was going to be a hell of a long trip.

By the time the ship reached New York, Mark found he was once more in command of himself. Somewhere during the journey he had made certain resolutions: the first order of business was to marry Julie; the second was to check out the family in California, at least for Valerie's sake, and the third was to go back to Prescottville and, with Julie at his side, undo the damage that the Prescotts and Miranda Latham had done.

Jason had been right enough about prohibition. But from what Mark had been able to gather, the wets were by no means finished. In the states that had failed or would fail to ratify, the anti-prohibitionists were particularly active. In California they must be downright mutinous. He tried to imagine San Franciscans accepting this imposition on their freedom, but he failed to envisage it.

According to the article in *Le Monde* that bewailed the curtailment of French wine exports, there was already a flourishing trade in illegal whiskey and wine. Once he himself was in control of Fontaine's again, he would see what ways could be used to get around the Volstead Act and the subsequent constitutional amendment.

The realization that he was once more able to plan for a future did much to restore his natural buoyancy and belief in his ability to make the world bend to his will.

The doubts and misgivings about Julie had vanished, although Mark could not successfully combat the waves of yearning for her. These doubts unsettled him more because his need surpassed the notion of pure physical love more than anything else. Worse, it left him indifferent to the charms of the women aboard the ship. Save for the battlefield, he could not remember a time when he had gone so long without a woman, let alone a time when he couldn't be reasonably satisfied with whomever happened to be around.

On the morning the boat docked, Mark stood at the rail and stared at the New York skyline, looming close by, his nostrils filled with the brackish odor of the harbor waters. It was early yet, but a summer haze rose over the city, softening the sky to a gray-blue. The sun burned fiercely through it in shimmering waves of heat.

He had cabled ahead to Lew Belmont. As the ship tied up at the dock he scanned the faces in the crowd below, expecting to see Julie momentarily. There was no sign of her, but he was not alarmed; she would be there. He turned and went below to gather his one suitcase and disembark.

He was through customs and out on the street in front of the terminal building when he spied Madeline James, leaning from her car, smiling and waving to him.

He hurried forward, smiling back at her. All must be well, he thought. Julie was around somewhere. He felt a surge of elation. Reaching the car, he said, "Where's Julie?" It took a minute to realize that Madeline had said precisely the same thing at the same moment.

"Where's Julie?" he repeated. "I thought she was back here in New York."

"And I thought she was coming back with you. The theater forwarded your cable to Lew. Lew . . . well, get in, Mark. Is that all your luggage?"

"Yes." He got in beside her, and the chauffeur began to move slowly through the crowd and the vehicles that choked the pier.

"I was sure she'd be back before I was," Mark said. "That's why I cabled Lew. How is he?"

"Lew is dead," Madeline said flatly. "Last winter he died during the flu epidemic. I wrote Julie about it."

"I haven't seen Julie since . . . since . . . it's been a year."

"Then that explains it," Madeline said. "She wrote me last month and said that she was going to visit Kitty, the girl she roomed with in Paris, and then she was coming home. So she . . . why, Mark, she still thinks you're dead. I nearly fainted when I found out you weren't. Where have you been all this time? Julie's letters . . . on top of what happened to Lew . . . they were almost too much to bear, except for the last one, saying she was finally ready to pick up her life again."

He was silent for a moment, assimilating the information: Julie still in France, but ready to leave. He smiled wryly as he remembered that sensation he had had that she was still in France. It was true, after all. Not that he believed in clairvoyance or second sight, but there must be something to the idea that when people were in love their senses were more acute.

". . . and at first she wouldn't believe you were dead. I knew how she felt. I was there with Lew when . . . and it took me a long time to accept it. Poor Julie. She kept imagining you would turn up. And then one day she wrote and said that one of your friends had finally convinced her it was true. Still, she wouldn't come home. I had an idea that she still thought . . . well, no matter. She was right, as it turns out. Where were you all that time?"

"Ill, delirious, half amnesic. It's a long, long story. If you still want to hear it, I'll take you to dinner tonight and tell you all about it—that is, if you're free."

"Yes, I am. I'd like that." Madeline smiled. "We can talk about old times and old friends. I start rehearsals next week for a new show. Meanwhile, I'm as free as a bird. My daughter is visiting a school friend, and I've been rattling around New York without a lot to do."

"That is going to make two of us. I need an army discharge, which means I'll be rattling around here myself for a while. You don't know just where in France Julie is visiting, do you?"

"She's down in Provence, but I don't know Kitty's address or her married name. Don't worry. I'll be hearing from Julie. She promised to cable upon her arrival."

"Would you mind dropping me off at the armory? I want to start that discharge as soon as possible."

"Where are you staying?"

He shrugged. "Hadn't thought beyond getting here."

"You're welcome to stay at my place. There are plenty of spare bedrooms, and I still have one of the best cooks in New York."

"Thanks all the same, Madeline. But I'd better see what the army has in mind for me. I'll call you when I'm settled. I'll let you know the time and place. All right?"

"Fine." She leaned forward and picked up the speaking tube.

"We'll drop Captain Douglas at the armory, Hoff."

Madeline was good company. Mark found her witty and entertaining. She was an undemanding kind of woman: easy to be with; not fussy over small points; undeniably attractive. She never grew coy or silly and, while she greeted him affectionately on the evenings that he arrived at the house to take her to dinner, she never was provocative with him. Occasionally it piqued his curiosity. From what Julie had told him, she had loved Lew devotedly. "But not in love the way I am with you," Julie had said. Even so, Madeline must still be in mourning for Lew. There were no other men around, as far as he could tell.

Mark had been in New York just short of a week when Julie's cable finally arrived. He and Madeline had come in rather late from a supper show and he was about to leave when she noticed the cable on the silver tray in the hall. She tore it open gaily, saying, "This is it. Julie's on her . . ." Her voice trailed off and she raised stricken eyes to Mark.

"What is it?" he demanded.

"I'm sorry," Madeline said, handing him the wire.

"Married," he ejaculated. "To René. Who is René?"

"I have no idea. She never mentioned him in any letters. It must have been very sudden. She'll tell me about it, of course. She says a letter is on the way."

Mark stood up, the paper still in his hand. All the blood in his body seemed to have rushed to his chest, so that his legs felt hollow and the pain in his heart was so acute that for minutes he felt as if he could barely breathe. His head was light, dizzy. He heard Madeline's startled exclamation, felt her hand on his arm. Yet he made no reply, his body rigid as he fought his emotions to a standstill.

"That is that," he said then, "not even the customary year." He smiled tightly.

"Let me get you a drink," Madeline offered. "I've still lots of stuff left. Lew had an eye for the handwriting on the wall."

She led the way into the living room, switching on lamps. "I'll be right back," she said. She disappeared for a few minutes and came back bearing a tray of decanters and glasses. He had not moved from his position near the windows.

"Please sit down, Mark," Madeline coaxed. He came over to the couch without answering her and sat down, accepting the whiskey with a terse thank you.

After a time, Madeline said, "You can't blame her, Mark. She didn't know you were alive. She really went off the deep end while you were missing. I know. She wrote me letters that were terribly despondent. And in that last one she said it was the fact that she'd been drinking too much that finally made her wake up and realize that she had to start her life again. This René, whoever he is . . . it may have been more out of desperation than anything else."

"I don't blame her," he answered. "And I don't want to talk about her. I want to know the name of the man, that's all."

"I'll let you know the minute I get the letter," Madeline promised. "It's a bit of a letdown for me, too, you know. I was looking forward to Julie coming back.

Funny, but I think she's the only woman friend I ever really made. Beautiful as she is, jealous as I was at first . . ." She gave a little laugh. "Here." She refilled his glass. "It's a good night for drinking."

Afterward, she knew it had been a secret she had hidden from herself during the week Mark had squired her around town, but that night she told herself she was only offering the comfort of a friend.

A hand on his arm, a light kiss on his cheek, and, as the night wandered on into its depths, more drinks and more sympathy, and, finally, the light affection deepened with the night and all at once Mark seized her in his arms and began to kiss her. "This is what's known as creature comfort," he said at one point. "We need each other." She led him up the stairs to her bedroom without any further words and they made love silently, expertly, in the bed she had once shared with Lew. It seemed to her as she lay dozing afterward that the room was peopled with ghosts. Beside her, Mark cried out in his sleep, but she could not make out the words. It was more than creature comfort, she thought. He's angry with Julie, knowing she's in another man's arms tonight. I am the punishment."

That night set a pattern. Mark would pick Madeline up after her rehearsal and they would go out to eat and perhaps take in a show and then they would come back to her house.

It was good to have a man around again and Madeline began to hope that nothing would happen to change the comfortable routine. Mark Douglas. Julie married and Mark Douglas here. She began to fancy that more would come out of it. She needed to marry, wanted to marry. Mark was undeniably a good prospect. What children they could make! All redheads. She would smile at this fancy and then think: that was my first downfall. Still, she kept on, and by the time the show opened she had convinced herself that this was what she wanted and what she could get.

In the middle of the week Julie's letter arrived. Madeline wrestled with herself a long time and then burned the letter. She had seen Mark confront Steven Randall and knew he had abducted Julie on the eve of her wedding to Steven. He was quite capable of heading back across the Atlantic and repeating his performance. She'd an idea that little things like marriage certificates wouldn't stop him.

It's better for Julie, she thought, but in her heart she knew it was not Julie's happiness that concerned her; it was her own. For the first time in a long time she felt alive and optimistic.

Mark only needed her now, but with time that need could become permanent, as it had with Lew, only this time there was no wife to stand between her and what she longed for.

It came as something of a shock, therefore, when Mark told her several days later that he was headed back out to California.

"It seems I am losing a lot of people," he said with an effort at a smile. She saw him swallow hard. "I've just had a letter from the ranch. My youngest sister, Valerie, died a few weeks ago. She had meningitis when she was about nine. It left her frail, sickly. She had influenza in March. She just never got well again, my sister Grace says." He stopped and coughed.

"Mark, I am sorry," Madeline said, putting her arms around him. She felt his body stiffening and withdrew at once.

"One of those things that happen," he answered gruffly. "With Val gone, there's no point in keeping the ranch going. My other sisters want to sell it, and they need me to do it."

"Will you come back to New York?" she asked.

"I don't know. My plans . . . the things I meant to do when I came back don't seem that important to me now. I might stay on the Coast for a while. I might go back to Prescottville. In the meantime, Madeline, this is my address in California. If you hear from Julie, write me, will you? I want to know where she is."

There was a bleak look in his eyes, a tightness in his face that bespoke deep sorrow. She felt a surge of guilt for having deceived him.

"It will all come out all right," she offered inadequately.

He smiled a little, raising one eyebrow ironically. "So the clergy tell us. You've been good company, Madeline. When or if I come back this way, I'll call you."

He bent down and kissed her lightly. "Take care of yourself," he said. "Thanks for everything."

"Thanks for everything," she echoed aloud when the

door had closed behind him, "as if I had helped him get
a job." In a sudden burst of frustration, she picked up a
pillow sham and threw it against the wall. It bounced
off a lamp-shade and she grabbed for the teetering lamp
base.

"Hell," she said. "And just as I was getting used to the
idea of him."

He'd be back, though. He'd be back if only to find the
name of the man Julie married. Sooner or later, if she
was patient . . . She let the thought drift off, remembering the sadness in his face.

What if she had told him, shown him Julie's letter?
She shook her head. It wouldn't have changed things.
There was no point in stirring up Julie or interfering
with her marriage. If Mark never came back to New York,
Julie would still be better off not knowing he was alive.

She knew that wasn't true and felt again the rising
guilt of her own interference. Later she compromised.
Later she would write to Julie and ask her if she wanted
Mark to know her married name. Yes, that was the idea.
Not now, of course. It would be better to wait until
Julie was settled into that marriage. Julie might not want
Mark back disrupting her life again. After all, who knew
better than she herself that time had a way of curing
just about anything?

19

Nothing that René had told her about himself or his
family had prepared Julie for life at Château de Brugarde.
Driving through to Lacon from Paris, she had been delighted with the exquisite views, mourned the still-evident
destruction of many of the vineyards, and grown increasingly anticipatory as they neared Hautvilliers. In
many ways it reminded her of home. Though the tiny
roads in Lacon, barely wide enough for the Rolls to

negotiate, the cobblestoned streets, and the narrow vertical houses clinging cheek by jowl to each other were picturesquely foreign, as they reached the outskirts of the Brugarde land and glimpsed the vineyards, she had almost imagined herself coming into Prescottville.

The château itself was set in a park covered with smooth green lawns, filled with formal flowerbeds and studded with old trees. The house rose in the distance among the trees, different from the other châteaus she had seen along the way. It was tall and graceful, built of delicately pink brick with white marble columns and shallow steps leading to its massive front doors.

All of it was like a fairy tale, up to and including the wrought-iron gates held open by nodding workers and the entry into the dim, vast reception hall, where a retinue of servants was standing by to greet her.

It was only later, on a tour of the house itself, that Julie began to perceive the shabbiness behind the splendor. Much of the furniture was in need of reupholstering or of refinishing, and many of the carpets showed noticeably threadbare patches. The damask portieres at the windows were frayed, and the lace curtains, while clean and mended, had been repaired too often and were now more patch than whole.

Much of this Julie could see for herself, but René explained that the war had made such serious inroads into his capital that the house had been too long neglected. He looked to the postwar boom to recoup his fortunes. Meanwhile, of necessity, he had been unable to rehire much of the staff of servants that had disappeared for one war effort or another.

"But you have so many servants," Julie said.

"Not for a château. It takes many more to keep it as it should be kept. That is why I have closed one wing and many of the other rooms. Now they are opened only once a year for airing. It saves time and work. And we do not need the space now, do we? When you have had five or six children, then we must think differently."

"Five or six?" Julie echoed, dismayed. "Please let me see how I get on with one or two first, René."

He had laughed at her, saying that he was only making a joke, but as time went on she realized that it was a joke in earnest. He followed her progress from month to month, saying cheerfully, "Ah, well, next time."

The first few weeks as La Comtesse de Brugarde were dreamlike. On the second day after her arrival, the old countess, René's mother, requested an interview.

"She was too tired last evening," René explained. "But now you must allow for her age, and for her fancies. She sometimes takes little fancies. You promise?"

"I promise," Julie said.

"Good. Then I shall come for you at eleven."

"Where are you going?" she asked.

"To my own room, of course. Presently Isabelle will come to you with your breakfast and she will help you bathe and dress, and then you will see, it will be eleven."

"But can't we breakfast together?"

"What? And have the servants chatter of how Monsieur le Comte was found in bed with Madame la Comtesse?"

"We're married."

"Exactly. But we do not stay together, for the benefit of the servants, only for each other. Is that not so?"

It was rather bewildering. She stood looking at the door he had closed between them. Last night he had come to her bed after she was asleep and had not awakened her. She had been surprised to find him beside her that morning, even more surprised that he had made no demands on her body. It was not that she minded his abrupt departure, but his concern for servants' gossip struck her as odd.

"Good morning, Madame la Comtesse," a bright voice said from the doorway, and Julie turned to find a young maid she had noticed last evening among the staff waiting to greet them.

Julie smiled and said, "Good morning."

There was something very appealing in the girl, a sweet pertness, a twinkle in her blue eyes, and a little cupid's-bow mouth that looked ready to laugh at any moment. Beneath her cap, stern efforts had evidently been made to repress her fat little sausage curls into smoothness, so that her hair, like her personality, seemed ready to pop out of restraint with the slightest encouragement.

"You are Isabelle?" Julie inquired as the girl arranged her tray and opened the draperies.

"Yes, Madame la Comtesse. I am to be your personal maid, unless you do not prefer me."

Julie laughed. "Well, so far, Isabelle, I prefer you."

Isabelle colored slightly and dropped a curtsy with a murmured thanks.

"Have you been here long?" Julie went on.

"Oh, yes, Madame la Comtesse. I was born here at the château. My father is the gatekeeper. My mother used to be the maid to . . ." There was a slight hesitation. ". . . and then she married my father," Isabelle finished.

"Maid to whom?" Julie asked.

Isabelle averted her eyes. "*Pardon,* Madame la Comtesse. I was not to mention that."

"Well, I shall tell no one," Julie said and smiled, "at least not as long as you satisfy my curiosity."

"To La Comtesse de Brugarde."

"Comte de Brugarde's mother?"

"No, Madame la . . ."

"Ah, I see," Julie said. "Well, you needn't worry. I shall say nothing." So, to René's first wife, Emilie.

"Shall I draw your bath?" Isabelle asked.

"Yes, please, Isabelle. But I require no assistance in dressing."

"Ever, *madame?*"

"Hardly ever." Julie laughed.

"But then what will my duties be, aside from keeping your clothes in order and mending and bringing trays and seeing to your room?"

"Well, if you find time on your hands too heavily, perhaps you can take a walk," Julie teased.

"Impossible. If Madame Arnaud, the housekeeper, finds I have time on my hands, she will soon find things to put in them."

"Then don't tell her. I certainly won't," Julie said. "And now, the bath, Isabelle?"

"Yes, Madame la Comtesse." And Isabelle hurried away to her task.

Shortly before eleven René returned, looking sober and formal, to lead Julie down the long corridor from her room.

At the end he steered her right and up a short flight of stairs and down another and then along another corridor. "I will definitely get lost here without a guide," she said to him.

"You'll get used to it in a few days," he assured her.

"I suppose so," she agreed, although privately she doubted it.

"Ah, here we are." René paused before a door at the end of the corridor. Julie stood a little to the right and behind him as he knocked. To her own right there was a large window overlooking the back of the château. Formal gardens bloomed for acres, and beyond them she saw other buildings. Some were stables, and she thought of riding again with a great surge of pleasure.

An elderly maid opened the door to the suite. She bobbed a curtsy to René and then to Julie as she was introduced. From the depths of the room, a high, imperious old voice crackled out, "Well, then, bring her in. Bring in the new countess, my dear count."

René ushered Julie into the room. At first she did not see the old woman. The room itself was crammed with furniture, mostly of the Louis XV period. There were endless small tables, some inlaid with marble, and all of them were covered with framed photographs and bibelots. At the end of the room there was a tall double window leading onto a wrought-iron balcony. In front of it there was a large game table before which chairs were drawn: three were delicately carved bergère chairs; the fourth faced away from the table. It was a tall-backed upholstered chair, of no period that Julie could determine, and in it, nearly dwarfed by it, Julie finally saw the tiny, birdlike frame of René's mother.

Julie moved forward under René's guiding hand. As they approached, René said formally, "I would like your permission to present my wife, Julie Fontaine de Brugarde." The old lady nodded her head and René went on. "Julie, this is my mother, La Comtesse Veronique de Brugarde."

I wonder if I am supposed to curtsy, Julie thought wildly. She took the skinny claw the countess extended to her and was surprised to find it strong and warm in her grasp. "You may kiss me," René's mother said and presented first one cheek and then the other to Julie, kissing the air near Julie's ear each time.

"Now go away and leave us alone," she said to her son.

"But I thought we would visit together."

"Nonsense!" his mother replied. "Go along now. You may send someone to fetch Julie in half an hour. Marianne," she said, summoning the hovering maid, "we will take some tea."

"*Oui*, Madame La Comtesse," Marianne replied, then hurried away, followed by René, who cast a backward glance at Julie that was a mixture of amusement and chagrin.

"So, we are alone. Who are you and where do you come from? Who were your parents? Fontaine? That is a French name. But you are American. What are you doing in France?"

The questions came in rapid staccato fashion and Julie answered them, scarcely finishing before a new barrage was fired at her. She had reached the end of the story of her service to the Red Cross with such swiftness that she was quite dizzy by the time Marianne returned with the tea cart.

"My daughter-in-law will pour," the old countess said to Marianne, who dutifully drew the cart up before Julie.

The porcelain was very thin, rimmed with gold bands and sprinkled gently with pale gold leaves. The silver was ancient, from the feel of it. The teapot was of somewhat sturdier construction.

René's mother sat silently. Julie poured the tea and had presence of mind to offer the sugar.

"Very nice," the old countess approved. "I see that you serve tea in the French fashion and not in that savage English way—plopping in sugar and pouring in water and adding lemon wedges. *Mon Dieu!* As if one wanted someone muddling about with one's tea."

And another bow to the nuns at St. Veronica's and Camp Joy, Julie said to herself.

"Now, about my son. He is too old to marry again. He is fifty and you are too young. Still, I suppose if he wishes an heir, he had better choose a young wife. But he should have done that years ago, fifteen years ago. My dear Emilie has been dead for twenty years. Five years of mourning was more than sufficient. Do you not agree?" She cocked her head at Julie, who was too startled by the sudden intimacy of the conversation to do more than nod.

"So, that is settled. Now, you were not married by the Church. That won't do. Tomorrow we must make arrangements. You may wear my wedding veil. You are too tall to wear my gown. It would not be seemly to wear

Emilie's and, of course, her daughter would object. So, you must have a white dress. Marianne." She clapped her hands and Marianne hurried forward again. "You will please send a message to Marguerite to come this evening and measure Madame la Comtesse Julie for a' gown. Take some of the old lace I have saved and line it with silk—a simple dress, I think, and the old lace is nearly a match for my veil."

Again the maid bobbed a curtsy, murmured her answer, and hurried away.

"There. It is done. Père Giroud will marry you, and I think my old friend the bishop will agree to waive bans. So, next Saturday. Yes, we will be ready then. Until then we will have no scandal. A civil marriage is not a marriage. And your children will be bastards. There is to be no question of succession to the title once the monarchy is restored."

She's quite mad, Julie thought, quite mad. Monarchy? Restoration? What on earth was she talking about?

"Once it is finished—the marriage—you will begin to have your son, my grandson, the future Comte de Brugarde. After all, René will not live forever."

Marianne entered the room once more, this time to come forward to say that Isabelle had arrived to show Julie to her quarters. Julie rose with relief and her mother-in-law said, "I enjoyed our little talk. You are very eloquent, my dear, yet you do not fatigue one with your conversation as so many young girls do."

Julie managed to control her laughter until she was back in her own room.

She and René dined alone that evening at a large table that surely could have seated twenty with ease. She said so to René and he laughed. "The big dining salon is below. This is for more intimate affairs." He laughed again at her astonishment.

Over the meal, seated at his right, Julie told him about her visit with his mother. "I couldn't believe she expects a restoration," Julie said.

"And why not? All good aristocrats expect a restoration of the monarchy."

"Do you?"

"I? Expect? No. I am a realist. I am a royalist at heart, but a republican in practice. As long as the Republic does not remove my lands and vineyards or confiscate my other property, I am content to be a republican. But my mother is different. You must remember that she was born and reared during a monarchy of sorts; at least, she was presented at the court of Louis Napoleon. That was not entirely to her liking. She fancies a Bourbon restoration, which is no more than the count of Paris fancies himself."

"But will it happen?"

"Probably not. But I indulge my mother and her fancies."

"And we are to have a wedding on Saturday. And I was told that I must be very circumspect until then and not chance the scandal of a child born before a church wedding."

She expected him to laugh, but he said, "You mustn't mind my mother. I have explained it all to her, but she forgets. Just go along with whatever she suggests. She is too old and too ill to leave her rooms. If she persists in the fancy of a village wedding, then I will say it has been accomplished."

"But she is ordering gowns and getting out her old veil," Julie persisted.

"*Alors,* if she insists, you can dress in whatever gown it is on Saturday morning and affix the veil and present yourself to her. Afterward, you can take it off and we will go about our business, although we are expected to attend Mass each Sunday. The priest is an old family friend. He thinks my presence encourages his backsliders."

"Every single Sunday!" Julie exclaimed.

"No. Of course, one may be in Paris or indisposed. Let us say *most* Sundays. Really, Julie, it isn't as if you have not been attending Mass all your life. You are like Hélène, who refuses to go, and we must coax her when she is here."

I will not need to be coaxed," Julie answered stiffly. "But I have not been what you might term a regular communicant, and de Brugardes or no de Brugardes, family friends or not, I do not intend to play the hypocrite."

He did not reply and she went on, expostulating her position for several minutes before she realized that he had no intention of answering her. She fell into an of-

fended silence and the meal ended without either of
them speaking again.

He escorted her into the drawing room afterward and
waited while she was served coffee and brandy, and then
he spoke for the first time. "You will excuse me this
evening, Julie. I have an engagement. I shall see you in
the morning." So saying, he withdrew.

It was the first time in all her experience that anyone
had simply ignored her so completely, certainly the first
time that any member of her family had refused to
speak.

Suddenly, sitting in the drawing room with its Louis
XV furnishings, its endless tables crowded with bibelots,
and with the dark whispering in the corners of the dimly
lit room, she was possessed of a desire to flee. What was
she doing here? What had brought her to this marriage
and to this house? Mark! He was vividly before her and
she experienced the old desperate anguish.

She must get away, at least from this room. She sprang
to her feet, upsetting the small demitasse cup, and went
out into the hall. Where could she go? Outdoors, away
from the lonely, shabby splendor of Château de Brugarde.
She went lightly down the wide main stairs and out the
front door.

For a moment she stood poised on the top of the broad
marble steps, and then she was down them, nearly running out into the dark, warm night. Avoiding the main
paths, she went around the house and down through the
back lawns and gardens, walking swiftly, as if there were
some goal and some purpose in her haste.

Coming to the gates, she opened them and went
through without knowing what was ahead. With nothing
but the moon to guide her, she made her way from field
to field until at last she was at the beginning of the vineyard. Here she stopped in her headlong flight.

Ahead and rising upward lay the terraced vines. She
could smell the essence of the thickly clustered fruit as
she made her way around the rows, now and again letting her hand trail along the foliage or touch the grapes
with light fingers. She turned her mind backward to her
old home and to rows such as these. It brought a curious
kind of comfort to her, for it made her heart ache with
memories, even as its very familiarity erased her sense
of isolation.

After a time, Julie turned back the way she had come. It had been easy enough to find her way in her headlong pace. Now, calmer, she was uncertain of her direction. She walked some distance before she realized that somehow she had left the grounds and was on a country lane. She could see a small house in the distance with lights flickering from opened windows, and she headed toward it.

A man answered her knock. He stood before her in his stocking feet, his undershirt showing beneath his hastily donned jacket. He was of medium build with thick, springy brown hair and intensely blue eyes. His face was weathered and tan.

"Excuse me," she said. "I have lost my way. I was out walking . . ."

"Good heavens!" the man returned in English. "You must be the new Countess de Brugarde. I thought I recognized you. I saw you the day you arrived. Excuse me, I'm Michael Lynch."

"Oh, yes. My husband told me about you. You train the horses and . . ."

"And buy them and sell them, as well." He grinned. "Well, now, Countess, if you'll hold on a minute, I'll get myself properly dressed and show you the way back."

He disappeared and returned a few moments later with his shirt on beneath his jacket and with boots on his feet.

"You aren't really very far away, you know," he said as he stepped outside and closed the door.

"I don't know how I got out of the grounds."

"You aren't out of the grounds. You must have come up on the other side of the vineyards. The house is just beyond that grove of trees. See?" He pointed it out to her.

She said, "I would never have guessed it. If I'd kept walking, where would I have gotten to?"

"Well, if you'd kept on long enough and passed through the gates at the end of the lane, you'd have been on the road to Hautvilliers—the back road, that is. You'd have missed Lacon altogether—going around it, you might say."

"I'm glad I saw the lights."

"You'd best wait to go walking at night until you've learned the paths by day. I got lost myself when I first came here, and in the daytime."

"How long have you been in France? You're not English, are you?"

"English? Not by a long sight. Irish. I've been here since before the war started."

"And were you in the war?"

"Not me. It was no Irishman's war, although many of them fought in it. And many of them at home fought England. They're still fighting England at home."

"And you stay neutral?"

He gave an amused chuckle. "In a manner of speaking, I suppose you could say that. Horses are my life. The count does well by me and I by him. No reason to change that. Well, now, Countess, and here you are. The house is just down that path. Do you see it?"

"Yes. Thank you, Mr. Lynch."

"You call me Michael, Countess. Only the count's servants call me Mr. Lynch. And if you know what to make of that, it's more than I do."

Refreshed by her exercise and heartened by the encounter with Michael Lynch, Julie felt her normal spirits return. That silly quarrel with René. She must make it up. It was only nerves, anyway, and strange surroundings.

As she went into the house, she began to plan her days. There were surely some household affairs that she could assume. And in the meantime she could ride, explore the countryside, familiarize herself with the village, and it was coming to harvest time. She could pick up again where she had ended that summer when Joe Damien had answered all her questions with endless patience. One day she would know a great deal about the winemaking. Thinking about that long-ago summer brought the old familiar pain, and she turned her mind hastily away. The past was the past. She had a future before her. She would make René a good wife and there would be children.

She heard René coming down the hall and heard him go into his room. She waited a few moments and then tapped on the connecting door, opening it as she did so. He was already in bed and she went over to him, saying penitently, "I'm sorry, René. It must have been nerves. Everything has happened so suddenly."

"It's all right, *chérie*," he replied in the dark. "I apologize for my ill humor. Come to bed."

She climbed in beside him, burrowing against him, taking comfort from his presence, feeling now that there was some cohesion in her life again.

The first few months of her marriage passed calmly after that. She began to understand the household functionings, and her days fell into a satisfying routine: breakfast in the morning in bed, coupled with light conversation with Isabelle, who upon closer acquaintance proved a cheerful companion; a consultation with Madame Arnaud, the housekeeper, one that she had learned to handle with tact, sensing early that Madame was suspicious of her American background and jealous of her own autonomy; the obligatory visit to René's mother, during which she would let the old woman chatter on in her irrational way and suffered herself to be called Emilie when the countess' grasp of the present slipped away and she floated into the past.

Most late mornings found her riding. After lunch she read, wrote letters, answered invitations, or napped. In the afternoons, she would walk out to the vineyards and watch the harvesting, and when that was over she began to haunt the winery. Here she experienced a little difficulty. The cuvée, Monsieur Bonnefous, did not have Joe Damien's patience. He was polite, but she could see that many of her questions annoyed him. Still, she persisted, ignoring his obvious dislike of her visits and her intrusion into the old caves where the wine was stored.

René had lost none of the early passion, and she marveled at the consistency of his lovemaking, as well as his endless innovations. Her body took on a voluptuousness it had not had before, and sometimes, when René was away or when Hélène and Guy came to stay at the château and their privacy was curtailed, she would grow restless with desire.

If she had any complaint, it was that while René was a gay and amusing companion for the most part, indulgent of her whims and fancies, he never spoke to her of important matters. When she questioned him, he would turn her aside with an amused, "But that is too complicated for you, my dear."

It was, in many ways, as if she viewed him in two parts. She was not obsessed with a need for his company, yet she was endlessly obsessed with the physical pleasures he brought her.

One Saturday toward the end of October, Julie met Michael Lynch as she was riding back to the château grounds. He had come out through a small lane up ahead and, seeing her, had reined his horse to wait for her.

"Good morning to you, Countess." He smiled as she neared him. "It's a fine day, isn't it? It was raining the whole time that I was in Dublin and pouring the whole time I was in England at the Haymarket sales."

"Yes, it is a lovely day," she agreed, unaccountably cheered at the sight of him. "I'd missed seeing you around. René thought you'd be gone longer, actually."

"To tell you the truth, I was anxious to get back. We did well on the stock I sold, but there wasn't much in the way of good horseflesh to buy. The war hurt the breeders as well as the farmers and growers. Ah, well, there'll be another sale soon, and we'll have to try at it then."

They rode along side by side in companionable silence for a while. Then nearing the château, he said, "It's yourself who should be learning more about the horses. You've a love for them. Now, you take the count. He's fond of breeding them and fond of selling them, but he has no fondness for the poor beasts themselves. He never so much as rides anymore. Why, if I were to break my neck, there'd be the devil to pay around the stables until he found a replacement. There's not a groom who could take over in the management, good as the lads are."

"I?" Julie said. "But I know nothing at all. Oh, I can ride, of course, and groom my own animal if it comes to that, and I've been known to clean out the stable. But as for breeding, bloodlines, knowing a good horse from a bad one, I have no eye for that."

"You could learn. After all, what did you know about wine until you began to haunt the poor winemaker at harvest?"

"I knew a bit. My own family had—has—a winery in America. In any case, that's different. Fontaine's and Château de Brugarde have all the experts they need. Fontaine's doesn't need me and, heaven knows, Monsieur Bonnefous certainly doesn't."

He laughed. "You unsettled him. The count never goes near the winemaking. He inherited this and he does all of the business, but the wine is like his horses. He hires experts for the real work."

"Well, you will definitely have to remain the horse expert," Julie said. "I'd love to learn about the differences in the new foals and how you can tell one from the other, and I wouldn't mind learning about bloodlines. But don't imagine you can groom me to replace you, Michael Lynch. Even if I were willing, René wouldn't hear of it. He likes the ladies in his family to remain above any ordinary concerns that might tax their intelligence."

Julie had meant it as a joke, but, once said, the words hung in the air like a complaint. Michael did not appear to notice it, however, and as they reached the stableyard gate, he fell back to let her precede him.

As Julie dismounted, Hélène appeared from the stable office.

"I didn't realize you were coming so soon," Julie called to her. "I am sorry, Hélène. I'd have put off riding if I'd known."

"Not on my account, surely," Hélène said, strolling forward indolently. "Good morning, Michael," she said, greeting Lynch.

"Good morning, *madame*," he replied.

"I was hoping to have a ride myself," she said. "As a matter of fact, I came down expressly to ask you to pick out one of the new mares for me. But I see you found a riding companion in my stepmother." She gave a disagreeable little laugh, looking directly at Michael. The pose of the daughter of the house and master of the horses held, but Julie saw a look of intimacy pass between them that belied the formality of their words.

"Well, *madame*," Michael said a shade too heartily, "I'll be happy to pick out a horse for you to ride later in the morning or whenever it pleases you."

"It would please me to ride tomorrow morning," she replied. "Perhaps you would care to show me my mount now."

"Yes, *madame*, of course," he answered. His face was flushed, as if he were angry, and Julie felt intuitively that it had to do with the arrogant tone Hélène was taking with him.

"I'll see you at luncheon," Julie said to Hélène, "unless you'd rather I waited for you now."

"Not at all," Hélène returned coolly. "You must be quite fatigued from your morning . . . er . . . exercise."

Julie felt her face flame at the intended insult, but

she managed to control herself. "I'm not fatigued in the least, Hélène. I ride each morning and have gotten quite used to it, although," she smiled sweetly, "I don't generally have the pleasure of Mr. Lynch's company." She turned to Michael and said with genuine courtesy, "It was nice to have met you today, Mr. Lynch."

"The pleasure was mine, Madame la Comtesse," he replied, openly amused. From the corner of her eye, Julie could see Hélène's face tighten in anger, and she thought, it serves you right, you little snob.

Walking back to the house, Julie found she was half disappointed, half annoyed that there was an obvious flirtation in progress between Michael and Hélène. Hélène was married. And, anyway, Michael was much too good for her. The thought sprang unbidden and she was slightly shocked at herself.

Still, Hélène had not improved on acquaintance, although until today she had not shown any open hostility in company or when they were together, and she actually had attempted to be pleasant lately.

That evening Hélène insisted on bridge, a new form of it that she had learned from some Americans in Paris and which she predicted would soon replace the old style. It was a lot more complicated. However, once the new rules were mastered, it became absorbing, and they played quite late into the night. At eleven, Guy suggested that they end the game with the next hand, and Hélène pleaded for yet another.

Julie, resigned to Hélène's penchant for keeping the household up half the night, agreed, and René, absorbed in the game, went along with it. It turned out to be an endless game filled with no-bid deals and part scores and sets. All save Hélène were barely stifling yawns when the conclusion finally came and, yet, at that moment, Hélène complained: "I should have listened to you, Guy. I am tired to death and have a dreadful headache."

Guy made no reply, but Julie saw a slight tightening around his mouth and realized that Hélène's passion for staying awake stemmed not from some childish intent on her own way, but it was, in fact, purposeful. Exhaustion and a headache required solicitude and abstinence on the part of her husband. Julie was swept with sympathy for Guy and pity for Hélène. She herself would hate to be married to a man who did not thrill her in their marital relations. Her eyes sought René's and she saw an answer flicker in them.

Tonight René accompanied her to her room instead of undressing in his own room, as he normally did. He seemed unusually excited, as if he were holding himself back with great effort, where, heretofore, he had been cool, controlled, building and building until the very end, when he would finally permit himself release.

He seized her as soon as the door closed behind them, leaning his back against it and pressing ardent kisses upon her parted lips, crushing her body against him. "I thought it would never end," he murmured between kisses.

"So did I," Julie answered, desire seizing her at his touch.

"Here," he whispered and led her to the mirror, facing her in it as he had that first night in the Delons' house in Paris.

He began to remove her clothing, watching in the mirror. When she was fully unclothed, he pressed her back against him and began to caress her body. It was strangely exciting to see it, yet something else stirred within her. He managed to unclothe himself, always touching her, and when she would have turned in his arms, he would not permit it, bending her body to suit his purpose, now forward, now backward, until a throb of pleasure caused her to moan. She felt her knees buckle but he pulled her back against him, holding her upright, running his hands over her body. Through half-glazed eyes, she could see each of his movements as well as feel them, and the two sensations became separate, as if what she felt was different from what she saw. His hands, moving downward to spread her thighs, were the hands of a stranger. His eyes were intent on the mirrored image of his own actions; his face was wet with perspiration; his mouth went slack in unholy excitement as he tried to enter her from this position. All at once she shuddered and he mistook it for excitement, redoubling his efforts until she began to shake almost uncontrollably. He stopped then and drew her away to the bed. "Tonight we will make a child," he whispered, his body pressed close to her own. In the very act of this final, frantic outburst of passion, Julie was filled with a suffocating sensation in her chest, and a deep revulsion convulsed her body so that she cried out piercingly. He mistook it for fulfillment and grew more agitated.

I can't bear it, she thought, biting fiercely on her cheek to keep from revealing the truth to him. It was over at last. As he lay panting on top of her, she restrained the impulse to throw him off and wriggle free.

He rolled away at last, exhausted, and she suffered his gentle strokes and murmurings until finally he slept. She moved away from him then and lay curled in a ball on the far side of the bed, clutching her body with her arms, hugging herself, as if something else might violate her integrity.

Why it had happened this way she couldn't fathom, and she lay dry-eyed and tense, falling asleep near dawn only to awaken alertly as Isabelle brought her breakfast.

The events of the previous night left her with scarcely any appetite, and she hurried through her toilette, sending a message that she would not see Madame Arnaud that morning and that she would call on her mother-in-law in the afternoon.

She headed out to the stables, not sending the usual request to bring her horse to her. She found Michael Lynch there and he greeted her with pleased courtesy.

"A bit early this morning, Countess. I'll saddle the horse myself since the grooms are busy."

"Thank you," Julie replied, unable to keep the tension from her voice. If he noticed, he gave no evidence of it, talking on quietly while he tightened the girth and led the horse out.

"I'll be back just before luncheon," she said. "I want a good ride this morning."

She swung up easily, feeling better as she felt the horse beneath her once she was in the saddle. She left the grounds decorously enough, but, once in the lane, she headed the animal on the road to Hautvilliers, away from her usual paths, and brought it from trot to canter and finally to a full gallop, riding that way for perhaps fifteen minutes when she slowed to rest the horse. She had no real destination and, now that the pace had slackened, she began to look around her. It was unfamiliar territory. As they went along, the road began to twist and curve and she could see other vineyards in the distance. There were few houses along the road.

At one rather sharp curve she brought the horse to a

slow and careful walk. To her right there were thick
bushes and hedges and tall trees, and a little farther on
there was a break in the foliage with a path leading
through. It was a narrow path with no room for more
than one horse. Should she meet another rider, she would
be forced to the shoulder in order to let him pass.

It invited her by its very isolated look, so she turned
the horse's head and it obediently walked forward under
her gentle prodding. The path was straight for the most
part, with gentle curves that soon hid the main back
road from view. Some few minutes later the path ended
against a forest fence. Julie dismounted to lead her
horse around again. To her left, half hidden in a tangle
of overgown hedges, were gates. Curious, she peered between the iron bars and caught a glimpse of an old manor
house, overgrown with ivy, its lawns ill kept, its ruined
flowerbeds relics of a past glory. The house looked lonely
and deserted, surrounded by woods and off the main road.
Its former owners must have fled the isolation.

Taking the bridle in her hand again, Julie led her
horse forward, not remounting until they were once more
outside the lane. For some reason the deserted house
reminded her of her childhood home. There was no one
living there now, either. She wondered if it had been
left to decay and she shuddered. She had not written to
the Prescotts since her marriage. It might be wise to do
so now. She had left her old life so completely that ever
since she believed Mark to be dead, she had not
thought about Prescottville.

There were things she needed to know, plans she
needed to make. Once, when she and René had first
married, she had thought that it might be a good idea to
sell the old place. Now she was unwilling to do that.
Last night had been so profoundly disturbing that she
was once more unsure of herself and her future.

She mulled over her predicament the rest of the morning. Perhaps it was only that one time. Perhaps it was
her own fatigue. Yet the thought that René might come
to her again soon filled her with the same sense of revulsion she had experienced the night before.

Coming back onto the château grounds, her mount
stumbled and Julie dismounted to examine the horse's
hooves. She couldn't see anything in the first three. As
she neared the left hindquarter, however, Tokay whin-

nied and shied away. Julie moved back to the horse's head. Stroking the animal and making soothing noises, she led it gently forward, noticing that it began to limp. She left it with one of the grooms, telling him to leave it alone.

Upon learning that Michael Lynch was in his cottage she went around to tell him about the horse's injury. As she stepped up on the small porch, she heard voices inside.

". . . stupid of you to come here like this in the middle of the day."

"Shall I steal out at night? I can more easily explain away the day."

Hélène!

"Unfortunately, I can't," Michael Lynch replied. "Look, be a good girl and go home to your husband. I don't fancy losing my job over this."

"You were willing enough a little while ago," Hélène said.

"Well, it was the war and the poor wife all alone and not knowing where her husband would be. A bit different."

"You're a coward." Hélène said this contemptuously.

"Ah, you've found me out. A coward is what I am—the worst you've ever seen," Lynch said cheerfully.

"You and your job! I can have you fired."

"I doubt that, *madame*. Your father isn't such a fool as to turn away one of the best men he can hire on your whim."

"And you are conceited," Hélène returned, her voice rising excitedly.

"See, you've found yet another fault. Isn't it enough for you, woman? What would you want with the likes of me, after all?"

"You know very well what I want. It's good for us together. You know that."

"What I know is that you've a husband sitting up at the château and a father somewhere around this very minute. Now, be a good girl and go home."

"I won't."

There was a sudden silence and Julie took advantage of it to rap loudly on the door. There was a scurrying inside, and then came Michael Lynch's voice, saying, "Yes, coming." A moment later he opened the door.

"Sorry to bother you," Julie said, "but Tokay's gone lame and I think you ought to see him. I've left him with a groom with instructions not to touch him until you have arrived."

"I'll come right away," he said, stepping out and pulling the door closed behind him. "Do you want to come along, or shall I send word?"

"If you'll just send word," Julie said. "I'm a bit late getting back, and luncheon is nearly ready. Thank you, Michael," she added politely.

Michael Lynch and Hélène. And poor Guy, none the wiser. Suddenly she dreaded facing the luncheon table with Hélène of the headaches, Guy the cuckold, and René of her late infatuation. She needed time.

Reaching her room, she rang for Isabelle and had her take down the message that she was ill with a bad throat and would not be down. "No, nothing substantial to eat, just soup and rolls and milk," she told the concerned Isabelle. "I'm sure I'll be fine in a day or two."

When the maid had gone, she undressed quickly and crawled gratefully into bed. The long, sleepless night and the morning's ride had left her thoroughly fatigued. She was asleep when René came up to see her.

20

When dinner was over that evening, Hélène came to Julie's room. She was the last person Julie wanted to see, but she put on as pleasant a face as possible, inviting Hélène in and urging her to sit down.

"No, thank you," Hélène said, standing just at the foot of Julie's bed. "I must say, you don't look especially ill," she remarked.

"That's good," Julie replied evenly. "I feel a bit better, actually. Sleep is a great healer."

"You heard us today," Hélène said abruptly.

"Heard you?" Julie repeated in feigned surprise.

"Don't pretend," Hélène said. "I know you heard us. Michael was sure of it. I just want to know what you propose to do about it."

"I? Why, nothing. I quite agree that Mr. Lynch shouldn't be fired. In any case, I don't carry tales, and, even if I did, I can't see any useful purpose in upsetting your father or your husband, since I don't imagine it will change much, aside from having Mr. Lynch fired, as I said before."

"And why are *you* so concerned about Michael? You scarcely know him."

"He's a good horseman. They aren't all that easy to come by. René trusts him with everything, including the purchase of new stock and the sales. He also has a degree in veterinary medicine, you know."

"I know all about Michael. We were lovers long before I married Guy."

Julie stared at her.

"Does that shock you? But Michael is a very good lover."

"Then, why did you . . ."

"Marry Guy? Well, I could hardly marry one of my father's servants, could I? Guy is an old family friend. I like him well enough. It suits me to live near the château, and Guy's house is not that far away. If I had married someone else . . . oh, Jacques Molinet, for example, I would have been forced to live down in Gascony —much too far away."

"So you chose a husband of convenience as much for his place of residence as anything else."

"Well, and why did you marry my father?" Hélène asked. "Convenience, wasn't it? After all, he is much older, and surely you've had other lovers. I know about actresses."

"They apparently aren't very different from spoiled daughters of the French aristocracy," Julie said quietly.

"You married my father because you wanted money and position. I despise you for it."

"Whatever my private reasons are for marrying your father, they had nothing whatever to do with money or position. I am not dependent on anyone for money. I may have less than you, but it's sufficient for my needs, which I might add are a lot more modest than yours."

Hélène laughed. "I'm glad it's out in the open," she said. "I never liked you, or imagining you having my mother's place. My mother was so different. Her people were not little merchants, nor was she an actress. She was beautiful and gracious and . . . oh . . ." She broke off. "When I think of you being called La Comtesse de Brugarde—you, a common little tramp," Hélène said hotly. "I don't know what possessed my father. You must have made him believe you were crazy about him. How did you do it? I'll bet you can't bear for him to touch you."

Julie, remembering the night before, paled, and Hélène said triumphantly, "You see!"

"I see nothing," Julie said, her temper finally aroused, "except that you are not only the most insulting, ill-bred person I've ever met, but you must be half mad, as well. You come to me because you are worried that I might tell what I overheard, and then you start a quarrel with me after I've agreed to say nothing."

"Say anything you like," Hélène replied, suddenly indifferent. "I'll lie and so will Michael. I'll say you tried to seduce him and that he was embarrassed and I was, too. I can change it all around."

"Don't be a complete fool, Hélène," Julie said tiredly. "Your father has good reason to know that would be a lie." The underlying truth caught at Hélène and she became very white and still.

"So, you see, Hélène, you were wrong about many things." Julie pressed her advantage. "But try it if you like. It's none of my business what you do with Michael Lynch, so if I were you I wouldn't stir up a storm, unless you're sure you won't end up getting blown apart. Now, if you don't mind, I'd like to be alone."

On Monday René went to London on business, mourning the fact that Julie could not come with him. To Julie it was a three-week reprieve. She had not been able to contemplate a resumption of her marital duties, and the fact that he would be gone so long gave her a sense of repose. Surely in that time she would either come to terms with the problem or find that it had only been a passing one, after all.

Freed of the necessity to pretend any longer, she made a remarkable recovery, and on Tuesday she resumed her regular routine. Aside from the fact that she spent more time with René's mother out of an irrational feeling that it would placate whatever fate had thrown her from her earlier contentment, she lived much as she used to.

Her first meeting with Michael Lynch since the "incident," filled her with trepidation. She knew Hélène must have reported their conversation, and she was half afraid he would mention it.

When he greeted her with the old, easy air of friendliness, saddling her horse himself, chatting amiably to her all the while, she was annoyed that he said nothing, and on impulse she blurted out, "Look, it really isn't any of my business, but Hélène has made it so by talking to me."

"Ah, that," he said, his eyes intent on tightening the girth. "Well, now, Countess, I'm sorry you were brought into it, although, truth to tell, I'd rather it was yourself instead of himself. He'd be taking a crop to me and I'd be having to fight him, and then where would we all be?"

Julie said nothing. She looked at the thick muscles of Michael's well-exercised body and thought of René's elegant slimness. There would be no match at all, either in physique or age.

"Of course, now, the man has an inch or so on me, but I've a bit more experience, you might say. So I'm glad that you won't be saying a word, Countess."

"Glad that you won't be fighting my husband? Glad you won't be fired?" she burst out. "Why, if you lifted a hand to René . . ."

He looked up at her with half a smile. "I lift a hand? Not I, Countess, not to start—only to finish. And what would trouble me most is that it would be the same as beating a horse that's dead and gone, if you take my meaning." He met her eyes levelly. There was no embarrassment in his look and a shred of remorse.

"I like Guy," Julie said suddenly.

"Aye, and so do I," he answered with such a look of surprise that she should have doubted it. "A fine lad. I never minded that Hélène married him. I never minded consoling the war widow." He laughed suddenly, as if it were a huge joke. "But I draw the line at smiling at a man every weekend while his wife is winking at me behind his back. I've made myself clear, I hope, Countess."

"You shouldn't be telling me all this," Julie said.

"I would never have mentioned it, Countess. 'Twas yourself that brought it up."

"We'll say no more about it," she said stiffly, feeling very foolish.

"Now, then, will you be wanting company on this ride, Countess? Shall I send one of the grooms, or would you like my own company?"

"Neither, thank you," Julie said, mounting up. It occurred to her then that she had been more abrupt than was warranted. After all, Michael had not given her any offense. She looked down at him and added, "I need a good canter and time alone. But, thank you, Michael." She smiled at him and spurred Tokay forward.

As she turned into the lane she looked back. He was standing where she had left him and he raised an arm in a half wave, half salute.

The week before René was due to return, Julie realized she was pregnant. A visit to Dr. Villon in Lacon confirmed her suspicions. She took the news with equanimity, not knowing quite how she felt about it. However, coming along the main street of the village, it suddenly hit her: something of her own; something to love again; someone. Why, she thought in a dazed wonder, now I will never be lonely again. In a mood of wild elation, she went into the pastry shop to buy some sweets for her mother-in-law. She bought quite recklessly and then proceeded to demolish a goodly amount herself on the drive home, stuffing herself with éclairs and petit fours and cream puffs—she, who had never cared very much for cakes or pastries.

Everything had changed now. Her pregnancy might easily explain the feeling of revulsion. It was something that happened, that was all, something caused by the changes in her body, which certainly would explain her sudden desire for sweets and the reversal of her usual response to René. Oh, René would be thrilled about the baby. She could scarcely wait for him to come home.

René was thrilled, far more than even Julie had anticipated. He was also unbelievably solicitous. There was to be no exercise of any strenuous sort. Riding was out. If she must have that sort of thing, then she could take the old dogcart, and he would buy her a tame

Shetland pony or she could use one of the donkeys. No going up and down stairs all day. The list went on and, in desperation, she finally had the doctor speak to him so that René had to permit some latitude.

"But you must be careful," René warned. "I don't want anything to happen to you."

"Nothing is going to happen to me," Julie said stoutly. "I'm young and healthy and women have babies every day."

A cloud passed over his face and he said, "Forgive me, *chérie,* I was thinking of . . . well, of the past."

"I am not Emilie," she said steadily. He put gentle arms around her. "No, of course you are not, my darling. All the same, you must take care."

Along about the second week after René's return, it occurred to Julie that, while he had not approached her at all, she had not missed him. That must be natural. She had never asked anyone, of course, but presumably one did not have sexual relations while pregnant. For the moment the idea suited her.

As the weeks went on, Julie felt a growing sense of well-being. Hélène, informed of the impending arrival, took it with ill-concealed resentment. Guy, on the other hand, was delighted with their news and came on his next visit with a gift of flowers from his hothouse. He had arranged them in a lovely antique cachepot.

The old countess immediately began to order all manner of clothing made up for the grandson and could not be moved from her position that it was a boy, and that was that. "So nice for you, dear Emilie," she said tranquilly, her trembling hands sifting rhrough laces and ribbons and bits of material. "If only I could sew as I used to," she complained. "I do lovely embroidery, and it would be nice to make something myself. Perhaps I might manage to crochet. Yes, that will be it. I shall crochet a blanket."

She called at once for yarn and a hook and set about quite happily. The blanket occupied her for several days, and then she forgot that she was doing it and forgot that there was going to be a baby at all.

"When she remembers I am Julie, she forgets the baby, and when she remembers the baby, she forgets I am Julie," Julie said one night to René.

"She is worsening. I know that. It can't be helped.

The doctor says it is progressive. But she is happy enough and well cared for. One cannot expect much more, eh?"

"It isn't always that way," Julie said. "When I was little my great grandmother was still alive and very clear to the end."

"She was fortunate," René answered. "And you," he added, "you are not at all bothered by this, are you?"

"If you mean by having the baby, no. I've never felt better."

"I meant it doesn't affect your health that my mother can be so . . ."

"Don't be silly. I'm not fanciful and, no, it doesn't bother me to be called Emilie by your mother. I'm not jealous of . . ." She paused, trying to think of a tactful way to end the sentence.

But René finished it for her. "Ghosts," he said.

"Well, yes, in a way. What is past is past. Ghosts, dead or alive, have no place in the present."

He laughed suddenly and kissed her. "I love you," he said. "How many more months?"

"A bit over six," she told him, and he made a mock groan.

"Is it so necessary to abstain?" she asked delicately, feeling a little unexplained tremor as she waited for his answer.

"It's better," he said shortly, then changed the subject.

Now that René had forbidden riding and the doctor had concurred, Julie was hard pressed to use her energies. If René caught her walking too long or moving about too much, he put a stop to it and it hampered her activities considerably.

She finally took to driving the dogcart with the donkey well away from the grounds, where she would get out and walk to her heart's content, coming back aglow from the exercise.

But those days, too, would be numbered. The first snowfall was light, but she was not allowed out while it lasted. When winter finally ringed the valley in, she would be more and more confined.

This constant concern and watchfulness was the only irksome part of the pregnancy. Only in Isabelle did Julie have an ally. When René came looking for her and found her out, Isabelle would say she had been gone only a short time and would be returning soon. It allowed for a bit of freedom.

"If I permitted it," Julie complained to the doctor, "he would have me carried about in a palanquin like an Arabian princess, curtained from drafts and borne everywhere so that by the time I had the baby I would be unable to walk because I'd be so fat."

"You must forgive him," the old doctor said gently. "He cannot help worrying, considering the problems and tragedies of his first marriage."

"What was she like?" Julie asked curiously. "Emilie, I mean. I've seen her portrait, of course, and one or two photographs, but it's difficult to know the person."

"Lovely to look at," the doctor said, "prettier than her daughter, but very like her—small, thin, volatile. Her moods were always changing. She was not very healthy physically—quite different from you, though, of course, you are also a beautiful woman." He made a slight bow. "And now, from what I see, you are very well. There are no causes for alarm. Let your husband worry if he must. You needn't."

An unexpected warm spell at the end of December sent Julie outdoors once more. Climbing along the banks of the roadside and across the fields, she kept one eye on the donkey and cart. It would not do to have the animal take it into his head to wander off.

It was lonely out in this part of the country, quiet, away from habitation, unseen, unwatched over. The secretiveness of her small deception lent a special enchantment to her forays. Well, soon enough, when her stomach grew bigger, she would be slowed down, anyway. She might as well enjoy what she could.

Climbing back into the cart, she clicked the donkey into motion. As they started forward there was a grinding snap as the trace broke and the dogcart turned over. Julie rolled clear and arose uninjured, but it was impossible to untangle the animal from the lines or right the cart alone.

She stared ruefully at it. It was a very long walk back. Suddenly she remembered the house at the end of the lane that she had discovered on one of her rides. It was only a short distance ahead. She could go there and beg assistance and, in that way, no one need ever know what happened. If René found out about this, her one escape would be cut off. And it would be endless strolls around the gardens instead of the free and easy rambles she was having now.

The lane was longer than she remembered, but perhaps that was due to her own impatience. As it was, she would be very late. The gates, of course, were locked, but beside them there was a bell pull and she pulled at it, hearing it clang with a sudden loudness.

"Hush," a voice spoke, quite close-by. "You'll wake the baby."

Julie peered through the gates; although she could see a movement behind the hedges at the left and the outline of a pram, she could not see the speaker.

"Sorry," she called softly. "I've had a bit of trouble. My cart turned over and I was wondering . . ."

"Hush," the voice said again crossly. "You will wake the baby. Just a minute, please."

"Sorry," Julie said again and waited. Presently, around the hedge came an extremely fat little woman dressed in white, only a little brighter shade than her powdered face. She appeared to waddle, and Julie perceived that it was due in part to her slender ankles' effort to support a bulk they were never designed to carry.

"Now, what is it you wanted?" the woman asked, coming forward.

"My dogcat overturned," Julie explained, "and I can't get the lines free from the donkey in order to right the cart. I was wondering if one of the men, the . . . er . . gardener or someone, could help me."

"No. Indeed, not. We can't let anyone leave here," the woman said. "Someone tried to leave here once and was severely punished." She put her head close to the bars and Julie, staring into the depths of the brown eyes sunken in a puffy, lined face, felt a little chill. Mad. The woman was mad. The place was probably a sanitarium of some sort.

She started to draw back from the gate, but the woman thrust her hand through and grasped Julie's wrist with steely fingers. "Don't go," she pleaded. "I'll help you if I can. Can you open the gate?"

Julie shook her head dumbly.

"Oh, do try. Then I can take my son and get away from here. It's a terrible place. We've been here so long."

"I . . . I'll go and see if I can find help," Julie managed to say.

"No, you mustn't go. You'll tell and then I'll be punished." Tears began to cascade down the fat cheeks, making rivulets in the white powder.

"I won't tell," Julie said as gently as possible. "I know how it feels to want to get out. Trust me."

From a distance Julie heard shouts, and the woman, hearing them, too, clutched Julie's wrist harder than ever. "They've found me talking," she said. "Quick. What shall I do?"

"Let me go," Julie said very quietly.

"What is your name?" the woman asked.

"Julie," she said.

"Julie? What else?"

"Julie de Brugarde."

The woman dropped her hold on Julie's wrist and brought her hands together gleefully. "Why, then we're relatives," she said. "I am Emilie de Brugarde." She drew herself up. "I am the wife of Le Comte René de Brugarde," she added. "And when you tell my husband where I am, he will come and get us out of here. He doesn't know we've been kidnapped."

Julie was too stunned to move. She stood staring while the woman prattled on. Emilie. It couldn't be. Fat, grotesquely fat. But with all that, she could see some resemblance to the woman who had once been beautiful, and worse, as the woman, still chattering eagerly and gaily, burst into sudden laughter, it was as if Hélène de Brugarde stood there, years older, pounds heavier, but very much the same.

"Good-bye," Julie whispered. Turning, she fled down the lane.

"Where are you, Emilie? What are you doing? Come away from that gate. Alain, help me," a nameless woman's voice called out, alternately pleading and peremptory.

Julie heard no more. Emilie was alive. Mad. Locked up. Emilie, who was supposed to be dead. A live ghost. A truly live ghost. Julie had an insane impulse to laugh. Why? Why had they done it? Divorce would have been possible. Perhaps there had been a divorce, a secret one. Could there be such things in France? She didn't know.

She hurried now that she was out on the road, passing the still tangled cart and donkey unheedingly.

She was nearly halfway back to the château when Michael Lynch, driving his small, wheezing car, found her.

"I thought something must have happened. Get in, Countess. There's the devil to pay if the count realizes there's been any trouble."

She obeyed him automatically, her mind still numb from the shock of her discovery. Her main objective was to find René and confront him with it. Bigamy. He had committed a bigamous marriage and . . . her child! She gasped aloud.

Michael Lynch, helping her into the car, said anxiously, "Something wrong, Countess?"

"Yes." Something was wrong. She was not married and her child would be the bastard René's mother feared it might be. She began to laugh and then weep.

Michael said, "Here. Easy, Countess, you're all right now. You didn't hurt yourself, did you?"

She shook her head, making a monumental effort to stem the hysteria that welled so alarmingly inside her. "No," she said. "No, I'm all right, frightened and tired, that's all." She got into the car and he closed the door and ran around to get in beside her.

"This motor goes out when it's idling," he said. "And there I am waiting for it to cool down so I can crank it up again."

"The dogcart broke and overturned and I couldn't get the donkey out of the lines or shaft. I was walking home to get help."

"You're sure you weren't hurt?"

"Positive. I saw it coming and I rolled clear. It's lonely on this road," she added with a barely repressed shudder.

"Aye, it is that. Not a road for you to be traveling on alone these days, if you'll forgive my presumption, Countess."

"I won't travel it again."

"We'll go along and check the donkey, if you don't mind. It won't take more than a few minutes, and we'll have you back at the château before the count comes in from the office."

She made no answer, leaning her head back and clos-

ing her eyes. Her mind could not seem to go beyond the
racing thought of René's deception and her own pre-
carious position. She thought of all the years that she had
flirted with the possibility of pregnancy without marriage and nothing had gone wrong. Now she had been
deceived into the very situation she had always sworn
would never befall her.

"There are some houses, you know," Michael was saying, "farther ahead on the road. One of them is deserted,
or nearly so. You wouldn't want to go there for help.
There's an old woman caretaker and her son, at least I
think it's her son. Anyway, they ran me off years ago
when I stopped there to try to find my way back to the
château. A proper old hag, the woman is. Nose like a
hawk's beak and gray hair and humped over. All she's
wanting is a crooked stick and a peaked hat, and she'd
go fair for frightening little children, or me, for the matter of that. And the son looks like her, only he's not
stooped. But he's got strange, mean eyes. Sometimes
you'll see him along the road. But she never leaves the
place. Ah, here we are, and there's the ass already into
the weeds at the roadside. Hungry are you, old son?" he
called out and received a bray in answer.

"There, now. I won't be a minute," he said to Julie
and got out of the car.

So Michael knew of the house, and he was warning
her off. Did he know that Emilie de Brugarde lived
there? Or was he just making conversation to end the
awkward silence.

"All fixed up now," he said on rejoining her. "And
my luck is holding with this car. Or maybe the car wants
to show off to so fine a lady."

"A foolish lady, anyway," Julie answered.

"Now, then, the ass is tethered and I'll send one of
the lads along to fetch it back. No use for the dogcart.
It's too old. The wood's rotten, which is why the trace
broke. Fix that and next it'll be the shafts and wheels.
We'll have to find you something better."

"I won't be riding out alone again," Julie said. "I did
stop at that house, and it was . . ."—she paused and
swallowed—". . . frightening."

"Ah, no wonder you were so pale. It was a terrible
experience for me myself, and I'm not afraid of most
things. For a lass like you . . ."

"Are the old woman and her son the only ones there?" Julie asked.

"As far as I ever saw, they are, although it wouldn't surprise me to find a den of thieves, as well, or perhaps a coven of witches and warlocks."

"There are worse things than thieves or witches or . . . or even murderers," Julie said enigmatically.

"Lord, and what would be worse than all of them?"

"Devils, I guess."

"Here, now, you want to watch that talk. My old grandmother used to say, 'Mention the devil and he'll pop up to meet you.' And then she'd cross herself to scare him away." He laughed.

I've met the devil, Julie thought. I married the devil.

"Thank you for bringing me back, Michael," she said aloud. "What made you come looking for me?"

"It was your little maid, Isabelle. She was worried and came to me. I promised I'd have a look. Well, here we are. You walk on up through the gardens. We'll say nothing to the count, if you like. I don't mind keeping a secret to stave off trouble."

Julie met his open gaze and gave a faint smile. "Nor I," she said.

He gave her a silent salute as she moved away.

René had not yet returned. Julie went straight to her room, where an anxious Isabelle was sewing industriously. She rose the moment Julie entered, saying, "Oh, madame . . . I . . ."

"It's all right, Isabelle. Thank you for sending Mr. Lynch. Will you draw me a bath? And then I want to rest before . . . until my husband returns."

Julie was lying on her bed, a peignoir over her undergarments, when she heard René moving about his room. She had planned for hours just what she would say, buoyed by her rage over the deceit and her horror over the unmasking of it. Now that the moment was imminent, she began to tremble. She rose a little unsteadily and went to put on her gown and comb her hair.

Her eyes looked dead in the mirror, and the white oval of her face was without any touch of color. She made no attempt at artifice, however.

Finished, she stood for several minutes at the connecting door trying to compose herself before she finally opened it and stepped inside.

René looked up in the act of tying his cravat, surprised to see her. "I understood you were sleeping," he said. "You look quite pale, *chérie*. Are you feeling well?" He came forward anxiously, his hands outstretched to take hers, but she stepped aside.

"You miserable liar," she said clearly and distinctly. "You deceived me. You've deceived everyone. Or have you? Do the rest know? How could you? What kind of man are you?"

A look of alarmed fear came over his face. "My God! What are you talking about? Are you . . . you . . . I've never heard you speak like that. You're irrational."

"Irrational? Is it irrational for me to accuse a bigamist of bigamy?"

His face went white. "You don't know what you're saying. Bigamy? I've committed no bigamy."

"Haven't you, René? I was riding today . . . out on the old back road to Hautvilliers, and the dogcart overturned. . . ."

"I knew it! I knew you shouldn't be allowed so much freedom. You might have killed yourself. Don't you realize you must be careful? How can you be so pigheaded?" His face had reddened as he spoke and he was breathing heavily.

"It's no use, René. I know now. It isn't me you want; it's this baby I'm carrying. I met Emilie. She's mad. I can even perceive why she must be mad, living with a devil like you. How could you do it? Locking her away with . . . my God! Why wasn't she put in a doctor's care? What kind of monster are you?"

He made no attempt to answer, and she went on recklessly, hurling accusations, her voice growing higher and higher until he moved with a rapier swiftness, grasping her around the waist and putting one hand across her mouth. She bit him fiercely and tasted blood, but he did not flinch, his eyes boring down into hers. "Shut up!" he grated. "If you speak of this, if you make any kind of scene, I'll kill you. Do you understand? I'll kill you."

His grip across her waist and his hand pressing cruelly against her mouth cut off her wind. She could feel herself growing faint and suddenly sagged against his arm. He let her go then, chafing her wrists anxiously, speaking rapidly in a low voice: "I'm sorry, *chérie*, sorry about it all. But, you see, you cannot make this kind of accusation. It would ruin me, kill my mother, and Hélène . . . Hélène would go mad herself. Hélène must never know. Why do you think I kept the secret? Doctors—Emilie had doctors. Hopeless, they said. Hopeless. She was physically weak. She couldn't last, they said. I wouldn't have her die in an asylum. Think what it would do to Hélène. Raving. Emilie was raving mad. I had to think. And then a stroke of luck, a great stroke of luck. A cousin of Emilie's, a remote cousin, orphaned and with no means, was living at the house. She was helping with Emilie, and Emilie . . . Emilie . . ." He stopped, peering at Julie's terrified face. "Emilie killed her. She ran a darning needle through the back of her head just so . . ." He pressed the soft spot at the base of Julie's skull. "There was almost no blood. It all happened inside, you see. I laid her out. I said it was Emilie. I demanded a closed coffin and I then took Emilie to . . . to where you found her. I paid the caretakers; I still pay them. I pay more each year because Emilie, weak Emilie, grew stronger as her madness deepened. Once I thought she would live longer than I. Now, well, you saw her. You know."

Julie heard it all with a growing sense of horror that she had never before experienced. Murder and madness, and René covering up both. Still, with it all, only one thing stood clear in her mind. René had threatened to kill her. Realizing the lengths to which he went to protect Emilie, Julie had little doubt that he meant it. She must get away.

With an effort she drew herself erect, loosening her wrist from René's grasp and saying as steadily as she could manage, "It's been too much for me to understand, René. I . . . I can't speak of it anymore. Please, I must lie down. I feel ill."

"You will say nothing," he repeated.

"I will say nothing."

"But we must talk. There are ways . . . I . . ."

"We will talk," she said, making herself lay a placating hand on his arm. "The shock—surely you understand what a shock it has been."

"I never meant you to know," he said. "If I had dreamed . . ."

"Please, René, please. Tell me the rest later. I . . . must lie down. Surely you don't want me to lose the baby."

"No, no, of course not . . . everything I . . ." He broke off. "Let me help you," he said gently. She suffered him to put an arm about her waist, to lead her to her room, to help her out of her gown and into the peignoir once again.

"I can't eat anything," Julie said wanly. "Later, perhaps Isabelle can bring me some soup and bread." She closed her eyes, sighing, as if she were unutterably weary. She heard him move away from her bed and go to his own room and close the door but some sixth sense told her that he had only pretended to leave, so she remained as she was for long minutes, finally turning over, as if she were actually going to sleep. It seemed that she lay there an eternity before she heard the soft click of a stealthily opened door and a corresponding click as it closed. She turned over then and opened her eyes to find the room was empty.

How she got through the next few hours, she never knew. All she could think of was escape, and her mind went feverishly over means to make that escape. Night— it would have to be at night. She couldn't take much with her, just her personal things. But to go from Lacon to Paris and beyond, she would need transportation.

It was not as it had been once before when she was running away. Then she had only been sickened by the Prescotts and the realization that they could never protect her against Holt. Then she had places to go, nearby places, if it had come to that. Here, though, she was an alien and among people whose first loyalty would be to René. Even if she could steal into the stables and saddle a horse, she would be at a loss as to direction, and then with the burden of her pregnancy . . .

All at once the baby she had carried with a sense of happy anticipation became a nauseating alien intruder, and Julie had to bite hard on her thumb to keep from screaming her anxiety to the heavens.

Who could help her? Michael Lynch. His name stood out in her mind like a sign from heaven. Michael Lynch. She would go to him, tell him the truth, and throw herself at his mercy. It was a poor chance, but the only one.

If he betrayed her . . . but she would not think of that. She must try.

Twice during the late evening René came into her room, but she continued to feign sleep, stirring restlessly when he touched her, as if he were interrupting some dream.

It was a long time before he went to bed. Julie could hear him pacing in his room. At last the lights went out under the rim of his door. Then, after another long wait, she stole from her bed, feeling through the dark for the clothes she had hidden beneath her bedclothes, together with the small packet containing her own jewelry, her bank book, her passport, and other identification.

When she was ready she stood hesitating at her door, her ear pressed against it, listening for some unusual sound. All was quiet. She opened the door soundlessly and crept down the hall, hugging the wall. She was at the top of the stairs, the dark foyer lying below, when she felt a movement behind her. She whirled about even as René grabbed her case.

"No!" she screamed in her terror. "No!"

"You aren't going anywhere," he said venomously. "I knew you were planning something."

She tried to wrench the case away and, as she did so, her foot slipped on the top stair and she went down backward, bumping her head on the carpeted risers, rolling over and over again, screaming as she went, until at last she hit the bottom and a searing wave of pain shot through her whole body.

I am going to die, she thought, I am going to die like Eileen. She could hear René shouting and then saw the lights come on. She struggled to rise, but the action was too much. As she managed to grasp the banister to pull herself erect, she fainted.

21

During the weeks of her convalescence after the loss of the baby, Julie lay spent and uncaring in her room, taking medication and sustenance dutifully from a much-subdued Isabelle and suffering René's visits without comment.

The nightmare of the miscarriage itself evaporated from her memory like most nightmares. Foremost in her mind was the remembered face of Emilie de Brugarde and of René's horrifying confession. Somewhere during the time between her fall and her return to some semblance of recovery, Julie had come to the conclusion that this was one prison from which she could never escape and that René would have no compunctions about killing her, or causing her to be killed, if she failed a second time.

Her physical ordeal and the subsequent infection had left her too helpless to formulate any rational plan, so she made no reference to the events preceding her fall, nor did she offer René any argument when he outlined the new beginning they would make. Once he said, "I know it was a shock, but you must see how much I wanted you. You remember how it was with us. It will be that way again." She was even able to hide her convulsive disgust and summon a wan smile.

Slowly over the weeks, and under Isabelle's devoted care, Julie's strength began to return, and along with it a ravenous appetite. All at once, she, who had supped gruel and soup and bland foods without interest for weeks, could not eat enough.

"You are getting better, *chérie*," René said one day. "That is good. Soon you will be up and about, and we will be as we were before the unfortunate accident."

In February, during a day of false spring, Julie was finally taken out of doors and placed on the back terrace,

327

wrapped in lap robes against any unexpected breeze. She turned her face to the sun and, for the first time since her illness, a sense of life came back to her.

As she lay there, half dreaming, an idea began to form. First she must get well. She must get strong again and begin to move about by herself again, and then—then—there might be some way to end this half-life that had been forced upon her.

But she could not do it rashly, impulsively, as she had done so many things from the beginning: stealing out of the convent; running away from Prescottville; fleeing from her despair over Mark's death and falling into René's cunningly set trap; and this last flight that had brought her to the brink of death. They had all been done without any thought of failure, and each in its own way had produced a failure.

This time she would plan as carefully and as cunningly as anyone had ever planned anything. First, get well, and then . . . and then she must con René into believing that she accepted the circumstances. How she would do that, she did not know, and trying to think about it made her head ache. She let the ideas go, let her mind wander again, and presently she napped, waking with an increased sense of hopefulness.

A month later she was beginning to see the fruits of her planning. She was fully restored now, able to ride and walk once more. She managed to put off René's demands on the grounds that it was "too soon." Three months, at least, Dr. Villon had warned. She told René six months; thus, she won a reprieve from his demands.

On the renewed subject of Emilie, Julie had been equally cautious. "You must see how I would feel," she said. "It was cruel of you, René, although I understand why. I love you," she said, barely feeling the lie, "and what of our . . . our children? If anyone should discover . . ."

He believed her because he wanted to believe her, but he mistrusted her at the same time. She could see it in his eyes. "Yet you were running away from me," he said.

"I was raging, hurt, humiliated. I kept thinking about the baby. What son would want to be called a . . ." She paused and let her eyelids bat rapidly as if holding back tears.

The mention of the word "son" had helped bring René

closer to believing. "I know, I know," he said distract-
edly. "Don't you think it torments me, too? But Emilie
. . . she can't live forever. You saw. You know. Then,
when it is over, we can arrange everything. Leave it to
me."

"But we need arrange nothing once Emilie is dead,"
Julie answered. "With no one to question it, our marriage
in St. Cloud will stand."

"Yes, yes," he agreed hurriedly, not meeting her eyes,
and she realized that the marriage was probably not valid,
that the mayor, the little, fat, happy mayor, was either a
paid performer or perhaps a bribed petty official.

Sometimes as she presided over the dinner table during one of Guy's and Hélène's visits, she would marvel
at the control she was able to exercise.

Once René said to her, "But you seem so much more
at ease. You are even gayer than you were before . . ."

"It's coming back to life," she assured him. "I was so
close to death. I saw a girl die once from a miscarriage.
When I fell . . . I thought I would die, too, and then
when I didn't, I suppose I appreciated life all the more."

"Can you forgive me?" he asked penitently.

"Of course I can. I know how you felt. I know how
I felt . . . feel," she corrected. But when he sought to
draw her into an embrace, she put him off, turning one
of his old phrases against him: "Slowly, darling. It's better to wait, and it won't be much longer."

Soon Julie knew she would not be able to put him off,
and she lived in fear and dread of another pregnancy.
That could not happen, or she would never get away.
Yet there was no way to use any preventive measures.
René wanted a son—that above all, she knew. But she
wanted no child of his, and, one way or another, she must
see that she did not have one.

Learning that Michael Lynch was away on one of his
buying trips, she felt less sure of being able to find a way
of escape. Michael was the key; she felt certain of that.
And if he wasn't . . . there would be a way. There had
to be.

Six months to wait, she had told René, and the six
months were nearly up. Yet she had devised no way to
leave. For all that she performed her duties sensibly and
quietly, and for all she forced herself to give René tokens

of affection, and for all she assured him that she agreed completely that to reveal the truth to Hélène would be to destroy her, she knew that she was still being watched closely. Even Isabelle, whom she once might have trusted to help her, was no longer willing to tell even the small fibs about her times of departure and arrival. And the case containing her passport, jewelry, and bank books had been unpacked, everything put neatly back into place, save for her passport and other papers of identification. René still held those and she had not asked for them, fearing to arouse his suspicions.

She never rode alone anymore; a groom always rode with her. When she wished for anything, it was brought to her. When she wanted to shop, she was sent in the chauffeured Rolls with Isabelle for company, or, in the car's absence, she went in the horse and carriage.

When Michael Lynch returned, Julie could find no way to arrange to see him. She feared to go to his house in the daytime, and, since the groom always brought the horses to the yard for mounting, she was never at the stables. And she dared not try to leave the house at night again.

Her days were marvels of pretense, but when they ended she often lay sleepless under the strain of pretending and the mounting realization that time was running out. She was as much a prisoner of Château de Brugarde as Emilie was a prisoner in the wooded, lonely manor house outside Hautvilliers.

Julie grew more tense. One night, any night now, she knew that René would come to her and that, short of murder, there would be no way out at all.

When it finally happened she was least prepared for it. She had drunk a lot of wine at dinner and sat up afterward with René, drinking brandy and coffee. Finally, pleading a headache from overindulgence, she had gone to bed. The effects of the alcohol had sent her to sleep rather soon. The next thing she knew, she was awakening with René beside her, caressing her.

Half drugged, she recoiled, and he soothed her, saying, "It's all right, *chérie*. You must get over your fears of having another child. Don't be alarmed." Julie stiffened and he pursued his intentions. Wide awake now, her disgust at his touch overcame her. She knew she must try to pretend she was aroused, but her revulsion was too great for her to succeed. She knew he must realize how she felt, and the fear the thought engendered made her tremble. Almost at once he moved away from her, rising and saying, "You are not fooling me, Julie. I am no callow boy who is so beset by his own desire that he takes anything for a signal of a woman's pleasure."

"I'm sorry," she whispered. "It's true. I am afraid. Give me a little more time."

"Time for what?" The words snapped like a whip as he turned on the lights. "Time to lull me into believing you so that you can leave and spread scandal and ruin us all?" He was advancing back toward the bed, his face livid with fury, his eyes glittering. "Afraid! You aren't afraid, except of me. And, Julie, you have every reason to be afraid of me. Do you imagine I could explain your leaving, even if you kept silent? Do you imagine I can make other marriages that will produce other sons? I waited for years, first hoping that Emilie would die, then looking for someone I could marry, someone who had no family to trouble me, someone who did not know our French laws. I want a son and heir. I will have one. And you will give me one."

He seized her and flung her face down upon the bed, leaping astride her and spreading her buttocks. With horror she realized that he meant to sodomize her. A vision of Holt rose before her dazed brain and she squirmed away, fighting silently, so that she was partly on her side, her legs tangled in René's. For minutes they struggled and then, without warning, he reversed his direction so that she lay on her back and he was above her. She stiffened to resist his entry. He persisted but without success.

In a flash, she realized the truth of those nights of endless excitation in which he had appeared to exercise such monumental control over his own desire. He was impotent, or nearly so. He had performed so expertly in those days that she had never thought to wonder why they never made love in any ordinary way.

Knowing he was losing the ability to penetrate her body, she took fresh courage and continued to resist. The longer it took him, the more furious he became. She began to be afraid that if he did not succeed, he would kill her in his rage.

She relaxed suddenly, taking him by surprise, and

then with a mightly heave she threw him off and ran for the door. He was after her at once, seizing her by the hair and forcing her to her knees. He tried to thrust his half-soft organ into her mouth, but she twisted away, screaming out her fear and revulsion.

This last struggle on her part increased his fury and he began to slap her, his hand striking her face from side to side so that her head rolled drunkenly and she could feel the stinging pain upon her hot cheeks. Then he picked her up like a rag doll and flung her across the bed.

"That is what you will have every night until you learn!" he rasped out, and then he left the room.

Julie lay huddled and weeping for several minutes. Then, with rage breaking through her humiliation, she rose and locked both doors. She was certain that she would never sleep again.

In the morning the effects of René's beating showed in the huge, puffy redness of her face. Along the top of her cheekbone a purple bruise crept toward her eye.

She dressed herself with some care and tried to cover the bruises with powder, but the effect was almost as bad as it was without it. Nevertheless, she went out of her room and down the stairs, heading out through the side terrace, away from the view of the bedrooms, making her way down the gardens and to the stables.

It was just past six. No one would be up yet. If she could gain the tack room and bring the saddle to her horse's stall, she had every chance of saddling Tokay and riding out well ahead of any pursuit that might be mustered at such an early hour.

To her dismay she found the tack room locked. She looked about for something heavy enough to pry the padlock loose, but everything that was heavy enough was too cumbersome. With only a glimmer of hope, she came out of the stables and turned the corner to the office. It, too, was locked. Dreading to go back to the house and, yet, with no help in sight, she went into the stables once more and up to the stall where Tokay stood. She reached up and patted the horse's neck and stood there, unable to think of what to do next, only hoping that Michael Lynch would arrive before the grooms, as was his custom. Please, she prayed silently, don't let Michael have gone abroad again, and don't let him be late this morning. She stood there, her face pressed against the side of the stall, and Tokay pushed his head out to nuzzle her hair.

Michael, coming into the stables shortly afterward, found her there. "Here, Countess, what is it?" he said, peering at her bruised and tear-stained face.

"Please!" she begged. "Please, you've got to help me! I've got to get away from here. I've got to get home. Please."

He gave a hasty look around, cautioning her to silence. "If they catch you here, it'll be worth my life. What happened to your face?"

Haltingly, she poured out the story, holding back nothing except the more degrading details. His face grew stony as he listened. "And she is alive. But he'll kill me if I tell anyone. Oh, if you don't believe me, see for yourself. If you'd ride up one day and wait, you'd see. She's out in the gardens. She's very fat—not like her old pictures. I was going to saddle Tokay and ride off. But the tack room was locked, so I waited for you. Please, Michael, please help me." He was silent a minute, chewing his lip, and she began to be afraid that it was all for nothing. "You won't, will you?" she said despondently.

"I will, of course," he said. "I'm only thinking how I can help you. I'm to go on my vacation tomorrow—a bit of business mixed with pleasure, you might say. I'm to look at some stock for the count while I'm there. He won't be expecting me back for a month. I'll tell you what. Can you manage until tomorrow afternoon?"

"I don't know, I don't know."

He looked at her, his face softening a little. "Poor lass," he said. "It's a desperate man would do that to your face." He reached out his hand and touched the bruise gently. "You'll be all right. I'll tell you what, you go on now and go back to the house. I'll send the groom as usual with your horse. Only, if you're going to bring anything with you, bring it then. It can't be much, mind you."

She shook her head dumbly. Now that he had promised to help, her will and her strength both left her. She felt helpless and unable to think for herself anymore.

"Here, now," he said. "It's no time to turn fearful. I've said I'll help, and I will. Holy God, when I think of the devil, well, he'll be paid for it one day. I'll help you. But you must be brave and sensible. Now, go on back to the house. Use your wits, girl. I'll take care of the rest. Oh, and say, you'll ride this afternoon instead of this morning. It will be easier."

"Thank you," Julie said between stiff lips. "I can't thank you enough."

"Don't thank me at all," he said gruffly. "I've no use for a man who beats a woman that way, no matter what she's done. I've no use for an unfair fight." He grinned at her suddenly. "Well, Countess, and wait till I tell you what that means. We've a long journey to go, and you might even enjoy the telling of the story. Go on, now."

René had not yet risen when Julie got back to her room. Her breakfast tray sat on the table before the windows. From her bathroom she could hear Isabelle humming as she filled the tub.

Quietly, she removed her clothing and slipped into her gown and robe, seating herself at the breakfast table, her back to the room so that when Isabelle reappeared she was able to speak to her without showing her face.

"I won't need anything more," she said. "Oh, Isabelle, will you send word to the stable that I will ride after luncheon today? Just a short ride—about three o'clock."

"Yes, *madame*," Isabelle replied.

Julie remained in her room during the morning, and shortly after eleven René came to see her.

"You are not riding this morning?" he began, as if this were any usual day and they were any usual married couple.

"I thought I would give the swelling on my face a chance to subside," she answered. "One little bruise can be explained. Huge, puffy welts cannot."

"And so you will remain indoors?"

"No. I'm better now. I will ride after lunch. But if you will excuse me, I shall have a tray sent to me here. I can wear a scarf outdoors; it would look strange to wear one at the luncheon table."

She did not look at him during the exchange for fear he would see her trembling and be alerted to her plans.

"You made me lose my temper," he said. "It is something I seldom do. I hope you realize that what happened last night was your own doing. You have been deceiving me with lies. You see, I spoke to Dr. Villon yesterday. Once I knew you lied, then why should I believe that you tell the truth about other things?"

"Leave me alone, René," Julie answered tiredly. "I'm sure you can always find some excuse for taking what you want or doing as you please. Speaking of lies, if you had acted truthfully years ago, Hélène was young enough to forget. In any case, you could have divorced Emilie. Incurable madness after a certain number of years would surely have given you some legal redress."

"And how would I have avoided the scandal of Emilie having killed her cousin?" She was silent and he went on. "I've asked your forgiveness in the deception. I have explained the circumstances. Perhaps . . . it is possible . . . I did not act wisely. Perhaps, as you say, the whole truth would have been better. But I had others besides myself to consider: my mother, who loved Emilie; Hélène, who adored her mother. Emilie was very gay, witty, and charming when she was rational. How to explain that with each child she became something else? I spent years trying to conceal her lapses. The last one was hopeless. I knew then she was incurable. If I had told the truth, she would have been locked away as criminally insane. What a heritage for Hélène!"

Julie looked at him then and, seeing his face so tormented, she felt a wave of compassion that in the next moment she stifled. He was adroit, clever, and he wanted something from her—sons. He wanted one heir at the very least. If he could persuade her to sympathy, he would go on playing the adoring older husband of his young countess. If not, well, she had seen last night, and she knew that there was no longer any hope of pretense. She loathed his touch as once she had thrilled to it, and he was too astute for her to feign emotions and responses.

"I will tell you this," she said coolly. "You can beat me, abuse me, and misuse me, as you did last night, but it will be no way to get a son from me. I asked you to give me time. All right, I did lie about the things Dr. Villon said. I wanted to . . . to spare you." He smiled thinly and she lowered her eyes. "Believe what you like," she said, "but if I had wanted to destroy you, I would have told the story to Isabelle, and it would have been all over Lacon within hours." She felt her muscles tighten, hoping he would not ascertain her real reason for silence was that she trusted no one on his staff—only Michael

Lynch. And with a nameless dread she realized such trust could be equally unwise. It was based on such flimsy reasons. He had been kind, and she knew he was grateful for her silence on the subject of Hélène—two rather dubious notions. When she realized her trust in him was partly due to the fact that he spoke her native language, she realized on what a frail basis her hopes rested.

"It wouldn't have done any good," René said smoothly. "When you were ill I told Madame Arnaud that you had fancies about seeing Emilie and that they arose from the terrible coincidence that you also had lost a baby."

Julie's eyes flew open. "You didn't!" she said. No wonder Isabelle was so watchful. But Michael Lynch had seemed to believe her—seemed. Perhaps he was only placating her, leading her to believe that he would help only so that she would not become too agitated.

"And if Isabelle had seen my face this morning?"

"Ah, but that is so easily explained. You fell in the bath yesterday."

"I see."

"However, I have taken some precautions. Emilie is being moved soon. In that way, no matter what you say, you will be thought very peculiar. I intend to have you remain. I intend that you shall behave. And I intend to see that you obey me in all matters. Years ago I was younger and more sentimental. I should have smothered Emilie myself as she lay sleeping. It would have spared all that agony and also saved the life of the poor cousin. I very nearly did do that. Something stayed my hand. I would not be so merciful with you, Julie. If my secret got out and my family was ruined, then life would be meaningless to me. I wouldn't hesitate to use a pistol on myself. But I would pay you before I died."

"Perhaps you would like to commence now, then," Julie said with sudden courage, "because, as you pointed out yourself last night, there is no way that I can fool you into thinking I welcome your attentions."

She saw the anger flare in his face and took an instinctive step backward.

"Brave words," he sneered, "but they are only words. I will dine out, but I will see you later tonight, Julie. And don't bother locking the door. If necessary I will break it down." He turned and strode from the room.

Despite his warning, Julie locked both doors after him and began to choose those things she could take with her this afternoon. She wrapped her personal jewelry, her bank book, and her small amount of cash in a kerchief and secured it with a pin to her suspender belt. She looked at the rings on her fingers. The wedding ring —she would keep it and throw it away once she was out of France. The other two she stripped from her fingers and tossed into her drawer.

She stuffed into her brassiere the old letters from Mark that she had saved. The other correspondence she discarded. There was nothing else. No change of clothing. She had better dress warmly, then. She put on heavy winter underclothes beneath her jumper and riding skirt, and she pulled on woolen stockings beneath her boots. She would wear the heavier riding jacket and take an extra scarf.

She had finished all her small preparations by the time Isabelle brought her tray. She sat down to eat, a book in her hand, a woolen afghan covering her.

"*Madame* is chilly?" Isabelle inquired. "Shall I light the fire?"

"No, thank you, Isabelle. I am fine as I am. Oh, Isabelle?"

"Yes, *madame?*"

"My blue gown needs pressing. I want to wear it this evening."

Isabelle went to the wardrobe and removed the gown in question.

And that took care of that. If her disappearance was noticed and René asked Isabelle for information, it would appear that she meant to return.

Shortly before two the groom brought up Tokay. Julie, wondering what Michael Lynch could be arranging and how she would be able to slip away from the groom, set off down the path, the groom following at a respectful distance. Not knowing what Michael had in mind, she hesitated at the open gates. Normally, she took the roads leading away from Hautvilliers and from the vicinity of Michael's house.

"If Madame la Comtesse would like a different ride today," the groom said quietly, "perhaps the back road would be pleasant."

She turned obediently, passing the stables and Michael's house without catching a glimpse of him. They rode for perhaps half an hour before Julie decided that the ride had gone on long enough.

"We will go back," she said, and the groom murmured agreement. Her earlier anxiety that Michael might, after all, have betrayed her returned. So it was to be just an ordinary ride, after all. They were very nearly home again and Julie, her heart heavy and leaden in her chest, felt her last hope flicker out.

Rounding the last curve in the lane, she could see the stables and the top of the château itself, and just then Michael Lynch stepped casually into the road. They reined up to let him pass.

"Good day, Madame la Comtesse," he greeted her. Then he said to the groom, *"Alors,* Michel, what's wrong with Tokay?"

The groom rode forward, looking anxious.

"Something with that left hindquarter; I am certain of it. Did you see him stumble there a minute ago when Madame la Comtesse reined in?"

"No, Monsieur Lynch. He's ridden well all day. I assure you that if he had been favoring a leg, I would have seen from my position behind the countess."

"You had better get down, *madame,"* Michael said. "I saw this just in time. I wouldn't want the horse to throw you." He helped her dismount and handed the reins to Michel.

"Walk her easy, please. I'll be along to look as soon as I've escorted Madame la Comtesse home."

"I can go alone," Julie said.

She saw Michael exchange a look with Michel and stiffened. "It's best not to, Madame la Comtesse. You know Monsieur le Comte. He still worries about your health. He would dismiss us all if you should stumble or fall on the way."

Julie set off beside Michael as soon as the groom had turned the horses into the stable yard.

"Easy, now," Michael said. "We'll go up to the trees and then slip through and circle around and head back for my house."

"I thought . . ." she began.

"Shhh!" he cautioned. "This is the worst part. If we should be seen, I've no explanation to offer. Just follow me."

She slipped behind him as they entered the grove and veered left away from the château lawns, bending low as they cleared the grove and came to the hedgerows.

"All the way down now," he whispered and went nearly on all fours so that they were crawling with the open, empty field on one side of them and the hedgerow protecting them from view on the other.

Julie tried to keep her eyes ahead, but the open field made her apprehensive and she kept darting her eyes to the side, fearful that someone would come into the field and see them. Crawling like this, it was endless; yet, once they reached the back of Michael's house, she heard him say with satisfaction, "That's it. Ten minutes. Now, inside quickly."

She scurried through the open door and he followed, only half closing it. "Give me something," he said, low voiced, "anything at all. A handkerchief will do."

Julie took one from her pocket and handed it to him.

"Good. Now, go into the bedroom and stay there. Don't light a light and don't move until I come back. If anyone comes to the door, get under the bed. The front door's bolted and I'll lock this. I've the only key. If I'm alone, I'll be whistling. If I have company, get under the bed, as I told you. You'll know if there's company. I'll be telling you as I come in." He gave her a pat and was gone.

She heard the key rasp in the lock and heard him moving away jauntily, whistling as he went. The first part was over. The relief loosened her tense muscles and she began to shake. It was with difficulty that she managed to walk into the bedroom and sit down upon the brass bed. It felt good to sit there and she had an overwhelming desire to lie down on the puffy provincial quilt, but, fearful of the fatigue that follows sustained anxiety, she remained bolt upright, staring into the dimness of the curtained gloom and trying not to let herself think of what would happen should Michael's plan fail.

The clock on his dresser ticked loudly in the silence. Four-thirty. She would surely be missed in another half an hour, an hour at the most. She stared at the clock, taking comfort in the slowness with which the hands seemed to move, and at the same time impatient to have the hands complete their course and to have Michael, succeeding or failing, return and an end to the worries.

It was after five when he finally returned. She heard the whistling as he came to the door, heard the key rasp again as the tumblers fell into place, and then he was inside, calling out softly, "It's all right. Come out now."

She rose and went into the kitchen. He looked very pleased with himself, and she could not help smiling back at him in spite of her renewed tension.

"All smooth as silk. But we've got to make haste. Now, you be a good girl and fix us up some food to take along. There's bread and cheese and some cold meat. Wrap it up in something. And take some of the wine on the shelf there. God knows I'll be glad of a pint once I'm home."

"They'll have missed me," Julie said.

"Not to worry yet. I took your handkerchief up to the château. Says I, 'The countess dropped this on the lawn as I was seeing her home.' So they'll think you're about. You see? And then I went to have a look at Tokay, who's as right as rain, bless his old black heart, but I ordered him rested and said that if you were wanting to ride in the morning you'd have to take another horse. And here I am. I'm to leave. They know that. By the time they realize you're gone, we'll be on the way to Brest."

"But suppose they follow you?" she asked.

"Here, keep up with the packing. If they follow me, it's to Le Havre where they'll be heading. I'm going to Dublin, remember?"

"But what about Brest? Why will we go there?"

"Because I've a friendly ship's captain who's going to run me and some good friends to Cork. He'll run you, as well, and from there, well, don't worry. There are other friendly captains, and you'll be sailing for America before you know it. Now, finish that up. I've some clothes for you to change into."

When Michael had got his own things together and the food was packed, Julie changed into the clothes he had brought for her: shapeless peasant garments and a long black shawl. The sky was darkening, and from the distant village they heard the faint toll of the Angelus.

"Running a bit late, we are," Michael said. "Come on, then. When you're in the car, get down on the floor and curl up. I'll be piling some packages and luggage in your seat and the lighter things over you. You're not to move now until we've cleared the place. Understand?"

"Yes," she said.

"All right, then, we're off." He opened the front door, peered both ways into the lane, and beckoned her silently. She was in the car, curled crablike under the lighter pieces of luggage, and Michael was cranking the motor when someone gave a shout. Oh, no, she thought, not now, not when I'm almost free. Over the roar of the engine she heard Michael shout back. And then he, too, was in the car and it was moving forward.

"Until next month," she heard him call out, and as they careened down the lane he said quietly, "No need to worry. It was only one of the lads come to say goodbye. I'll miss it here."

"You aren't coming back?" she asked, her voice muffled.

"No, and never meant to. You see, I'm not such a Sir Galahad, after all, Countess. Were I coming back, I might not have helped you."

22

It was dawn of the second day before they reached the small Breton fishing village of St. Malo. Julie, who had dozed fitfully throughout the last long night, felt drained and exhausted. Michael, who had driven all those hours, save for a few hours the preceding night and the time they paused by the roadside to eat the food Julie had packed and drink the wine, looked fit and elated.

"There she is," he said, pointing one hand as they drove slowly along the quay and Julie saw the black outline of a trawler.

"It's a fishing ship," she said.

"Aye, it is that, and a good one. We'll leave the car

here. Have to carry the things onto the pier. You can
lend a hand, can you, Countess?"

"You had better start calling me Julie," she answered.
"I'm not a countess. I never was. And anyway, only
René's servants call me 'Countess.' "

He laughed. "You're all right," he said. "Here, then,
Julie. You're going to Cork as my wife, a nice little
Irish girl who can't speak French and is too shy to speak
at all. Pull your shawl around you so they can't see all
of your face. The captain's all right, but I couldn't
speak for the rest."

"What if the guards stop us?"

"There's no guard here. There'll be only the man on
watch. Come along now."

He gave her the lightest pieces to carry, but they
bogged her down, nevertheless, and she was panting by
the time they had boarded the vessel. The sailor on watch
had a few words with Michael and then went away. He
came back presently with the captain, a large, portly
man, grumbling and buttoning his jacket.

Julie listened quietly to the exchange, her head bent.
Michael Lynch was certainly a smooth liar. Here was
his little Irish wife, and frightened to death, poor thing,
coming all the way over from Cork only to find out she'd
have to go back. Surely the captain wouldn't leave his
little wife sitting on the pier? For if he did, Michael
would have to sit with her. Then who would arrange the
transfer outside the harbor, and then where would they
all be?

The captain complained but, at the mention of the
transfer to be made, he gave grudging acquiescence.
"There's only my cabin," he said. "You can't put her in
with the rest of the men. It would cause a disturbance.
This means I will have to give up my cabin and bunk
below."

Michael's voice dropped and she couldn't make out
what he said next, but presently he came back to her,
helping her with the packages she had carried aboard
and leading her down to a small, snug cabin.

"It's one bunk for two," he said, grinning. "I suppose
you'll be expecting me to sleep on the floor."

"I'll sleep on the floor," she answered.

They argued amiably for a few minutes and then he
said, "Never you mind, we can always sleep in shifts.

Lie down now. I've business with the captain. I'll sleep later."

After he left, Julie lay down, fully clothed, on the top of the bunk. Outside the water lapped against the sides of the ship and the sun dawned as she lay there. It was a beautiful day, cool and clear, and the salt air coming in through the open porthole was sharply cleansing. After a while she dozed off and awoke again to find that, as she slept, the ship had sailed and was now well out of the harbor. Someone had come in and closed her porthole —Michael, she suspected. She sat up and looked about. There he was, sitting in the captain's chair, his feet propped up on the inboard desk, fast asleep.

The first day went smoothly enough. Julie had risen on awakening and aroused Michael sufficiently to guide him to the bunk before she went above. The fishermen eyed her curiously as she walked about, and finally one of them came and said in halting English, "It is to be hard; the sea. To the bottom is better."

She smiled as if she did not understand and went on about the deck, loving the roll of the ship's motion and the cold winds that cleared her head and restored her spirit. They had done it. In a few days she would be on a ship bound for America. She must find a way to wire Madeline.

That night in the cabin, she asked Michael why it took so long to get to Ireland. "It isn't that far away, is it?" she asked.

"Speed arouses suspicion. The men are here to fish, not to take people on cruises from port to port." He smiled.

"And where are your good friends?" she asked. "The ones that were coming with you?"

"Down in the hold, all of them I hope, and behaving themselves, I trust."

"It's something you're smuggling, isn't it?" she asked.

"It's better you don't know," he answered. "Now, then, which of us will have first turn at the bunk?"

"You," she said promptly, starting to get up from it.

But he pressed her back. "I couldn't," he said regretfully. "I'd be thinking of what my poor old mother would say, should she know I was letting a lady sit up while I snored like a great beast in the only bed."

He smiled down at her, his eyes compassionate, and

without knowing how it came about, Julie began to cry, tears rolling down her face.

"Here, now, that's a terrible thing," he said. "I do you a kindness, and you behave as if I've beaten . . ." He stopped. "I'm sorry," he said gently, and, seating himself beside her, he put an arm about her shoulders and pressed her head against him. "There, now. It's a brave girl you are and a fine one. Spirited. I liked that about you from the first." His hands were alternately smoothing her tumbled hair and stroking her wet cheeks.

It was so soothing and pleasant to have a man's strong arms hold her with tenderness again. In all the months with René, there had never been any tenderness. All his caresses had been geared to rousing her passions and his own to fever pitch—to tormenting her sexually until she couldn't think of anything except the ultimate release. It made her cry harder and Michael pressed her back upon the bunk, lifting her legs so that she was lying supine. He sat beside her, still smoothing her forehead and making comforting sounds.

After a while her tears stopped flowing and he mopped her cheeks. "I'm so tired," she murmured.

"Hush. You go to sleep now," he said and started to get up, but she held his arm. "Don't go, Michael. Stay here with me."

He settled down again. "You're as hurt as a child," he said.

"Yes," she whispered, opening her eyes and smiling up at him. "You've been so good to me." She turned her face to the hand that still stroked her hair and kissed it, holding it still against her cheek.

After a while she said quietly, "There's room for two, Michael." She moved over against the bulkhead to allow him a place to stretch out. For a time they lay there, not touching, he with his arms crossed beneath his neck and she with her hands clasped loosely in front of her.

"It won't do, you know," he said when several minutes had passed. "I wouldn't take advantage of a lady in distress, but I'm not made of stone."

She turned her head to look at him and found his face very close to hers. It happened quite naturally after that. His kisses were soothing even when they became less gentle, his hands on her body healed the memories of that last furious attack by René, and in the ultimate consummation she felt the stirrings of sweetness again, like a tiny opening in her tightly closed heart.

Sex without any affection, however exciting, cloyed and sickened after a time. There had to be something more, even if it was only the gentle affection and friendship she felt for this man who had rescued her from her entrapment.

"There has to be some soul to love," she said aloud.

"Ah, and the lady has poetic thoughts, as well," he said. "It's more than I imagined when I used to see you riding and walking and playing the countess."

"Did you like me then?"

"Who wouldn't? And I don't mind telling you that you'll be hard to forget," he said.

"But we will say good-bye in a few days?"

"Aye, you to follow your star and I mine." He kissed her tenderly on the forehead. "We'll both sleep now," he said.

Once they had left the shelter of St. Malo bay, the crossing was turbulent. The trawler rolled and pitched with increasing violence as they approached Land's End, where the ocean dashed itself upon the rocks of that stark promontory and threatened to cast the ship up on the reefs. Julie, lying in her bunk and clinging to the sides, had a brief but unpleasant surge of seasickness, which, by a strong concentration upon the actual ship movements and a willingness to let her body go with it, she managed to partially subdue.

Late in the morning of that second day, as the coast of Ireland rose dim and beckoning on the horizon, the sea was quiet once more. Coming on deck, Julie saw that they were heading away from the coast. Alarmed, she went back to the cabin to query Michael.

"We can't sail into the harbor in broad daylight," he told her. "We'll head out a bit, as if to pass. There's a rendezvous with another vessel some miles off the coast tonight. Don't worry about it. We've hours, yet. And I hope you're agile enough for the Jacob's ladder."

"What is a Jacob's ladder?" Julie asked.

"You'll see soon enough." Michael grinned. "Don't fret. I'll see you make it safely down."

His words had been reassuring, yet close to midnight, with the trawler anchored and the waves beginning to hurl themselves up against the sides again, Julie was

more doubtful. Next the trawler lay another smaller
fishing vessel. She stood alone, braced against the rail,
and watched while with muffled, good-humored swearing the fishermen passed sailcloth-wrapped bundles to
the sailors waiting in the boat. It took nearly half an
hour, and then Michael, who had been supervising and
helping in the transfer, came back to her.

"Time to cross over to the mainland," he said. "Julie,
see there?"

She peered down and saw a wavering, sea-drenched
rope ladder lying over the side of the ship. "It looks
as if it might blow away," she said doubtfully.

"Not at all. I'm going down it first. You follow. It'll
be all right. Just hold tight to the ropes above you and
get your footing before you move down. And keep your
eyes front. Don't look up or down. Watch me."

He was over the side in a flash, skimming lightly down
the tossing ladder and then climbing halfway back up,
beckoning her and calling softly: "There, now, that fellow will help you. Down you come. Brave girl."

The fisherman beside her motioned her to follow
Michael, helping her over the side, holding her by the
shoulders until she nodded before he let go. Julie felt
her feet slip on the ropes, balanced precariously for a
heart-stopping moment, and then found her footing again
and descended gingerly, inching her way while Michael
murmured encouragement just below her. She longed to
glance downward and assure herself that he was close at
hand, but, remembering his warning, she kept her eyes
in front. The spray was reaching the hem of her skirt
and the wetness clung about her ankles, impeding her
descent. Any minute now she would feel Michael's
hands reaching for her. She would make it. Yet, as she
went down, it seemed that his voice was always just below her. When at last she felt his arms grasp her, she
discovered she was already on the tilting deck of the
Irish fishing boat.

"You kept going down as I did," she accused, her
voice rough with relief.

He laughed, his teeth gleaming in the torchlight, his
face alive with an elemental joy. It reminded her of
Mark, and her anger evaporated.

"Anyway, I made it," she said.

"Yes, that you did. This will be some adventure to tell

your grandchildren, now, won't it? And more to come. Quick now, into the hold. We've the run into Kinsale."

He helped her below, settling her among the packages that had been passed on earlier. They rose level with her on either side, making a small, narrow nook. The hold was dank and dark and smelled strongly of fish.

"I'll be going topside again," Michael told her. "You must stay quiet. If by chance we're stopped and boarded, this will serve to keep you from Mountjoy Prison." He was moving about and, as he did, he said, "I'm going to bind your wrists, not tight, mind you, but leave the ropes alone. It'll be proof that you discovered my smuggling operation and I was forced to abduct you to keep you quiet."

"But . . ." She shrank back as his hands touched her.

"Easy," he said. "It's for your own safety. If we're caught, it's prison for the lot of us, and worse. You wouldn't fancy being hanged, would you?"

"I'll be quiet," Julie said tremulously.

"Good girl. I'll be down now as soon as we're in the harbor."

She suffered her wrists to be bound behind her, stilling the tremors of uneasiness that rose along her nerves. "There now, you'll do," he said, giving her a light pat before he went back up the ladder. He left the hatch open so that she felt less isolated, but it was frightening to lie there between the bulky parcels, unable to make out more than the dim shape of gray that marked the open hatch.

There were no sounds from above. Even the muffled voices she had heard during the transfer of cargo had died down. A light wind blew in through the hatch and the boat tacked its way through the moonless night, rolling and pitching toward port. The packages kept Julie erect, bracing her against the boat's movement.

At some point she began to hear sounds above the creaking of the timbers. First there were sharp, squeaking noises and then came the scrabble of claws across the floor. Rats. Her mind recoiled and she bit the inside of her cheek until the pain brought tears to her eyes. She must not cry out. Hanged. They would be hanged. She felt a light tickling across her legs and realized with horror that one of the rodents was examining her. The tickling ceased and she heard the animal's claws scratching across the planks. She began then to thrash about, making as much noise as she dared. She continued to move, bringing her heels down in alternate light taps on the deck of the hold, shrugging her shoulders and moving her head back and forth and trying not to think what it would be like if one of them were bold enough to approach her face. Her face, dear God. The hysteria welled sharply within her and she thought that if she did not scream, she would go mad.

In another moment the dim light of the hatch was blotted out, and for one terrorized moment she thought the hatch had been closed. But then came the sound of feet descending and an increased squealing and clattering as the rats sought the safety of their holes.

"Julie?" It was Michael. She began to sob with relief, shuddering and leaning against him as he sought to quiet her. "Rats," she blurted out. "Rats." He fumbled at his jacket and presently she saw the dim flicker of a match. The light caught the gleam of two beady eyes in the far corner. There was another scrabbling and then all was silent. Still she sobbed and clung to Michael as he untied the ropes that bound her.

"Hush," he said. "I'm truly sorry, I am. I'd forgotten about the beasts. Shhh! We're nearly into port. Be a good girl. Tonight you'll sleep in a decent bed, and the worst is over."

As they walked through the dark and silent streets of Kinsale, the sky above began to turn a deep violet, and Julie said, "But it's dawn already."

"That's Irish spring for you," he answered. "It's only four o'clock. The sun will be up in another hour and a bit more. But don't worry. We'll be tucked in by then. It's just here," he said, as they turned into a narrow lane in which rows of small houses faced each other. Michael steered her into one of them, opening the door softly and closing it behind them.

"Is this your house?" she asked.

"It's a friendly house. We're expected . . . at least, I'm expected, and I'll explain about you come morning. Shhh! We don't want to wake them up."

She followed him obediently through a small hallway

and then a kitchen, and then they were briefly out of doors before a turn to the right brought them inside once more. "We'll have a look," he said, and struck a match. A kerosene lamp flickered on the interior to reveal a narrow bed, a washstand, and a chair.

"We seem to be doomed to one bed, you and I." He laughed. "Come on, then, Julie."

"It doesn't matter," Julie sighed. "I'm so tired I could sleep on a board."

"So could I," he agreed. They undressed silently, Julie stripped down to her slip and Michael to his underwear. She was in bed first, and he came in beside her shortly after he extinguished the light. He slipped an arm under her shoulders and in moments she was asleep, her head against his broad and solid chest.

The sun was high in the heavens when Julie awoke. Michael had already left the room. She washed and dressed, trying to make some semblance of order out of her hair in the tiny cracked mirror against the wall. She wondered whether or not she should go in search of him.

There was a faint odor of food cooking, and the smell of it reminded her that she was starved. She opened the door and looked out into a narrow alley that ran on the left as far as a wall and on her right a short distance to a door leading into the house proper. Just across from her was a small shed, which she realized was the outhouse.

There were no sounds from the main house, but the smell of cooking was stronger and Julie decided to chance it. She went to the door and opened it, stepping into a large, all-purpose room. A square table sat against one wall and there was an old broken sofa against another. Chairs stood about and a smaller table laden with dishes was just to the right of a large old coal stove, on which two pots were simmering. She was crossing to the stove and peering into the pots when Michael came through from the hall.

"Ah, you're up," he said in normal voice. "Mrs. Nagle has stepped out for a few minutes on some errands. She'll be along presently and we'll eat."

"I'm famished," Julie said.

"Here, then, have a bit of bread and some tea." He

motioned to the teapot sitting on the warming panel of the stove and went to fetch her some bread. The bread was brown and crusty and mealy, and she fell on it ravenously, gulping down huge mouthfuls of lukewarm tea and refilling her cup.

As she ate, Michael outlined the itinerary he had managed to arrange for her.

"It won't be a luxury voyage," he said. "But I've had a talk with the captain and you'll be all right. He'll take you into New York. It's a cargo vessel sailing from Cork Harbor tomorrow night. She's British. But the captain's an Irishman and so is most of the crew. And the captain is one of us, so you've nothing to worry about."

"It was guns that you smuggled in, wasn't it?" Julie asked.

"It's better you don't know that," Michael assured her. "Let's say it was something to aid the cause. It's dangerous down here in Cork. The British have sent a guerrilla force in now that their own little war is over. You wouldn't know whom to be trusting. And some Irishmen are British informers," he added bitterly.

"Why?" Julie asked.

"Sure, it's a long story, Julie. I've done my bit in France now. This would be my last trip out of France, and I won't be going back. There have been many Irish rebellions, so many since the first Saxons came in that I wouldn't be able to name them all. But this one—ah, this one is a fight to the finish. Britain's hard pressed from the war, and the British themselves have had a bellyful. It might be that they'll be able to see the waste of it, for as long as they're here, there'll be a rebellion of one kind or another."

"Why did you want to have them gone?" Julie asked.

"Why did America fight a revolution?" he asked.

"To be free, and to have our own government," she answered promptly.

"Well, it's the same here, with one difference—we didn't come from other lands to settle a new country. Ireland was civilized when the Saxons lived in caves and painted their faces blue. Reasonably enough, we want it to ourselves."

"I see," she said.

"Well, and that's enough politics. I'll be gone part of

the day and looking for something else you can wear, for those clothes you've got are sadly torn and filthy."

"You've been very good to me, Michael. How shall I repay you?"

"Speak a word in Ireland's defense when you're back in America. Send us something to buy rifles with."

"I will," she said. "I will do that. I promise."

Mrs. Nagle returned just then, her arms laden with bundles. "It's dearer and dearer at the shops," she sighed, scarcely acknowledging Michael's introduction. "But I've a bit of ham for tonight and, dear knows, with the money you gave me, Michael, there's enough spuds and cabbage and flour and tea to keep us for a month."

"I'll be gone long before that," Michael said, "and Julie is leaving tomorrow."

Mrs. Nagle turned her attention to Julie then, a smile on her face. "What will you ever think of me?" she said. "And me barely saying hello, and you so good helping Michael and the lads. It's a pity I didn't know you were coming along. I'd have fixed up a bed for Michael in the parlor. Well, I will tonight. Poor man, having to bed down on the floor after that voyage. How is your back, Michael?" she inquired solicitously.

"Still sore," Michael said blandly. "It'll be good to have a bed to myself tonight."

Julie kept her face turned from him, knowing full well there would be a spark of laughter in his eyes.

"We'll be having lunch now," Mrs. Nagle said briskly.

Later, Julie said to Michael, "You'll tell the most inventive lies. On the floor, indeed!"

"What's the harm in that? We were innocent enough last night. And, anyway," he added with an impish grin, "it isn't that the good woman believed me for a minute, but it's only that to tell the truth would have been brazen, and she'd be forced to treat you with appropriate coldness to observe the proprieties."

"And what about my helping you and the lads?" she mimicked.

"Well, and didn't you say you would?"

"I did. But that was after you told your story."

"Sure, but I knew you would. I was, as you might say, anticipating."

She laughed at him. She couldn't help it. During the

time she had known him, he had taken all hazards with a lighthearted air that she had only lately come to realize masked a deep and deadly purpose.

"You're a strange man, Michael Lynch," she said now.

"Yes, I suppose I would seem so," he answered. "Look, now, stay put until I get back. You'd best keep to the room after supper."

"Will you be gone that long?"

"I'll be back about ten or eleven, with your new clothes. And I hope I get the sizes right. It'll be a new thing for me, buying women's clothes."

He was back closer to eleven than ten. Julie, who had had a long and lonely evening, greeted him with unusual warmth.

"You've been missing me, eh?" he asked.

"I've been alone since supper. Mrs. Nagle went to a meeting at the church. I heard her come back a while ago with some people, but I stayed here."

"Good girl. There was a bit of a fight this evening and two of the lads were wounded. Mrs. Nagle has them now in the parlor and the doctor has just gone. They'll be all right, those lads. One boy was killed, not fifteen yet, either."

"A boy of fourteen? But . . ."

"We're outnumbered as it is," Michael said shortly. "It's everyone who can and will. The boy wasn't in the battle. He was coming with a warning and he was shot by the Black and Tans. They're looking for the others now, making a house to house search."

"But then they'll come here," Julie said. "Oh, we'll all have to get away."

"They won't come here," Michael answered. "This is the home of an R.I.C., Mrs. Nagle's son, Desmond."

"What's an R.I.C.?" Julie asked.

"A Royal Irish Constable. You see, if we didn't have some of our own men in their outfits, it'd go hard. Desmond Nagle is totally loyal to the Crown, as far as they're concerned, and Mrs. Nagle, too. You could say that most of this street is. Some of them are honest royalists, of course. But the rest . . ." He shook his head. "We've other safe areas, some far grander than this. There are titled Irish. Would you believe that? And they aid us. Their peerages may have been handed out at

Buckingham Palace, but Ireland's the land that bore them, and some few of them remember that."

Julie sank down on the bed. "It's all so . . . so strange," she said. "It seems so complicated. Why don't all the people who think Ireland should have its own government line up against the rest?"

"Openly, do you mean?" And at her nod he gave a grim laugh. "Yes, the British would like that. They could add their troops to whoever here was for them, and in one month of bloodshed or less it would be over. We're outnumbered. I told you that. We've always needed help from outside. The French arrived too late to save us from William, and never at all when Wolfe Tone might have claimed victory. Now it's only this way that we'll win. No fancy uniforms and forming fours on proper battlefields. We'd be mowed down. No, it's by stealth and in secret and with the silent aid of those friendly to the cause that we'll win."

"And if you don't?" she asked.

"We will," he answered. Then, taking the two packages, he tossed them on the bed beside her. "Here, now, enough talk. Let's see if the finery fits."

Julie undid the first parcel, taking from it a skirt and blouse in a pretty blue color. The other parcel held a warm cloak of heathery tweed.

"The best I could do," Michael said. "But you'll look respectable walking up the gangway, and no one will take you for a stowaway. Go on now, try them on."

Without thinking, Julie slipped out of the peasant dress, standing unconcernedly in her bra and suspendered belt and knickers. She reached for her skirt and suddenly became conscious that Michael was very quiet. She looked up and saw that he was looking at her body with an expression she had not seen before on his face. He had made love to her that night aboard the Breton trawler and she had welcomed the sweetness of it, but this was different, and the look on his face made her own nerves tingle.

She placed the skirt back on the bed without realizing what she was doing and he glanced at her, saw she was watching him, and the blood came up in his face.

"I haven't really looked at you before," he said softly.

"Nor I you," she answered. She stood waiting, feeling her body come alive with anticipation and, as if he read her thoughts, he moved forward slowly. She could smell the strong, masculine odor of his body and it increased her desire.

When he reached out and touched her breasts, she drew her breath sharply at the sensation of pleasure that swept through her. His arms went down and around her and she pressed against him, feeling his desire rising. His mouth was on her, and these were not the soothing kisses of the other night but deep, probing kisses that parted her lips and explored her mouth. She returned those kisses with growing excitement, and when he moved her away from him she gave an unconscious cry of protest. But then he was stripping her of her underwear and his hands were squeezing her breasts and running over her body. He bent his head to kiss her breasts and she swayed against him. Gently, he forced her back on the bed and in one swift movement he had slipped his jersey over his head and his eyes feasted on her body.

She moved on the bed, whispering, "Hurry."

She watched him undress, finding increased pleasure at the sight of his naked body, the broad chest and hard arms and the thick muscularity of his thighs. He came back to her then, half sitting, half lying on the bed beside her, and his mouth was on her again, everywhere, leaving darting tongues of fire wherever he touched her. Once she moaned, tugging at his hair, pulling him back beside her.

"You like that?" he whispered.

"Yes," she said, "oh, yes."

It was as if her whole body had come piercingly alive. She could not be still. She began to move about, her hands reaching out to touch him, feeling pleasure in that as much as in what he was doing to her. He knew instinctively when she was ready and she welcomed him, her body moving under his with increasing agitation and his organ growing rigid and his breath hoarse and uneven. There was a moment when she thought there would be no end, and then waves of pleasure swept over her, jerking her body uncontrollably. Even as the cry formed in her throat, his mouth was on hers, muffling the sounds of ecstasy that escaped from them both.

He lay there, spent, for several seconds and then rolled away, gathering her in his arms and kissing her hair and face until she was quiet. They lay silently for a long time, half dozing, and then Michael said, "It's the last night. Julie. Let it be a good one." She turned back to him gladly, eagerly, reveling in sensations she had for so long been denied.

They slept, and in the morning they joined together again as naturally as if they had always been lovers. Afterward, he lay watching her as she rose and washed, saying, "It's almost a work of art, your body. I said you'd be hard forgetting. I didn't know then what I said at all."

There was a poignancy in their parting that evening. One part of her wanted to stay with Michael and share whatever the future brought, and yet she knew that it was time to go.

"I won't forget you," she said as they kissed good-bye in the cabin of the H.M.S. *Seeker*.

"Ships that pass in the night," he replied. "That's all there was for you or me, all that was meant to be. Mind yourself. And let me know you've gotten home safely."

"I will," she said again. At the last moment she clung closer to him so that he moved her away with effort.

"You'll be all right now," he said. He touched her cheek briefly, adding, "You see, the bruises are healed already." And then he was gone. He did not linger on the pier. The last glimpse Julie had of him was as he walked rapidly away, hands thrust deep in his jacket pockets, his head thrown back, whistling a bit of a tune.

PART FOUR

23

Madeline James was alone in her house and preparing to bathe when the doorbell rang. She wasn't expecting anyone, so she continued removing her outer clothing, thinking that whoever it was would become discouraged and go away. It rang again, more insistently, and she hesitated briefly. It might be important—a telegram from Cecelia, who was due home this weekend, or it might even be Mark Douglas. He'd arrived unannounced the last time he was in New York.

She pulled on a dressing gown and went down the stairs, hoping it might be Mark. She had not seen him since February. And then the strain of continuing her fabrication about not having heard from Julie made her uneasy and spoiled her pleasure in the time they were together. He had left sooner than expected, headed this time for Prescottville.

She had at first been afraid that Julie might have written to her relatives and they would be able to tell Mark Julie's married name. But when he made no mention of it in the two letters she had received from him, she decided that Julie hadn't been in touch with anyone in her hometown.

Around Christmastime she had finally written to Julie, telling her that Mark was alive and back in the States and asking if she wanted her address given to him, but there had been no reply to that letter or to the subsequent ones she had sent. Julie, in a new life, apparently wanted nothing to do with the old. It had made her feel justified in withholding the information.

By the time Madeline reached the door, she was intent on the idea that it must be Mark or a telegram, and when she opened the door she was surprised to find a shabbily dressed, countrified-looking woman. It took her a moment to recognize Julie.

"Good God! What happened to you, Julie? You look . . ."—she caught herself up—"so different."

"Hello, Madeline," Julie said, trying to smile. In the next instant the two women were hugging each other, both trying to talk at once.

"Come in, come in," Madeline said, drawing Julie into the house and closing the door. "It's wonderful to have you back. You . . ." She broke off as she saw tears falling down Julie's cheeks. "Why, Julie, what is it? What's wrong? You look awful."

"The same old tactful Madeline," Julie said, half laughing, half crying. "I'm sorry," she murmured, wiping her eyes. "Oh, it's so good to be back. It's so good to see you, Madeline. It . . . there's so much to tell you."

"Why didn't you answer my letter?" Madeline asked. "I wrote to you at Christmas, but . . ."

"Letter?" Julie broke in. "But I never had a letter from you. I wondered why not, but . . ." She made an effort to stop crying and gain some measure of composure. "It's a long story," she said at length, "but I suppose that the letter . . . I mean, after I was so ill, they must have kept the mail from me."

"Who kept mail from you? Ill? Ill with what?" Madeline asked. "Oh, never mind, don't tell me this minute. We'll talk later. Look, why don't you go up to my room and freshen up, bathe, whatever you like. I'll fix us something to eat. No servants today, you see—today, of all days. Go on," she urged as Julie stood there. "Borrow anything of mine you like. Those clothes! Where did you get those clothes?" She knew she was talking feverishly, but she wanted time to think. If Julie hadn't gotten her letter, then she still didn't know Mark was alive.

"Coffee would be fine, and I don't need to bathe. I really want to talk."

"First things first," Madeline insisted. "Go on. The bath water is still hot. I ran it just before you rang. Come on down into the kitchen whenever you're finished and I'll have something ready. Go on, Julie. I get distracted when anyone watches me in the kitchen."

"All right, Madeline. I'll have the bath. Heaven knows I can use a change of clothes. There weren't many facilities for ladies on that cargo ship."

"Cargo ship?" Madeline raised her eyebrows. As Julie started to explain, she said hastily, "No, it can keep. I want the whole story from start to finish, not in bits and pieces."

As she assembled a lunch of sorts in the kitchen and measured coffee and set the table, Madeline's mind went around and around. Should she tell Julie about Mark, or shouldn't she? It was clear she didn't know he was alive. Perhaps she did, though. Surely someone from Prescottville must have known where she was. Yet Mark was still ignorant of Julie's whereabouts. So, perhaps not. She paused in the act of pouring sugar into the bowl and thought, if she doesn't know, I won't tell her. Not now.

By the time Julie came downstairs, Madeline, her mind made up, was composed. "Now you look more like your old self," she said to Julie. "Come on, sit down. Everything's hot."

Madeline ate with good appetite, but Julie, telling her story, picked at her food despite Madeline's urgings.

The story was a long time in the telling. When it was ended, Madeline said, "I can scarcely believe this. It's like a melodrama mixed with one of those new Cecil B. De Mille two-reelers; in fact, it would make his latest effort, *Why Change Your Husband?*, look like a child's puppet show. On second thought, maybe it's more to the taste of Erich von Stroheim. His characters are always so deliciously wicked."

"Someday I may even laugh," Julie said in a tired voice.

"If you ask me, that Michael Lynch is the one you ought to have kept hold of. You liked him, didn't you?"

"Yes," Julie answered, "more than *liked* him. But I don't know . . ." She gazed off into space, adding slowly, "I suppose I'll never really care for anyone the way I did for Mark. René . . . well, I was lonely, desperate, and even if Emilie had not been alive . . . I was already over my infatuation. If the baby had lived, of course, there would have been that. Now I can't even think of what I mean to do next."

"What you need," advised Madeline, "is rest, and you also need to get back into things again. We'll go shopping tomorrow. You ought to cut your hair, too. See how mine is? It's the very latest fashion." She ran her fingers through her red waves.

"Very nice. But I don't know. What if I don't like it?"

"It can always be allowed to grow out again if you fancy that come-into-the-pasture look." Madeline laughed. "Cheer up, Julie," she said vigorously. "You'll see. Once you've begun to live decently again, everything will work out."

"Yes, I suppose you're right," Julie said listlessly. Now that she had reached the end of her journey home, further goals eluded her. Perhaps Madeline was right. Rest was what she needed first.

Madeline allowed Julie the first few days without comment on her lack of interest in doing anything more vigorous than moving from her room to the dining room or living room, but on the fifth day she said, "All right, Julie, the time for moping is over. You've had enough rest. We're going on that shopping spree, for one thing. And then you're going to have that audition with Ziegfeld, if I can arrange it. I think I may sign for his new show. Work is what I need, and work is what you need. You've definitely got to start getting out more. You're pale as a ghost moping about this way."

Julie, still disinterested in any plans, acceded out of politeness. The idea of going downtown and milling through the shops, of seeing dressmakers and of having endless fittings, was a tiring one. She was sure that she would not enjoy it.

However, once she was actually in the process of doing something again, she began to feel better, and by the following weekend she had become thoroughly involved in the new routine. She shopped with Madeline and alone. She began to accept invitations to go out in the evening with Madeline and with some of the new friends she had acquired since Lew's death.

Finding that the trust money Jason had transferred to her New York bank had grown over the past year, she bought recklessly, even extravagantly. There were so many new fabrics—luscious taffetas in brilliant colors and filmy chiffons. There were clothes for so many different activities; comfortable clothes especially designed for a particular occasion or sport; tennis outfits; motoring costumes; the new beach things that were made in one piece, gathered at the waist and with little capped sleeves and legs that reached only a little over halfway down the thigh and had sheer black silk hose to go with them. It was even rumored that some women weren't wearing the hose at all, like the Mack Sennett girls, whose stockings sometimes stopped at the knee.

Long hair did not suit these fashions, so Julie had hers cut. Freed from its weight, the waves curled about her head and face, giving her a gypsy look.

New York had changed. There were far more motorcars and fewer horses and buggies on the streets. The postwar boom was to be found everywhere, and there were many new and taller buildings being built farther uptown on Fifth and Park avenues and along upper Madison.

To Julie, feeling like herself again, the city was exciting in a way that it had once been—noiser, different, with some of the old theaters being turned into movie houses with new movie houses being built—but sometimes even more exciting than it used to be.

Passing a newsstand one afternoon on her way back to Madeline's, she saw the much-talked-about new tabloid. The New York *Daily News,* and she stopped to buy a copy.

An old lady next to her sniffed and said, "It's a scandalous paper!"

Julie said. "But it is fun to read."

"Young people these days," the woman muttered under her breath. "What's the world coming to, anyway?"

Julie laughed to herself, started to fold the paper, and put it under her arm when her eyes caught the headlines across the top:

FRENCH COUNT IN MURDER-SUICIDE SCANDAL

Her heart hammering, she turned to the inside page, heedless of her surroundings or the fact that she was being jostled by other customers as they came and went.

René was dead. The manor house where he had kept Emilie all those years had burned to the ground. The two keepers had pulled both bodies from the flaming house.

The whole story was there, or almost the whole story. She read avidly but could find no mention of her own name. At the end there was a paragraph on the "rumored second countess," but the count's daughter had denied it, saying only that it had been some actress friend of her father's and that there had been no marriage at all.

Dazed, Julie refolded the paper and walked on. The Sûreté in Paris had been alerted by an anonymous letter from St. Malo. Michael! She could almost hear him saying, "One day he will pay for it." But the detectives arriving at the château to investigate had been taken in by René's charming protestations. They waited while he presumably went to change so he might lead them to the house. Instead, he had gone on ahead of them. By the time they realized they had been duped, it was too late.

Poor, mad Emilie. Poor Hélène, arrogant and willful and so proud and now faced with the truth about her mother. She could feel sorry for all of them . . . all of them save René. He was dead and she was glad.

"You were lucky, Julie," Madeline said that night after hearing the news. "But then, you were always lucky. If that had been me, my name and date of birth would have been part of the story."

Julie looked at her. "No," she said quietly, "you don't know Hélène. The château, the vineyards—they're all hers now. She must have bribed the servants or threatened them, or both. She wouldn't want any more scandal than she has already, but more than anything she wouldn't want my name and face in the press. It would lead to further investigation and even more notoriety."

"I still say you're lucky," Madeline persisted, "more than you know," she added.

"What does that mean?"

"I have something to tell you. I was afraid to say anything when you first came back, but I've been living in dread that you'd find out before I could tell you myself. This is going to be a shock, Julie. Prepare yourself."

"Prepare myself? Shock?" Julie asked in bewilderment.

"Mark Douglas is alive," Madeline said abruptly. "He's been back in America since last August."

"I don't believe it," Julie breathed. "It's too much. No, I can't . . ." She stopped and turned pleading eyes to Madeline. "You . . . it is really true? I couldn't bear to have it . . . I mean . . ." Her face was paper white, her eyes enormous.

"I've seen him," Madeline said. "I'll tell you about it."

It had taken her weeks to reach the decision. Now that the words were out, Madeline became nervous. She stumbled in the telling, unwilling to let Julie know that she had betrayed her and, yet, feeling somehow that in the end Julie would know anyway. She watched Julie's face as she spoke, seeing it begin to come alive as her words poured out until finally it was aglow with an almost unearthly radiance.

"Where is he now?" Julie asked. "Still in California, or . . ."

"He's back in Prescottville, staying at your old house," Madeline told her. "But, Julie, there is something more."

"What? Nothing bad? I couldn't stand that now."

"It's Mark. He changed a lot after he heard you were married and after his sister died—the young one, the one he really cared about."

"Changed? How?"

Madeline shrugged. "I can't explain. He was angry at first and then sad, and the last time I saw him he was closed up . . . not . . . well, I can't explain."

Julie stood up, suddenly throwing her hands wide, and saying. "It doesn't matter. It doesn't matter. He's alive. Oh, I knew it!" Her voice rose exultantly. "I knew it! I said I'd feel it if he were dead. Remember? I wrote you that. But, then, that seemed like lunacy and I believed . . . but it isn't true. It never was true. Oh, Madeline, he's alive. Why didn't you tell me before this?"

"I was afraid," Madeline said, looking away. "You'd been through such a bad time. I was afraid of the shock . . . what it would do to you, and then . . . well, I've told you now. I thought you knew. I didn't realize you hadn't gotten my letter."

"The Christmas letter? God, that was a terrible time. René must have read it and been afraid I'd contact you or . . . Christmas," she repeated. "But if you got my letter in August, why didn't you write me immediately to tell me Mark . . ." She stopped, eyeing Madeline's downcaast eyes, and then said, "Why didn't you, Madeline?"

"If you must know, it's because of Mark. He wanted your name and where you were living. He was angry. I remember the way he took you away from Steven

Randall. I didn't think he would just say, 'Well, that's that.' And you—you were settled, married. I wouldn't tell Mark, of course. Then, afterward, I thought you ought to decide whether or not you wanted him to know where you were. I wrote you then. When you didn't answer, I thought you wanted to forget all of us. I thought you were happy. I mean, a château for a home, a titled husband . . . I certainly wouldn't have blamed you."

"You never really liked Mark, did you?" Julie asked.

"That's not true," Madeline said, raising her eyes.

There was a tense silence as they stared at each other. Madeline looked away too late and Julie said quietly, "No, it isn't true. You did like him. You do like him. It wasn't me. It was Mark. You wanted Mark."

Madeline stood up, saying defensively, "All right, supposing I did. You seem to forget that he was free and I was free. It was you who were married—at least as far as anyone knew."

"If you'd told Mark, he would have come after me. And even if he hadn't, then he would have once I . . . oh, before I found out about Emilie, even."

"Just think for a minute, Julie. You always have had what you wanted. You've never really had to fight to earn a living or, for that matter, fight to keep a man. There's always been someone to help you, beginning with Lew. Oh, yes," she said and raised a hand, "Lew wanted you, too. Do you suppose I enjoyed knowing that?"

"I never . . ." Julie began.

"Never mind. It's all in the past now," Madeline interrupted. "I've been a good friend to you, Julie. I still am. And, after all, no matter what I wanted, I did write to you in the end."

"Yes," was all Julie said. They parted after that, Madeline to keep an appointment, Julie to spend the rest of the night packing her clothes in the new luggage she had bought during her shopping spree.

The scene with Madeline coming hard on the heels of learning that Mark was alive had left her somewhat numbed. But through everything was the conviction that she must leave at once for Prescottville. It was not until she had finished her packing and gotten into bed that the full force of it struck her. "He's alive, alive," she murmured over and over to herself. She would see him in less than twenty-four hours. Tomorrow she could take the morning train. She'd be in Prescottville before evening. She began to make mental notes. She'd hire a hackney in Hammondsport, that was it, and go to . . . go straight to Mark. If he was back in Prescottville and staying at her old house, as Madeline said, then he must be back at the winery, also. She could see herself waiting for him as she used to do, watching him ride across the fields and down the drive. She began to tremble with excitement. The feelings she had for so long suppressed suddenly surfaced: to touch him; to hold his hand; to be able to put her head on his shoulder and feel the rough texture of his jacket beneath her cheek. Memory, unleashed, came flooding back and her heart ached unbearably with happiness.

Oh, nothing mattered except that they would be together again. Nothing that had happened before could touch them now. She tried to imagine his face when he saw her and couldn't. Her brain whirled with thoughts she could not control, and it was a long time before she slept.

Rising early, she found Madeline up before her, already seated at the table, having coffee and nibbling on toast.

"I'm going home this morning," Julie said to her. "Madeline, I'm . . . well, I'm sorry about last evening. You have been good to me. You and Lew always were and . . . anyway, it doesn't matter."

Madeline said nothing for a moment, eyeing Julie over the rim of her coffee cup, which she finally put down.

"I'm sorry, too," she said finally. "Oh, not for trying to snare Mark Douglas. I'm not such a hypocrite as to pretend that. You know me, Julie. You wouldn't be fooled, anyway. No, if there's any chance that we'll stay friends, the truth is better. But neither am I such a pig that I can't wish you happiness this time. God knows, you've earned that after these past years. In fact, while it hurts my pride to admit it"—here she stopped and grinned in the old way, as if the joke was on her— "you might as well know that Mark didn't want me, anyway. I don't think marriage is his first choice."

"I don't care about that either, anymore," Julie said. "All I care about is being with him, married or not. I guess that doesn't sound very clever, but it's the way I feel. And you, are you going into the new Ziegfeld show?"

Madeline shook her head. "I'm going to Hollywood. The famous Players-Lasky made me a handsome offer. I don't really want to stay in New York anymore. Cecelia's so big now and away so much. She'll be out of school in another year. She can come to me just as easily out in Hollywood as she can in New York, although, heaven knows how I'll like living in that little village of Hollywood after New York, or how I'll take to the wide open spaces of Los Angeles. Still, it'll be different."

"Will you sell this house?"

"Not right away. If I fall flat on my face out there, I'll want a place to run to. No, I'll sell the Rye house. We've almost never used it since Lew died. I'll close up here, and if everything goes well I should be in California by September."

"That's harvest time at home," Julie said. "Someday you'll have to come to visit us in Prescottville during the harvest."

"That's someday," Madeline said. "In the meantime, if you're planning to catch a train, you'd better drink that coffee and get started."

Madeline drove to the station with Julie and came aboard while the valises were stowed away. She looked at the stack of luggage that was finally placed in Julie's compartment and said, "I thought I was clothes hungry, but this beats anything I ever did in my life. Take care of yourself, Julie, and give my best to Mark."

"I'll see you soon," Julie said. "You'll be coming up for our wedding."

"Yes, well, you may think differently once you're there," Madeline answered cryptically.

"What do you mean?" Julie asked. "Is Mark, I mean, has he . . ." She couldn't say it. "You've told me everything, haven't you, Madeline? I'm not going home to find out that Mark is married?" There. She had said it and her mouth was suddenly dry.

"No, no, of course not," Madeline answered hurriedly. "Good-bye, Julie. I wish you the best of luck." She did not wait for a reply but went away quickly, leaving

Julie to spend the entire journey home alternating between a fear that Mark was somehow unattainable or in love with someone else and an inner conviction that nothing would ever change between them.

24

"It is like old times," Joe Damien said, "a good spring again, a fine crop." He touched the burgeoning vines and smiled.

"And not like old times," Mark answered, "but it will be—if I have to bootleg the reserves and increase still wine production and wrest sacramental wine contracts from every diocese in America."

Joe shook his head. "Steuben's is far ahead of us. I tell you, Mark, we may never be able to prove it, but I am certain Jason Prescott is a major stockholder in Steuben's."

"It doesn't matter," Mark said. "If everything goes according to plan at tomorrow's meeting, it won't make any difference what the Prescotts own."

"You're sure you can count on Miranda Latham this time?" Joe asked.

"I'm sure," Mark said shortly. "Do you still have that last letter from Julie? That's going to be tricky. No one's heard from her since she married that Frenchman. Jason could protest on that score and, if he wanted to, he could make a court case out of it and hold us up until there wouldn't be any chance at all of saving the company."

"I know, I know. But I have the letter and I have the proxies. With Miranda on our side, I think we can push through your reinstatement. I can't believe that you smoothed the feathers of Miranda." He laughed. "Eh, Mark, what did you promise her?"

"Not the moon," Mark said drily. "I'm not worried

about tomorrow so much as I am about realizing some margin of profit while the drys have the country by the throat."

"If only you had been here sooner. I couldn't persuade the Prescotts to try to buy up Germania when they closed. Speaking of bootlegging, ah, there was a brandy!"

"What made the Freys sell? Pleasant Valley is still operating; Taylor is still operating. Germania was doing a good business. If people are willing to take medicinal champagne, why not medicinal brandy?"

"They had an offer from a fellow in New York and I think they believed that it was sell or go under. Now, if old Jacob Frey had still been around, it might have been different. I remember him from when I was a boy. He was a friend of my father's." Joe sighed. "Ah, times change. Who would imagine that wine drinking would one day be a sin, eh?"

"It's sin that pays off in the marketplace," Mark said cynically, starting to walk back along the rows.

Joe fell into step beside him. "We'll have Peter back, too," he said. "He's done well at Taylor's, but I would like him here with us."

"I want him with us," Mark agreed. "Don't worry, Joe. When I'm finished, Fontaine's will be in good shape. Nothing lasts forever. Someday that Eighteenth Amendment will be amended."

They parted at the foot of the vineyards, Joe to return to the winery, Mark to mount his horse and ride over to the Douglas Dairies to see his cousin Art.

It had been a long four months since his return. There was nothing Jason or anyone else could do about keeping him out of the winery proper, and his daily presence had had a marked effect on Avery Bertram.

Slowly but surely, with Mark physically present, the employees had turned more and more to him. It infuriated poor Avery, but he lacked the courage and physical strength for a confrontation with Mark. He spent his days scuttling to and fro like a worried rabbit.

It hadn't been easy to win Miranda over to his side. She expected penitence for his treatment of her in California. She had been too frightened during his first overtures and then had played a long, boring game of expecting repentance from him and made coy reference to how it had been in the old days.

He had known that the longer he was circumspect with her and the longer he refused to apologize, the more she would be drawn to him. So far he had not bedded her, but, if it took that, then tonight he would bed her. He had to have Fontaine's back in his control, and if that meant sleeping with Miranda and every girl out at Viola's . . . He paused in his thoughts and laughed. No, he could count on Miranda. Her "yes" had been reluctant, but he was dangling the plum of marriage before her dazzled eyes and he didn't think she would change her mind.

He turned off the side road into the dairy proper. If possible, he hoped to avoid Lillian and to talk to Art alone. He found his cousin leaning against the fence near the bull runs, talking to Sam Howard.

"Just the man I wanted to see," Sam called out as Mark dismounted. "Think I've got a line on the Steuben stockholders for you, Mark. I'm not sure yet. It's hard to find out just who owns what in these private companies, but one of my spies tells me that Prescotts are heavily invested."

"Any real proof?" Mark asked.

"Not yet, worse luck," Sam said, "but I will have soon. So if that meeting goes against you tomorrow, you can count on the *Banner* editorial. Collusion, I believe it's called. Perfectly legal to point it out."

"Too bad we haven't got it to threaten Jason with tomorrow in case of trouble," Mark said.

"Trouble?" Art questioned. "You've got the votes, haven't you? Has anything changed? Miranda? Anything like that?"

Mark shook his head. "The one weak spot is still the fact that no one knows Julie's whereabouts. She used to keep in touch with Joe, but he hasn't had a word from her in nearly a year."

Sam and Art exchanged a brief look, and Sam said, "Well, she'll turn up one day. Meanwhile, Joe has her proxies. I think you're worrying too much about this, Mark. Jason isn't going to make a case out of it. If he does, there's always the possibility of threatening to force him under oath in court to reveal his Steuben holdings. Same thing that happened when they tried to have you arrested for those beatings out at Viola's. None of them dared get on a witness stand. Why, when I suggested to Jason that it would mean finding out everything about Viola's, he went so purple I thought his time on earth had ended." He laughed and clapped Mark on the shoulder affectionately. "Let me know how the vote turns out."

"Staying for dinner, Sam?" Art asked.

"Can't. Still have that paper to get out. I want it all set so I can run that story about Mark taking over again. I've got the faith." He grinned at Mark. "You keep it."

When Sam had left, Art said, "Well, you're staying for dinner, aren't you, Mark?"

"I don't think . . ." Mark began.

"Oh, come along. Lillian's almost convinced you aren't that bad, after all. You know Lillian; she blows whichever way Miranda blows."

"Which will be mighty cold once this vote is in," Mark said, "or soon afterward."

"I wonder what it feels like to be a devil with the ladies," Art joked. "Is it hard work, Mark? Come on, you can tell your old cousin."

"Nothing to it, really," Mark deadpanned. "Just help them into carriages and motorcars and tell them how pretty they are. Surely you know that?"

Art clasped his forehead in mock despair. "That easy! And when I think of the way I had to chase Lillian!"

"I chase no woman," Mark said succinctly and, unbidden, Julie's face was before him, as it had been that night in New York, the night he had waited outside her house. It might have been yesterday. He turned away, striding ahead of Art toward the house, calling back, "Well, come on, then. I'm starving, and Lillian does set the best table in Prescottville."

It was nearly nine when Mark reined up before Miranda's house. He saw a movement in the upper window and realized that she had been looking for him. He could almost predict the exact sequence of events that would now follow. Carmen would let him in, looking nervous as she always did at the sight of him. Miranda would remain above for a suitable interval, as if his arrival had interrupted her from some more important task.

He smiled to himself as Carmen opened the door with a barely contained little sound of fright.

"Is Mrs. Latham at home?" Mark asked.

"I will see, *monsieur*," she replied. She showed him into the living room and hurried away, returning some minutes later with the announcement that *madame* was engaged but would be in presently.

Mark settled himself on the sofa. About ten minutes, perhaps a little longer. The unvarying performance when he called both amused and irritated him. The more he saw of Miranda these days, the less appealing he found her. And yet once they had been good together. She had even excited him.

He wondered idly if Miranda realized that there were other women who made themselves available to him. Surely she must have been curious when he had made no move toward her, but then it was hardly a question she could put to him.

"Oh, Mark," she had said, "you'll never settle down."

And he had replied, "Don't be too sure. In fact, I've been thinking it's high time I did take a wife to my bosom."

She had not pursued that, fluttering her lids at him, coloring when he had stared meaningfully at her. It caused him no discomfort whatsoever to lead Miranda down the garden path. He had only to remember San Francisco and the loss of Fontaine's. From his standpoint, he was paying her out in far better coin than she deserved.

He heard the living room doors open and he quickly got to his feet. Miranda was sweeping in, wearing something long and flowing and not at all in the current fashion. "Very charming," he approved suavely.

"Thank you. Do you like it? It's one of those Grecian robes that Isadora Duncan wears. Carmen is very clever with a needle. I love the freedom of this sort of thing. Actually, it's a lot more modest than the newer styles."

She swirled to the sofa and sat down, patting the seat beside her invitingly.

"I'd hardly call it modest," he said, raising an eyebrow. "Quite the opposite, actually—very alluring." He looked pointedly at her bosom where it thrust against the drapery of the bodice and showed its mounded, soft curves just above the neckline.

"I wish I looked alluring to the Prescotts. You've no

idea how they've been after me to vote with them tomorrow. I'm having a dreadful time trying to keep them
off the scent."

She swayed toward him, pouting a little. Nothing
for it, he thought. Conquering his cold distaste, he took
up her invitation, leaning forward and kissing her parted
mouth. Her tongue darted out at once, and he caught it
between his teeth, biting it lightly. She gave a little
squeal and drew her head back, looking at him archly.

"I've missed you, Mark," she said with heavy meaning.

He did not reply but bent his head dutifully again,
this time encircling her waist with one arm and moving
his free hand up and over the bodice of her dress. A
moment later he pulled away and, still holding her,
looked down at her face and said, "No, Miranda. It
was different when only the old couple you used to have
were around. But Carmen—I worry about Carmen."

"I don't care," she said.

"I do," he said firmly. "We need privacy. And we
need time—away from Prescottville. What would you
say to a trip somewhere for a weekend?"

"Oh, Mark, I'd love it. When?"

"Soon," he temporized. "And, maybe . . . well, it's
too soon to talk about that. But I've quite a surprise
for you."

"Oh, Mark, tell me what it is."

She had drawn away from him, sitting up and smoothing her hair, smiling animatedly.

He rose. "If I tell you, it won't be a surprise." He
smiled. "I'm going to run along now," he said. "You're
definitely too exciting in that gown. I'll see you at Fontaine's tomorrow."

"Tomorrow," she agreed. "Eleven, isn't it?"

"Eleven. And don't worry about the Prescotts," he
added. "After all, I'm there to protect you."

She followed him to the door, but Carmen, coming
down the stairs, forestalled any clinging goodnight kisses.

"I'll see you tomorrow, then," Mark said and shook
hands with her, grinning at her look of balked annoyance.

There, it was done. He felt immeasurably tired as
he rode slowly across the fields through the dark. He
was close to winning. He would win. He thought of the
plans he had made coming back from France. He had
been sure then of meeting Julie, of seeing to Valerie,

and of regaining Fontaine's. At least one goal was in sight. And tomorrow he would win it. As for the rest, with Val gone and Julie married, living God knew where. . . . He frowned. That part of his life was over, closed and finished. "I am thinking of taking a wife," he had lied to Miranda. Nothing was further from his thoughts. Never again would any woman come close enough to him to matter.

That day in Madeline's apartment, reading Julie's cable, he'd have turned around and gone back to France and abducted her, if necessary. Now it was different. The pain had dulled, the hurt was healed. Now he wouldn't drive to New York to win her back.

He spurred Rusty forward, taking the last field at a gallop and reaching his stable shortly thereafter. He unsaddled the horse and rubbed him down before throwing a blanket over his back.

As he came out into the yard he saw a light glimmer from the house and wondered who could be there at this time of night. Sam, maybe, or Art. He quickened his pace. He hoped there was no bad news, not just as the thing seemed settled.

He saw Julie the moment he entered the house and the shock hit him with the force of a blow to his midsection. "You," he managed to get out.

And then she was flying across the room to him, saying, "Mark, oh, Mark! It *is* really you! You *are* alive!"

She stopped short as he made no move toward her, his face very pale, as if the color had flowed upward to his hair, making it redder than ever. His eyes were staring into hers with a look of bewilderment, and something else—anger, she thought.

"Oh, Mark, don't look at me like that," she pleaded and put her arms up to encircle his neck. "I never thought I would see you again."

"Julie, I can't believe it. What are you doing here?" he was saying almost simultaneously, and then she lifted her head, her eyes shining with tears, her mouth trembling. And his lips fastened hungrily on hers.

With his touch everything faded away. There was nothing now except that roaring in her ears and the achingly sweet feeling his lips evoked. She clung closer and closer and, when he lifted his head to look down at her face, she said in the barest whisper, "Oh, Mark, it's been so long."

"Yes," he muttered his response, his mouth buried now in the hollow of her throat. Suddenly he drew back. "You, why are you here?"

"Not now," she whispered, "not now." And he was half carrying her, half pulling her back into the bedroom.

But he was different, changed. She knew it when he was beside her. Somehow the tenderness of those first kisses had faded and he seemed almost angry. "What is it?" she asked, but for answer he began to move down her body, evoking the feelings no one ever evoked, making her want him desperately and yet leaving her languorously sensual and willing to let time stand still as long as his touch did not stop, as long as his mouth burned so fiercely on her skin.

She began to moan and gasp and writhe upon the bed and he said, "Now, now," and she felt his weight upon her. They were locked together, moving in unison, clasping each other. He pulled roughly on her body and the pain was unbearably good. When at last the final throb of pleasure engulfed them, she felt as though they floated together somewhere far above the earth.

Later, his back turned toward her, she fell asleep with one arm around his waist, her body pressed close against his. It was like a continuous love-making, for they slept and awoke without a sensation of the passage of time.

In the morning the sun burned at Julie's eyelids, forcing them open and closed. She threw up an arm to cover her eyes and turned her back to the windows. She reached out for Mark and found the bed empty. She sat up and looked around the room. She could hear him then, splashing water in the bath, whistling lustily as he washed, and she smiled. She wanted him to come back to her and she lay propped up, waiting.

Presently, she heard the door open and his footsteps coming down the short back hallway. He entered the room, a towel wrapped around his waist, and, finding she was awake, he said a brisk good morning.

Something was wrong . . . Something. . . . This wasn't the Mark she had always known. Last night . . . he had said very little to her last night, none of the words of love he had used before.

"Mark," she said tentatively.

"Yes?" He had flung off the towel and was climbing into his clothes.

"I have so much to tell you," she said, "so much I want to hear, so much to explain."

"No need for explanations," he answered coolly. "Save those for your husband. You got what you came for. When are you going back?"

"Back? I'm not going back. I have no . . ." She broke off as she heard a car stopping at the back of the drive.

"Who could that be?" she asked, sitting up and clutching the blanket around her.

He made a sign for her to be silent and left the room. Seconds later she heard Miranda Latham's voice saying, "Good morning, darling. You left so early last night." There was a hint of reproach in her voice. "I thought I'd come around and . . ." Her voice stopped and, after a short silence, she said on a laughing, breathless note, "I'll never know what to make of you, Mark Douglas. Are you going to keep me standing in the yard?"

"I'm just on my way over to the winery," Mark said. "I want to be there early. It will look better if we aren't seen together. I'll meet you at eleven."

"And then we can pick up where we left off," she purred. "You know how shameless I am, Mark."

"I know how shameless you are," he answered. There was another long silence and then a squeal of pretended outrage from Miranda.

Julie sat there shivering, unable to accept the facts. Miranda. He had been with Miranda last night, had come to her from . . . Her face flamed and her heart squeezed itself dry.

She got out of bed, heedless of the noise, and dressed hastily, intent on making her appearance, but, even as she was buttoning her dress she heard the car crank to life, and before she reached the kitchen door it was turning out onto the road at the top of the drive. Mark stood looking after it, waving a hand and smiling.

As he turned back to the house, he saw her standing there. His smile faded at once and, with a startled oath, he hurried toward her.

"You cad!" she flung at him. "You miserable, cheating . . ."

"Cheating?" His eyebrows went up. "Cheating on whom, may I ask? I'm not married to you. Some French gentleman named René is married to you. If anyone is cheating . . ."

"You came from her last night and then you . . . Oh!" She flung up her hands, shame and disgust struggling for possession.

"I didn't invite you here," he said coldly. "You arrived. I came home to find you all ready for bed. You always were a tempting sight, Julie. But, then, you must know that by now. Or are you going to tell me that your marriage to René was for purely platonic reasons? Or that he was the only other man in your life?"

"I don't need to be invited here, as you put it," she flared. "You seem to forget—this is my house. I don't need your invitation or anyone else's to come into it. I'm planning to live here."

"Live here?"

"Yes. You don't imagine I care to go back to the Prescotts, do you? Perhaps Miranda can put you up. All that talk about Miranda and you being enemies. Enemies! 'Oh, Mark darling, you left too soon last night,'" she mimicked. "Oh, I wouldn't care . . . that you'd . . . patched it up . . . anything. I . . . I could forget that you went from one to the other of us . . . but not after, after . . ." She could feel herself breaking down and took a firm grip on her emotions. ". . . after last night, you could stand out there and kiss her and make a promise to see her later. What kind of man are you?"

"One who may lose his temper any minute," Mark said in a steely voice. "This, as you say, is your house." He made a slight bow. "I'll pack up my things as soon as I get back."

It was only after he drove off that she realized she had not told him anything at all and that as far as he knew, she was married. "Let him think it, then," she said stubbornly. "He and his Miranda." Well, if that's what he wanted.

Don't be foolish, she told herself, you know better than that. Last night . . . but last night had been different. She had dreamed of pouring out her heart to him during the journey home and, yet, once with him, his own silence had silenced her.

She was pacing the house aimlessly. On the third

turn past the silent rooms with their dust-covered furnishings, she was seized with a need for action.

Moments later she had changed into her riding clothes and was out in the stables, saddling Mark's horse. Now was as good a time as any to let the Prescotts know she was home. Holt and Jason would be at the bank, and that would leave only Millicent. She could talk to Margaret, as well, and see if one or another of her many nieces, cousins, and friends might not be available to come and work for her. The house needed far more attention than she could give it alone.

As she came to the crossroads where the wider street led into town, she continued across. It would be better to call on the Prescotts first. There was no point in having them learn from neighbors that she was back.

Ahead she could see Deer Hill, and she spurred the horse forward, anxious to get this first order of business out of the way.

She tethered Rusty to the old hitching post and went up the walk. Time rolled back as she did so. It was almost like that spring five years ago when she had returned from the convent. The park was flowering, the pond was gleaming in the sun, and the scent of lilacs filled the air. Then she had been a girl, untried and foolish and headstrong. Well, she was no longer a girl. She was not quite as foolish, and, as for headstrong, even some of those edges had been blunted and thwarted by the passage of time and by the war and the experiences that had sent her on her odyssey.

She tried the door, found it unlocked, and walked in. There was a curious stillness in the house. She walked through, opening doors only to find the common rooms empty. In the kitchen she could smell the results of recent cooking. Someone must be about. It was only ten-thirty. Margaret was probably in the kitchen garden.

Julie went back to the front hall and up the stairs. Her old room looked as it had always looked, the spread neatly drawn up, the curtains clean. If she were to put a few personal articles around, it would look as if she had never left it. Holt's door was closed, as was Jason's. She tapped, not expecting a response, and when none was forthcoming she peered in each room, anyway, to reassure herself of the owner's absence.

Aunt Millicent's door was slightly ajar and she tapped

at it, waiting for Millicent to reply. She tapped again and then Millicent's voice, sounding weak and reedy, answered.

"It's me—Julie," she said, stepping into the room, darkened by drawn shades. Millicent lay in the middle of her bed, looking unutterably ill and old. Her hair, which had scarcely been marked with gray when Julie fled the house, was now snow white and her face terribly lined.

"Julie," Millicent said weakly, "I, I heard you were married and living in France."

"I was living in France," Julie answered, coming forward to take Millicent's outstretched hand. It felt dry and hot and boneless in her own firmly fleshed palm.

"I've been very ill," Millicent said. "I had that influenza in 1918. My heart." She tapped her chest lightly. "I've never really recovered. Have to stay in bed so much now, nearly all the time. Or in that wheelchair." She nodded, and Julie followed her gaze and saw the chair with a plain lap robe folded neatly over it. "My legs," Millicent said. "They haven't been right since then. I'm an invalid," she said and a tear trickled down her cheek.

"You need more air and light," Julie said. "This room —it's stuffy and close. That's very old-fashioned. I learned a lot of things in the Red Cross hospitals. Let me open the windows and pull up the blinds. You'll see; you'll feel better."

"I'm not allowed. Dr. Vincent says drafts aren't good for me."

Julie forbore saying that Dr. Vincent was an old fuddy duddy and said, instead, "Well, drafts, of course—but not fresh air. Look, I'll close the bedroom door, like so, and then you'll see."

Julie moved about the room, talking soothingly, opening the blind and fetching a shawl before she drew up the windows.

"There, you see," she said. "Just smell that air. Isn't it glorious?"

"You've changed," Millicent said as Julie came back to prop her up against the pillows and to settle the shawl around her. "You're older and, well, softer, I think."

"I'm older, anyway," Julie said. "I'll be twenty-three next week."

"Where are you staying?" Millicent asked. "Not here." she added in sudden fear.

"No, not here. I'm going to open up the old house."

"Mark Douglas is back," Millicent said. "He's staying at your house."

"I know," Julie said. "I've seen him."

"And your husband?" Millicent asked.

"I have no husband," Julie said steadily. "It was all a mistake. I'll tell you about it another time. I was never married, that's all."

"But . . ."

"Another time," Julie repeated gently. "You know, you ought to get out of the house, too, Aunt Millicent. You could go for drives on nice days and sit in the garden in a sheltered spot. It would do you good. I was very ill this winter after I . . ." She stopped. She had almost told Millicent about her pregnancy. No. She had come back here remembering the old Millicent, the one capable of cruelty and deceit and unspeakable behavior. and she had found this pitifully frail old woman. Millicent might have been eighty or more. She appeared to cling to her life by the most tenuous threads. It would serve no purpose to be cruel in return. Holt was a different matter, and so was Jason.

"Don't quarrel with Holt," Millicent said suddenly. "Holt is . . . Holt can be . . ."

"I know all about Holt," Julie said. "Don't worry."

"That's why . . . why I sent you away." Millicent spoke tiredly. "I knew Holt hated you. I never knew why, but . . ."

"Shhh! Don't worry yourself, Aunt Millicent. That was all long ago. I'm not likely to put myself into the way of a fight with Holt now."

"Good." Millicent leaned back against the pillows and closed her eyes. "That air does feel good," she said, "and I'm not a bit chilly. I get chilly sometimes lying here with all the windows closed."

There was a bustling noise from the hall and Jenny came in, still in street clothes and carrying a parcel.

"Oh. my goodness!" she exclaimed. "The windows are open. Miss Prescott, you'll have a chill, for sure. Why. Mr. Prescott . . ." She stopped, goggling as she spied Julie. "Why, my goodness, Miss, I wouldn't have recognized you," she said.

"Leave the windows, Jenny," Millicent spoke up. "Did you get the medicine?"

"Yes, ma'am, here it is." She undid the parcel and placed the apothecary jar next to Millicent. "I'll fetch some water right away." She bustled off and Millicent said, "You were good to visit me, Julie, but I'm very tired now. Come back again, will you?"

"Yes, yes, I will," Julie answered.

She stopped on her way out to find Amos or Margaret, and found Margaret in the kitchen. She spoke to her briefly about the possibility of hiring someone and was gratified to learn that Margaret had a niece widowed by the war who would be glad of a good job.

"Things have changed around here, Miss," Margaret said. "Your aunt is so sick and ailing. Ever since Mark Douglas came back and began to fight with them, your uncle hasn't been all that well, either. And Mr. Holt, well, he never was easy," she sighed. "Amos and me, we're due to retire. Why, Amos is near seventy, and I'm not far behind him, but whenever we talk about it, it just upsets things more."

"Is Mark back at Fontaine's as manager?"

"I heard them talking at breakfast today. Mr. Holt was real angry, and your uncle said he'd make a fight to keep Joe Damien from voting for you . . . whatever that meant. But, of course, no one can do much hollerin' around here these days, what with your aunt and all. If she hears voices raised, she takes one of her spells. So we all walk around like we're in church. Jenny don't seem to mind, but Amos and me, well, we need a bit more life around us. Now that my daughter Abby is widowed, she'd like us to come live with her, and we've a little saved. There'd be grandchildren and then the new baby. I'm a great-grandma now, you know."

"I didn't know." Julie smiled. "Congratulations. You don't look it, Margaret."

"Feel it, though," Margaret grumbled. "My sciatica acts up on cold mornings, and, poor Amos, his rheumatism is something awful."

Julie reached across the table and took an apple from the fruit bowl. "You'd better not pay any attention to upsetting Holt or Uncle Jason," Julie advised. "You and Amos deserve a rest."

"I know, but when you've been with people so long,

it isn't easy to tell them good-bye just like that." She looked at Julie and said, "Miss Julie, are you going to eat that apple or not?"

"It's for Rusty," Julie said, tossing it back and forth between her hands. "He's tethered out front."

"Mr. Douglas' horse? Where's your husband?" Margaret asked suspiciously.

"I haven't a husband," Julie said. "I never did have a husband. It was a mistake."

"Just like Mrs. Latham and Mr. Douglas, you mean?"

"Not quite," Julie said. "Just a misunderstanding, a bit of gossip."

"Well, not that Mrs. Latham and Mr. Douglas aren't friends again," Margaret said. "I heard she was likely to vote with him from now on. I swear I don't know how Mr. Douglas managed to get her back on his side. She was awfully afraid of him a few years ago and never had a kind word to say about him. Why, do you know, he was nearly arrested for attacking her? And there was some business about Viola's roadhouse, too. But then something happened. I don't know what. Seems Mr. Art Douglas and Sam Howard did something and the whole thing was dropped after a while. Your uncle was furious about that. And Mr. Holt . . . I thought he'd take a fit. Then, of course, Mr. Douglas comes back as smart as you please. War hero. You could have knocked Prescottville over with a feather. We all thought he was dead. Had a memorial service and everything. Next thing we know, he's back. Gave your Aunt Millicent a real attack. Surprised the sight of you didn't, too."

Julie patted Margaret's arm. "I won't be around here very much, Margaret. Now, don't forget about Pauline. I'll be expecting her tomorrow."

"Don't you worry. Pauline's living at home and just dying to get away. My brother watches her like a hawk since she's widowed . . . a lot more than he watched her before she was married. She'll be glad of a job with you."

"Good. I'll drop in to see you again, Margaret, when the house is quiet like it is now."

"Yes, well, that would be best, especially after the meeting this morning. Guess you won't be voting against Mr. Douglas."

"Meeting? This morning?" Julie queried.

"Why, sure. Didn't you hear about that? I'd have

thought Mr. Douglas would have said something to you, or Mr. Damien."

Meeting. So that was it. And that was why Miranda had come by. And that was what Mark meant about meeting her at eleven. She looked at the kitchen clock. Nearly eleven-fifteen. If she hurried . . .

Aloud, she said, "Oh, yes, that meeting. I almost forgot. I'd better hurry. I'm late as it is."

She raced Rusty down the roads to the winery. Twenty minutes later, flushed and breathless, she was standing outside the closed office door. She waited a minute, listening, trying to catch her breath.

". . . and I tell you we haven't got all the facts in." Jason's voice. "You can't just walk back in after all these years, Mark."

"But I have walked back in after all these years," Mark replied. "What facts do you need? I can see that Willis Bradford and Mr. van Houten and you and Holt might be a bit unhappy. But we've got the votes, Jason."

"You have Julie's proxies," Jason began.

Julie straightened her clothes and drew a deep breath and opened the door.

"Not anymore, Uncle Jason," she said. "I'm back now, and I'm quite able to vote for myself."

The effect of her entrance was electrifying. Every face turned toward her and she saw the expressions frozen for that brief moment: Jason, his jaw sagging in astonishment; Miranda with widened eyes; the mayor and Mr. van Houten looking as surprised as Jason; Holt, a look of venom in his eyes and then a sudden movement toward her; Mark, with his head back, his eyes half closed. Only Joe Damien smiled.

"Ah, Julie, you are back," Joe said. "That's good. I think you will solve all of our problems."

"I hope so," she said quietly. "Surely this isn't one of those meetings to sell Fontaine's?"

"No," Joe answered. "The problem is the reinstatement of Mark as manager. The problem seems to be that Mr. Prescott questioned the legality of my voting the proxies you gave me when no one knew where you were."

"Now, Julie," Jason said heavily.

"Do you need my vote to reinstate Mark?" Julie asked.

"Of course they do," Jason said eagerly. "I can't see

that it would make any difference to you, Julie. Er . . . I presume you'll be leaving again, going back to your home in France."

"I won't be leaving again. I intend to open up my house and refurbish it and live there."

"What about your husband?" Miranda asked. "Will he be living here, as well? I can't wait to meet him."

"I have no husband," Julie answered her, but she looked directly at Mark when she spoke. She saw him stiffen, saw the mask come over his face, but she could tell from the deepening color of his eyes that he had been affected by the news.

"Why, my goodness," Miranda purred. "We heard from Mark that you'd married a Frenchman."

"I was never married." From the corner of her eye she saw Mark shoot a quick, guarded look at her.

"Not married?" Jason blurted out.

Julie was still standing in front of the door and, in a belated recognition of her presence, the men rose to offer her a chair. She selected one that left her facing Jason and Holt. "Now," she said, "since I am back, I suggest you go on."

"I'd like a word with you in private, Julie," Jason said.

She rose from her chair at once. "Very well, Uncle Jason." He stood up.

Holt said, "I'll come along, if you don't mind."

"No," Julie said. "I'll speak to Uncle Jason in private, or not at all."

"As you wish." Holt settled back, his face tight, a muscle working spasmodically in his jaw.

Outside the office, Julie said, "If you've brought me out here to enlist my vote for your cause, Uncle Jason, I must tell you . . ."

He raised a hand to stop her. "Hear me out. It's true that we did try to fool you about Mark, all for your own good." She gave him a coldly amused look and he said in a testy voice, "Well, and our own, too, of course. But you're making a fool of yourself this time. He's got Miranda Latham safely in his pocket again. In fact, I had it in the strictest confidence that there is going to be an announcement soon."

Julie laughed. "Not again, Uncle Jason. I'm not an easily fooled eighteen-year-old."

"Believe it or not, as you will," he answered. "But I don't intend to let Mark Douglas run this company again. We will make a court case out of it if we have to."

"On what grounds?"

"Gross mismanagement. Don't forget, it's Avery Bertram who kept the books and can show how the profits dwindled while Mark was manager."

"And what of Fontaine's since? You aren't suggesting it's showing a profit?"

"Well, prohibition, of course."

"I'm voting for Mark," Julie said. "And I'm still voting to keep Fontaine's. There isn't any point in talking about it. If you do decide to make a court case of it, I'll be on Mark's side. You've lost, Uncle Jason." Without waiting for a reply, she went back inside.

He followed her, fuming, and said to the rest, "Julie is convinced that Mark deserves this job. I think we'll have to face the fact that court action is all that's open to us. When I think of the way the value of my shares went down during . . ."

"You hypocrite," Mark said with barely suppressed anger. "You've done your level best to ruin Fontaine's and drive it into bankruptcy. I've seen the operation since I got back: a few small contracts to produce medicinal champagne; one or two to supply cooking wine; and half the juice grapes allowed to rot for want of a market, while Steuben's is getting rid of all its crops, one way or another. You've never made a single effort to get into the sacramental wine business. If anyone is guilty of gross mismanagement, it's you and your handpicked manager, Avery Bertram. You've maneuvered everything in favor of Steuben's through Prescott Bank, and all for your own personal gain. You gentlemen," he said, swinging around to Mayor Bradford and Mr. van Houten, "surely you can see you've been just as misled as the rest of us."

Holt made a low, angry sound deep in his throat and started to rise. His father's hand shot out and he grasped Holt's arm. "Let it go, Holt. Let it go."

"Now," Mark went on when Holt had subsided sullenly, "my proposals, gentlemen, and—I beg your pardon—ladies, my proposals are that we take what advantage we can of the present prohibition laws. Fontaine's can stay alive if it goes after the sacramental wine business, if it markets juice grapes, and if it increases its medical and cookery contracts."

"Juice grapes are a fraud," Jason said angrily. "Why, bootleggers buy them and . . ."

"I don't care who buys them or what they do with them after they get them," Mark cut in. "Every apple farmer in the valley and down the length and breadth of the state is selling more apples than ever before. And the farmers themselves are making cider. I'll bet nearly every orchard for miles around has got jugs of hard cider buried somewhere. As for grapes, the housewife may be putting up more jams and jellies than before, but I'd say her husband is brewing some kind of wine in his own cellar. Just tell people they can't have something and that's when they want it. Hell, people who never drank before in their lives are drinking bootlegged whiskey and wine and beer. That's why the illegal operations are making so much money."

"I warned you about prohibition." Jason was still fighting, seemingly unaware that he had been beaten.

Mark bowed toward him. "You did, indeed, Jason. And it appears you were right. It also appears that it's going to be with us a long time. With the illegal operators joining up with the righteous and holy in order to keep their profits flowing in, it will be an uphill battle to get that amendment repealed."

"So you admit there won't be a chance of recovery," Jason said.

"No. I admit nothing of the kind. Sooner or later the people who are buying the rotgut that is being offered them will want decent stuff to drink again. In the meantime, I intend to keep Fontaine's afloat. I think we might even turn a profit if I can get the diocesan contracts I've been angling for. Just think of all the churches in the country, and then think of how many Masses are said each morning. It's not the biggest market in the world, but it will do for the time being."

"Steuben's has offered us enough to allow a margin of profit on the Fontaine stocks," Holt argued. "They've even offered some stock options according to what we individually hold in Fontaine's. Now, that's *real* profit, not some *dream* of profit. Miranda, you ought to think about that. So ought the rest of you. My cousin ought to give it some thought, as well, although I doubt that she will."

"There you have it," Mark said suddenly. "Throw in with me and we'll put Fontaine's on its feet. Follow Jason and take your margin and run. But, I promise you, one day in the not too distant future wine is going to be really big business. What you hold today will be worth double, triple, maybe even more."

"I vote no," Jason said. "And if I lose, I will take it to court."

Mark stood up. "Take it to court," he said. "You'll find yourself having to testify as to your holdings at Steuben's—yours and Holt's. And you'll find yourself testifying as to how you used Prescott Bank and the mortgages it holds to undermine Fontaine's. Collusion, I believe it's called. And just how is it that Steuben's can afford this purchase? Are they bootlegging themselves?"

"I own no stock in Steuben's. Holt doesn't, either," Jason blustered, but his face had turned a trifle pale. "As for Steuben's bootlegging, where did you get an idea like that?"

"I have my sources," Mark said evenly. "Bring all the suits you like. But you aren't going to win them."

"Jason," Willis Bradford said uncomfortably, "I certainly would like to know if there's any truth to what Mark said."

"Nonsense. No truth to it at all." But there was a lack of credibility in his manner that belied the firmness of his voice.

"I'm afraid I have to vote with Mark," Miranda said.

"Joe?" Mark turned to him.

"Yes. I vote with Mark."

He went around to the rest, receiving a sullen "no" from Holt and uncertain "no's" from both van Houten and Bradford. "Julie?" he said at last.

There was a heartbeat of silence before she said, "Yes, of course. I want Fontaine's to go on. I vote for you, Mark."

"Let's get out of here, Father," Holt said, rising and shooting a murderous look at Mark. "Julie never did vote with her own family. I hope we aren't going to have the pleasure of your company at home, Julie," he added. "You won't be welcome."

There was a murmur of embarrassment from the others
and Jason said, "Julie is my niece. We don't put our
family out, Holt, whatever they do." He looked at Julie.
"I presume you saw your Aunt Millicent when you arrived this morning."

"I saw Aunt Millicent," Julie replied, "but I didn't
arrive this morning. And, in any case, I will be staying
at my own house. My things are there now. I arrived
last night."

There was a startled intake of breath from Miranda.
"Last night," she repeated. "But, why, Mark is living
there."

"There are twelve rooms," Julie answered quietly,
but she allowed the faintest gleam to appear in her
eye as she met Miranda's glance.

"And all of them Julie's," Mark interposed smoothly.
"I have moved out to my cousin's house." Check, his
eyes said to Julie, and there was a look in them that
forestalled any further comment from her.

They left one by one. Holt followed Jason out, and
Mayor Bradford and Mr. van Houten remained to offer Mark congratulations with some diffidence, but they
seemed decidedly more cordial now that he had won.

"It is good that you are home again, Julie," Joe
Damien said as he was leaving. "I suppose now you
will be back here at the winery and asking questions
and growing into an old winemaker."

"No, I don't think so. Oh, I'll be asking questions,
but I think I better leave the winemaking to the Damiens."

He held the door to let her precede him, but she said,
"No, thank you, Joe. I want to speak to Mark first."

Miranda, who had been waiting, standing near Mark,
looked annoyed, but she showed no sign of departing.
"If you don't mind, Miranda," Julie said, "it won't take
long."

"I have to be getting back, anyway," Miranda answered. "I'll see you tonight, as usual, Mark?" He
nodded, his eyes on Julie. Then with a little toss of her
head, Miranda swept out.

"Why didn't you tell me about this meeting?" Julie
demanded when they were alone.

"Frankly, it slipped my mind last night," he answered.
"And you were hardly in a mood this morning to hear

anything. I didn't want to risk you coming in and voting out of emotional rage."

"As if I would," she answered heatedly. "As if I did."

"No, you didn't," he replied.

"Mark, I must talk to you."

"There isn't much to talk about," he said. "I gather you weren't married. I suppose I should ask why."

"It's a long story, but I can make it brief," she answered. She outlined the details as quickly as she could, anxious to get it over with, not wanting to dwell on her relationship with René or make any sudden confession. Yet, in the telling, some of the horror of those last weeks at Château de Brugarde crept into her voice and Mark began to question her about her escape.

"And so the lovely maiden was rescued by the knight in shining armor," he said when she had finished. "I suppose it was all pure gallantry on his part, and he'd have rescued you even if you were ugly and old and misshapen."

"He was . . . he is a very kind man." Julie defended Michael.

"Ah, yes. Michael Lynch, gentleman," he answered. "All for the cause of knight errantry, not a bit because he had any interest in you as a woman."

She felt her heart quicken a little and knew the telltale color was creeping into her cheeks, but she said, "We were friends. He was good to me."

He made no answer, going to the window and looking out.

"Mark, it was a terrible time, and when I got to Madeline's and found out she never told you . . . that is, she had a letter from me. But she never wrote to tell me you were alive until it was too late."

"We seem doomed to cross each other's paths briefly from time to time, don't we, Julie?" he said.

"No!" she exclaimed. "It's over. We're here. It . . ."

He looked back at her. "Julie, I don't want to go into all of this now. I'll see you later. We can talk when I come back to the house to get my things."

"You mean you are still going?" she asked, incredulous.

"Yes. I think Prescottville has enough to talk about without adding us to the list."

"But you . . ."

"Later, Julie," he repeated. "I've got a long day ahead of me. Be a good girl and let it wait until tonight. I'll be by around eight or nine."

She started to protest but thought better of it. He was closed off from her. She had sensed it last night, and now she saw that it was true. It gave her the same sense of desolation she had felt when she had heard he was dead.

Julie spent the rest of the day keeping herself occupied with mundane tasks: shopping for groceries; taking off dust covers and airing out the closed rooms; finally resorting to washing the kitchen windows and scrubbing the floor.

As evening came on, she bathed and changed and tried to eat, but her stomach rebelled against the food. It would be all right once Mark arrived. She had made a mistake in trying to tell him about René in the office. Alone in this house, where they had so often been together, it would have been easier. Somehow, tonight she would make that withdrawn look disappear and they would be as they had always been.

The hours crawled by and it was shortly after eight-thirty when she heard the motorcar in the driveway. She flew into the bedroom to peek at herself in the mirror. She felt anxious and unsure, as if no matter what she said or did, the night would end in heartbreak and disaster.

As she came out of the bedroom, she heard the back door open and hurried toward it, saying, "Mark. I've been waiting for hours. You . . ." She stopped, stunned. In the doorway, flexing a whip in his hands, stood Holt Prescott.

25

In the first shock of seeing Holt, Julie stood there, mute and unmoving, hardly aware of the mounting fear beneath her breastbone. Holt's lips were drawn back in a smiling rage.

Her mind began to work frantically. Where could she run to? He was blocking the door. She had little hope of reaching the front of the house ahead of him, and, if she did, he would surely catch her. She drew herself up and managed to say in a relatively calm voice, "What are you doing here, Holt Prescott? This is my house. And Mark will be in any minute."

"Mark is at Miranda's house. I guess he wants nothing more to do with you, either. Even a whoremonger tires of whores."

"Get out of here!" Julie said fiercely, trying to keep the fear out of her voice. "If Mark finds you here, he won't usher you out the way Fred did at the Belmont. You could have been arrested then if I'd chosen to call the police."

"You weren't thinking of me, just of yourself and what a scandal it would make with your new lover. Who was it that time? Oh, yes, Mr. Randall. You seem to have a lot of trouble getting any man to marry you, Julie. Now you're back without a husband, after all—back to create a disturbance. Out talking to Aunt Millicent and trying to upset her. Opening windows, telling lies . . ."

"Get out!" Julie said again, feeling more confident now that he had made no move toward her.

"In good time," he said softly, "in good time."

He cracked the whip and it just missed her cheek. She drew back, terrified now but holding on, knowing that flight would only excite him.

"You won't get away with it this time, Holt," she said

clearly. "I won't save you. I won't run away scared. I'll stay right here in Prescottville and tell everyone what you are."

"Not when I'm through with you," he said in the same soft voice. "Mark's the one. Everyone knows that. Everyone knows you stayed with him last night. He beat you, just like he did Miranda. Tried to strangle her a few years ago. Oh, Art and Sam worked it out to get him off the list of suspects out at the roadhouse, but the town," he laughed, "the town is going to remember once they find out about you. War hero!" he said mockingly. "Wait until they see what their precious war hero did."

He moved forward so quickly that she could only stumble backward and, as she did, her panic surfaced fully and she turned to run. He brought the whip down then, hard and stinging across her back, and she screamed in pain. Again and again it flashed until she was half fainting. "Oh, this isn't all," he was saying madly. "There's more to come. You won't be alive to tell any tales when I'm finished with you."

The next blow knocked her to the floor and he stood over her, panting with excitement. He flung the whip aside and, reaching down, hauled her to her knees and his hands reached down to her. She saw his purpose and screamed again, twisting desperately to get away from him. The more she fought, the more excited he became. She was silent now, trying to use all her strength, but his hands finally seized her around the throat, choking the breath out of her. Desperately, she clawed at him, but he was too strong for her.

She felt the power going out of her arms and legs. He will do this to me. He will kill me, she thought, and she began to pray silently in a jumble of Hail Marys and Our Fathers, scraps of the Apostle's Creed, and finally the scarcely remembered Act of Contrition. There was a terrible searing pain in her chest and her mind grew dim, and the lights in the room were graying.

All at once there was a rush of air into the room and footsteps pounding across the floor, and then Holt let her go and she sank into a heap on the floor. She heard the desperate struggle above her and also her own rasping, painful breath. She pulled herself over to the stove and tried to take hold of it, but it was still hot and she drew back, the pain of the burn diverting her from the searing agony of her back and throat. Through eyes dim with sweat and fear, she saw two men locked in mortal combat—Holt and . . . oh, God, Mark.

As she watched, Mark wrenched free and she saw his fist go out in a quick, short chop that connected. Holt went down groggily. Even as he tried to rise, Mark was on top of him, picking him up by the shoulders and banging his head against the floor.

Julie rasped out, "No, Mark, no! In the name of God! You're killing him! Don't! Don't!" She scrambled to her feet and ran to catch Mark's arms, tugging at them, begging, saying, "Mark, if you kill him, they'll hang you! In the name of sweet heaven, Mark, if you love me at all you'll stop!" She was crying and pulling at him, and all at once he let go and she staggered back, falling against the table.

Mark got to his feet, breathing heavily.

"Get up!" Mark said tensely to Holt. "Get up!" But Holt lay there unmoving; his eyes were closed, his body limp.

"Mark, please," Julie said, faintness overcoming her once more. "Mark, I'm hurt." He was beside her in an instant, picking her up and carrying her into the bedroom, where he laid her down. She cried out, "My back!" He turned her over and swore. "What did he do to you?"

"He . . . he used a whip," she said. "He was going to kill me. He thought . . . he said everyone would believe it was you. Oh, Mark, it hurts, and I'm all sticky and . . ."

"Shhh!" he said. He was at the commode, dipping water from the basin and coming back to her. "This will hurt," he said. As the cold water touched her back, she moaned. "It's bad, but not deep," he told her. "Easy, let me get the rest of your things off. You'll be all right, darling."

"Mark, I have to . . ."

"Wait," he interrupted. They both heard the motorcar start and Mark, with an oath, raced for the door.

Seconds later, he called back to her, "Stay there. I'll send someone. I'm going after Holt."

She lay shivering for a long time after he left, but finally she heard a car in the drive and Art Douglas'

voice calling, "Julie, it's all right. It's Lillian and me."
She began to sob quietly.

They tried to take her to their place, but she wouldn't
leave. "Not until Mark comes back," she said, "please."
She sat gingerly on the edge of the sofa in the living
room she had managed to clean out only that morning.
Lillian, between silent clucks of sympathy and prim
disapproval, had cleaned and bandaged Julie's wounds
and helped her to wash and change into a loose gown
and robe.

"At least he didn't touch your face," she said now.

"For God's sake, Lillian, what difference does that
make?" Art asked irritably. He was pacing the floor,
stopping now and then to look out the window.

"It makes a lot of difference. He could have scarred
her. What's wrong with you?"

"Sorry, Julie," Art muttered. "Of course I'm glad
you're not hurt worse. What's keeping Mark?"

"He'll be here," Lillian said. "He's just waiting out
at Viola's for the police."

"Viola's?" Julie questioned, alarmed. "Police?"

"Lillian, can't you learn?" Art said, exasperated, and
went to calm Julie. "When Mark called us he told us he
had followed Holt out to Viola's and lost him. He
knows he's there but, with Jason owning half of the place,
Viola isn't going to tell Mark which room Holt is in."

"Uncle Jason?" Julie asked.

"Yes—Uncle Jason. And Holt's his son. And that's
why no one ever tells anyone about Holt's little ways
with the . . ."

"Please, Art!" Lillian exclaimed in a shocked voice.
"We don't want to hear about things like that."

"I do," Julie said. "I want to know. Mark isn't in any
danger, is he?"

"You're very concerned about Mark, aren't you?"
Lillian said. "What about your husband? Where is he?"

"I have no husband. I have never had a husband,"
Julie said in a slow and distinct voice.

"That's very funny," Lillian began.

Art stopped her. "Be still, Lillian. If Julie says she
isn't married and hasn't been, then she isn't and hasn't.
Let it be."

"Well, I must say." Lillian's voice was injured.

"Please," Julie interrupted. "Is Mark in any danger?"

"No, no, of course not . . . only . . ."

"Only what?"

"Nothing," Art said shortly.

"Only you hope he waits for the police," Julie said, and he gave her a rueful smile of agreement.

"So do I," she said, "so do I." She began to twist her fingers together, trying to imagine just where Mark might be at that moment, praying that he was all right.

Mark at that moment was standing at the bar at Viola's, talking to Tom Parrott, the policeman who'd come along with Sergeant Little on his call.

"Holt's around, and he's murderous. I don't care what Viola told the sergeant," Mark was saying for the twentieth time. He felt angry and frustrated. Damned fools. He should have forced the truth out of Viola himself. He saw her standing next to the sergeant, laughing with him as he was fingering his cap in the gesture of a man about to take his departure.

"Sergeant's about ready," Tom said.

"You mean to tell me you're going to walk out of here?" Mark asked. "I've already told you. He beat his cousin tonight."

"Family matters?" The sergeant had come up behind them. "If his cousin wants to come down and press charges, that's one thing. But we can't go around here tearing up this place. No warrant, Mark, sorry. Anyway, I don't think Holt is likely to beat up anyone here."

Mark held himself in check with effort. "Just who do you think is so prominent around here that he can come in and beat up these girls the way it's been done half a dozen times, and not one of the girls will mention his name?"

The sergeant began to look disgruntled. "Now, see here. That's slanderous. We came out here in the interests of preserving the peace. We know there's bad blood between you and the Prescotts. But I don't see Holt Prescott here. And Miss Viola . . ." Mark laughed and the sergeant stiffened.

"You aren't going to suggest that you don't know what the business here really is, are you?" Mark inquired insolently.

"Now, that's another slanderous remark," the sergeant said.

"Withdrawn," Mark said lazily. "And apologized f——"

There was a violent commotion at the door, and then one of the girls, half dressed, came tearing through, crying, "Oh, my God, he's killed her! Francie is dead!"

"Shut up, you fool!" Viola shouted and raised a hand to smack the girl across the face.

Mark inserted himself between them and the slap fell harmlessly against his broad back.

"Who killed Francie?" he asked into the hushed room.

"I . . . I don't know," the girl whimpered. "I heard . . . I seen a man run out . . . noises from her room . . ." She was sobbing now. "I seen him running and I went to look, and she's lying there and her face . . ." Here she began to scream, and it took the combined efforts of Viola and two or three customers to get her back to her own quarters.

"Julie!" Mark shouted. "He'll go back for Julie!" He raced from the bar and went to his motorcar. Behind him he could hear the police shouting at him to wait, but as he cranked his motor, he saw Holt's car turn from the lane out into the road heading south. He leaped in his own car, shouting back, "There he goes!" And then he was out on the road himself, pushing the pedal all the way to the floor. Ahead he could see the disappearing tailgate lights of Holt's car, and behind him he heard the police siren's wail.

Julie. He shouldn't have left her. But he'd had Holt in his sights all the way, all the way until he saw him turn into Viola's and rocket down the rutted lane through the woods to the clearing where Viola's better-class citizens parked when they were visiting the girl of their fancy. He'd seen Holt go in the back entrance of the house, but when he tried to follow him, Viola's guard barred the way.

Julie. Julie back and all hell breaking loose. The perfect timing, he thought bitterly—Julie back on the eve of the final takeover at Fontaine's. It was too good an opportunity for Holt to miss. Mark should have thought of that. It was Miranda he'd expected Holt to go after; Miranda, he'd warned. Miranda! Holt was far ahead of him on the road that paralleled the one to the Fontaine house. If he stayed on it, it would take Holt out to the main road and he would have to circle around to get to

Fontaine's. If he'd wanted Julie, he'd have turned north to the crossroads.

Mark blew on his horn, signaling that he was going to slow down. Behind him the police car tooted its answer and moments later sped past him.

"Fools," he muttered aloud. Mark pulled the car up to the front of Miranda's house. Holt's car was not in sight, but he left his own and ran up the walk to pound on the door. There was no answer and he twisted the knob, not surprised to find that it opened.

There were muffled sounds coming from the living room. As he entered, Miranda's maid, Carmen, her face a mixture of fear and curiosity, was coming in from the back hall. She saw him and gave a faint shriek. He raised a warning finger for silence and she nodded dumbly. Moving stealthily, he tried the living room door handle. Locked!

The windows—he would have to try to get in through the windows. He ran back outside and around to the front, looking for a rock or anything that would break the windows wide enough for him to get through. There was a loud scream from inside and he smashed his fist through the pane and pulled at the broken glass, heedless of the quick spurts of blood that sprang from his hands. He was inside, groping through the draperies when he heard the police siren. So they decided to come back, he thought grimly.

Within the room he could hear hoarse obscenities and a lock turning. Footsteps ran along the hall and burst through to the porch. At that moment the draperies parted and Mark saw Miranda. She was on the couch, her clothing half torn away, her eyes pools of horror. But she was alive.

"You're all right?" he questioned.

"Mark, it was awful. He . . . he . . ."

"Stay here," Mark ordered, and he went out to the hall. "Go to Mrs. Latham," he ordered the cowering maid and then ran back outside in time to see Holt Prescott, hands manacled behind him, being led to the waiting patrol car.

He went forward to the sergeant. "Mrs. Latham is all right," he said.

"How did you know it was Mrs. Latham he was going after?" Sergeant Little asked.

"We had a vote at the winery this morning. Mrs. Latham voted with me and against the Prescotts. I suppose Holt considered that disloyalty. Look, Sergeant, if you don't mind, I'd like to see to Mrs. Latham and then get back to Julie. I'll be at my cousin's if you need me."

"Have to make a few statements," the sergeant said. "This is going to kill his father," he added with a jerk of his head at the car.

"Yes, I expect it will," Mark answered indifferently. "Excuse me, Sergeant, but I'd like to get back."

". . . and he had some crazy idea it would all be blamed on you," Miranda was saying.

"Not surprising, considering all the trouble before the war," Mark answered evenly.

She looked away. "I thought we'd agreed to forget the past—start afresh, you said. You even suggested something more."

"I wanted your vote," he told her.

"You . . . why, you came here . . . you pretended the past was over . . . you even said . . ."

"I said only that we had the future to look forward to," he interrupted her. "You dreamed up the rest by yourself."

"But you, you acted as if . . ."

"As if I wanted you?" he asked. "Yes, I did, didn't I? Tit for tat, Miranda. You used me, and I used you. However, I did save your life. We were all on the road to Julie's. By the time anyone might have thought to come here . . . well, I don't need to tell you."

She clutched her arms across her breasts, shaking. "He . . . Holt . . . he was a pig, a monstrous pig. He called me a . . ."

"Spare me." Mark held up a hand. "I'm glad you're alive, Miranda. But we're finished now—for good. I wish you luck," he added. Without waiting for her to answer, he left the house.

Driving back down the road toward Julie, he was suddenly fatigued to the point where for a minute or two, he thought, he would surely have to pull over and sleep right where he was.

Now that the worst of it was over, he faced the business of Julie herself. He remembered his anger that morning, an anger that had grown over the months since he had read Julie's telegram in Madeline James' living room. It was an anger, however, that had not withstood the impact of seeing Julie again or of making love to her. He shook his head to clear it.

He pulled up before the Fontaine place and saw Art at the door, beckoning him.

"Is she all right?" Mark asked tersely, coming into the house.

"Hurt, of course. She'll be a time healing, but nothing too bad. See for yourself."

Art followed Mark into the living room, and at their entrance a volley of questions arose from Lillian and then from Art. Julie sat silently, staring at Mark, her eyes large and bright with relief.

He tried to answer the questions, but at last he said, "Look, it's over. Holt's in jail. I'll tell you anything you want to know tomorrow. But I've got to sleep. Julie, you should go back to Art's place."

"I'm staying here," she said.

Too tired to argue, he sent Art and Lillian on their way, saying, "I'll stay with her, of course." He was barely able to summon a smile when Lillian said something about appearances.

Julie met him in the doorway of the living room when he came back. "I want to go to bed, too," she said. "I can't talk tonight but, Mark, one thing."

"Yes?"

"I love only you, no one else."

He yawned hugely. "So you've told me," he said, and, taking her hand, he brought her back to bed, settling her gently upon it, and then, pulling off his shoes, he lay down beside her and was instantly asleep.

26

In the weeks that followed Holt Prescott's arrest for murder, daily life in Prescottville came to a virtual standstill. Reporters arrived by the trainload, and every inn, boardinghouse, and hotel from Elmira to Penn Yan was crowded with them and with the curious who had enough money and leisure time to satisfy their macabre fascination with murder. And such a murder—scion of the town's leading family killing a prostitute at a house that belonged to his own father. Attempted rape and murder on one of the town's lovely young widows. A whipping given to his young and beautiful cousin, Julie Fontaine, heiress to Fontaine Wine Company, who had once been Miss Angela Grant. Both of the ladies who had been saved on this murderous rampage had been saved not by the local police, but by the handsome war hero, Mark Douglas.

Jason fought hard to keep the news from Millicent and succeeded in some measure from letting her learn the worst. There were whispers that she had collapsed and was dying but, to the disappointment of the sensation seekers, she managed to pull through yet another time.

Just before the trial began, Jason came to plead with Julie not to testify. "It won't matter in the end," he said heavily, "but it will spare us something."

"I can't," Julie told him. "I promised. I'm under subpoena, in any case. And, Jason . . ."

He lifted dull, watery eyes to her face.

"It may be easier this way. Holt is clearly insane," she said. "That should be how he pleads, his attorney told me."

"No," Jason said violently. "I don't want him confined to a madhouse. I'd rather he . . . I'd rather see him dead," he finished. "Disgraced," he muttered. "Disgraced. You and Mark . . . you . . ."

"Don't blame me, Jason, or Mark. Blame yourself."

A sly look came over his face and he said, "You know, Julie, if it were to come out about you . . . well, I'm not such a fool as you think. There was that acting career. As it is, people—well, some people—probably think you invited Holt's advances and then repelled him. And there is that business in France. I know what you've said, but I think a little searching for the truth . . . a word to the reporters here and there . . ."

He was threatening her, actually threatening her. Her silence for his, was that it? Julie felt her anger boil up and she said, "If it comes to that, Jason, I really have nothing to hide, only things that might cause me some unwelcome attention. But if you want to wash every last bit of the family linen in public, then listen to me. I saw Sara Prescott in New York. And I know how to get in touch with her. And I saw you and Aunt Millicent the night I ran away. If I hear one word of gossip, one bit of slander against me or against Mark, I won't hesitate to retaliate. Think that over. Think about Millicent getting wind of it."

He sagged visibly and it seemed that his huge bulk began to wither, as if the spirit that supported it had started to shrink away. "I am ruined," he said. "I am ruined." And he turned and walked out of the house.

She watched him go with dispassionate pity. He and Millicent had made their lives the way they wanted them, not caring whom they used, not caring that they had taken Sara's life from her and set her on the path to a living hell. They had conceived and nurtured a son who was proof enough that such close interbreeding could produce the misbegotten. Holt could have been an idiot. Instead, he was a twisted, criminally dangerous human being who had finally resorted to murder. The trial was not something she wanted to face, either.

In the end, Julie was spared the ordeal. On the day before the trial began, Holt Prescott hanged himself.

"It's over at last," Mark had said.

Mark. Mark had been aloof since the night Holt was arrested. He had waited until Pauline came to housekeep for Julie. He had treated her with tenderness and care, but he had kept her at a distance. When she questioned him about his long disappearance in France, he told her of his illness at Les Deux Croix and the Frenchwoman who had nursed him. He spoke to her as if they were merely old friends, and as if passion had never flamed between them. Never once did he mention a life together again.

All during the time that she was mending, he had come by each day, sometimes with flowers or with a book or with a box of bonbons. He wouldn't stay, wouldn't talk about anything serious. He always left her with a cool kiss on her cheek or forehead.

Now that she was up and about, the visits were very infrequent. Once or twice she had gone over to the winery to see him and he had been almost formally polite. Often she had looked up to find him staring at her with a half-speculative, half-sad look in his eyes, and once she said, "Mark, what is it? Something's wrong."

"Nothing," he told her. "You are imagining things."

Well, it couldn't go on. She was mended now and well and ready to take up her life, and Mark *was* her life. Sooner or later, they would have to talk, and the sooner the better.

Suiting her decision to immediate action, Julie went to the telephone and called Mark at the office. He was not in and she left a message that something urgent had come up and she would meet him at the house at seven.

She was glad he had been out. This way she wouldn't have to attempt an explanation on the telephone of just what was so urgent. She dressed then and went into the kitchen to tell Pauline that she could have that day and the next day to herself.

Pauline, who looked rather like a very young Margaret once must have looked—small, skinny, and pretty in a sharp-featured way—was thrilled but a bit apprehensive. "It's not that you're not satisfied, Miss Julie?" she asked.

"Of course not. I'm very satisfied. Look at this house! It's the way it used to be. You're a marvel, Pauline. I just hope I won't lose you soon."

"No, ma'am, not me. I don't feel like marrying no one again just now. Bob, he was the . . . well, no use talking about that. Someday, maybe, but not now. To hear my father talk, you'd think that was all I had on my mind, though." She smiled.

"You go along, then. I'll see you tomorrow afternoon," Julie said. "Oh, and if anyone calls before you leave, I've gone out for a bit. I'll be back around seven."

When Mark arrived that evening, he found her on the front porch, sitting quietly in the glider, a book of poems open on her lap.

She had taken some thought to her dress and was wearing a soft blue chambray. She had threaded a blue ribbon through her curls to hold some of them back from her forehead. She looked, she decided, cool and pretty.

"Hello, Julie," Mark said as he came up the steps. He was still wearing his jeans and shirt and riding boots, and she guessed he had not gone home before coming to see her.

"Hello, Mark," she replied demurely. "Will you sit down?" She gestured to the place beside her, but he took a wicker chair and drew it up so that it faced her.

"What is the urgent business?" he asked, a faint smile on his face. "You look anything but pressed or harried or troubled."

"I am, though," she countered. "It's you—us. You've kept me at arm's length since the night Holt . . ."

"I know," he said, looking away from her.

"Why, Mark?"

"I . . . I don't know," he answered. "It's . . . it became too much. There was . . . well, for one thing, there was your life. Oh, I know about the bad count, and I suppose under the circumstances that I can't expect that you wouldn't have tried to make a life for yourself. But, somehow, Julie, I always seem to find you either in or just fresh from another man's arms."

"That's not true. René . . ."

"Forget René," he said in a sudden heat. "What of Michael Lynch? You were not the innocent girl being rescued by a gallant Irishman. Spare me the retelling of that."

"I won't try to tell you anything," she said, hoping she could keep her temper in check. "And what of it? What were you doing all those years? Waiting for me? You knew I was alive. How many women have you been with since . . . well, since that Frenchwoman who was so good to you? That young widow only helped you escape and stole money for you? What was she? Just a saint who liked befriending people? And Miranda." She could hear her voice rising and she knew she had lost control, but suddenly she didn't care. "What were you doing with Miranda? Making love to her! I don't care what the reason was. And what about Madeline?" she added suddenly. "I can tell, Mark. I know you. I know why you don't want to bring up the past. It isn't me—it's you."

He was on his feet and she rose to face him. "It's different with men. You wouldn't understand," he said. "Other women, they didn't mean anything to me. I ... men need that."

"Well, so do women!" She flared up. "What makes you think women are any different?"

"They are," he said.

"They're supposed to be—all of us. We're told from the time we can understand how it's all right for boys to be boys, but girls must be little ladies. Ha! Even Eileen gave in. Flesh and blood can stand just so much."

"It's different," he said doggedly. "I can't think of you in another man's arms. I heard the way you talked about that Lynch. Wasn't it on that trip that you told me you'd finally decided the fact that love makes the difference?"

"Yes, it does. It does for me, but not for you—not for René, either. There are men who don't give a damn."

"Don't compare me with your phony husband," Mark said very quietly.

"Why not? You've just said it doesn't make any difference whom you make love to."

"Don't twist my words," he warned.

"I'll do as I please. I'm in love with you. And you're in love with me, too. Just try to look me in the eye and deny it. Just try."

"I'm denying nothing," he said in that same quiet voice.

"Well, look at me, then." She placed her hands on her hips and stared at him, meeting the flinty look that struck a spark of fear in her at last. Maddened by that, she rushed on: "All right. If you don't want me, there are other men, lots of other men. Men always like me. You said . . ." She stopped as he grasped her.

"That's enough," he said hoarsely. "That's enough! I ought to wring your neck."

He was holding her cruelly hard in a vise-like grip so that one of her arms was pinned to her side. His face was inches from hers, his eyes dark now and smoldering. She lifted her free arm and put it around his neck and, pressing close to him, she raised her mouth to his.

There was a tense moment. She could smell the sweat of his body and feel his breath hot upon her own. His muscles were rigid and the cords of his neck were taut. In that split second she had just enough time to wonder whether she had won or lost, and then his mouth came down on hers, bruising in its harshness. She took it that way, took the harshness and the cruel pressing of her flesh, and in return she gave him all the softness of which she was capable. At last she felt the pressure lessen and he was kissing her slowly, his arms gathering her tenderly, his hands moving gently over her back and shoulders.

"I love you," she whispered. "I've never truly loved anyone except you. I never could." She stroked his neck and let her hands slide down his back, pressing him to her.

Finally, he said thickly, "It's never any good to fight this. I need you, Julie."

With one accord they turned and went inside the house, passing through the rooms without seeing them, finding their own place at the back. There had been times when he had loved her tenderly and times when he had been fierce and demanding, even harsh, but there had been no time like this one.

"My love," he said to her. "Never anyone else."

"No," she murmured, and she gave herself up to the rapture of his embrace.